Romantic Suspense

Danger. Passion. Drama.

Colton Undercover
Jennifer D. Bokal

Second-Chance Bodyguard
Patricia Sargeant

MILLS & BOON

Jennifer D. Bokal is acknowledged as the author of this work
COLTON UNDERCOVER
© 2024 by Harlequin Enterprises ULC
Philippine Copyright 2024
Australian Copyright 2024
New Zealand Copyright 2024

First Published 2024
First Australian Paperback Edition 2024
ISBN 978 1 038 93527 4

SECOND-CHANCE BODYGUARD
© 2024 by Patricia Sargeant-Matthews
Philippine Copyright 2024
Australian Copyright 2024
New Zealand Copyright 2024

First Published 2024
First Australian Paperback Edition 2024
ISBN 978 1 038 93527 4

MIX
Paper | Supporting
responsible forestry
FSC® C001695

Published by
Harlequin Mills & Boon
An imprint of Harlequin Enterprises (Australia) Pty Limited
(ABN 47 001 180 918), a subsidiary of HarperCollins
Publishers Australia Pty Limited
(ABN 36 009 913 517)
Level 19, 201 Elizabeth Street
SYDNEY NSW 2000 AUSTRALIA

Cover art used by arrangement with Harlequin Books S.A.. All rights reserved.

Printed and bound in Australia by McPherson's Printing Group

Colton Undercover

Jennifer D. Bokal

MILLS & BOON

Jennifer D. Bokal is the author of several books, including the Harlequin Romantic Suspense series Rocky Mountain Justice, Wyoming Nights, Texas Law and several books that are part of the Colton continuity.

Happily married to her own alpha male for more than twenty-five years, she enjoys writing stories that explore the wonders of love. Jen and her manly husband have three beautiful grown daughters, two very spoiled dogs and a cat who runs the house.

Books by Jennifer D. Bokal

Harlequin Romantic Suspense

The Coltons of Owl Creek

Colton Undercover

Texas Law

Texas Law: Undercover Justice
Texas Law: Serial Manhunt
Texas Law: Lethal Encounter

The Coltons of New York

Colton's Deadly Affair

Wyoming Nights

Under the Agent's Protection
Agent's Mountain Rescue
Agent's Wyoming Mission
The Agent's Deadly Liaison

Visit the Author Profile page
at millsandboon.com.au for more titles.

Dear Reader,

I always love being a part of any Colton continuity. I love working with other authors and the editorial team to bring you all a great series! And *Colton Undercover* is no different.

But there is something special about this book: Liam Hill and Sarah Colton were honestly one of my favorite couples to write. Liam is a dedicated FBI agent, but he's let his work take over his life. Sarah is struggling to find work-life balance after completing a graduate degree. She's also dealing with the death of her father and the realization that she has ten half siblings whom she knew nothing about.

Then when Liam and Sarah come together, they find what they need in their life—each other.

This book also has a lot of fun elements. Liam was Sarah's childhood crush. There's also an undercover operation, along with a fake relationship. Bonus: the villain is someone whom you'll love to hate.

As always, I hope you have as much fun reading *Colton Undercover* as I did while writing it!

All the best,

Jennifer D. Bokal

To my forever love, John.

Chapter 1

Special Agent Liam Hill, FBI, sat at his desk in a cubicle. His workspace was located in the middle of a group of similar cubicles. The large, windowless room located in the FBI's headquarters was affectionately referred to as the Rat Maze. The Hoover Building itself was named for the organization's longest-serving director, J. Edgar Hoover. Squat, plain, yet imposing, it was reminiscent of its namesake.

His cubicle mate, Constance Hernandez, sat at a desk across from his own. For the past two weeks, Liam and Constance had been tracking down documents associated with a church outside Owl Creek, Idaho. So far, they hadn't found enough information to bring charges. They'd received a report that the pastor was coercing his followers into giving him their life savings.

"I don't like this as a federal violation," said Constance. "It's not against the law to give away cash. If people want to give all their money to this church, so be it."

"But what if they feel as if they don't have any choice?" He paused. "Besides, he advertises online. Communicates with potential followers through the internet. That could be wire fraud."

"Weak sauce," said his colleague.

He knew her opinion already. Still, Liam was determined to conduct a full investigation. It was more than his job. It was his duty. "You know, they put Al Capone in jail for tax fraud."

Every FBI agent knew about the mob boss from the 1920s. The agency that put him in jail was a grandfather of what would become the modern-day Bureau. "In case you forgot," said Constance, "we don't investigate tax crimes. That's the IRS."

"All I'm saying is that Capone committed much worse crimes than tax evasion. But that's what got him locked up. And jail is jail."

Constance pursed her lips. He couldn't tell if she was considering what he said or thinking up a new argument.

"Hill. Hernandez." The two names were fired, like bullets. Liam looked up to find his supervisor leaning on the cubicle wall. Wayne Parsons, a Black man from Detroit, fit his name. He was the son and grandson of preachers. What's more, he'd inherited a clear and deep baritone voice that was perfect for the pulpit. "Tell me everything you know about the Ever After Church. Start with how you came across the information."

It was Liam who'd gotten the lead two weeks earlier. He said, "My mom's former receptionist, Helena, joined the church after a nasty divorce. She eventually moved to their compound in the mountains. Since she had secretarial skills, she was put to work in the church's administration building. Once she realized that the church's leader, a guy named Markus Acker, kept most of the money being raised for personal expenses, she became disillusioned and left. She reached out to me because she remembered I was with the FBI. According to Helena, Markus has his financial records on a separate computer that is never connected to the internet."

"That's odd," said Wayne.

Constance picked up the story. "I've been piecing together Acker's background. He's a shady dude, even if he's never been charged with anything. Been pastor at several failed churches over the years."

"Collect all your information," said Wayne. "Kate Dubois wants a briefing."

Assistant to the Director, or A-DIC, Kate Dubois oversaw all units that investigated financial crimes for the FBI. Constance lifted her brows. Giving a briefing to the A-DIC was a big deal. She asked, "When does Dubois want to hear from us?"

"She wants a presentation now," said Wayne. "But I convinced her to give you ten minutes."

"Are you kidding?" There was no way he could put together a coherent presentation in such a short amount of time.

"No joke. Get to work." Wayne took two steps, stopped, and turned around. "Just so you both know, I put in my retirement papers yesterday. On May first, I'll be a free man. The career board is meeting in the next few weeks to pick my replacement. The two of you are at the top of the list. Do a good job on this briefing and you might just end up with a promotion."

For years, Liam had worked with Constance. She was a smart agent, and the closest thing to a friend he had in Washington, DC. It was a shame that she was now his rival. For too long, he'd been stuck in the warren of cubicles. He wanted the promotion and intended to get it.

"Whoever the career board picks," he said, "no hard feelings."

Constance sighed. "Get to work, Liam. We only have nine minutes left."

Liam stood in front of a screen. A large conference table with room for eighteen took up most of the floor space. Chairs on casters surrounded the table. Only seven seats were filled. Aside from Liam, Constance and Wayne, the A-DIC sat at the foot of the table with her entourage of two special agents and a financial analyst.

Everyone in the room was an employee of the FBI. It was true that the Bureau didn't assign uniforms, like in the military. But there was an unspoken dress code for those who worked at the Hoover Building. Everyone wore a dark suit. All the men were also in a white button-down shirt and a necktie. The women had all donned blouses along with understated jewelry.

Liam held a tablet computer that controlled his part of the briefing. He pointed to the enlarged image of a tax document that filled the monitor. "This is the last return filed with the

IRS by the Ever After Church. As you can see, they claim only modest income. According to our sources, the church has taken in well over a million dollars this year alone through member donations." In his opinion, the donations were coerced from those people.

"Upstairs, you mentioned something about the church's leader having a computer that never goes online," said Wayne. "Tell us more."

"The CI thinks that Markus enters all his correct financial information into that device." It felt odd to refer to Helena, a lady who used to make him cookies, as a confidential informant. But this was work—nothing personal. "Acker is the only person with access to the device."

"So, the only way to see the information is to physically have the computer?" asked Wayne.

"That," said Liam, "or copy the hard drive."

"How would we do that?" asked Constance.

"Someone has to infiltrate the church," he said.

"But that will take months—maybe even years." Constance continued, "Does the Bureau have the resources to spare on such a small case?"

True, most financial crimes the FBI investigated were worth several million dollars or more. But other things were also true. "First, we don't know how much Markus Acker has taken from his followers." The amount could be astronomical—but he'd serve nobody by speculating. "Also, he's doing more than depleting bank accounts. He's ruining lives."

"This case merits our attention. Markus Acker is suspected of laundering money for some nefarious organizations. The church is also connected to several deaths," said Kate Dubois, the first words she'd spoken since the meeting began. She continued, "I'd like to hear how you plan to get an agent into the church."

In that moment, he knew what he needed to do to get out of the Rat Maze. And how he'd get the promotion. "I wouldn't just send any agent," he began. "I'll go undercover."

"You?" Constance's tone was filled with concern. "You haven't been in the field, well, ever. How're you going to handle an undercover operation?"

The thing was, she wasn't wrong. Liam had passed his CPA exam after his first try—an unheard-of feat. He'd then applied to the Bureau and been hired at the age of twenty-four. In the last seven years, he'd been assigned to the financial crimes unit. While he'd worked a variety of cases, he spent most of his time in the Hoover Building. It left a gap in his résumé that would be filled by being the undercover agent on the case.

"But why are you the one to go undercover?" asked Wayne.

"For one," he said, "I'm from Idaho. I grew up in Boise. It's close to Owl Creek. So, I'll know how to talk to the locals."

The A-DIC said, "I don't like it. You might run into someone from your past. Or someone who still knows your family."

This was his moment. If he could convince the A-DIC to let him go to Owl Creek, the next move in his career would be assured. Inhaling, he began, "My parents moved to Arizona five years ago. I have one sister, Allison, who's stationed on an airbase in Okinawa. She left seven years back when she got into the Air Force Academy."

For a full minute, Dubois said nothing. Then, she slowly shook her head and his stomach dropped. "It's still too close. We can't give you an alias if it could be easily blown." Then, with the next breath, she looked at Constance. "You have information on Markus Acker?"

Constance sat up taller. "Yes, ma'am." Her presentation was already loaded into the smartboard and was controlled by her own laptop. She typed a few keystrokes and Markus's face filled the screen with a professional headshot.

One couldn't tell by the photo, but Liam knew that the other man was tall and still fit. He wore his dark blond hair short, and by the looks of it, cut by an expensive stylist. In the photo, he wore a black suit, white shirt and yellow tie.

"Markus is fifty-five years old," Constance began. "He has degrees in both communication and finance."

He knew all the information already and was hardly listening. How had he blown his chance to work undercover? Then again, he should be asking a different question. How could he get the A-DIC to change her mind?

The first photo was replaced by another. "I pulled this recent picture off the church's website. The woman in the picture has been identified as Markus's fiancée. Jessie Colton."

His gaze snapped to the screen. He recognized the woman at once. "Damn," he said without much thought. "She hasn't changed at all."

"You know Ms. Colton?" Constance asked.

How many years had it been since he'd spoken to anyone in the Colton family? The last time would've been the summer that Allison graduated from high school, and he entered the FBI Academy. "I used to know her, at least. She's the mom of my kid sister's best friend. My dad used to joke that if Sarah came over for one more sleepover, he'd be able to write her off on the taxes." Sure, it was lame dad humor but there'd also been a nugget of truth to the jest. Sarah was constantly at his house.

"To be honest, I'm surprised that you didn't know the subject was dating the mother of a former friend," said the A-DIC.

A sick feeling dropped into his stomach, like he'd just stepped into something unpleasant. "Like I said, after my parents left Boise, we really haven't kept in touch with anyone from Idaho."

"That's not what I meant, Special Agent Hill. You've been building a case on Markus Acker and the Ever After Church, have you not? You should know about his personal life," she snapped.

There was only one thing for him to say. "You're right, ma'am."

"If I may," said Constance. "Liam and I divided the work duties. Since he's been working so closely with the financials, I did a background investigation on Acker. To be honest, this is the first time we're sharing information."

"I expect my teams to work as a cohesive unit. But I understand that this investigation is moving quickly. From now one, consult with one another. We're the FBI, not the Keystone Cops for chrissake." Leaning forward, Dubois rested her elbows on the tabletop. "The fact that you know Jessie Colton is interesting."

"I wouldn't say that I know her," he said carefully. Correcting a superior was the same as swimming in dangerous waters.

"But as a teenager, I knew her daughter well. Hell, she used to go on vacation with us."

"Why is that?" asked Wayne. "What was the Colton home like?"

To be honest, Liam hadn't thought about Sarah since he left Idaho. But now that she was top of mind, it was amazing how much he could remember. She'd been a sweet kid who liked to read. In fact, her taste in books was well beyond her years. He recalled a specific weekend that he'd come home from college. Sitting at the kitchen table, he read *War and Peace* while eating breakfast. Sarah wandered into the kitchen and pointed to the book in his hand. *Tolstoy, huh? I liked* Anna Karenina *better.* They'd spent the next hour talking about literature.

The squeaking of casters brought him back to the conference room. He'd been quiet for too long. He could feel Wayne's question hanging in the air. *What was the Colton home like?*

He let out a long breath. "Sarah's home life was crap. Her parents weren't abusive, or anything like that. But her mother and father split up when she was in elementary school. Dad was only around sometimes. Mom always had a flair for the dramatic. Her brother was a good guy—older than her, younger than me."

"Do you think she'd remember you?" A-DIC Dubois asked.

"I'd hope so," he said, offended that anyone suggest Sarah forgot about him. "I was the one who taught her how to drive."

Dubois leaned back in her seat. The image of Jessie Colton still filled the screen. "Special Agent Hill, you're certain that your family hasn't kept in touch with the crowd from Boise?"

He wasn't sure if it were a question or a comment. Still, there was only one thing he could say. "That's correct."

"What about your sister?" she asked.

When the family gathered for Christmas last year, Liam and Allison had sat outside in the balmy Tucson evening. Lamenting the heat, she'd complained, *"I miss Idaho. It's not Christmas without a little snow."*

"You're on leave," he'd said. *"You could take a week and visit old friends."*

Shaking her head, Allison had said, *"I lost touch with everyone when I graduated. The Air Force Academy doesn't leave much time for socialization—especially for people who live hundreds of miles away."*

"Even Sarah?" he'd asked, incredulous.

"Even Sarah," she'd echoed. *"I think we're social media friends. But I never use those apps so I'm not even sure."*

Liam's memory came and went in the span of a heartbeat. He didn't hesitate to answer the A-DIC's question this time. "Allison hasn't had any contact with the Coltons, either."

"So, neither Sarah Colton nor her mother know that you're in the FBI." Again, not quite a question, not quite a statement.

"Well, that's not entirely accurate," he said, measuring his words. "Sarah and my sister had just graduated from high school right before I headed off to Quantico for training. I assume she remembers that I was going to the academy." Liam becoming an FBI agent had been a big deal for the family. His parents had thrown a going-away party. Of course, Sarah had attended.

"But she doesn't know what you're doing now."

He knew what Dubois was thinking. His pulse began to race with excitement and apprehension both. "We haven't been in touch personally since that summer, so I doubt she knows any more about me than I know about her." Which was absolutely nothing.

"Do we have any intel on Jessie Colton's children?" Dubois directed her gaze at Constance.

"Um, no, ma'am." Her shoulders were shrugged in tight, probably preparing for another brutal comment.

Using his tablet computer, Liam accessed his sister's little-used social media accounts. From there, he found the friends list. Sarah Colton was among those with whom Allison had connected. He followed the link to Sarah's profile. The lanky kid with braces had been replaced by a statuesque woman. "Sarah still lives in Boise," he said, reading the details listed on her profile. "She graduated from Boise State with a master's degree in library sciences. She works at the downtown library. Never married. No kids. No current romantic partner. But she does have a cat named Tolstoy."

"Where'd you get all that information?" Wayne asked.

"My sister's social media profile," said Liam.

"I thought you said your sister and Sarah weren't friends anymore," said Wayne.

Liam exited Sarah's profile and opened his sister's. He checked for the latest post. "Allison hasn't accessed the account for three years but it's still online."

Dubois picked up a pen and tapped the end on the table. There was no other sound in the room and Liam's heart began to beat with the tempo. "You've got your wish, Special Agent Hill. I'm sending you to Idaho, but you won't be undercover per se. You'll go to Boise and contact Sarah Colton. From there, I want you to rekindle your friendship. If she trusts you, her mother might, too. These two women are the shortest path to Acker, I can feel it."

Liam was getting exactly what he wanted. Why was his gut twisted into knots of unease? "Sarah knows that I'm with the Bureau. Even if she's not suspicious, her mother and Acker will be."

"Leave that to us," said the A-DIC. "We'll change your life, online at least. You'll be given a new background." She paused, seeming to consider what to say next. "You'll be a banker who's in Boise looking for real estate for a client."

"It should work," he said. Still, the apprehension coiled in his gut.

"Of course it will work." Dubois stood. Everyone else in the room got to their feet, as well.

Liam rose slowly. "Thank you for this opportunity, ma'am."

"Don't thank me yet. I expect results, Special Agent Hill. And soon."

Dubois left. Her retinue followed.

Only Constance and Wayne remained.

"I'll be in touch with the particulars of your background and some training to get you up to speed on undercover work," said his supervisor. "But go home and make arrangements to leave. You'll be out of DC soon. A word of advice?" Wayne dropped his hand on Liam's shoulder. "You're a good agent but don't screw up. What happens over the next few weeks has the power to define your career for good or bad."

"Point taken."

With that, Wayne left the conference room.

Constance quietly packed up her laptop. For a moment, neither said anything. Finally, he cleared his throat. "I should probably thank you for covering for me with Dubois."

She gave a quiet laugh. "You probably should." She zipped up her bag before saying, "Looks like that promotion will be yours when you get back."

She was probably right. Still, he knew enough to say, "You never know. You're a hell of an agent."

"It's probably for the best. My wife doesn't like all the late hours I'm keeping now. Although the raise would've helped to pay for IVF." His work friend had shared the cost of each round of in vitro fertilization. The cost was astronomical. It almost made him feel guilty for wanting the promotion so damn bad.

Slipping the strap of her computer bag over her shoulder, she continued, "I'll keep looking into Markus Acker's personal life. Anything I find that's germane will get passed on."

"I appreciate having you in my corner."

"Just remember me when you're assistant to the director and get to pick your own minions," she joked.

He laughed. "It's a deal. Although, you'll never be a minion."

With a small wave, she slipped through the door and was gone. It left him alone. He knew he should be happy about the case—elated, really. He'd gotten the chance to prove that he was a capable field agent and not just another bean counter with a badge and gun.

Yet, blood hummed through his veins and left him jittery.

Was it because this would be his first foray out of the confines of Washington, DC? Or was there more?

He picked up his tablet computer and pressed the home button. His sister's social media account was still open. Instead of exiting the app, he found Sarah Colton's profile for a second time. In the picture, she wore a light blue dress and held her striped tabby, Tolstoy. Her light brown hair brushed the tops of her shoulders, and the corners of her green eyes crinkled with her smile. The last time he saw her, she'd been a skinny kid, barely out of high school and only eighteen years old. The long lines of youth had been replaced with womanly curves.

Looking at her profile, he sighed. He knew what was bothering him and why.

It was no secret that Sarah had harbored a huge crush on Liam when they were growing up. For years, he didn't care. After all, she was just a kid. But all of that changed right before he went away to the FBI Academy. Sarah, who'd recently turned eighteen years old, mentioned that she was legally an adult but still hadn't gotten her driver's license.

He remembered the conversation like it happened last week and not over seven years ago.

"Why no license?" he'd asked.

Sarah sat at the breakfast bar in the kitchen. *"Nate tried to teach me,"* she said, mentioning her brother. *"But we fought. Mom tried, but she freaked out."* She sighed, her shoulders slumping. *"I make progress with Dad, but he's not around much."*

"I'm home for a few weeks. I can take you out," he offered, happy to fill his days somehow.

It had only taken a week's worth of lessons and she passed the test on the first try.

Outside the DMV, she proudly held up her temporary license. With a big smile on her face, she'd announced, *"I couldn't have gotten this without you."*

He'd been so proud that he'd opened his arms for a hug.

She stepped into his embrace, and an instant later her lips found his.

Even now, his face burned with shame. Over the years he'd seen the looks on Sarah's face each time she glanced in his direction. He'd been a fool to ignore her longing.

He stepped away. *"Sarah,"* he mumbled, the feeling of her kiss still on his lips. *"I can't. We can't. I'm so much older than you."*

Her eyes flooded with tears. *"I just thought. I hoped."* She wiped her cheeks with her sleeve and dropped her gaze. *"Ohmigod, I'm so embarrassed."*

"Don't be embarrassed," he said, trying to sound soothing. *"It happened once, but it can't happen again."*

She ran off crying. In the moment, he convinced himself

that it was best to let her go. Even then, he knew that he should
have done or said something.

He left for the FBI Academy a week later. Sarah attended his
going-away party but the two didn't speak to the other.

He glanced once more at her profile picture. Soon, he was
going to have to face the grown-up version of Sarah Colton.
And to be honest, he wasn't sure what kind of reaction he was
going to get.

Chapter 2

One week later
Boise, Idaho

Sarah Colton's office was on the third floor of the Boise Public Library's downtown branch. The building, built in 1908, was made of local stone and filled half a city block. The residents of Boise affectionately called it The Castle. The multitude of rooms was perfect for reading areas, separating fiction from non, children's books from YA, and YA from fiction for adults. But the downside of such a large structure was that it was hard to keep temperate. In the summer, the building was sweltering. In the winter, the rooms were like iceboxes. And on this gloomy Tuesday in March, the damp had settled into the cramped spaces.

Huddled behind her desk, she gripped a cup of tea for warmth with both hands and stared at the screen of her desktop computer. The latest gas and electric bill had just landed in her inbox and honestly, she wished it hadn't.

"Knock, knock." Her friend and coworker Margaret Rhodes stood on the threshold. A Black woman, she wore her long hair in braids. Today, she'd donned a bright pink sweater with a lipstick to match. "So? How'd it go?"

Of course, Margaret would want all the details of last night's date. Taking a sip of tea, Sarah made a face.

Margaret's smile faded. "That bad?"

"He was fine," Sarah sighed. "Just a little young."

"Young?" Margaret echoed. "He's twenty-four. You're twenty-five. There can only be twelve months between your birthdays."

"He's a grad student at Boise State but he acted like an undergrad."

"I'm not saying that you should marry the guy—or anyone at all, for that matter. But you keep saying that you want to find someone to care about. Was he really *that* bad?"

Sighing, she took the last swallow of her tea. "He called me bro all night."

It was Margaret's turn to make a face. "Okay, that's bad."

"Tell me about it." She gave her friend a quick wink. "Bro."

"What're you working on? Anything I can do to help?"

"We just got the heating bill. If you have a million dollars just lying around, I'll take it," she joked.

"Sorry, no extra cash," said Margaret.

She sighed and looked at the amount due again. The budget was already stretched thin. Sarah had no idea how she was going to find the extra money. And yet, she had other things to worry about beyond the tight budget and her lousy romantic life. Her father had passed away only months earlier, and his death had sent out shock waves that still reverberated. Sarah and her brother, Nate, had ten half siblings. Of course, her parents' illicit affair had caused heartache for all the other Coltons. She was still trying to navigate her newfound family relationships. Then, there was her mother's new boyfriend. *Ugh.*

Pushing all her problems aside, she tried to smile. "What're you up to this morning?"

"Last night's shift didn't put away any of the returns. I'm going to get all the books on the shelves before it gets too busy."

"I'll help you put the books away." Anything was better than looking at the bill she didn't have the funds to pay. After exiting her account, she slipped on the loose cardigan she kept in her office. Standing, she said, "You take nonfiction and I'll take fiction."

"Deal," said Margaret.

On the first floor, two trolleys filled with books sat behind the circulation desk. "This one is yours," said Margaret, wheeling a cart toward Sarah.

From the number of volumes, she figured that the task would take the better part of an hour. It was 10:03 a.m. The library had opened only minutes before. If history served, patrons wouldn't start arriving for another thirty minutes.

She scanned the titles. Not only had the late shift failed to reshelve any books, but they also hadn't organized them alphabetically, either. Sighing, she realized that this task might take her closer to two hours. She picked up the first book.

The Gospel According to the Son. Mailer, Norman.

Pushing the cart through the stacks, she found the correct shelf and replaced the book.

Riffling through the titles, she found five more that should be placed close by. She picked up the next book in the pile, a heavy tome. *War and Peace. Tolstoy, Leo.*

Honestly, she couldn't look at a work by the Russian writer without thinking of Liam Hill. When she was in middle school, she'd talked to him about books. He was the first person she'd ever related to through literature. It had led directly to her current profession.

Then again, she couldn't look at another guy without thinking of Liam, either. Unquestionably, he was the yardstick she used to measure every other man. She'd yet to meet a guy who was his equal.

Maybe it was time to let go of her preoccupation with Liam.

The front door opened and closed. The sun caught on the glass and reflected on the back wall. She peered through a gap between the books and caught the glimpse of a man. He was tall with dark hair. She only saw his profile before he disappeared behind another shelf. Her heart skipped a beat.

Had it really been him?

She dropped her gaze to the book in her hand. Of course, it wasn't Liam. After all, he'd just been on her mind.

After setting the book back onto the cart, Sarah smoothed down the front of her button-up blouse. She needed to find the early-morning patron and offer help. She walked to the end of the stacks and turned the corner. The middle of the library's main room consisted of the checkout/help desk. A double shelf of fiction books ringed the perimeter. Periodicals were to the left and computer workstations were to the right.

The man she'd seen was gone.

Certainly, she wasn't imagining things—even if he had reminded her of Liam Hill.

Perhaps he'd gone to one of the other rooms. Well, if he needed anything, he'd find Sarah.

Retracing her steps, she rounded the corner at the end of a tall shelf and stopped. The man stood next to her cart. He held the volume of *War and Peace*. Her heart thundered in her chest, a wild beast trying to break free of its cage.

He was still tall with the same dark hair and brown eyes. She hadn't seen him in years, yet it was unmistakably him. Her throat tightened. She squeaked his name. "Liam?"

Looking up slowly, his eyes widened in surprise. "Sarah Colton? Is that you?"

"It is. Wow. I haven't seen you in forever." Her pulse still raced—it was a combination of shock and the fact that Liam had actually gotten better-looking since she'd seen him last. "How have you been? How's Allison? I haven't spoken to her in ages, either."

He wore his winter coat unzipped. Underneath was a white oxford shirt and pair of gray trousers. A pair of black loafers completed his outfit. "Allison's good. Still in the air force. Stationed in Japan right now. Parents are good, too. Life in the desert suits them." He paused. "It's so weird to run into you. I just got into town for work and need to do a little research on some property. I figured I could pick up a book to read, and who knew we'd both be at the library as soon as it opened?"

"Actually." Sarah held the fabric of her loose cardigan taut. Her name tag was no longer hidden in the folds of fabric. "I work here."

He peered at the metal tag affixed near her chest. "Head Librarian. That's impressive. Congrats."

"What about you? The last that I remember, you were heading to the FBI's training academy in Virginia."

He sighed and gave a quick shake of his head. "It didn't work out. Living on a civil servant's salary is hard. A bank offered me a job managing their investments and I took it."

"Oh." She choked on a kernel of grief. Yet, why did his job choices cause her any angst? She remembered Liam as being such a principled person, it was a shame to see him give up his ideals for cash. Then again, he was right. Even as head librarian, living on a civil servant's salary was hard. "Well, congrats on your new job."

"It's not really a new position, but thanks anyway. How 'bout you? How long have you been working for the library?"

"It'll be a year in May." She'd been hired right after finishing her master's degree. "So, you said you were here doing research. Can I help you with anything?"

"I'm looking for information on some buildings downtown. I have a client who wants to expand his business."

"Let me put you in touch with Margaret. She's our research librarian and can help you find all those things that aren't on the internet."

The nonfiction room was adjacent to the main room. Margaret was easy to find. The cart of books she was sorting was nearly empty. It reminded Sarah of all the tasks she'd yet to complete.

Her friend and coworker looked up as she approached. "Hi. Something I can help you with?"

"This is an old friend of mine. He's looking at some investment properties and wants to see what we have on file. Liam, this is Margaret. She can help with any of your questions."

Holding up one finger, Margaret said, "Let me put away the last of these books. I'll be right back." Wheeling her cart to the end of an aisle, she turned the corner and disappeared behind a set of shelves.

There was really no reason for Sarah to stay. But it brought up an interesting question. What did she do now? Shake his hand? Give him a hug? Since the last time they'd embraced had led to the most embarrassing moment of her life, she held out her hand. "It was really great seeing you."

He slipped his palm into hers. A tingling traveled up her arm, leaving her pulse racing once more. "Well." She was breathless. "Take care of yourself." She walked away. The feeling of his eyes on the back of her neck was like a lover's caress.

"Hey, Sarah."

She turned back quickly. "Yes?"

Damn. Why'd she have to look so eager?

He said, "I'm going to be in town for a few days. Any chance we can grab dinner one night? We can catch up more. You'd save me from a week of eating alone."

"Yeah, sure." The feeling of Liam's hand in hers still danced along her skin. Pressing her thumb into her palm, she rubbed a small circle into her flesh. She couldn't decide if she was trying to preserve the sensation or get rid of it. "That would be nice."

"Is tonight too soon?"

Honestly, she didn't have any plans after work. But did accepting a date last minute make her look desperate? No. This wasn't a date, despite the fact that her skin tingled from a single touch. Liam was simply an old acquaintance. "Tonight's fine. Meet me out front at six thirty. There are some nice restaurants nearby."

"Six thirty it is," he repeated.

Margaret approached. "Sorry to keep you waiting. What can I help you find?"

Sarah gave Liam a small wave and walked away. Her day started off lousy. But seeing Liam after all these years had definitely improved her morning. What's more, she hoped her love life was about to rally, as well.

By 6:10 p.m., Liam had checked into a downtown hotel not far from the library. His orders were to brief A-DIC Dubois daily. He'd called three minutes and forty-seven seconds earlier only to be put on hold. Sitting at a small table, he propped his socked feet on the bed and watched the seconds ticking by.

Before leaving DC, Liam had attended a crash course in

working as an undercover agent. The first rule was to always maintain his cover. It meant that he'd spent hours looking for a property that he would never purchase for a client who didn't exist. To him, it seemed like a waste of time. Especially since he only had one objective: to reconnect with Sarah Colton.

He'd achieved that goal. But there was more.

If he wanted Sarah to reintroduce him to her mother—and Markus, as well—she had to think they were more than friends. A make-believe romance felt slimy. He hated to fool Sarah, especially since she'd been a good friend to Allison.

"Special Agent Hill." Dubois came onto the line, pulling him from his thoughts. "What have you got for me?"

"To start with, I made contact with Sarah Colton." He spent the next several minutes filling in the A-DIC on the particulars of his run-in at the library. He also outlined how he'd worked with her colleague to find out information about several of the buildings in downtown Boise. "I'm meeting Sarah for dinner soon."

"Good job. I'll let you get back to work, unless there's anything else."

There was, but did he bother bringing it up to A-DIC Dubois? "When we were younger, Sarah had a crush on me. When I saw her today, I could tell that her feelings haven't changed much." It was more than the electric charge that shot up his arm the minute she placed her hand in his. He'd paid attention to her reaction. All the physical signs were there. Her pupils had dilated. Her pulse fluttered at the base of her neck. "It seems smarmy to use her crush against her."

After a moment, Dubois said, "I suppose using Sarah Colton's old feelings for you is grubby. But sometimes, you need to get a little dirty if you're going to clean up a mess. Trust me, the Ever After Church is one huge effing cluster. Let me know if you aren't up to the task. We can send in another agent. But like it or not, Sarah Colton will be used to access her mother and Markus Acker."

"I'm in," he said. "Forget I had any hesitation."

"You're a decent man, I won't forget that. But for now, stow away that decency."

"Will do." He glanced at the time. 6:27 p.m. "Crap," he cursed. "I'm sorry, ma'am, but I have to meet Sarah."

"Go," she ordered. "Keep me updated."

He ended the call while scooping up the keycard for his room. A hooded parka hung on the back of the chair. While wrestling his jacket free, he shoved his feet into his loafers. He was out the door in seconds. At one end of the hall was a bank of elevators; at the other were stairs. He didn't have time to wait for an elevator to make it to the tenth floor and back to the lobby. He jogged to the stairs and pushed the heavy fire door open. Descending, he took the steps two at a time. His footfalls clanged on each metal step.

The stairwell ended at a side entrance, and he stepped onto the street. Fat gray clouds hung low in the sky. Cold air bit into his skin. Zipping his jacket, he strode purposefully down the street. By the time he reached the corner, he was at a jog. On the next block, he started to run. A clock hung outside a bank. 6:38 p.m.

Damn it. He was more than a little late.

He sprinted down the empty sidewalk as fat snowflakes started swirling in the sky. The front doors to the library stood in the middle of the block. A long figure, clad in a puffy coat and voluminous scarf, stood in a pool of light cast by a lamppost.

"Sarah," he wheezed. She turned at the sound of his voice. He waved, slowing to a jog. "Sorry for being late. I had to call into my office and the time got away from me. I didn't have your number to let you know. Hope you haven't been standing here long."

"Not long," she said. Her words were clipped. "In fact, I just stepped outside and since you weren't here, I was worried that you'd come and gone." The strap to a small bag was draped across her torso. She unzipped the bag and pulled out her phone. Holding up the device, she said, "Enter your contact information. Then we can text each other if you need more help with your research."

He entered a number from the fake account set up by the FBI.

"Here you go." He handed Sarah her phone.

She tapped on her phone's screen.

His phone pinged with an incoming text a second later. He glanced at the screen.

Sarah had sent him a message with a book emoji.

"Now you have my contact information, too." Slipping her phone back into her bag, she asked, "Anywhere special you want to eat?"

For the first time in years, he was back in Boise. True, he'd never live in Idaho again. But still, this place would always be his home. "How 'bout some finger steaks?"

"I thought you might want some of those." Deep-fried strips of beef, finger steaks were a local delicacy. They were also something he'd never find in Washington, DC. Sarah smiled, and his pulse jumped. She really had gotten pretty. "Come with me. I know a place."

She started to walk, and he fell in step beside her.

During his undercover training, Liam had learned about more than just how to stay undercover. He'd become an expert in Sarah Colton, as well. Like, he knew that she spoke to her coworker Margaret Rhodes every evening for an hour. On Wednesday nights, Sarah attended a barre class and then had dinner with friends. She was a member of two different book clubs. The last guy she dated had been a match on an app. Sarah's father, Robert, had died several months ago. Jessie joined the Ever After Church not long after Sarah went to college. He also knew that each parent had abandoned a family of their own to be together. Combined, Jessie and Robert had ten other children. Most of them lived near Owl Creek.

Knowing so much about her was supposed to make it easier to connect. The thing was, he wanted to hear it all from her.

A cold wind sent snowflakes skittering across the sidewalk. Liam shoved his nose into the collar of his coat.

Well, the weather was always a safe topic. "In Washington, it's already spring. Sunny days and mild nights. The cherry blossoms will be blooming by the end of the month."

"Must be nice," said Sarah. "You remember how it is here. We might get snow in June."

"Spring is nice," he agreed. "But summer in DC is brutal. It's too hot and humid to go outside during the day."

She stopped in front of a restaurant. The front door was made from tempered glass. Light spilled onto the sidewalk. "This place is new, but they have the best finger steaks in the city." She pulled the door open. The scent of cooking meat wafted into the night air.

"Heaven," he said, crossing the threshold. "This must smell like heaven."

She laughed and followed him inside. "You have an interesting take on the afterlife."

The room was filled with two dozen round tables. Only half were filled. A wooden bar ran the length of one wall. A sign on a post read Seat Yourself.

"Let's grab a table by the window," Sarah suggested.

"After you."

She wound her way to an empty table set for four. After slipping out of her coat, she draped the jacket on one of the chairs. Dropping into the seat, she sighed.

"Long day?" he asked, taking a seat across from her.

"Let's just say it's been a long few months."

Was Markus Acker a part of the problem? "Anything you want to talk about?"

Sarah scrubbed her face with both hands, letting her palms drop to the tabletop. "There's a lot going on in my life. Too much, really."

"I know we never really kept in touch after my family moved, but that doesn't mean I don't care. You were able to count on me when we were younger. I hope you know that you can count on me still."

She shook her head and sighed. "It's just that..."

"It's just what?" He reached for her hand. A current of electricity ran from his fingertips to his shoulder.

Sarah met his gaze, her eyes wide. She looked down at the table, letting her hands slip into her lap. "I don't want to bore you with all my problems."

Before he could press her for more, a female server approached.

She set two menus on the table. "I wanted to drop these off. I'll be back in a second to get your drink order."

Sarah studied her menu. Liam picked up his own menu. True, he knew what he was going to order. But the conversation was over—at least for now.

Another rule from undercover agent training was to be patient.

Had he been too pushy?

Then again, she was still at the table. It meant he was still in the game.

Relaxing, he watched Sarah. Her light brown hair fell to her shoulders. She tucked a strand behind her ear and sighed. The sound landed in his belly, and he dropped his gaze once more to the menu.

His arm still buzzed with the current of energy that passed between them. It was an interesting physical response and one he didn't want to analyze. In fact, it was best if the reaction was just ignored.

Chapter 3

Sarah pressed her back into the chair to make more room at the table. The server set a large tray on a stand next to the table. There were two identical orders on the platter. Finger steaks, cooked carrots and fries. Steam wafted off the plates as the savory scent of meat mixed with the sweet smell of the carrots.

"Enjoy," said the server as she set plates in front of Liam and Sarah. Tucking the tray under one arm and holding the stand in the other hand, she walked across the restaurant.

"I never realized how much I missed these." Liam lifted a strip of beef from the plate and popped it in his mouth. "Tease me if you want about the afterlife, this *is* heaven."

"Maybe they just remind you of Boise," she said.

"Could be." He unrolled a set of silverware and placed the paper napkin on his lap. "For me, home and heaven are kinda the same thing."

"You've been in DC for so long, that must be home for you now."

Liam took a sip of his beer. "I live and work in DC. But it's not home."

"Well, at least you're here now." She lifted her glass of soda from the table and held it up. Liam touched the edge of his bottle to the rim of her glass.

"Cheers," he said.

She took a sip of soda and tried to calm the excited butterflies that started fluttering in her middle. If DC didn't feel like home, she doubted that he was in a relationship. Picking up her own roll of silverware, she removed a fork and stabbed a piece of beef. She popped it into her mouth, chewed and swallowed. "How's Allison? She never posts anything on social media, so I don't know what's going on in her life."

Liam washed down a bite with a swig of beer before speaking. "She's good. Still in the air force. Still flying jets. I saw her at Christmas. She was complaining about the heat in Arizona. She wanted some snow for the holidays."

"Next time you talk to her, remind her that we get snow in June." Sarah picked up a French fry and bit off the end. "And tell her I said hi. How're your folks?"

"They're good, too. After my parents retired, they started traveling. With Allison being in Japan, they've been all over Asia. Mom's hoping that she gets stationed in Europe next."

She tried to swallow, but her throat was filled with regret. She washed her food down with a drink of soda. At one time, the Hill family had been a major part of her life. Now, she knew next to nothing about them. "Your parents always liked to travel. I'm sure they love getting to see the world."

"Remember when we all went to Disneyland?" he asked. "I still have that group picture of us in front of the castle."

She recalled the trip well. The Hills had packed up their minivan and taken a road trip to California. They booked a suite at a fancy resort on the park's property. She and Allison shared one of the beds. Mr. and Mrs. Hill had been in another. Liam had been relegated to a pullout sofa in the living room. The family had covered all the expenses for Sarah. At the time, she was just excited to go on a fun trip. Now, she knew how much they'd truly given to her. "Your folks were good to me. They were like a second set of parents."

"They thought of you as one of their own, so I guess the feeling was mutual."

"I hate that I lost touch with everyone." She'd finished half of her meal. The rest could be saved for leftovers. After wiping her lips with a napkin, she said. "But I guess that's life."

"It's hard once everyone moves and there's nothing tethering you to a place." Liam finished the last swallow of his beer. "But I do miss Boise. I didn't think I would…" With a shake of his head, he placed the empty bottle on the table. "Being back has brought up a lot of memories. Well, I guess living here wouldn't be the same without family around."

Family. The one word was a punch to the chest. Sarah always knew her family was imperfect. It was part of the reason she was so drawn to the Hills. But she hadn't realized how many secrets both her parents were hiding. "My dad died a few months back," she said, without much thought.

"Oh, Sarah. I'm so sorry. What happened?"

Since her father passed away, she'd heard enough sympathies to last her a lifetime. But with Liam they seemed more sincere. Or maybe she just wanted him to care. "It's more than losing my dad." Though that was bad enough. "But I found something out after he died."

"Really? What?"

In all these months, she hadn't shared the entire truth with many people. Nate, her brother, obviously knew. She'd told Margaret. Sarah's mom refused to discuss her own past. And yet, "My parents had families before they got together. The kicker is—Mom was married to Dad's brother and Dad was married to Mom's sister. Between the two of them, Nate and I have ten half siblings."

Liam stared for a moment. "Are you joking?"

She shook her head. Her eyes burned but she refused to cry—not anymore, at least. "The worst of it all is that things are so awkward with the other Coltons. I worry that they blame us for stealing their parents."

"That's crazy. You aren't responsible for anything your folks did."

"I wish you could talk to them," she said with a listless laugh.

Liam sat taller. "Here's what I want to do. Go to Owl Creek right now and clear everything up." He poked the table with his finger, emphasizing his final two words.

Her meal sat heavy in her stomach. "How'd you know they all live in Owl Creek?"

"What?"

"You just said that you wanted to go to Owl Creek and chat with all my siblings. I never told you where they live."

"Oh, that." He paused. "I remember that's where your parents had lived before Boise. I guess I just assumed."

Her cheeks warmed. Had he remembered that much over the years? "You have a stellar memory."

A bead of sweat rolled down the side of his cheek. He wiped it away with his thumb. "Thanks."

The server approached the table. "Can I get you two dessert or coffee?"

Liam looked at Sarah. "You up for anything else?"

Pulling back the cuff of her sweater, she checked her watch for the time: 8:42 p.m. "I better get home. My cat was expecting his dinner more than an hour ago."

To the server, Liam said, "We'll take the check." Then, to Sarah, "Looks like the weather's gotten nasty." The percussion of sleet against the window had been a constant. He continued, "I'll order us a rideshare. I can drop you off at work before going back to the hotel."

"A ride back to work would be nice."

Liam pulled his cell from a pocket. After opening an app, he tapped on the screen. "The car will be here in three minutes." The waitress returned with the bill on a mobile payment device. Liam used his phone to pay. As he signed for the meal with a finger, his phone pinged. Glancing at his phone once more, he said, "Looks like our ride is here."

Sarah slipped on her coat as she walked through the restaurant. Outside, a black sedan sat at the curb. Icy rain fell in a sheet. Ducking down, she sprinted to the car. She settled in the back seat. Her hands were numb with the cold. Liam sat beside her. His strong thigh pressed into her knee.

A wave of desire washed over her. For a moment, she was lost in a fantasy of his mouth on hers.

Lifting her gaze, she looked in his direction. He was watching her.

The temptation to place her lips on his was strong. Then, she remembered the last time she tried to kiss Liam. Shifting, she pulled her leg away from his.

Within minutes, the rideshare driver pulled into the parking lot behind the library. Her small station wagon sat next to the building. An exterior light reflected on a thin layer of ice that coated her car.

"Thanks for everything," she said, reaching for the handle. "It was great to catch up."

Liam opened his own door. "Looks like you can use some help. Get in the car and start the engine. Do you have an ice scraper?"

Using a fob, she unlocked the door and started the engine. She kept an ice scraper tucked into a pouch on the back of the driver's seat. Back in the storm, she ran the blade over the windshield. Liam reached for her. His hand covered hers. "Let me."

The icy rain soaked her hair and dripped down the collar of her coat. But she didn't mind the wind and the cold. In the moment, there was nothing beyond Liam and his touch.

Then, another image filled her mind. This time, it was a memory and not fantasy. Liam's arms had been around her waist. Her hands were clasped behind his neck. She'd given in to the moment and placed her lips on his.

He'd broken away the instant the kiss began.

"I can't. We can't. You're a great girl—but I'm so much older than you."

"Six years, that's not much," she tried to reason, even as her eyes burned with unshed tears.

"Maybe one day, it won't be. Right now, it is."

Then, she was back in the parking lot and in the middle of the miserable weather. Her cheeks burned. "You should go. Your ride's waiting."

"I'm not leaving you by yourself."

"I'll be fine. You go on."

Liam spoke to the driver through an open window. The black car slipped into the dark. Soon, the only thing she could see were the taillights. Then, even those were gone.

"Get inside," Liam urged. "I'll clear the windshield. You can drive me back to the hotel."

This time, she slid behind the driver's seat. The inside of the car was already warm. She turned up the heat and held her fingers in the slipstream of hot air. Liam ran the scraper's blade across the glass. With the defrost turned up to its highest setting, the ice had already started to melt. It took only minutes to clear all the windows.

Liam opened the passenger door. "I forgot how the cold can slice into your bones," he said, getting settled into the seat.

"I'll drop you off before the weather gets worse."

She eased out of the parking lot and turned onto the road. Holding tight to the steering wheel, she stared into the headlights. The beams captured the sleet, making it look as though they flew through outer space. The hotel came into view, and she parked at the curb.

"Thanks for everything," she said, keenly aware that he watched her still.

"I'd like to see you again," he said.

Did he want another friendly dinner? Or was Liam interested in more?

"Reach out anytime while you're in town."

"What about tomorrow night?"

"Tomorrow night?" she echoed with a laugh. "You must really be bored. Don't you have friends to see while you're here?"

"I guess there are, but I want to see you."

She studied him. When she was a kid, she always thought that Liam was the best-looking guy in the world. Now, she was a grown woman. Still, he was the most handsome man she'd ever met. "I can see you again tomorrow."

He smiled. A breath caught in her chest. "Good. Great. Tomorrow, it is. I'll meet you outside the library."

Sarah remembered almost nothing of her drive home. As she opened the front door, Tolstoy launched himself off the sofa in the adjoining living room and ran toward her. Her apartment was modest but comfortable. Aside from the living room, there was a kitchen to the left and her bedroom suite to the right.

"Hey, buddy." The cat wrapped his body around her leg. She picked him up and he tucked his head under her chin. "Miss me?"

With a meow, he wiggled from her grasp. Then, he ran straight to his food dish.

"I know. I know." After slipping out of her coat, she draped it over the back of a chair. Continuing to chat with the cat, she walked toward the kitchen. "You must be starved."

Tolstoy's dish sat on the floor. A layer of kibble filled the bottom of his bowl, so the cat wasn't exactly famished. Still, he'd become used to eating a can of food promptly at 7:00 p.m. It was rare that she made him wait. She emptied his food into the dish. Purring loudly, he stuck his face into the bowl.

Sarah scratched the cat's back before wandering to her bedroom. She flipped on a bedside lamp. It filled her room with a warm glow. Outside, sleet continued to tap against the window. The storm outside made her small apartment feel cozy. But for the first time, Sarah was more than alone. She felt the shadow of loneliness creeping in from the corners.

She shrugged off the mood. After all, she'd always been fine with her own company.

After setting her phone on a charger, she stripped out of her work clothes and threw them into a hamper. A pair of flannel sleep pants and a sweatshirt—the same set she'd worn the night before—lay on her pillow. She put on her pajamas and completed her nighttime routine. With her face washed and her teeth brushed, she settled into bed. Books, stacked into a tower, teetered on her bedside table. From where she sat, Sarah scanned the titles. They were a combination of genres: mystery, literary fiction and a few romance novels. None of them piqued her interest.

She padded quietly into the living room. A floor-to-ceiling bookcase sat in the corner. She knew the shelf without looking. Sarah reached for her favorite book. Holding it to her chest, she returned to her bedroom and slipped under the covers. Sarah opened her copy of *Anna Karenina* and tried to read. The words meant nothing, and her thoughts kept slipping back to her evening with Liam.

True, he was just in town for one week. It was also true that they'd only gone out to dinner once and he hadn't even tried to kiss her. It could also be true that he still only saw her as his kid sister's friend. Tolstoy jumped onto the mattress. Purring, he shoved his nose under the book, making himself impossible to ignore.

Setting the book aside, she lifted the cat onto her lap. Since starting the job at the library, she'd spent many evenings at home with a good book and her cat. While she loved her furbaby with everything inside her, she wanted more from life.

She wanted a house. Kids. A husband.

Liam's face flashed through her mind.

Lifting her phone from the charger, she found her mom's contact and placed a call. Without a single ring, voice mail answered.

"This is Jessie." Her mom's voice was bright and cheery. "You know what to do."

"Hey, Mom. It's me. You won't believe who I saw today. Liam Hill. He was Allison's big brother. Anyway, he left the FBI and is a banker now, and is looking for investment properties for a client who wants to relocate in Boise. We had dinner." She sighed. Leaving a message wasn't the same as chatting with her mother. "Call me back when you can. Love you."

She ended the call.

Liam's reappearing in her life seemed like news that should be shared. It was too late to call Margaret, but they'd certainly chat about it tomorrow. Her brother, Nate, was a good guy. Even with his new girlfriend, Vivian, he was too practical to be romantic.

She opened a social media app and scrolled through her list of friends. Allison Hill, Liam's sister, was easy to find. From there, she typed out a direct message:

You won't believe who I ran into today. Your brother!! He's in Boise on behalf of a client who wants to buy an investment property. Liam and I had dinner. It was good to catch up. I'd love to hear from you, too.

Take care of yourself.

She hit Send and pressed the phone to her chest.

Her favorite childhood daydream had been to become Mrs. Liam Hill. Now, she was an adult and couldn't help but wonder—*what if?*

Jessie Colton leaned back into the sofa and sipped her wine. She loved a French rosé. Cold wind whipped down from the mountain peaks and rattled the windows in their frames. A fire danced in the hearth and warmed the chilly room. This house, with its floor-to-ceiling windows and beautiful views, was the first permanent property for what would be the Ever After Church's complex. It's too bad that not everyone who belonged to the church could live in such a large and well-appointed house.

In fact, many braved the bitter night in not much more than a tent.

But as Markus said, the Lord provides. Everyone was working so hard to create a utopia for all members. Soon, they'd all have lovely homes—although none would be quite as nice as hers.

A pang of guilt stabbed her in the chest. She took another sip of wine. It turned to vinegar in her mouth. Inhaling, she counted to ten, before exhaling. The feelings of remorse slipped away with her breath.

They were replaced with another thought. Really, it befits the church leader to have the nicest accommodations, right?

She took another sip of wine and sighed. The vintage was perfect.

Her phone pinged and she glanced at the screen.

She'd missed one call and had a single voice mail.

Both were from Sarah.

Spotty cellular coverage was one of the things she loathed about living in the woods.

Still, Markus felt that too much technology separated people from the divine. He was probably right. But it made getting calls difficult. She opened the message app and read the transcript.

Hey, Mom. It's me. You won't believe who I saw today. Liam Hill. He was Allison's big brother. Anyway, he left the FBI and is a banker now, and is looking for investment properties for a client in Boise. We had dinner. Call me back when you can. Love you.

Jessie closed the app and took a long swallow of wine. She remembered the Hill family well. Besides Allison being a permanent fixture in Sarah's life from kindergarten through graduation, the Hills had taken Sarah on several vacations over the years. The back of her throat pricked with envy.

Sarah had been fortunate to go on all those trips, especially since Jessie couldn't afford to go anywhere.

The large diamond solitaire on her engagement ring caught the lamplight, sending rainbow sparkles through the room. Now, it was her turn to be lucky. Markus really was a generous man.

Like her thoughts had made him manifest, Markus walked into the room. He moved like a predatory cat with loose limbs and a steady gait. "What are you doing?"

"Sarah just called but the phone never rang. She left a message, though. Seems like she re-met an old friend. He's a banker, in town for business." She paused, memories of the Hill family coming to her from over the years. "It's odd that he works for a bank."

"Why's that?" he asked. "Lots of people work for banks."

"Well, he used to be an FBI agent is all." She recalled his going-away party. The Hills had deemed to invite her, too. She'd awkwardly stood on the patio and tried to make small talk with the other guests. Sarah moved through the crowd like the Hill's third child. And if Jessie wasn't her daughter's mother, then who was she? That night, she'd gotten on the internet and found the Ever After Church community.

"You're right," he said, a scowl creasing his brow. "That is odd. I don't like your daughter dating a fed."

"They aren't dating." Markus and his constant suspicions were enough to make her head throb. She rubbed her brow. "I'm sure there's a reasonable explanation about why he changed jobs."

"Then why did you say it's weird?"

"It was a big deal that he'd gotten into the Bureau so young.

Could be that he just didn't know what he was getting into," she suggested.

"Maybe," he echoed.

She could tell that he wasn't convinced. "I can ask Sarah. I was just going to return her call."

Markus slid next to her on the sofa, his body fitting perfectly next to hers. "Oh, okay." The two words were filled to the brim with disappointment.

"What's the matter?" She felt the heat of anger rising in her cheeks. "You said that if I moved here with you, you'd never keep me from my kids."

"Of course, you're right. It's just that I was feeling a little lonely and wanted some time with my blushing, future bride."

Leaning into his side, she laughed. "Blushing bride. That makes me sound like an eighteen-year-old virgin."

"You know that every time that we're together is like the first time."

He stroked her breast through her shirt. Her nipple hardened. Honestly, Jessie had never known a man who wanted sex as much as Markus. It was just another way she had gotten lucky. Not every woman her age was with a man as virile as her fiancé.

He laid her back on the sofa and situated his hips between her thighs. He was already hard. She was already wet. They really were perfect for one another. In the moment, nothing else mattered.

Chapter 4

A-DIC Dubois had set up a daily briefing on the Ever After Church case. At 9:00 a.m. on his second day in Boise, Liam sat at the small table in his hotel room. His laptop was open, and a secure connection had been established with the Hoover Building. His screen was filled with the same image those in the conference room saw on the smartboard.

"We were able to get approval for aerial photographs of the compound," said Constance, narrating from off-camera. "After obtaining a warrant from a federal judge, we deployed a drone last night." A dark image filled with a jumble of darker shapes appeared on the screen. The same image appeared again. This time, there were three circles—red, yellow and green—around the largest shapes. "The red circle is around the home that belongs to Markus Acker and his fiancée, Jessie Colton. The yellow is the building that doubles as a cafeteria and sanctuary. The green is the church's administrative building."

"What else is in this image?" asked Dubois. "It looks like all the toys my kid leaves on the floor at night."

"Those are dwellings where the rest of the church members live. It's a combination of tents and shacks made of whatever's available." Constance continued, "I was able to access other images of the compound." She rotated through several photographs of the compound. Armed guards, dressed in black, were posted at the gate and wandered throughout the compound. People, lean and dirty, huddled over a small camp stove for warmth.

The images lit a fire in Liam's chest that burned with anger. He had a small printer in the room and would print off the pictures. They'd serve as a reminder as to why he'd returned to Idaho.

"For the privilege of giving Acker all your worldly possessions, you get to live in squalor." Dubois's tone was filled with snark. "It's our job to nail this bastard. Any updates from you, Special Agent Hill?"

"I arrived in Boise on Sunday night and made contact with Sarah Colton yesterday morning. We had dinner together. We also made plans to go out again tonight."

"That's decent progress," said Dubois. "But we need results. Did she buy your story about being in town for work?"

Constance stopped sharing her presentation. The image of the Ever After Church property was replaced by a view of the conference room at the Hoover Building. Liam's own image also appeared in a smaller square.

Dinner with Sarah had been one of the best dates he'd been on in months. She was easy to talk with—not like in DC where everyone was posturing. She'd been charming, funny and had taken him for finger steaks. Too bad it had all been a lie.

"I think she believed every word I said, ma'am. Of course, she remembered that I'd been with the FBI. When I told her that I left the Bureau for better pay, she seemed disappointed, not doubtful."

"What are you going to do tonight?" asked Constance. "I hope you're taking her somewhere special."

"Honestly, I haven't put much thought into where we're going. Last night, she picked the restaurant. The food was good."

"The FBI didn't send you to Boise on a gastro tour. Get tight with Sarah Colton again and quickly," said Dubois.

From her seat in the conference room, Constance held up her phone. "I found just the place for you. Chez Henri is the highest-rated restaurant in Boise."

He didn't remember any place called Chez Henri. It must be new. Or, newish. "I'll look it up and make a reservation."

"I've already taken care of it for you," said Constance. "I booked you a table for two at seven."

"You'll keep me informed of your progress," said Dubois, rising from her seat. The rest of those in the room stood, as well. They filed out of the conference room.

Constance remained in her seat. "How's it going?" she asked. "Honestly."

He wasn't going to tell his friend that he felt like a jerk for lying. He'd already tried that with Dubois and almost got pulled from the investigation. Instead, he said, "I didn't think I'd enjoy being back in Idaho, but I do. Plus, it's good to catch up with Sarah."

"Plus, plus," she added. "She's cute. That can't hurt."

"She's more than cute," he said.

"That's what I thought," said Constance. "Well, have fun. But not too much fun."

He ignored whatever she meant to imply. "I'll chat with you later," he said.

Then, his computer screen went blank.

With the briefing complete, he had hours until his dinner date but nothing to do with his time. Looking out the window, he surveyed people on the street. From ten stories up, their lives seemed uncomplicated.

As he watched, he understood the schism between his real life and his undercover persona. If the real Liam Hill had been in Idaho for work, he'd reach out to old friends. But undercover Liam knew enough to stay away from people who would ask questions he'd never answer.

Moving from the table to the bed, he placed a call. His mother answered after the second ring. "Liam, honey. It's great to hear from you. Everything okay?"

Damn. Had someone seen him in town and called his parents already? "Why would you think something's wrong?"

"You never call in the middle of the day, is all."

"I'm fine, but I have a favor to ask. If anyone from Boise asks about me, don't say anything."

"That seems rude."

"It's not rude. It's national security."

His mom sighed. "I guess you can't tell me what's going on, then."

"I can't," he said. "Sorry."

"Anything else I can do for you?"

Actually, there was. "I've been trying to get a hold of Allison." Since she was stationed overseas, the family used a messaging app to keep in touch. Once the investigation had been approved, he'd tried to reach his sister several times. He needed to alert her to ignore any messages from Idaho, as well. So far, she hadn't messaged him back. "Any idea why she's incommunicado?"

"Your sister's part of a joint military exercise in Asia. It's all very hush-hush. She told me not to expect to hear from her for a few weeks."

Liam exhaled and sank back in the chair. Allison's being off the grid for the Air Force explained everything. It also meant that Sarah wouldn't be able to get in touch with her, either. "Looks like both your kids have to worry about national security."

"You know that your father and I are very proud of you and your sister, even if we don't always get to know what you're doing."

"Thanks, Mom." He was tempted to give his mother an update on Sarah Colton. Before he got into real trouble, he said, "I need to get back to work. Give Dad my love."

"Take care of yourself, Liam."

The call ended and he rose from the seat. Sure, he wanted to avoid people whom he used to know. But he couldn't just sit in the hotel room all day and wait for his date. Slipping into his coat, he shoved his phone and room key into his pocket. Liam turned for the stairs and came down all ten flights. At the ground level, he pushed the door open and stepped onto the street.

Every building he passed held a memory. There was the building where his buddy's dad had a law practice. Over the years, they'd stopped by his work more than once. A nice assistant always made the boys a cup of hot chocolate. Across the street was the building where his mother practiced medicine until she retired. At the corner, where his favorite diner had been, a used bookstore.

As he walked, he realized something important. For seven years he'd devoted himself to his job. He believed in the Bureau's mission. *Fidelity. Bravery. Integrity.* But he'd spent so much time at work that he hadn't bothered to make a life. Even his mom, who'd been a doctor, had gotten married and had kids. When was it going to be his turn?

No, that wasn't a fair question.

He should be asking something else.

When was he going to make having a life his priority? At the end of the block, a striped awning hung over the sidewalk. Years ago, it had been one of his dad's favorite restaurants. Was it still the same, or had that changed, too?

A sign was taped to the door: Now Serving Breakfast.

Back in DC it was 11:27 a.m.—almost time for lunch. He'd already burned off the bagel he'd eaten at the hotel. A second breakfast wouldn't be the worst thing. Pushing the door open, he stepped inside. The room looked just like he remembered. Dark paneling covered the walls. Chairs, wrapped in green vinyl, surrounded twenty-plus tables draped with white cloths. A set of stairs led to a balcony that also served as a private party space. His mom had hosted a surprise fiftieth birthday party for his dad on the upper level.

A young man stepped up to the host's stand. "Can I help you?"

"Table for one," said Liam.

It was easy to find a seat. Aside from Liam, the restaurant was empty. The host led him to a table next to a line of windows overlooking the street. He handed Liam a menu. "What can I get you to drink?"

"Coffee and an orange juice," said Liam.

"Be right back."

Alone, it was time to get back to work. Pulling out his phone, he found Sarah's contact information. He sent her a text.

Hope your cat wasn't upset that I kept you out late last night.

She replied immediately.

Once Tolstoy got his dinner, all was forgiven.

He typed out another message.

I made us a reservation for tonight, so it might be late. Chez Henri. 7:00 p.m. I'll pick you up at your work.

Sarah replied:

Chez Henri? I'm impressed. If I'd known we were going someplace that fancy, I would've dressed nicer for work.

He chuckled as he read her text. She was funny and smart. Besides, he couldn't imagine her looking anything other than beautiful.

You looked fabulous to me last night.

Standing behind the circulation desk, Sarah read Liam's text. He definitely knew how to flatter a girl, that's for sure. A dozen flirty responses came to mind, but with him, she wanted to play it cool. Slipping the phone into the slouchy pocket on her loose cardigan, she smiled.

"I saw that expression," said Margaret while scanning a book into the system. "Let me guess. You just got a text from a handsome banker."

Margaret was a good friend and the only other full-time employee at the library. It meant the two shared a lot of their lives, but they had an unwritten rule to never gossip at work. Since the room was empty, Sarah decided it was okay to break their rule this once. "Liam made us reservations at Chez Henri."

"Très fancy," Margaret said with a fake French accent. "What're you going to wear?"

She shoved her hands into the pockets of her sweater and

opened the front. "He's picking me up from work, so I'm wearing what I'm in."

"Read Banned Books?" Margaret read the front of her T-shirt out loud. "I love your sentiments, but you cannot wear that to Chez Henri. Quin took me there for our last anniversary. That place is swanky. You'll want to dress up." Her husband, Quin, was an engineer for the city, and one of the most considerate people Sarah had ever met.

"Of course your husband took you to Chez Henri because he's amazing." She wasn't ready to give up. "But Liam said I looked fabulous just the way I am."

"Well, isn't he a sweet talker? That just gives you another reason to look your best."

"It's not all about looks," she countered. Then again, she couldn't remember the last time she wanted to look good for another person. But she did want to wow Liam. "Besides, our reservation is at seven. I can't stay here until six thirty, go home and change, and be back to meet him."

"Go home early," Margaret suggested. "Take a shower. Put on that floral dress you wore to the last library trustees meeting. Then, have him pick you up at your place."

"I can't leave you alone."

Margaret said, "I am perfectly capable of running the library by myself until we close. Nobody's here now, and if we get a rush, I can handle it. I'll even have Quin stop by on his way home to keep me company."

Most people didn't consider it wild to leave work early to get ready for a date. But Sarah was conscientious and dependable and going home before closing time felt reckless. "Only if you're sure."

"Not only am I sure, but I insist."

Pulling her phone out of her pocket, she sent Liam another message.

Change of plans. I can get out of work early. Can you pick me up at my place?

She also gave him the address.

Her phone pinged with his reply.

Sounds perfect. See you at 6:30

A swarm of butterflies flitted in her stomach. Seriously, she shouldn't be this giddy over a guy. But Liam wasn't *a guy*. In fact, he was *the guy*.

She didn't believe in fate or luck or a higher power—especially after her mother got involved with Markus Acker. But something good had brought Liam back to her life and she was eager to see what would happen next.

At 6:25 p.m., Sarah checked her reflection in the bathroom mirror. Her hair fell in loose waves to her shoulders. Her makeup brought out the green of her eyes and her lips were full and glossy. Margaret had been right to suggest that she wear her floral dress. The bodice hugged her breasts before the skirt fell in folds around her legs.

It was the most effort she'd put into her appearance in months—hell, maybe all year.

She couldn't help but wonder if Liam would appreciate her effort.

A knocking came from the front door. Tolstoy, who sat on the back of the toilet, jumped down from his perch and scampered to the living room. Sarah followed her cat to the front door and looked through the peephole. Liam stood on the stoop. He held a bouquet of pink roses wrapped in cellophane and a small paper bag.

Placing her hand on the doorknob, she tried to remember the last guy who brought her flowers. Then again, it didn't matter. None of the guys were Liam. She pulled the door open. Cold air rushed into her apartment.

Liam's gaze met hers. Time turned into molasses in the winter. A smile spread across his face. "You look fantastic."

She couldn't help but smile back. "Thanks."

He handed her the roses. "These are for you." The sweet scent of flowers filled the air. Then, he held up the small bag. From inside, he removed a bag of cat treats. "These are for your cat."

He shook the bag. "It's the least I can do since I'm taking you out two nights in a row."

Tolstoy heard the treats and wound his body around Sarah's ankles.

"You know," she said, "most guys just send a text when they show up and expect me to meet them in the parking lot. Not only do you come to the door, but you bring gifts."

"I'd like to think that I'm not most guys."

Oh, he was far from average. Stepping back from the threshold, she said, "Come in for a second. It'll give me time to give Tolstoy some treats and put the flowers into a vase."

Sarah dumped a few treats into the cat's dish. The cat ran to his food bowl. Sticking his nose inside, he started to purr as he ate.

"I think he likes them."

"I hope so," said Liam. "I figure with a name like Tolstoy he'd only want the best."

"Some cats are picky," she said, pulling a vase from a cabinet. She placed the container in the sink and filled it with water. "Not him. He's like a dog and will eat most anything."

"Next time, I'll pick up dog treats."

So, he thought there'd be a next time. That was promising. She bit her lip to keep from smiling again. Sarah unwrapped the flowers. She placed them in the vase and set the arrangement on the middle of the kitchen table. "There," she said. "They look perfect."

Liam knelt next to the cat and ruffled the fur behind his ears. "I've always been a big fan of Tolstoy's work."

"Yeah, I remember," she said.

"You do?" He smiled. The expression lit up his whole face. Even the corners of his eyes turned up in their own version of a smile. Sarah's heart skipped a beat and he continued, "I'm surprised."

"You shouldn't be. We talked about Tolstoy a million years ago. You were in college. I was in middle school. That conversation made me realize that literature and reading and books could be more than a hobby but a career. It took me a bit to figure out that I wanted to be a librarian. But here I am."

The last words tumbled out of her mouth. Once she started speaking, it had been impossible to stop. Why had she decided to be so honest?

"I'm humbled that anything I said made an impact."

"It's more than just the one talk or the fact that you taught me how to drive. You've always done so much for me. From the time I was a kid, your family was my shelter in the storm. If it weren't for all of you, I'd be a very different person."

Liam worked his jaw back and forth. "There's something I need to tell you."

Her interest was piqued. "That sounds ominous."

"Well, it's not horrible. But I need to clear the air." He paused.

In the silence, a million different disasters came to her at once. One of his parents was gravely ill. He was the one who was sick. He was involved with someone else. He was married. "What—" she began. The word came out as a croak. She cleared her throat. "What is it?"

He dropped his gaze to the floor. "We have a reservation, and the rideshare is waiting. We really need to get going."

Obviously, that wasn't what he was going to say to her at all. What was she supposed to do now? Argue with him until he confessed? Demand that he tell her the truth? Neither option was her style. "Let me get my coat and my purse." Both were tucked into a small closet. After slipping on her coat, she draped her purse over her shoulder. "You ready?" she asked, opening the door.

Liam nodded and walked out of the apartment. Sarah followed, pulling the door closed and twisting the handle to make sure the automatic lock engaged. It had. She walked across the outdoor landing toward the steps. All the while, she tried to ignore the nagging thought that there was more to Liam's story.

Her apartment was located on the second floor of an apartment building with sixteen units. There were four floors and an open stairwell that bisected the building. A frigid gust blew up the steps and the icy wind bit her flesh. Zipping her jacket to the chin, she asked, "When will winter end?"

"According to the calendar, spring is about three weeks

away," he said. "But in DC, the weather's already warm enough for flowers to bloom."

"You keep saying that. Sounds to me like you're bragging."

"Maybe a little bit," he said.

Glancing over her shoulder, she gave him a fake scowl. She turned and took a step down. That's when it happened.

Her foot hit the edge of the stair. She slipped, pitching forward. Then, gravity took over and she started to fall. As she went over, Liam reached around her waist. He pulled her back, holding her to his chest. Her pulse thundered in her ears.

"Are you okay?" His words tickled her neck.

She was keenly aware of him. His arms were strong. His pecs were hard, and his legs were long. But it was more than his toned physique—although that was impressive enough. "Thanks for catching me," she said.

"I've always had your back. You know that."

She wanted to believe that was true. But there was something important that he wanted to tell her and at the last minute, he changed his mind. True, she hadn't seen Liam in years. Even before then, she was hardly entitled to know everything about him. She drew in a deep breath. Icy air froze in her nose. The cold was bracing and brought with it a sobering thought.

She could not get lost in a fairy tale.

She and Liam were not going to have a happily-ever-after.

"We better go," she said, stepping carefully on the next stair.

Liam followed but said nothing.

A blue SUV sat in the parking lot. The driver flashed his lights as they approached. "That's our ride."

Liam opened the passenger door for Sarah. "My lady, your carriage," he kidded.

Yeah, the joke was cheesy. Still, she laughed. "Thank you, kind sir."

She climbed into the back seat. Liam closed her door and rounded to the other side of the car, sitting behind the driver.

The SUV pulled out of the parking lot. After a minute, she glanced in Liam's direction. Resting his chin on his hand, he stared out the window. The glass caught his reflection. Lines of worry ran along his forehead.

"Rough day?" she asked.

"What?" he started, obviously lost in his own thoughts.

"You look worried. I wondered if you'd had a rough day."

Liam sighed. "Jet lag is catching up with me." He gave a wan smile. "Besides, I'm not having much luck finding the right building for my client."

"Tell me about your job." She knew next to nothing about banking.

"There's not much to tell," he sighed. "It's boring and complicated."

To her it sounded awful—no matter how much money he made. "Why'd you leave the FBI, then? You used to want to save the world. What changed?"

"I don't know how to answer that question. It's just that..."

In the darkened back seat, he pinned her with his gaze. She had the feeling that whatever he said next was going to be important—not just for him but for her, too. Holding her breath, she waited for him to keep speaking. He didn't. "It's just that, what?" she prodded.

The car slowed to a stop.

"It's just that I think we're here," he said.

She glanced out the window. Dual electric sconces, made to look like flames, stood on either side of a wooden door. Located in a renovated home, the white stone structure was built by a silver baron in the late 1800s and Chez Henri had kept much of the Victorian-era charm. From the sconces to the wrought iron railing to the room with the round turret and peaked roof on the third floor, everything was as it had been in Boise's heyday.

Liam opened his door and stepped from the car. Leaning into the auto, he held out his hand. She placed her palm in his. Her flesh warmed with his touch. Together, they walked up the stone steps to the front door.

Inside, a hostess stood behind a wooden stand. "Good evening," she said with a smile. "Do you have a reservation?"

"Hill," said Liam. "Party of two."

"Can I take your coats?" Sarah removed her jacket and handed it to the hostess. Liam did the same. The hostess disappeared through a door marked Coatroom. She returned a moment later and handed Liam two plastic tickets. "Follow me."

She led them down a short corridor. Smaller rooms branched off the hallway and were set with two and three tables each. Most of the tables were filled with patrons. The crystal stemware at each place sparkled.

"Liam?" A male voice boomed from one of the dining rooms. "Is that you?" A man in a dark suit with thin, blond hair approached. He smiled wide, "Damn. It is you. How ya been?"

"Topher." The two men shook hands. "I didn't expect to see you here."

"Why wouldn't I be here? I still live in Boise. Still working for my old man at the law firm. What're you doing? Or can't you say because it's top-secret for the federal government."

Liam worked his jaw back and forth. "I left the Bureau a few years ago to go into the banking industry. I thought you knew that."

"Last I heard, you were still a G-man."

"Topher, do you remember Sarah Colton? She was one of Allison's friends."

The other man offered his palm. "Actually, I do remember you. Nate's little sister, right?"

"I am. Good to see you again." She recalled Liam's high school friend who played on the football team. Allison thought Topher was dreamy. Sarah was never interested in anyone other than Liam.

She shook Topher's hand. His skin was clammy, and the antiseptic scent of alcohol surrounded him. Turning his attention back to Liam, he asked, "So, what're you doing since you left the FBI?"

"Me?" Liam seemed surprised by the question. "I'm here for a client. They're looking for a building."

Topher's smile grew. "My law firm handles that kind of transaction. Who's your client? What kind of property do you need?"

Liam said, "I can't really talk about that right now."

"We need to meet, then. There are lots of properties I can show you. Give me a call."

"Yeah. Sure." Liam shook hands with Topher again. "I'll reach out."

"Don't you want my number?"

"What? Of course." He removed his phone from his pocket before handing it over. "It'd be great to catch up."

"It'd be even better to do some business. Between me and you, my dad's always on my case about bringing in new clients," Topher confided as he entered his contact information. After handing back the phone, he extended his thumb and pinkie. Putting his hand to his ear, just like he was talking on a landline, he said, "Call me."

"Will do." Liam gave his friend a quick wave before walking away.

"That seems like a lucky break," she said as soon as Topher was out of earshot. "You two used to be tight, and now you can work together."

"Yeah," he said. "It'd be great."

Sarah might not know everything about Liam or his life. But she suspected that he wasn't in Boise to find property for a client. It brought up an interesting question. Why had he come home in the first place?

Chapter 5

Sarah and Liam sat at a table in the main dining room of Chez Henri. A marble fireplace, big enough to fit her car, dominated one wall. Flames danced in the grate. Several tables, covered in pristine white cloths, were scattered around the room. The walls were covered in golden wallpaper. A crystal chandelier hung from the ceiling.

"This place is beautiful," she said.

"It's almost as attractive as the company."

Picking up a pre-poured glass of water, she took a sip. "Now you're flattering me."

Liam lined up his silverware, although the table was perfectly set. "Can't a guy give a compliment?"

She held up her hands, surrendering. "You're right. I'll take the compliment."

"You're welcome."

Before he could say any more, the server approached the table. "My name is Douglas and I'll be taking care of you this evening." He handed them each a menu. "Can I get you started with something to drink?" The server continued, "We have a special on a French rosé."

French rosé. It was her mother's favorite wine. In fact, this was the exact kind of place her mother always wanted to patronize. But money had been tight in the Colton household. She also knew that her mother felt the lack of cash like a physical pain. Suddenly, the cozy room was stifling. Her throat closed like a fist. "I think I'm okay with water for now," she croaked.

"Make that two. But leave the drink list."

Sarah tried to scan the food menu but saw nothing.

"Listen," Liam began. "My compliment made you uncomfortable. I was trying to be flirty but overshot the mark. You do look great, though. So, I'm not going to apologize for that."

"It's not your flirting. It's just..." She paused, not sure what to say. How was she supposed to explain her family? Then again, he knew a lot of the story—more even than most of her current close friends. "It's just that the wine recommendation reminded me of my mom."

"You think that's a bad thing."

"It's not bad, it just touches a nerve." She paused again. "My mom started dating a new guy. He's a minister, and his church is really successful. He has all sorts of money. My mom can buy all the things now that she couldn't afford before. French wines are one of those things—and rosé is her favorite."

"Sorry that it got brought up."

She waved away his apology. "You couldn't have known," she said. "How could you?"

He sat quietly for a moment. "So, what do you think of Markus?"

She lifted her shoulders. Ready to let them drop in a shrug, she stopped. "How'd you know his name is Markus?"

Liam looked up from the menu. "What's that?"

"My mom's fiancé *is* named Markus. But I never mentioned that."

Liam regarded her but said nothing.

"How'd you know his name?" she pressed.

Shaking his head, Liam smiled. She really did love his smile. "You caught me. After we ran into each other, I looked at your social media page. I found your mom and Nate, too. I'm not a creep. I was just curious about your lives." He paused. "I hope you aren't too mad."

Was she? "I guess everything we post online is meant to be seen. Did you send me a friend request?"

"I really don't get on social media much, so, no."

Funny, his sister was rarely online, either. Must be a Hill family thing.

The server approached and stood at the side of the table. "Are you ready to place your order?"

She'd barely glanced at the menu. Looking at the selections, she picked the first thing to catch her attention. "I'll take the chicken piccata."

"Soup or salad?"

It was too cold outside to eat a salad. "I'll have the soup."

Liam ordered a pork chop with apricot glaze. He also took the soup. Finishing the order, he said, "We'll take a bottle of local merlot."

After the server left, Liam said, "I hope you like red wine. I figured that it wasn't imported, and it wasn't a rosé."

"I'm sure everything will be delicious." As it turns out, Sarah was right.

The wine was earthy. The soup was a hearty tomato bisque. Her chicken was tender. The sauce was a perfect blend of creamy and tangy. For dessert, they shared a flourless chocolate torte.

Scraping her fork across the dessert plate, she hummed with satisfaction. "If that meal had been any better, it'd be illegal."

"The only thing better than the food was the conversation." Liam opened his phone and tapped on the screen. "I just ordered a car to pick us up. But excuse me for a minute. I'm going to the men's room."

Sarah watched him walk away before pulling the phone from her purse. During the evening, she'd missed several texts and a call from her mother. Calling her mom back would have to wait, but she opened the texts. They were all from Margaret.

How's the date?

What outfit did you wear?

What do you think of the restaurant?

When are you going to text me back?

She sent Margaret a message: He brought flowers and cat treats. Wore the floral dress. Chez Henri is amazing.
Margaret replied instantly.

How's the date going? Do you still like him?

Sarah stared at the screen. Honestly, she wasn't sure how to answer the question. But she had to tell someone the truth.

Something seems off.

The text bubble was open for several seconds before Margaret's message appeared.

Maybe you're looking for a reason not to like him.

Sarah slumped back in the seat. Could Margaret be right? She sent another message.

I'll call you when I get home.

Her friend replied with a thumbs-up emoji.
She closed the conversation and that's when she noticed her social media. She had one new message. She opened the app and read. Her mouth went dry, and her pulse started to race. She read the message a second time and all the pieces of the puzzle clicked into place.
"Are you okay?" Liam stood next to the table.
How long had he been standing there? Then again, she was blind to everything other than her phone.
"Are you okay?" he asked again. "You look flushed. Do you have a fever?"
"I don't have a fever," she snapped. "But I'm not okay."

As if struck, he rocked back on his heels. "Okay," he said slowly. "What's going on?"

She read the note from Allison one more time.

Sarah!! It's so great to hear from you. I never get on social media, and I should. It's the best way to keep up with friends. It's weird that you ran into Liam. But are you sure it's him? When we talked about a month ago, he was still with the FBI. No mention of leaving the gov't to work for a bank. Let's keep in touch.

She handed Liam the phone. "Maybe you can explain all this."

Liam read his sister's message. Like falling off a cliff, his stomach dropped to his shoes. He hit the bottom, and it left him stunned and breathless. There was no way to salvage the investigation now.

Underneath his concern was a single thought. It was a patch of blue sky in the middle of a hurricane. At least Sarah knew the truth.

He hated lying to her from the beginning.

"Say something," she hissed.

"I'm sorry you had to find out." He held the phone out to her.

"That's the lamest thing I've ever heard." She rose from her seat and jerked the cell from his hand. Anger, like dancing flames, rolled off her. "I thought you were one of the good guys. What I don't get is why you lied."

Ouch. He was one of the good guys. It's just that he couldn't tell her what he was doing. Then again...

His phone pinged. He glanced at the screen. "Our ride's waiting. Can we talk about this at your place?"

"I'm not going anywhere with you. And you certainly aren't coming back to my apartment."

The more time he spent with his newest idea, the more he liked it. "I really think we need a few minutes alone."

She shook her head. "I'll get my own ride. Thank you very much." She turned and walked out of the dining room.

Liam followed her into the corridor. "Wait," he called out. "Just give me five minutes to explain."

Stopping at the hostess stand, she glared at Liam. "Do you have the ticket for my jacket?"

He fished the plastic tabs from his pocket before handing them over to the hostess. Once she disappeared into the coatroom, he lowered his voice. "Give me two minutes. If you don't like what I have to say, the rideshare is yours. I'll have this ride take you home and order my own car."

The hostess returned with their jackets. "Here you go."

Liam placed a tip on the stand before reaching for the coats. "Two minutes," he repeated.

"Talk quick." She held up the phone so he could see the screen. The timer had been set for 120 seconds.

He moved to a corner, far enough from the hostess that he wouldn't be overheard. He didn't have time to think about his decision or consider the consequences. He said, "Allison's right. Topher's right. I'm still with the FBI."

Sarah gaped. "Why didn't you say that from the beginning?"

"Because." He rubbed the back of his neck. His muscles were taut with tension. If this didn't work out, he'd lose more than this case. Certainly, Dubois would fire him. "I'm working undercover."

"That doesn't make sense. Why send in someone who used to live in Boise? Obviously, you were going to accidentally run into people you knew, like me and Topher."

He had to be honest with her. Playing games wouldn't work—not anymore, at least. "Meeting you wasn't an accident."

Her gaze hardened. "It wasn't?"

"I meant to find you. To get close to you."

She shook her head. He could feel her slipping away, like grains of sand through his fingers.

"Me?" She gazed at him. "Why am I important to the FBI?"

"I need Markus Aker."

"My mom's fiancé."

Liam wasn't sure how much time he had left, but he was determined to say his piece before the clock ran out. "He's not the pastor of a rich church. He's been extorting money from his followers for years."

"There's no way," she began. "That's not true..." Her words trailed off. "My mom would never..." And then, "How would you know?"

"I'm with the FBI, remember?"

"How can I forget?" For a moment, she stood without speaking. "What about my mom?"

"Right now," said Liam, "your mom isn't in any trouble with the FBI. The longer she stays, the more criminal exposure she'll have."

Her complexion paled. He imagined the reality of the situation was settling on her. "Do you think she's in physical danger?"

Liam had to tell her the truth. "To be honest, I'm not sure about your mom's safety. He is manipulative. It's possible that your mother doesn't know what's going on."

She raked her fingers through her hair. "I've always hated that bastard."

The question was, did she hate Markus enough to willingly betray her mother? There was only one way to find out. "I need your help."

"My help?" she echoed.

"There's a lot you don't know about Markus. He's not a good man. But I need more evidence before any charges can be filed." How much time did he have left? "I need to get onto the church compound. There's a computer with his financial records."

She shook her head. "My mom will be beyond pissed if she ever found out I helped you."

"She'll be upset if you let her stay involved with a criminal, too," he said.

Sarah's phone began to beep. His time was up. He'd told her everything. But was it enough?

Sarah had agreed to hear everything Liam had to say. Together, they'd returned to his hotel room, and now she stood next to the bed. Funny that a few hours earlier, she shaved her legs in case her night ended at his place. Here she was, but this wasn't the evening she had hoped for at all.

The comforter was covered with papers and photographs. For the past hour, Liam had outlined the evidence.

The story was easy to follow. Members of the Ever After Church lived in desperate poverty as Markus extorted money from those same people and their families. He claimed the money was all for the good of humanity.

In every picture of Markus, her mother was at his side.

There were too many questions for her to think straight. Sure, she wanted to know how her mom got involved with a con man like Markus. Yet, there were other things she wanted to know, as well. Finally, she settled on a single question. "What was your plan before your original plan went to hell?"

Liam leaned against the wall. He folded his arms across his chest and stared at the pictures on the bed as he spoke. "I had hoped to rekindle our friendship. Once we were established, I'd talk you into connecting me to your mom. Then, your mom would introduce me to Markus."

"Friendship," she echoed. "That's a funny word choice for how aggressively flirty you've been. Flowers. Cat treats. Nice restaurants."

"Okay, fine. I was playing the romance card. And I am sorry for hurting your feelings."

Her feelings weren't just hurt. They'd been crushed to dust. "How could you do this to me?"

"I've got a confidential informant who used to be a member of the church. Markus coerces people into giving him money. There's no way to file charges because he didn't steal the cash. But he uses the internet to lure followers to him. That's wire fraud. Aside from that, there's speculation that he's laundering money for some seriously bad people. His real transactions are kept in the church's admin building. To find those documents, I need access. But…" He picked up another picture. In this one, a guard armed with a rifle stood next to a road leading to the Ever After Church. "Obviously, I can't sneak onto the property. What I need is an invitation."

In a way, she understood why he'd come to her. She was the

most direct path to Jessie and, therefore, Markus. Knowing didn't help ease her hurt. In fact, the void inside her yawned wider.

The shambles of her love life aside, Sarah had to help her mom. She picked up a photograph. The image was black-and-white. Taken from a distance, the subject was grainy, yet unmistakable. In it, her mother stood next to Markus. Jessie gestured to the large house where she lived. Sarah recognized the floor-to-ceiling windows from a video call when her mom gave her a virtual tour.

In the background of the picture was something her mother hadn't bothered to share. Shacks, constructed of boards and plastic tarps, were scattered around the beautiful home. People milled about in the picture. Everyone was thin, dirty and looked hungry—everyone, that is, other than Jessie and Markus.

Setting the photo back on the bed, she looked at Liam. "Tell me what you need."

Chapter 6

Sarah studied one of the photographs taken at the Ever After Church's compound. In it, her mother embraced Markus, the two of them laughing. The diamond in her engagement ring sparkled in the sun. In the background, a child with a dirty face cried.

How could Jessie happily ignore such suffering?

Then again, she knew the answer. Markus had money. Her mom had always wanted the security that came with a boat-load of cash.

Maybe she should be asking another question—one that she didn't know how to answer. Was she willing to set up her mother with the FBI?

Sure, Jessie wasn't perfect. But what kind of daughter betrayed their mom?

Liam sat on the corner of the bed. "I know this a lot to take in."

"A lot to take in?" she snapped. Anger burned her from the inside out. She was furious at him for disrupting her boring life. She was furious at him for making her choose between helping to put a criminal in jail and deceiving her mom. But mostly, she was furious with herself. She'd trusted Liam completely. And even now, she couldn't walk away. "What can't I take in? The fact that my mom is dating a criminal or that you set me up?"

"Both, I guess." He was so damn calm, it made her want to scream.

She drew in a shaking breath. "If I were to help, what would you want me to do?"

"If?" He lifted an eyebrow.

"If," she repeated.

He exhaled. "You know I wouldn't ask you to do this if it wasn't important, right?"

"The thing is, I don't know anything about you." She didn't bother to keep the anger from her tone. "I used to know you. But now?" She shrugged.

"I've already shared a ton of confidential information about my case. If you aren't interested in helping, I really can't say anything else." He paused. "Just do me a favor and don't say anything to your mom about running into me."

"It's too late for that." Sarah shook her head. "I was so excited that you and I accidentally bumped into each other, I called her last night."

"Did you speak to her? What'd you say?"

"I had to leave her a message." Oh, yeah. Her mom had returned her call during dinner. "She called me back. We just haven't spoken yet."

"What can I say to get you to agree to help me?"

She didn't have much fight left in her. Still, she wasn't ready to give up or give in. Shaking her head, she said, "Give me some time to think things through."

"Fair enough. Can I call you in a few days?"

Oh, whom was she kidding? She couldn't let her mom stay involved with someone like Markus. Even if Jessie wasn't personally charged with a crime, her life would be ruined. Suddenly exhausted, she slumped back in the chair. "I'll do it."

Liam slipped off the bed and knelt in front of her. He placed a hand on her knee. His touch sent energy buzzing through her veins. He asked, "Are you sure?"

"No, but I'm going to help my mom anyway. I want one thing from you," she said. "If my mom is implicated in any of this, you need to help her out."

"I'll do what I can to shield your mother." He pressed a hand to his chest. "I promise."

It wasn't the complete assurance she hoped for. Yet, it was the best she was going to get. "Now what?"

"You need to convince your mom that you and I are in love. More than in love. Tell her that we're talking about making the relationship permanent. With me as a future son-in-law, she'll have to introduce me to Markus."

Liam's plan was so simple, she knew it'd work.

Standing, she went to the chest of drawers. Her purse sat next to the TV. She dug through the bag until she found her phone. After pulling up her list of recent calls, she found her mom's number and placed the call. Turning on the speaker function, she counted each ring.

One. Two. Three. Four.

"They have really bad service," she said, not bothering to look at Liam. "It's why we have a hard time speaking to each other."

Before Liam could say anything, her mother's voice came out of the speaker. "Hi, hon. Are you still there?"

"Hi, Mom." Guilt twisted in her gut.

"Well, you know how big this house is. I heard the phone ringing but had to run to get it."

In that moment, she knew something to be both unpleasant and true. Her mother would ignore a lot to live in a large home and have lots of money. "I'm glad you answered. I've got news. I told you how I ran into Allison's older brother, right?"

"Well, I got your message," said Jessie. "What was his name? Ian?"

"It's Liam. We've been out twice, and Mom, I can't believe it. I'm in love."

"Love," her mom echoed. "Are you sure? You've only been on two dates, that's pretty quick."

"It is." She continued, trying her best to sound dreamy. "Kind of like you and Markus."

"That's great for you both," said her mom, sounding like she didn't mean a word.

She leaned against the dresser. The edge bit into her flesh.

The pain seemed to be a recompense for what she was about to say next. "I was thinking since you don't work, you could come to Boise. I'd love for you to see him again."

"You know I can't get away from the church on short notice. Markus needs me. The congregation needs me, too."

Did her mother really believe she was helping? "Oh, that's too bad. Liam's going back to DC at the beginning of next week. He has meetings with his other clients," she added. Any mention of business—and therefore money—was sure to get her mom's attention.

"You never said why Liam is in Idaho."

"He works for a bank and is here trying to find a building for a client that's expanding their business," she said, repeating his well-worn lie. Then, she added one of her own. "He's even looking to donate money to local charities. You know, make a good impression for his client."

"Markus and I really can't get away from the church for long. We're going into Owl Creek on Thursday. He promised to take me to Hutch's Diner. We could meet for brunch at ten."

Just like Sarah had dangled a hook in front of her mom, Jessie saw the possibility of money and had taken the bite. "I'll have to check," she said, knowing full well that she was going to use a personal day. "Can I call you back in the morning?"

"Sure thing," said her mom. "Love you."

"Love you, too." The words caught in her throat. After ending the call, she slipped her phone into the pocket of her dress. "I'll take Thursday day off and we can go to Owl Creek together."

"I hate to ask this, but can you take off Friday, too? If we're lucky, I'll be able to get onto the compound. But getting an invitation will take more than one day."

The weight of the world dropped onto her shoulders, leaving her flattened. Then again, what was another day? "I'm sure I can take off two days."

Liam exhaled and smiled. Her heart skipped a beat. After everything, how could she still find him attractive? He said, "You did great on the phone, by the way. I really appreciate what you're doing for me."

"It's not for you," she snapped. "This is for my mom. She needs to get away from Markus before he causes her real trouble."

"I get that," said Liam, his tone conciliatory. "But you're the key."

She took out her phone and opened a rideshare app. "There's lots to do before Thursday. I have to get home."

Liam already had his phone out, too. "I'll get you a car. It's the least I can do." She started to argue. After all, she was an adult and could order her own ride. Then again, why should she incur expenses on the government's behalf? Saying nothing, she watched as he tapped on the phone's screen. "Looks like someone can pick you up in five minutes."

She had done the unthinkable by deceiving her mother. True, someone needed to save Jessie from her own bad decisions. But there was more. Deep down, Sarah knew that she hadn't made the call just for her mother's benefit. It was Liam. She'd had feelings for him her entire life. It was a habit. An addiction. And quitting Liam wasn't going to be easy. The room suddenly felt too hot. She started to sweat. "I'll wait in the lobby."

Liam rose from the bed. "I'll come with you. Make sure you get home safe."

Shaking her head, she said, "Everything you've told me is overwhelming. I need time to process. And besides..." She let her words trail off, knowing full well that it was better to keep some thoughts to herself.

"*And besides*, what?" he pressed.

She picked up her purse and coat, draping both over her arm. "Good night, Liam."

He stepped in front of her. "If we're going to work together, we need to be honest."

Honest? Until now, everything he'd said was a lie.

Before she could say anything, he added, "Besides, making sure you get home safely is the right thing to do."

"This isn't a real date. Stop acting like you care."

He stepped toward her. His scent, soap and sweat and pine of his cologne, washed over her. "Tell me what to say that will make this better between us."

"It's not my job to tell you how to fix things." She continued, "And there is no us."

His phone pinged. He glanced at the screen. "Your ride's here."

She shifted the coat from one arm to the other. "Well, then, I better go."

She maneuvered past him. Her shoulder brushed his chest. The side of her arm grazed his abs. Her pulse began to race.

He placed his fingers on the back of her hand. Electricity danced along her skin. "Look at me."

She couldn't lift her gaze. Her obsession had to end. "Good night, Liam."

Slipping away from his touch, she opened the door and stepped into the hallway. She walked down the corridor and drew in a deep breath. And then another. By the time she reached the elevator, Sarah's heart rate had slowed. She pushed the call button and the doors opened immediately. Stepping into the car, she rode the elevator to the ground floor. By the time the doors opened into the lobby, she was able to think.

The rideshare waited next to the front doors. She verified her driver before settling into the back seat. Looking out the window, she knew why Liam hadn't been honest with her from the beginning. Still, she hated that he'd lied to her. She also hated that she bought his lie. What she hated worst of all is that in being around Liam, she started to hope that all her adolescent dreams were about to become true.

Her phone pinged with an incoming text from Margaret.

Message me so I know you weren't kidnapped or something.

Instead of texting, Sarah opened her phone app and placed a call.

"Hey," said Margaret as she answered the phone. "I didn't mean to be a pest, just wanted to know that you were okay."

"I'm better than okay," said Sarah, forcing her tone to be bright. "I think I'm in love."

"Love?" her friend echoed. "That was fast."

"Not when you think about it. We've known each other our

whole lives. Finding Liam was like coming home." Her chest tightened. Sarah was prepared to lie, but it was the truth that hurt. "I'm going to take a few personal days—Thursday and Friday—to take Liam to Owl Creek. That way he can meet my mom as my boyfriend, not just Allison's older brother."

"Well, you've got it bad."

Sarah tried to laugh. "You make it sound like I've come down with the flu."

"In a lot of ways, being in love *is* a sickness. I'm going to say one last thing, and then I'll stop. You know that he lives in DC and he's only here for work?"

It didn't matter. Once she helped Liam, the fake relationship would become a bogus breakup. "Yeah, I know. Can you stop by Friday and Saturday to check on Tolstoy?"

"Of course I can take care of your fur-baby, so long as you promise to be careful."

"You're the best." Would she ever tell her friend the entire truth? "I'll see you tomorrow," she said before ending the call.

Staring out the window, she watched her reflection in the glass. She tried to be an informed person. She watched the news. She read legal thrillers and nonfiction books on criminals and crimes. It was naive to think that she could slink away from the case like she was sneaking out the back door. If Markus was arrested, there'd be a trial. Sarah would be called as a witness. The minute she agreed to help, she became involved until the end.

Her phone pinged as another text landed on her phone. Sarah decided that if it was Margaret again, she'd tell the truth and ask for advice.

The text was from Liam.

I know there was a lot to absorb tonight. I wish things could be different.

Hoping for some kind of real relationship with Liam was like trying to grab fog. Sure, it seemed like something solid was there, but in the end, it was only mist.

She typed out a message, asking the only question that mattered.

Different, how?

He replied right away.

I wish your mom wasn't involved with Markus.

Well, that made two of them.

Agreed.

He sent another message.

I am sorry that I lied but there was no other way.

She typed out another text.

I'll be able to make the trip to Owl Creek on Thursday and Friday. I have the weekend off, too, if we need extra time.

Liam sent another message.

Thank you.

Another message followed the first.

I'll do what I can to help your mother. I swear.

He'd lied to her about…well, about everything. Was this another one of his fibs?

The car stopped in front of her building. Sarah unbuckled her seat belt. "Thanks for everything."

"You have a good night," said the driver as she opened the door.

"You, too," she said, stepping into the parking lot.

She jogged through the cold and up the stairs to her apartment. At the door, she unlatched the lock. The scent of roses filled her apartment. It seemed like it had been days since Liam showed up at her apartment, not hours.

Tolstoy ran across the room as she opened the door. She bent down and picked him up from the floor. Purring, he tucked his head under her chin. "Did you miss me, buddy?" she asked, scratching under his chin. She walked into her room and set him on the bed. "Then you're going to be unhappy with the next few days. I'm going on a trip."

Setting both her purse and coat on the end of her bed, she sat down on the mattress. The cat nudged her side. She ran her hand over his silky fur. "You love me, right?"

He offered her the underside of his chin for a scratch.

"I'll take that as a *yes*."

Maybe Sarah was no good at love. Maybe it was her destiny to be alone—a librarian and her cat. Maybe she overlooked the good guys and was only interested in those who'd never love her back. She missed her father, truly she did. But he hadn't been around much when she was growing up. Of course, now she knew why. Maybe that was why she'd been so fixated on Liam. He'd showed her the attention she craved.

That was the biggest irony of them all. For years, she wanted Liam to need her. Now that she was crucial to his investigation, she wished that he'd forget that they knew each other at all.

Chapter 7

Two days later
7:35 a.m.

Liam shifted his duffel bag from one shoulder to the other. Standing on the sidewalk in front of the hotel, he scanned the long line of early-morning commuters that clogged the downtown street with traffic. Sarah was supposed to have picked him up already. He glanced at his phone, checking for the time: 7:36 a.m.

A hard knot formed in his gut.

True, Sarah had agreed to help him. But he also knew she wasn't fully on board.

He didn't blame her.

He didn't like the lies or betrayal, either.

But like his boss said earlier, sometimes you have to get dirty to clean up a mess.

If truth were told, A-DIC Dubois was another reason for his roiling gut. By bringing Sarah Colton into the case, he'd opened a proverbial pandora's box. Instead of being filled with curses and evil, he'd found paperwork. Then again, paperwork was a curse all on its own. After several heated discussions, Dubois had given the okay to continue the investigation.

He exhaled, and his breath caught into a frozen cloud. The

sky was already a brilliant shade of blue. Today was going to be one of those beautiful Idaho days that started the transition from winter into spring.

Being in the place where he grew up brought back all the reasons why he loved his home state. The weather was crisp and clear. The people were friendly and inviting. He had friends who shared his history, not just workmates who knew him professionally. Besides, Boise was the only place he could ever find good finger steaks.

Then, there was Sarah Colton.

He hadn't seen her since she left his hotel room on Tuesday night. They'd communicated, but only through texts. He had to brief her more about her undercover role but figured his instructions could wait. They would have time to go over things while stuck together on the drive to Owl Creek.

On Tuesday evening, he'd brought her flowers. When he stopped at the market to get the bouquet and the cat treats, he understood his motivations. Then, she opened the door, and he knew that he was in real trouble. It was more than her brown hair, her green eyes or the way her dress hugged her curves. It was her smile. It was her scent. It was the way she'd felt in his arms as he'd held her in the stairwell.

He rubbed his forearm, the memory of her body pressed against his still lingered on his flesh.

Oh sure, it could just be loneliness. After years of working in DC, Liam didn't have a single friend outside of work. Aside from Constance, those people were just friendly colleagues. Seeing Sarah, and being here, reminded him of all the things he'd missed.

The phone began to shimmy in his hand a moment before caller ID flashed on the screen.

Sarah Colton.

The knot in his middle hardened. Had she changed her mind? After fighting to bring her onto the case, what would happen if she backed out now?

Drawing in a lungful of icy air, he swiped the call open. "Hey."

"Sorry I'm late." She was breathless. "It took forever to decide what to pack. Now, I'm stuck in traffic. I'll be there in five minutes. Ten minutes, tops."

"Thanks for letting me know." A café sat across the street. He'd been so focused on getting out of town that he hadn't bothered with breakfast. Now he had a few minutes to spare. "How do you take your coffee?"

"Coffee?" she repeated, as if the word held no meaning for her. "I really don't drink coffee. I'm more of a tea person."

The café would have tea, too. "How do you take your tea, then?"

"Green tea with honey and lemon."

The cars on the road stopped for a traffic light. Liam stepped from the curb and wound his way past the bumpers. "I'll see you in a few."

On the opposite side of the street, the Winding River Café sat between an ophthalmologist's office and a shoe store. A sandwich board boasted fresh smoothies, açaí bowls, organic coffees and teas, and a used bookstore. He opened the door and was greeted with the sweet scent of warm blueberry muffins. His stomach grumbled. Ten tables were scattered around the room. Most of them were filled. The server stood behind a long counter that was attached to a pastry case. She wore her hair pulled back in a blue bandanna and looked up as he entered. "Morning," she said. "What can I get started for you?"

"I'd like a medium green tea with honey and lemon, along with a black coffee."

"Anything else?"

The scent of the muffins was too much to ignore. "I'll take a muffin, as well." Sure, he didn't have to woo Sarah any longer. But really, she was doing him a solid favor. For that, he really was grateful. "You know," he said to the server. "Make that order for two muffins."

"I'll get those for you." As the server poured his coffee, Liam used his phone's app to pay.

"Here you go." At the end of the counter, the server set two cups in a drink container next to a paper bag. "The muffins are fresh from the oven."

Picking up his order, he hustled out the door. Traffic was

stopped once again. Three vehicles back, a car beeped its horn. From the driver's seat, Sarah waved. Balancing the drink tray, the paper bag and his duffel over his shoulder, he hustled to where she idled.

After setting the drinks on the roof of her car, he opened the back door. Once his bag was set on the rear seat, he opened the front door and slid into the passenger seat. As he slammed the door shut, traffic started moving. "Your timing was perfect."

She inhaled deeply. "Are those blueberry muffins?"

"They are." He set the tea and coffee into the car's cupholders. Then, he opened the bag. "You want one?"

"Yes, please." He handed her a muffin. "Thanks for picking up a tea."

Traffic stopped again. She eased her foot onto the break while peeling away the paper wrapper. She took a bite of muffin and hummed with satisfaction. The sound reverberated in his chest. He cast a glance in her direction. A piece of muffin stuck to her lip. She licked it away. The gesture was unassuming and, still, undeniably sexy. The car's interior suddenly became sweltering. He closed the heating vents and blew onto his coffee.

In front of them, traffic rolled forward.

"Here." Sarah held out her muffin. "Hold this."

Liam placed his hand under hers. Their gazes held. For a split second, he swore that she saw into his soul. It was the first time he'd been seen in years. No longer was he a cog in the machinery that was the FBI.

From behind, a horn blared.

Pulling away his hands, he said, "I got it."

Eyes forward, Sarah clenched the steering wheel with both hands, and drove.

Easing back into the seat, Liam tried to relax. Yet the feeling of his hands on hers still vibrated from his fingers to his wrist. He placed the muffin back in the bag and picked up his coffee cup. He took a long swallow, hoping that the caffeine high would reset his system. Because Liam knew one thing—if he was going to spend the next few days with Sarah and be professional, he was going to have to get his libido in check.

* * *

Sarah had never taken the trip from Boise to Owl Creek by herself. But when she learned about her numerous siblings, one thing was clear. They were part of the fabric that held Owl Creek together. If she wanted to see them, she'd be driving this way more often.

Leaning into the seatback, she sighed.

Liam looked at her from the passenger seat. "Everything okay?"

"There's a lot to deal with, you know? It's more than my mom being involved with Markus." Even his name tasted foul. "It's that Owl Creek is where they're from…"

"You mean all the other Colton kids?"

There was so much to say, but her throat was tight with emotions. "Yeah," she grumbled the single word. "I'm not sure what to do if I see one of them. Things still feel weird."

"What caused all the hurt feelings?"

"Honestly, I don't know why this is so difficult." Her shoulders slumped. "Since I don't know, anything I say will be a guess."

"You know, my middle name is Speculation."

"Your middle name is James," she said.

"Liam James Speculation Hill," he said. "I had it legally changed last year."

She didn't want to find him charming. But he was. With a quiet chuckle, she shook her head. "I forgot your corny sense of humor."

"You remembered that my middle name was James but forgot how I'm the King of Bad Jokes?"

Her shoulders relaxed, releasing some of the tension she'd been carrying for days.

"Honestly," he continued, "I'd like to hear what you think."

The highway ran between a forest on one side and a steep mountain peak on the other. Keeping her eyes on the road, she said, "I guess they were shocked to find out that Nate and I existed. Plus, who'd want a living and breathing reminder that your parents have been lying to you for years?" She lifted the tea from the cupholder and took a sip.

"I'm sure they don't blame you and Nate," said Liam. "How could they? You guys didn't ask to be born."

That was true. It was a thought that kept her awake on sleepless nights. "But we're a complication they can't ignore."

"I'm sure things will change," he said. "Once they get to know you, they'll come to love you."

She glanced at Liam and gave him a small smile. "I wish I had your optimism."

"We might not even run into any of your siblings."

"Now I know that you're optimistic. The Coltons are everywhere in Owl Creek." Like the fact that one of her Colton siblings, Ruby, was the local veterinarian. There was also Fletcher, an Owl Creek police detective. One sister owned a bookstore, and another owned a catering business. "It'll be me against them."

The tea in her stomach churned.

"I'll be with you." Liam smiled. The roiling changed to a quickening. "Besides, I am an FBI agent. They can't mess with you if I'm around."

She looked back at the road. "But they won't know that you're an agent. Besides, one of my brothers was with the FBI, too, I think."

He rubbed his forehead. "There are a lot of Colton kids. It's hard to wrap your head around all the siblings."

"Nate and I make a dozen."

She drove for several miles, neither one of them speaking. Finally, Liam cleared his throat. "We should probably discuss our cover story."

Cover story? "What do you mean? Are we supposed to have a made-up background? Because I'll be honest. I'm not going to be great with a lot of new details."

"For the most part, what we'll tell people is the truth. I'm Liam Hill—Allison's older brother. I came back to Boise for work and ran into you. We went out twice and realized that we have an amazing bond. Since we knew each other before, there's no awkward getting-to-know-you phase." He hooked air quotes around the words *getting to know you*. "So, sure, the relationship is moving fast, but who cares?"

"There are a lot of lies in our story. We aren't in a relation-ship." Picking up her tea, she took another sip. Working the cup back into the holder, she continued, "We don't care about each other."

"I get that you're mad at me still." Shifting in his seat, he turned to face her. "But if you carry your anger around like an accessory, nobody will believe that we're in love."

She inhaled and exhaled. "What will I have to do?"

"You and I will have to hold hands," said Liam. "Gaze into each other's eyes. Kiss in public."

Over the years, she'd wondered what it would be like to re-ally kiss him. Was she about to find out? But there would be no real emotions in the act. In a lot of ways, it would be worse than never knowing. "What about the hotel situation?"

"I booked us one room but there are two beds." He paused. "Nothing will blow our cover quicker than someone not believ-ing that we're a couple."

"Great. No pressure." Her hands ached. The ridges of the steering wheel pressed into her palms. She loosened her grip. "So how does this whole investigation thing work?"

"Once I have the evidence, Markus will be arrested. Then, there'll be a trial to determine his guilt or innocence."

"I'll have to testify, right?"

"You will."

How would Jessie feel when Sarah took the stand? Actu-ally, she didn't need to ask that question. She already knew the answer.

Her mom would be furious. She'd hate Sarah. It might de-stroy their relationship.

Might, hell.

Sarah couldn't worry about that right now. Instead, she asked another question. "Do you do this a lot? You know, work on undercover cases?"

She turned to glance in his direction. The sun caught him from behind and surrounded him with a golden halo. Then again, for much of her life, he'd seemed more like a deity than human.

"I barely get out of the Hoover Building," he said. "Most of my work has been analytics."

She asked, "Do you like it?"

"Define *like*," he joked. "Right now, it's all I do. It's all I know."

"You know the old saying about all work and no play."

Shaking his head, he gave a quick laugh. "Who knew a nursery rhyme was going to be the original slogan for a work/life balance?" He stretched his legs out. "I really don't have any kind of balance in my life. I only work. Right now, I'm hoping to get a promotion. Then again, the new job will mean longer hours and more responsibility. All the sacrifices will be worth it in the end."

"It's none of my business how much or little you work. It's no secret that I've always liked you. I just don't want you to have regrets." She waved a hand, as if erasing her words from the air. "Forget I said anything. You have a right to live the life you want. I'm not in any position to judge."

With an exhale, he looked out the window. Without turning to face her, he said, "Being back in Idaho made me realize all the things I've given up for my work." Liam leaned his chin on his fist and continued to stare out the window. "At the end of my life, I'll be able to look in the mirror and say, 'I worked hard.' Not a bad accomplishment. But think of the things I've missed already. Friends. Family. Love. The whole time, I've been so busy that I forgot that the whole point of life was to live."

She wanted to say something wise. Too bad she couldn't think of any advice. "Will this case help you get your promotion?"

"If I can bring down Markus Acker, my career is set."

"That's a good thing, right?"

"Yeah, it's a good thing."

She wasn't convinced.

A mileage sign stood on the side of the highway.

Owl Creek 20 Miles.

"Almost there," said Liam. "If you want to bail, now is the time. Call your mom and tell her we had a huge fight. Tell her that you're taking me back to Boise."

His plan was tempting. What's more, it would work.

Did she want to turn around now? Honestly, there was a part of her that just wanted to return to her uninteresting life. But could she live with herself if she ignored the people who lived at the compound? Also, what about Liam? Sure, she was hurt that he'd lied to her. But the wound was deep because she still cared.

She felt as if she stood on the edge of a cliff, wondering if she should jump. There was no turning back once she committed.

Rolling her shoulders back, conviction straightened her spine. "I'm in."

Chapter 8

Liam sat in the passenger seat and gazed out the window. A mountain peak rose in the distance and tall pine trees stood on either side of the road. The view was breathtaking. Or it would've been, except for the fact that he'd been asking himself a single, important question.

Was he ready to work as an undercover agent?

True, he'd fought to open the case and to be assigned as the special agent in charge. It had been another fight to bring Sarah on board. But he'd spent his whole career in the Rat Maze at headquarters. He didn't even have experience working with a criminal unit and out in the field—let alone being a singleton.

A large wooden sign surrounded by a dormant flower bed stood at the side of the road.

Welcome to Owl Creek, Idaho.

A Great Place to Visit. A Better Place to Live.

Owl Creek was like many towns in the Mountain West. Their economy was based on tourism. Skiing in the winter. Boating and hiking in the summer. Early March would be their low season, and it explained why the streets were all but empty. The buildings that lined Main Street were an eclectic mix of Victorian-era brick and new constructions.

Sarah eased her car next to the curb and put the gearshift

into Park. "We made it," she said. "Hutch's Diner is on the next block. It's the one with the blue-and-white-striped awning."

Liam opened the car door and stepped onto the sidewalk. The scent of pine hung in the air. "It's nice here." He slammed the door closed. "Not at all like DC."

Sarah had exited the car, as well. She stood next to the front bumper. "I thought you loved your city. What about spring coming early?"

He chuckled. "I guess I'm more of an Idaho boy than I thought."

Sarah stepped up onto the sidewalk and stood next to him. She was so close that he could touch her if he wanted. And honestly, he wanted to wrap his arms around her waist and pull her to him. But what did she want?

"I've never been to DC." Twisting from side to side, she stretched. "Obviously, I've read all about the monuments and museums. I'd love to see it one day."

For an instant, he wondered what it would be like to wander down the National Mall with Sarah. She'd want to read the entire quote wrapped around the inside of the Lincoln Monument. But what would she think of the words? Or if they visited the National Gallery, which exhibit would she like best?

The invitation clung to his lips.

He didn't know how to describe their relationship. Years ago, Sarah was his sister's best friend. Now, she was helping him catch a crook. She wasn't a coworker. She wasn't a friend. They weren't involved. Although he hoped they could fool everyone—including her mother—into thinking they were in love. Maybe their association was too complicated to define. "You should go one day."

"But only if it's in the spring, right?" She winked to show that she was teasing.

"We should probably cover some ground rules." The street was empty, but he lowered his voice to a whisper. After all, he couldn't be too careful. "Unless we're alone, we have to stay in character. You're you, Sarah Colton. I'm me, Liam Hill. We were childhood friends, and now we're in love. You don't have to say anything much about my job. But so long as you remember I work for a bank, we'll be okay."

"Got it," she said. And then, "Anything else?"

"We should probably hold hands."

"Yeah, sure." She slipped her palm into his.

An electric current ran up his arm and left his pulse racing. He wanted to think that his reaction was just natural tension. A lot was riding on this case. But he knew better. It was being close to Sarah.

They walked down the block. The restaurant's door opened. "There you are." Jessie Colton rushed toward the sidewalk with her arms opened wide. "I've missed you so much," she said, pulling Sarah into an embrace.

Stepping back, Sarah reached for his hand. "Mom, you remember Liam Hill. He's Allison's brother."

"It's been a while, but you haven't changed much," Jessie said, smiling.

"Well, you haven't changed at all."

Jessie squeezed his shoulder, and said, "It's good to see you, Liam." A large diamond ring flashed in the sunlight. "I saw you from our table and had to come out." She pointed to a window that overlooked the street.

"C'mon." Sarah's grip on his hand tightened. "Let's introduce you to Markus." Turning to her mother, she continued, "His client wants to invest in some nonprofits in Idaho. Since Markus is the pastor of a church, I thought that he might know some worthy charities."

Jessie's eyes went wide. "Of course Markus can help you. Tell me, would your client want to invest in a house of worship?"

Liam didn't need to worry about Sarah. She was a natural at working undercover. Turning to Jessie, he smiled. "That depends on the church."

Grasping his elbow, Jessie pulled him to the door. The snare had been set and it seemed like Jessie was interested in the bait. Only one question remained. Was the trap enough to fool someone as devious and dangerous as Markus Acker?

* * *

Jessie studied her daughter, looking for signs that Sarah was really in love.

She was dressed nicer than usual—none of those T-shirts with sayings that she found so humorous. For the day, she had on turtleneck sweater in deep red. It matched her lipstick perfectly. She also wore a pair of black slacks and boots.

But more than Sarah's clothes were different.

Her cheeks were rosy. Her hair was shiny. She stood tall and proud—not slouched over like she spent too much time hunched over books. The changes were slight but unmistakable. Sarah had fallen for Liam—again.

Inside, questions practically bubbled up and out. How did Sarah's old crush happen to waltz back into her life? What kind of clients did he represent? And most important—how much money did he want to donate?

Unlike all her kids who lived in Owl Creek, Sarah and Nate were different. Maybe it's because those two kids had been Jessie's alone. She didn't have to share them with either of her exes, Buck or Robert—she'd left Buck and Robert hadn't been around all that much. She never had to raise those two in the shadow of her sister, Jenny—the saint.

Liam held open the door for Jessie and Sarah to pass. She glanced at his watch. The timepiece was expensive. She knew the brand. Markus wore one, as well.

As they squeezed across the threshold, she leaned in close to her daughter. "You and I need to find some time to talk. There are obviously some things you haven't told me."

"Oh?" Sarah's eye went wide with feigned innocence. It was the same look she'd used since she was a kid and trying to blame her brother for her own misdeeds. "What's that?"

"You didn't tell me how handsome Liam had gotten." She paused. "Or that he was so successful."

Sarah glanced over her shoulder. "You know I don't really care about money."

True, she didn't care about money. If she did, then she would have majored in prelaw or premed or even business. But no,

Sarah insisted on library sciences. It didn't matter that she'd be poor her entire life. She loved books and wanted to be happy.

But Jessie knew different. Happiness without money was impossible.

"Well, he certainly is a catch," she said, her voice not much more than a whisper. She led them through Hutch's Diner.

It was the same place she'd come for years. The walls were filled with memories, both good and bad. She was working as a waitress in this very restaurant the first time Buck asked her on a date. Years later, they'd brought Malcolm here to celebrate his first birthday. The original owner, Hutch, had still been alive and the celebration dinner had been on the house. The first time Robert suggested they leave Owl Creek was on the sidewalk in front of the diner. That last memory stabbed her in the side. Yet, she was intent on only being happy. And speaking of happiness, Markus waited at a table near the window.

"Darling," she said, placing both her hands in his. "I want you to meet Liam Hill. He's an old family friend and is in Idaho on business."

Markus didn't like new people, she knew. He had a hard time trusting others. Then again, who could blame him after all the lies that circulated on the internet? In fact, he hadn't wanted to come to brunch at all. But Jessie had insisted and now, she was happy that she had.

Smiling sweetly, she tossed her hair over her shoulder. "Liam's client is looking for a charity that might need a donation. Sarah thought of you and the church." That wasn't exactly what her daughter had suggested, but it was close enough to the truth. Besides, it was exactly what Markus would want to hear.

Her fiancé's face went slack for a moment. Then, he smiled. It was the same charm he exuded from the pulpit. "Sarah, honey," he said as he stood. "Good to see you." He pulled her in for a quick peck on the cheek. "And Liam." Markus held out his hand to shake. "Nice to meet you."

"Nice to meet you, as well," said Liam. "I hate to mix business and family, but Jessie and Sarah think you can help me out."

Drawing his brows together, Markus nodded slowly. It was

his grave-and-concerned look. She'd seen it more than once. One of the things she loved most about Markus was that he always knew what people wanted to see and hear. "I'll help if I can. Have a seat and tell me what you need."

Jessie waited until Liam sat next to Markus. Sarah sat to Liam's right. Finally, Jessie took her own chair. As she looked around the table, she felt light with contentment. This is what she'd always wanted—a loving relationship with her children, and a devoted man in her life. Sure, she'd made some mistakes. But she'd been treated poorly, too. Now, all the difficulties were in the past and she could finally live the life she wanted.

From here on, nothing could go wrong.

Liam sat between Markus and Sarah. Just like he'd sprinted the last leg of a race, adrenaline surged through his system. Then again, sitting across from the target of his investigation was akin to crossing the finish line.

He picked up a pre-poured glass of water and took a sip. The gesture gave him a minute to get an initial read of Markus. He wore his dark blond hair short. Even for this lunch, he wore a well-tailored charcoal gray suit, white shirt and blue tie. Serious. Conventional. Trustworthy. In short, he dressed the part of a man who led a successful church.

But he'd seen the bank statements. According to the paperwork filed with the IRS, Markus and his church didn't take in much money. It was up to Liam to get the evidence proving all of that was a lie. So, he hadn't crossed the finish line at all. In fact, he'd just completed the first leg of a grueling multistage endurance event.

Markus watched Jessie as she chatted with her daughter. He smiled. The expression filled his eyes with genuine warmth. Did the pastor really love Sarah's mom? It seemed so.

Leaning toward Markus, he lowered his voice. "I remember Sarah's mom from when I was a kid. She was always anxious about one thing or another. Just seeing her for two minutes now, I can tell that she's more relaxed. Seems like she's a changed woman."

Markus sat straighter. "You think so?"

"I do." A twinge of guilt caught in his throat. He didn't like using Markus's feelings for Jessie against him. Then again, if he wasn't going to put Acker in jail, why was he in Owl Creek at all? "Seems like you showed up at the right time to save Jessie."

"Save Jessie," Markus repeated. "I'd like to think that I, along with the members of the Ever After Church, helped her through her grief."

"I'm sure it was more you than anyone else."

"Tell me." Markus turned to face Liam. "Are you a religious man?"

Liam sighed. "I don't go to church if that's what you're asking. But I do have a strict set of beliefs."

"Oh?" Markus picked up his own glass of water and took a drink. "What are those?"

"I do what's right for my clients—especially if we can both profit."

Throwing back his head, Markus laughed. "Who do you work for now?"

"My bank's headquarters is in Washington, DC." Liam gave Markus all the information from his undercover profile.

"What client has brought you to Owl Creek?"

"Well," he said, "it was Sarah who brought me to Owl Creek. I was working in Boise."

"Fair enough. But you still haven't told me much about your client."

Liam exhaled. "I'm sure you understand confidentiality—being the pastor of a large church and all. My clients expect discretion from me, much as your congregation expects it from you."

"I understand completely," said Markus. "What's more, I value a man who can keep his own counsel." He paused. "I understand that you used to work for the FBI."

Liam nodded. It'd be impossible to escape that truth. "I did."

"Can I ask why you left the Bureau? Don't most people stay with the federal government until they retire?"

"Have you seen how much FBI agents get paid?" he asked.

Markus shook his head. "Can't say that I have."

"Let's put it this way—it's not nearly enough money to live in a place like DC."

Markus chuckled. "Jessie mentioned something about investing in a charity."

The charity investment wasn't part of the original script, but something Sarah had added. Even though he'd never worked in the field, he knew that to be a successful undercover agent, he needed to improvise. He said, "It's one way to create a connection with a community."

"Does this charity have to be in Boise? I have some contacts in churches there, of course," Markus continued, wiping sweat from the side of his glass. "But if you could work with an organization closer to Owl Creek, I could personally help you out."

Liam recalled one time he and his father had gone fishing on the Payette River outside Boise. It had been boring just standing on the riverbank, waiting for a fish to bite. But one had.

Pull him in but slowly, his father had advised. *Otherwise, he won't swallow the hook all the way and might get loose. Make him think that he's coming for you. The fish has gotta think it was his idea all along.*

He had to follow his dad's advice from all those years ago. "I appreciate your offer to help locally, but this really isn't where my client plans to relocate." His mouth was dry. Picking up the water, he drained the glass in a single swallow. "But if you can make any introductions to organizations in Boise, that'd be great."

With a sigh, Markus smoothed down his tie. "Of course. There are plenty of worthy charities. How much do you plan to invest?"

A server, clad in a white shirt and black pants, walked past. Liam waved. "Do you have a slip of paper and a pen?"

"Of course." They removed both from the apron that was tied around their waist. Placing them on the table, the server said, "There you go."

Liam wrote a sum on the square of paper: $500,000. He slid it toward Markus. "This is confidential, of course."

"Of course," the pastor repeated. He removed a pair of reading glasses from the inside pocket of his suit jacket. After donning the glasses, he looked down at the sheet. His eyes widened for an instant. The change was gone as quick as it came. But Markus had swallowed the hook. "Let me make some calls on your behalf. Until then, maybe you'd like to see where we're building our next church."

"I'll have to talk to Sarah and see what she has planned..."

"I insist," said Markus. "Besides, I don't think that Sarah's been by our new home. I know that Jessie's proud of what we've built."

Yep, the hook was in very deep. "I'm sure we can figure something out. Sarah and I are in town until Sunday."

"Come by tomorrow morning. By then, I'll have a list of worthy charities for your client." He wiped his mouth with a napkin and stood. "Excuse me a minute. I need to make a call."

Jessie looked over as Markus rose. "Where are you going?"

"I just need to check on something."

"Now?" Jessie asked. "After Sarah and Liam came all this way to meet us? Can't it wait?"

Markus placed his lips on Jessie's cheek. Closing her eyes, she leaned into the kiss. He said, "I won't be gone for a minute. Order food. You know what I like. We're here to celebrate since Sarah's come to visit."

Sarah gave a tight-lipped smile.

Markus strode across the dining room. From a nearby table, two men with short haircuts and thick necks rose. They followed Markus from the dining room. He'd seen the photos from the church compound and the armed guards at the gate. It appeared that Markus had his own security detail, as well.

"What's up with the bodyguards?" he asked, as they left the restaurant.

Jessie sighed. "Markus has gotten some threats recently. It's like that with important people. We felt it best to put extra protection in place."

"What kind of threats?" asked Sarah. "Are you safe?"

Jessie patted the back of her daughter's hand. "I didn't want to mention anything to you, hon. It's just trolling on the internet. Nothing to worry about."

Before Jessie could continue, Markus returned.

Smoothing down his tie, he smiled. "Crisis averted. Have we ordered yet? I'm starving."

"You look like you're in a good mood," said Jessie, leaning into Markus's side. "What's up?"

"I got some really great news, that's all."

Liam's phone pinged with a text. He checked his watch for the message. It was from Constance. "Someone searched you on the internet. The background we planted was all they found."

He wasn't surprised. Obviously, Markus had left the table and conducted a search for Liam. The fact that he'd only found what the FBI wanted him to see meant that everything was going as planned.

It also meant that Markus really had swallowed the bait completely. Now, it was up to Liam to reel him in.

Chapter 9

Sarah hooked her arm through her mother's elbow as they left the restaurant. A black SUV was parked at the curb. A man jumped from the passenger seat and opened the back door.

"That's our ride." Jessie gave her arm a squeeze. "I'll see you tomorrow."

"Looking forward to it." She pulled her mother in for a quick hug. When had her mom gotten so thin? Thin, hell. Jessie felt frail. "How are you, Mom?" she asked, whispering into her ear. "Honestly?"

Jessie held her at arm's length. "Right now, I'm thrilled. I love having you here. Liam seems like a nice guy. Markus likes him, too. I'm delighted for us all."

She studied her mother's face. "But are you always happy?"

"I always live in the now. And this moment is filled with peace and bliss."

Her mother was with a man who needed armed guards. How could that be peaceful? Liam and Markus stood up the block. Heads bowed together, they talked.

Sarah felt the irrational need to tell her mom everything. How Liam was actually with the FBI. That the feds had Markus in their sights for stealing from his followers.

Then again, it wouldn't make a difference.

As soon as she got the chance, Jessie would tell Markus everything.

Her mom needed to see that he was a total creep for herself. Otherwise, she wouldn't believe what anyone—even Sarah—had to say.

"Earth to Sarah." Her mother waved her hand. "Come in, Sarah."

"Yeah, sorry," Had her mother been talking to her? "I zoned out for a minute."

"I'd say you did. I asked if you'd seen my new bag." Her mother held up a leather purse with red and green trim. "Markus bought it for me last week."

Sarah knew little about expensive brands, but she recognized the designer. "Wow, Mom. That's really nice. I bet it cost as much as my car's worth."

"Don't be silly." Jessie smoothed her hand over the glossy leather. "This cost twice what your car is worth."

Ouch.

Markus and Liam approached. Both men were laughing. Markus slid into the waiting SUV. "Let's go," he barked from inside the vehicle. "I have to stop at the post office before we go back."

Jessie reached for Sarah's hand. "Take care of yourself and I'll see you tomorrow."

Her mother's hand started slipping away. Sarah tightened her grip on Jessie's fingers. "Mom, you know I love you, right?"

"I know." She squeezed Sarah's hand once more before letting her fingers slip from her grasp. Her mother got into the SUV. The door closed and the vehicle drove away.

"As far as the Bureau is concerned, this brunch was a rousing success."

"Well, I'm super happy for your successes," she said, knowing that her tone was less than super happy.

"You don't sound pleased."

That was an understatement. "How am I supposed to feel? My mom is cozied up to the world's biggest scumbag. Why? Is it really for all the designer bags and flashy jewelry?"

"I'm sorry," said Liam. "I wish I could…"

She waved away his apology. "It's not your fault."

But that wasn't exactly true, either. As crazy as it sounded, even in her own mind, she wouldn't betray her mother for anyone other than Liam Hill.

"I know my mom," she said, her voice small. "She's never been a good person." Was she allowed to say that out loud? Sure, she'd thought it before. Even when she was a kid, her mom wasn't like most parents. She wasn't proud when Sarah or her brother did well. Instead, she was jealous of their accomplishments. And, of course, Jessie had been hiding a whole other family. "How could she keep me and Nate away from all our siblings?" But there was more. "How could she abandon all those kids?" The last word came out as a sob.

"Hey, hey, hey." Liam gripped her shoulders. His hands were warm and strong. She wanted to lean into his chest. Yet, she didn't dare. Because if she did, she'd never leave his side.

"I'm okay." She drew in a shaking breath. "I'll be okay." At least her second statement was closer to the truth. Whatever her mother did, Sarah always rallied.

"We've got a few hours before we can check in to the hotel. Owl Creek looks like a nice little town. Want to wander?" He pointed across the street. "There's a bookstore."

An hour of roving through stacks of books was the exact salve her soul needed. "You do know how to woo a lady—at least a librarian."

He reached for her hand.

For a moment, she ignored his outstretched palm. Then again, they were supposed to be a couple. Sarah slid her fingers between his. They fit together perfectly, like they'd been woven into a single being. She lifted her gaze to him. He was watching her with his big, brown eyes. She wanted to kiss him— just to see how his lips felt against hers. She moved closer and tilted her chin up. He moved closer still, erasing the distance between them.

A truck, its exhaust pipe rattling, roared past.

Sarah stepped back. "That was loud."

Liam ran a hand over his mouth. "Tell me about it." Another car passed. "Looks like it's all clear. Let's go."

Hand in hand, Sarah and Liam jogged across the pavement. Book Mark It. It sat in the middle of the block. The front windows were filled with a variety of titles—both newly released bestsellers and well-known classics. Liam reached around Sarah to grab the handle and pull the door open. His chest pressed into her back. His breath washed over her shoulder. A little shiver of excitement danced down her spine.

In the bookstore, the scent of paper and ink mixed with the aroma of coffee. Sarah inhaled deeply, and her shoulders began to relax. Her jaw loosened. At least for a few minutes, she could let her tension slip away.

"Are you okay for a few minutes?" Liam asked. "I want to find a quiet corner and text my boss. They're waiting for an update in DC."

"Go ahead," she said. "At least you have good news to share."

"Thanks a million." He pressed his lips onto her cheek. Her heart skipped a beat. Then again, it didn't matter what she felt. Any affection was part of the act.

The shop was filled with neat rows of books. The genre fiction section filled three of four walls. Mystery. Romance. Sci-fi and Fantasy. Nonfiction shelves were toward the back. Tables, heavy with discounted reads, were scattered throughout.

Running her fingers over a shelf, she scanned the titles.

"Excuse me," a woman called out. "Can I help you find anything?"

Sarah turned to the sound of the voice. Her heart ceased to beat.

Standing in the middle of the store was her sister Frannie Colton.

Hands on hips, she stared at her sister. "Sarah," she said, the single word ringing out like a thunderclap. "What are you doing here?"

Pulse racing, she stared at Frannie. Her sister wore her golden hair loose around her shoulders. For the day, she'd donned a pair of jeans, a cardigan and a T-shirt emblazoned with Read Banned Books. It was nearly identical to the shirt Sarah owned and loved to wear.

"I, uh, well, I..." Her mind froze up, spluttering, like a car that wouldn't start. She glanced over her shoulder, looking for Liam and some support. He'd disappeared into the racks. Great. She had to face her sister alone. "I didn't know you owned this store. I mean, I knew you owned a bookstore, but I never heard which one." She realized her mistake, but only once it was too late. "I should've looked you up or asked Jessie just now."

Frannie narrowed her eyes. "Your mom was here?"

After Robert's death, Jessie had tried to sue for his estate. Her mom's plan didn't work but it had certainly made Sarah and Nate's attempt at any relationship with Robert's other children more awkward. Still, Sarah couldn't deny the truth or ignore the question.

"Yeah, I met her here for brunch." She wondered if roadkill felt as beat up and flattened as she did right now. "I better go."

"No, wait." Her sister reached for Sarah's arm. "I don't want you to leave. I mean, you can, if you don't want to stay. I'm not kidnapping you or anything. It's just, well, we've never had a chance to chat." Frannie inhaled. She let out a long exhale. "Sorry. I was rambling. Can I get you a coffee? I mean, you just had brunch, so maybe you aren't really thirsty or anything…"

Was Frannie nervous, too? "Do you have tea?"

"I have so many different types of tea. What kind do you like?"

"I'll try your favorite."

"Aw, that's so sweet of you." Frannie walked toward the café. It was just a few tables on the far side of the bookstore with a pastry case and espresso machine. "Do you like hibiscus green tea?"

"As long as you have honey."

"How could I call myself a bookstore café if I didn't have honey?" Frannie slipped behind the counter and filled a mug with hot water from an electric kettle. She dropped in a tea bag and placed the mug on the counter. As the tea steeped, she said, "I heard you're a librarian in Boise."

Sarah nodded. "I started my job after finishing up grad school."

"Must be exciting to run a big library—all those books." Frannie sighed and leaned her forearms on the counter.

"I love my job. My favorite thing is to put a reader together with the perfect book. But administration is a lot of unglamorous work."

"Obviously, running a small business is hard. Owl Creek is supportive of the store, so we do okay," said Frannie. "But I'm with you. The best part of my day is when a book shows up at the store and I know which customers will love it." She paused. "It's nice to meet a fellow Colton who's also a bibliophile. I never fit in. Everyone else is so active and physically fit."

Honestly, she didn't know much beyond the basic details about her other siblings. "In Boise, it was just me and Nate." Then again, Nate was a police officer. He went for a run every morning and visited the gym several times a week. If there was ever a fight, he was in the middle, trying to break people apart. So yeah, he was definitely one of those active Coltons. "When we were kids, he was the athlete. I was just happy to sit in a corner and read."

"It sounds like I finally have someone who understands me. What a relief." Frannie slumped comically. For a moment, neither woman spoke. Frannie pushed the mug of tea across the counter. "Looks like this is ready. The honey's over there," she said, pointing. A ceramic sugar dish, cream pitcher and matching honey pot all sat on a table at the end of the counter.

Sarah picked up her tea and walked to the table. As she put a drizzle of honey into her tea, she said, "I love your shirt, by the way. I have the same one. Mine is blue."

"Oh my gosh, really?" Her sister approached with her own mug of tea in hand. "We'll have to wear them at the same time and get a picture. I'll hang it up behind the cash register in a frame and call it 'The Colton sisters against censorship.'"

"I'd like that," she said. She'd love to have a picture with Frannie. She took a sip of tea. It was warm and sweet. "This is really good."

"Glad you like it," said Frannie with a smile.

When she smiled, her sister looked just like their dad. For a moment, grief filled her chest. Sarah couldn't breathe.

"How long are you in town?" her sister asked.

"My friend Liam has some work in Owl Creek. We're here over night, for sure. After that?" She shrugged.

"Can I be honest?" Frannie asked. She didn't wait for an answer and continued, "I'm so happy you stopped in today. It's kinda like fate. I've been thinking about you a lot." She nodded toward a table. "Do you have a minute?"

"Sure." Sarah carried her cup to the closest table and slid into a chair. Frannie took a seat across from her and set down her own mug. "What's up?"

"Well, it's about what happened after my dad—correction, our dad—died. Everything was so chaotic. Jessie came looking for money, and then we all found out about you and Nate." She paused, blew on her tea and took a sip. "Well, none of us Coltons behaved the way we should have. You're part of our family. You lost your dad, just the same as me, and Fletcher and Lizzy and everyone else." She took another sip of tea. "I know you came to the wedding, but I wanted to call over the past few months. I wasn't sure if you wanted to hear from me. Sorry for not reaching out."

Sarah's throat tightened, filling with emotions. "I appreciate your apology and I accept."

"Are you sure you forgive me? I don't want you to just to be polite."

"I absolutely forgive you."

Frannie reached across the table and gripped Sarah's wrist. "I couldn't bring a baby into the world knowing that I had a sister out there and we weren't speaking."

She looked at Frannie again, taking her in from the top of her head to her feet. How had she not noticed the baby bump before? "A baby? That's so exciting!"

"I'm sure he or she will love their aunt Sarah very much."

"Aunt Sarah?" she echoed. "That's not something I expected to hear today. Or tomorrow. Or for a long time."

"Well, we'll all have to wait for this little one to start talking first." Frannie placed a hand on her middle.

"And, of course, we will get the little one reading," she joked.

Frannie said, "Dante loves books, so it'll be in our baby's DNA."

"There you are," said Liam, approaching from the bookstore side. "My one text turned into a long exchange. When I looked up, you were gone." She imagined that his superiors with the FBI would have questions about his progress.

"Liam, I want you to meet Frannie Colton, my sister. She's one of Robert's daughters."

"Sarah said you were here for your job," said Frannie. "What kind of work do you do?"

Liam repeated his cover story. He worked for a bank and was looking for property for a client. There was extra money for a local charity, maybe one in Owl Creek. Blah, blah, blah. "We just had brunch with Jessie and Markus."

"Oh, him." Frannie rolled her eyes.

"Sounds like Markus isn't your favorite person," said Liam.

Sarah wasn't going to let her sister get dragged into the investigation. Rising from her seat, she reached for Liam's arm. "We should probably get going. You have work to do, I'm sure."

Her sister stood, too. "Maybe we can get together before you leave. What're you doing for dinner tonight?"

There was a lot she didn't know about an undercover investigation—like what was she supposed to do until they visited Jessie and Markus in the morning. "I'm not sure what we have planned."

"Our night is pretty open," said Liam. "Getting together for dinner would be great."

She hated to be suspicious. But she had learned the hard way that Liam was always focused on his investigation. So why was he so keen to have dinner with Frannie and Dante? In the end, it didn't matter. Pulling the phone from her pocket, she opened the contact app. "Give me your number," she said, handing the phone to her sister. "I'll send you a text."

Frannie typed in her contact information, then held out the phone to Sarah. "Here you go."

After saving the contact, she typed a long line of hearts and hit Send. "Now you have my number, too."

Frannie's phone pinged. Pulling it from the back pocket of her jeans, she checked the screen. "We'll keep in touch. There's a lot of missed years to make up for."

She opened her arms and her sister stepped in for a hug. "I'm so glad that I wandered into the store today. It feels like a new chapter for me."

Her sister squeezed her tighter. "It's a new chapter for everyone."

She wanted to believe that everyone would get a happy ending, even her.

There was more to the story. How would all the Coltons feel once they understood the plot twist? Would Frannie still want to make up for lost time when she learned that everything Sarah just told her was a lie?

Chapter 10

Sarah and Liam stood on the sidewalk that ran between the bookstore and Main Street. A cold wind blew from the mountains. Tucking her nose into her collar of her coat, she trudged down the sidewalk.

"Anything you want to do right now?" Liam asked. "We still have time before check-in."

"After sitting in the car all morning, I'd like to walk. We can explore Owl Creek a little bit."

"Works for me," he said.

They walked without speaking. With each step, it was easy to let her mind wander. How different would her life have been if she'd grown up in a place like this, surrounded by family?

"You seem happy," said Liam, nudging her side with his elbow.

"I guess I am," she confessed. "I was worried about coming to Owl Creek. My mom. Running into one of my half siblings. The fact that we're pretending to be dating for the sake of your case." She glanced over her shoulder to make sure they were alone on the street. They were. "So far, this trip has gone better than I hoped."

"You think your mom will be okay once she knows the truth?" Liam asked.

Staring at the concrete as they walked, she stepped over a

break between the slabs. Even now—as an adult—the childish rhyme filled her head.

Don't step on a crack or you'll break your mother's back.

As a kid, Sarah was terrified of hurting her mother in any way. Because of her father's frequent absences, Sarah always felt responsible for her mother's happiness. Time had changed a lot of things. Like now, she was working with the federal government to send Markus to jail. Her mother's life would be upended when that happened.

"There's no getting around it. My mom's going to be furious when she knows that I helped the FBI. But she needs to be saved, too. Otherwise, she'll end up in jail with Markus." She stepped over another crack in the sidewalk. "Running into Frannie has made this trip special. Not only is she my sister, but we have a lot in common."

"I noticed," said Liam with a wide smile. "You'll get to know her better at dinner."

His smile left her heart racing. She dropped her gaze back to the sidewalk. "Maybe we should cancel." She kicked a stone, and it skittered over the curb.

"Cancel? I thought you liked Frannie. Don't you want to see her husband?"

"I like her, and I'd love to see Dante again. But getting together means continuing the lie." She added quickly. "You and I aren't a couple. It's all pretend. I might get to know more about her, but she won't know anything about me."

"Go without me," he said, shoving his hands deep into his pockets. "That way, I'm not part of the equation."

Sarah glanced up, but she forgot whatever she planned to say. A black SUV sat at the end of the block. Her hands went icy, and she started to tremble. Looping her arm through the crook of Liam's elbow, she pulled him closer. "Look at the next block. Do you see it?"

The muscles in his arm went taut. "You mean the vehicle?"

The shadows of two people were visible in both the driver's and passenger seat. "What're the chances it's the same one that brought my mom and Markus into town?"

"That's definitely the same SUV." He paused. "It means that

they took your mom and Markus home. Then, turned around and came back to Owl Creek."

"Why'd they do that?" she asked, although she already knew the answer.

"They're spying on us," he said. "On me."

It was just like Markus to be suspicious. "Then we have to give them something to report," she said. "We should kiss."

"Are you sure?"

She stroked the side of his face and smiled. "Remember, this isn't for me or you. But for them." She tilted her head toward the SUV.

He wound his arm around her waist and pulled her to him. Her breasts pressed against his chest. He placed his lips on hers. She was keenly aware of the security guards at the end of the block. Were they watching with binoculars? From a distance, would they be able to tell that the kiss was a fake?

She wrapped her arms around Liam's neck, pulling him closer. He moaned, his breath mingling with hers. Sarah couldn't help herself and she parted her lips. Liam understood the invitation. He slipped his tongue inside her mouth and kissed her hard. It was a kiss meant to conquer and claim. With a sigh, she surrendered.

He moved his hand from her waist to the small of her back. He pulled her closer, until there was no room between them. The muscles in his shoulders and pecs were tight. His abs were hard. His legs were long and lean. In short, he was everything a man should be.

Then again, the kiss was only for show. By now, the guards had seen enough.

She placed her hands on his chest and pushed back. Running her teeth over her lower lip, she peered down the street. It was empty. "They're gone."

Liam pressed his forehead into hers. "Should we talk about what just happened?"

"I think that this kiss was better than the last time," she said, teasing even though he'd sent the butterflies in her belly into a frenzy. "I'm sure we fooled the guards."

After drawing in a deep breath, he blew it out. "Very convincing for anyone watching."

"Good." The ghost of his kiss lingered on her lips. Hot blood ran through her veins. How was she supposed to work with him now?

"The thing is…" Liam began. His cell phone began to ring. Pulling it from his pocket, he glanced at the screen. "It's the hotel." He swiped the call open. "Hello?"

The speaker function wasn't turned on, but it didn't matter. Sarah could clearly hear the caller on the other end of the line. "Mr. Hill, this is Rakai Paku, the manager of The Inn on the Lake. I wanted to let you know that your room is ready. You can check in anytime you like."

The Inn on the Lake overlooked Blackbird Lake. The front porch was surrounded by white railing. Tables and chairs were clustered in groups. If the weather was nice, it would be a perfect place to sit and enjoy the view. The lake was to the left and the mountains rose beyond the water. At one time, it had been the home of Owl Creek's founder. Made of golden bricks, the luxurious estate had been renovated to a resort. An outdoor pool, closed for the winter, sat behind a wrought iron fence. A tennis court was on the other side of the pool.

Liam sat in the passenger seat of Sarah's car. She maneuvered the station wagon into a parking place marked with a sign: Reserved for Guests.

His pulse pounded, echoing in his ears. The memory of Sarah's body pressed against his own still warmed his flesh. The scent of her soap and floral shampoo clung to him, as well. He inhaled deeply.

"This place is nice," she said, misreading his intake of breath.

It was better if she didn't know that the kiss left him drunk with lust. Because Sarah was like a fine wine—sweet, light and intoxicating. He'd only gotten a taste of her, and now he wanted more. Spending the night in the same room would be a special kind of torture. Then again, he had recruited her, so he was wholly to blame for his own mess.

She continued, "I wonder how much a place like this costs for a night."

"It's expensive," he said, happy to keep the conversation neutral. "I live in DC, where everything is pricey. But booking the room brought a tear to my eye and I was paying with an expense account."

"I guess this is one of the perks of working undercover." She pressed a button on her steering wheel and the trunk opened with a pop. "Let's go."

Liam exited the car and then grabbed his duffel bag from the back seat. Sarah rounded to the rear and got her small suitcase from the trunk. After setting the luggage on the ground, she extended the handle and slammed the trunk closed.

A set of glass doors opened automatically as they approached the front of the hotel. The check-in desk was at the far side of the room. A grouping of chairs, upholstered in buttery-yellow fabric, surrounded a low table. A TV hung on a wall that separated the lobby from a restaurant. The television was set to a local news station. A meteorologist stood in front of an Idaho map. "A storm system is moving down from Canada. Expect more snow over the next few days. Seems like Old Man Winter isn't done with us yet..."

A dark-haired man stood behind the registration counter. He wore a name tag that read Mr. Paku, General Manager. He smiled as they approached. "May I help you?"

"We have a reservation under the name Hill."

"Nice to see you, Mr. Hill," said the manager. He slid a small envelope over the counter. "You're in room 317. The keys are inside here—" he tapped the envelope with a pen "—along with the password for the Wi-Fi. If you need anything, just press zero on the room phone. It rings to the front desk. The elevator is at the end of that hallway." He pointed to the corridor that ran to the left.

Liam scooped up the keycards. "Thank you so much," he said, giving Mr. Paku a small wave.

With Sarah at his side, they walked to the elevator. He waited as she pushed the call button. The doors opened automatically, and they stepped into the car. She pressed the button for the third floor and the doors slid closed. She stood a few feet in front of him. It gave him the perfect view of her from the back. Her round ass. Her hips. The way her jeans hugged her thighs. The light from overhead shone down, bringing out the fiery highlights in her hair. His fingers itched with curiosity. If he touched her hair, would he get burned?

In the small elevator, Liam was trapped with the truth. Sarah was more than pretty, smart and funny. She was even more than someone with whom he had a shared history. She was the kind of woman he'd choose to date if he ever made time for a relationship.

It was too bad that she and he were separated by an entire continent. If they were together, things might be different. But he hated the idea of a long-distance relationship. To him, loving someone from afar was worse than being alone.

The door opened. Sarah stepped out of the elevator, her rolling suitcase trailing behind her. Liam followed. A plastic sign hung on the wall. Rooms one through twenty were to the right. Twenty-one through forty were on the left.

"Looks like our room is that way," she said, before turning. He followed her, his feet suddenly too heavy for his legs. She glanced over his shoulder. "Are you okay?"

"Just tired, I guess," he lied. Because there was one other truth he had to finally admit. He wanted to take Sarah as his lover. It didn't matter that the relationship was a sham. His desire for her was real.

But there was something else he knew. If he slept with Sarah, he'd lose more than his chance at the promotion. He'd lose his job, as well. It meant he couldn't let anything happen between the two of them. Remaining professional was going to be the hardest part of an already complicated investigation.

Sarah stood in front of the door to room 317. Liam tapped the keycard on the lock before pushing down on the handle. As the door swung open, she had a clear memory of sitting in Allison's childhood bedroom.

The two girls sat on the bed, crisscross-applesauce. Each girl held a pillow.

"Now, you have to hold it like this." Using the pillow as a fake torso, Allison continued, *"One hand behind the head. The other behind the back."*

Sarah copied the hold.

"Now, you lean in and kiss." Allison smooched her pillow. She set the pillow down, an unmistakable slobber mark on the case.

"I'll try." With an inhale, she puckered her lips and brought the pillow to her face. Like a million bubbles came out of her middle, she started to giggle. Burying her face in the pillow, she squealed, *"I can't."*

"Yes, you can. And you have to. How else are you supposed to know how to kiss when it comes time?"

At twelve years old, it was a reasonable question.

"I guess I'll just figure it out," she said, already thinking of the love scenes she'd read in the romance novels that had been purloined from her mother.

"It's not something you can read in a book. It's something you have to experience."

In seventh grade, Allison was already the star of the middle school lacrosse team. There were rumors she would be moved up to JV in the spring. Sarah usually stood on the sidelines, only playing when it was a blowout, and she couldn't do much damage. Even then, her feet always got tangled and the ball never stayed in the pocket of her crosse.

"Try again," Allison urged.

More giggles.

"Honestly," Allison huffed. *"Concentrate."*

"How is this even practice? I know the difference between a pillow and a person."

"You gotta use your imagination. Close your eyes."

Sarah did as she was told.

"Now, think of a guy you really like. And not my brother. That'd be so gross if you practice kissed Liam with my pillow. It has to be someone from our grade."

How was Sarah supposed to find any of the guys in her class attractive? All of them were defined by the three S's. Skinny. Spotty. Smelly.

With her eyes still closed, Sarah's mind filled with an image of Liam standing next to the pool in the Hills' backyard. Wearing nothing but swim trunks, his abs and pecs were defined. A thin line of hair ran from his navel down the front of his shorts. He smiled. His teeth were brilliantly white against his tanned skin.

"Do you have someone in mind?" Allison asked.

"Yes."

"Is it Liam?"

"I'm not thinking of your brother," Sarah lied.

Allison continued, *"Keep your eyes closed and imagine what it's like to kiss him. Then, kiss the pillow."*

Sarah brought the pillow to her face and puckered her lips. In her mind, Liam's hand rested on her cheek. Her fingers were wrapped in his hair. *"Oh, Sarah,"* he'd whisper. *"You are so beautiful."* And then, he'd place his lips on hers.

She set the pillow on her lap.

"How was that?" Allison asked.

"Not as bad as I thought." Her pulse raced, as the pretend kiss still buzzed through her mind.

Flopping onto her back, Allison asked, *"What'd you think your first time with a guy will be like?"*

Sarah lay on her side. *"I dunno. Awkward. Messy."*

"You're too literal. Don't you want romance?"

"Okay, what's your first time going to be like?"

"Prom night with Topher."

"No way. He's the same age as your brother. When we're eighteen, he'll be—" she paused and mentally did the math *"—in law school. No way will he take you to prom."*

"See, there you go, being all literal." Allison swatted Sarah with her pillow. *"Come on, what do you think your first time will be like?"*

Again, she thought of Liam. *"We'll check into a fancy hotel, where it's just the two of us. He'll be gentle and loving."*

"See, that's romantic. Who with?"

"Billy Frierson," said Sarah. Billy was an interesting combination of cute and smart.

As it turned out, her first time had been with Billy on prom night. It had been awkward and messy and sweet. But now, standing in the hallway of a fancy hotel, it was like her pre-teen fantasy was about to come true. But there was one huge difference.

Now, Sarah knew what adults did behind closed doors.

As she crossed the threshold, her luggage rolling behind her, the phone in her pocket began to vibrate. She pulled out her cell and glanced at the screen.

Caller ID read: Frannie Colton.

She swiped the call open.

"Hey, Frannie," she said. "What's up?"

"I hope I'm not interrupting but I was wondering if Malcolm could join us for dinner. He stopped by the store today and I told him about meeting you and how we had plans for dinner. He asked if he could tag along. I didn't know what to say, but figured I should call you and ask." She paused. "No pressure, though."

"Of course," she said. It was funny that she'd been wor-ried before about being rejected by her Colton siblings. Now, it seemed like they wanted to get to know her. "I'd love to see Malcolm."

"Great. I'll tell him. He'll be so stoked. Let's meet at Tap Out Brewery at seven."

"See you then," she said before the call ended.

With the phone pressed to her chest, she pivoted.

Liam stood right behind her, hanging his coat in a small closet. She stumbled back. Her thighs hit her bag and she started to fall. He reached for her, catching her wrist before she went down.

"You okay?"

"Yeah, thanks. It's the second time you've kept me from going ass over tea kettle."

He smiled and let go of her arm. "Glad to help."

"I'm a bit of a klutz. I guess that's why I've always been such a book nerd."

Gripping her suitcase, she rolled the bag toward the room. Liam moved at the same moment. She placed her palm on his chest to keep from colliding. His heartbeat raced beneath her touch. Dropping her hand, she said, "Sorry for touching you."

"I don't mind." His voice was deep and smoky and sounded like sin.

She swallowed. "What's that supposed to mean?"

"I… Well, I mean, it's no problem, I guess." He worked his jaw back and forth. "I feel like I'm covered in road grit. Unless you need anything, I'm going to grab a quick shower."

"I'll just get settled, then."

"Pick whichever bed you want." He set his duffel bag on the chest of drawers. Rummaging through the contents, he pulled out a pile of clothes. "I'll be done shortly."

She moved to the bed at the far side of the room and hefted her suitcase onto the mattress. The sound of the water's spray coming from the bathroom was unmistakable. An image of the two of them, naked and covered with water, came to her. Liam's mouth was on hers.

Without thinking, she crossed the room and placed her hand on the door. It would be so easy to go inside. If she did, would he send her away?

Chapter 11

Liam wanted to kiss Sarah again. But that would be wrong on so many levels. Standing under the shower's spray, he set the temperature to scalding. He really didn't need to get clean—what he needed was time away from Sarah. It wasn't like he hated her or her company. That was part of the problem. But there was a bigger issue. He knew how she tasted. He knew how her lips felt, how her body fitted perfectly with his, and how she sighed when he put his tongue in her mouth.

He could still feel the imprint of her palm on his chest. He scrubbed his breastbone with a cloth, but the echo of her touch remained. Over the past several days, she'd seeped into his pores until her scent was part of his own.

Ironic how he'd worried she'd redevelop feelings for him. After all, she'd had an epic crush on him when they were younger.

Who knew that he'd be the one who wanted her?

A vision struck him with a startling clarity. In it, he wore nothing other than a towel. Sarah's shirt lay on the floor of their current hotel room. The cup of her bra, lacy and pink, was lowered. He ran his thumb over one nipple as he licked the other one.

Without thought, his hand drifted to his groin. He stopped before gripping his length. He wanted Sarah, not just time alone in the shower. Maybe he was just horny, and he'd feel the same intense draw to any attractive woman. The last time he had sex was six—no, make that eight—months ago. He'd dated an analyst from the violent crimes division. Turns out, the only thing they had in common was their job with the FBI.

With a curse, he turned off the spigot. The shower stopped and a trickle of water leaked down his face. "Get it together, Hill." He emptied his lungs in one breath. "You cannot screw up now—not with everyone in DC watching the case."

He ran a towel through his hair before buffing his body dry. His strokes were hard and fast—a punishment for wanting Sarah so damn bad. His clothes sat on top of the vanity. Stepping from the tub, he reached for his skivvies. There was a single pair of jeans and a button-up shirt and nothing else.

Damn it. How could he have forgotten underwear?

Well, he wasn't going to walk through the room in just a towel, his fantasy aside. He'd have to go commando, at least for a minute. After stepping into his pants, he opened the door. A cloud of steam rolled into the room.

The first thing he saw was Sarah. She lay on her side, her head in her hand. A curtain of chestnut hair fell, hiding half her face. A book lay on the bed in front of her.

His fantasy from the shower was fresh in his mind. He couldn't help it, his arousal growing. Perhaps he should've taken care of things in the shower. At least it would've taken the edge off his sex drive.

She glanced up, her gaze meeting his. "That was fast."

He moved his duffel bag from the dresser to the unoccupied bed. "I forgot some things is all..." He found a pair of boxers tucked into a side pocket. "How are you, by the way?"

She drew her brows together. "What?"

"You tripped over the suitcase just a minute ago. I was making sure that you didn't get hurt."

She waved away his concern. "I'm fine. I've just never been graceful on my feet is all. You probably remember from when we were younger. Like the time Allison and I lost Bruno."

Oh, yeah. The two girls had walked the family dog. Sarah

got tangled in the leash and Bruno had run as soon as he was free. "Who knew an arthritic Labradoodle would be so fast?"

She laughed while setting her book on the small table that separated the beds. "On the lead, he could barely walk. Off the lead, it was like he'd been launched out of a cannon or something."

"I haven't thought about him in years. He was a good dog. I still miss that old guy."

"He had a good family who loved him a lot," she said.

For a moment, he was surrounded by the ghosts of everything he lost when he left Boise. Friends. Family. Pets. A home. "I guess the only real guarantee we get is that time changes everything."

"Funny." She swung her legs around to sit on the side of the bed. "I still feel like the same old dorky kid."

"Trust me, you're fully grown up."

"I can't tell. Is that a compliment?" she asked, "Or are you saying that I'm old?"

"You've become a beautiful woman. Smart. Funny. Perfect." Sure, everything he'd said was true. But he hadn't meant to share so much. He ground his teeth together to keep from saying anything else.

"Wow," she said, rising to her feet. "That's one of the best compliments I've gotten from a guy."

"Sounds like you need to hang out with better men." He moved toward her.

"If you know any good men, let me know."

She was flirting. Inviting him to do more. To say more. To be more. The question was, did he want to cross that line? "I lied to you once," he admitted, "but I promise to be honest from now on. And honestly, if anything happens between us physically, there would be consequences."

She closed the distance between them. "Because if your superiors knew, things would be bad?" she asked, her voice sultry as a starless night in the summer. His cock grew to its full length.

The heat from her body warmed his bare chest. He took a step toward her. "It would be very bad if they knew."

"There's only one way to solve that problem," she said. "Just don't tell them."

"What do you want from me?" he asked.

"I want you to kiss me."

Liam turned off the part of his brain that knew he was making a huge mistake. Pulling her in close, he placed his lips on hers. He ran his hand over the fabric of her sweater and gripped her breast. She mewed with desire.

He didn't think it was possible, but his dick got harder.

"I want you," he said, breathing the words into her mouth.

"I want you, too," she said. "Make love to me, Liam."

He didn't need any other invitation. Lifting her from the floor, he set her on the mattress.

Sarah lay back, her hair spread out like a halo. "Come here," she purred, opening her arms.

Kneeling on the edge of the bed, Liam stretched out next to Sarah. Starting at her collarbone, he traced her body from shoulder to thigh.

"You are so unbelievably soft." Kissing her again, he explored her mouth with his tongue. He knew that if anyone ever found out, he'd be in a hell of a lot of trouble. The thing was, to be with Sarah he was willing to sacrifice it all.

Sarah pressed her hips into Liam's pelvis. He was hard. She was already wet. He kissed her slowly, seemingly prepared to take his time. Usually, she was fine with a leisurely round of sex, but with him it was different. She'd always had a fiery passion burning for Liam. For years, that flame only smoldered. But with him, here and now, that tiny spark had burst into an inferno.

She wanted him inside her.

She unfastened the top button of his pants before pulling the zipper down. She reached into the open fly. "Oh," she said, surprised to find his hard length and nothing else. "Do you always go without underwear?"

"Just today," he said, placing his lips behind her ear. "Just now."

The sensation sent a shiver of desire down her neck. "Is this a special surprise for me?"

"I wish I was that creative." He slipped his hand inside her sweater. His touch skimmed over her skin as he moved to her breast. His hand slipped into the cup of her bra. Brushing a finger over her nipple, he said, "Let's see if there's anything else I can do to astonish you."

He gently bit her other nipple through the fabric of her sweater.

She sucked in a breath, pleasure mixing with pain.

"You like that?" he asked.

She nodded. "Yes."

"Take off your sweater." He stretched out on the bed.

She lifted the garment over her head. After tossing it to the floor, she lay down at his side.

He gently pulled down on the cup of her bra, kissing her nipple before scraping her with his teeth. The pain was almost too much.

"You like that, too?"

"Yes," she said, arching her back and pulling him closer. She needed to feel Liam, skin to skin. He kissed her, harder this time. She reached for him again and ran her hand up and down his body.

"I want to be inside of you."

She wanted him inside her, too. Sitting up, she pulled the bra straps over her shoulders and unhooked the latch. "Do you have a condom?"

"In my wallet." He pointed to his duffel bag on the other bed. "Give me a second."

He rose from the bed and kicked off his pants. Naked, he crossed the room. His shoulders were wide, tapering down his back to the tight muscles of his ass. The sight of him left her mouth dry.

Standing quickly, she stripped out of her own pants. When she looked up, he was watching her. A slow smile spread across his face.

"What?" she asked.

"You are so damn sexy."

Sarah never thought of herself in that way. "You can't be serious."

"Look at you. Your long hair, tumbling over your shoulders. Your breasts are perfect." He came toward her, a condom packet in one hand. "Seeing you in just your panties is too much."

Maybe she did feel a little sexy. After removing her underwear, she stood in front of Liam. "What do you think of me now?"

"I think I'm going to enjoy being inside of you."

She sat down on the bed and opened her thighs. "I think I'm going to like that, too."

Liam opened the foil wrapper before rolling the condom down his length. She scooted back and he knelt between her open legs. He pressed his thumb onto the top of her sex. She was already swollen with want. A wave of pleasure rolled through her.

"You know what else I'm going to do?" He didn't wait for her to answer. "I'm going to like finding out what else it is you like."

"You're doing a good job so far." She placed her lips on his, kissing him softly.

"Do you like this?" he asked, slipping a finger inside her. "Or this?" He added a second finger to the first.

Her muscles tightened around his fingers. The wave of pleasure grew. "Oh, yes."

"What about this?" Still rubbing her, he slid his length inside her.

"Oh, God, yes." Sarah felt like she was being carried away onto an ocean of longing.

"This," he asked, sliding in deeper.

He was in deep, but not deep enough. "Harder, Liam. Harder."

He slid inside her all the way, and she moaned. Closing her eyes, she let the sensations wash over her. His mouth on hers. His hand on her breasts. The heat of his body and feeling of him inside her. Every part of her was alive.

But for her, it was more than just the merely physical.

This was the exact moment that had occupied her daytime fantasies and filled her nights with erotic dreams. Yet, nothing she imagined over the years compared to this moment. Wrapping her legs around his waist, she pulled him in deeper. "Oh, Liam."

"You like it like this." He drove in hard.

"Yes," she said. Her orgasm was starting to build. She still felt as if she were riding a wave on the ocean. The swell rose higher, moving faster.

He lifted her leg, setting one calf on his shoulder.

God, she couldn't stop herself from having an orgasm. "Harder," she panted. "Deeper. Faster." Like a wave crashing on the shore, Sarah cried out with her climax. Her pulse thundered in her ears, making her deaf to every sound save Liam's ragged breath.

He drove into her faster. Throwing back his head, he let out a low growl. He came. Then, he slumped on top of her, his body melding with hers. Liam propped onto one elbow and kissed her slowly. "That was fantastic," he said, gazing at her. "You are fantastic."

"I feel pretty fabulous right now," she said. Funny, Sarah thought she had memorized every part of Liam's face long ago. But with him so close, she saw that his dark eyes were more than brown. Streaks of gold, like rays of the sun, radiated out from his pupil. "You should probably take care of the condom."

"I probably should." He rose from the bed and padded across the room. Then, he disappeared into the bathroom, before closing the door.

Sarah sat up. Her panties lay on the floor. Her bra was on the bed, next to her sweater. As she redressed, the fog of lust started to clear. Without all the tingles and throbbing parts, it gave her space to think.

She and Liam were supposed to be working together. What's more, he didn't have some regular job. He was an FBI agent. Sure, she had reasons for wanting to have sex with him. But she should have ignored her yearning.

Jessie sat on the sofa and looked out over the mountains. The internet was working, *thank goodness*. With her tablet computer propped up on her knees, she scrolled through one of her favorite clothing websites. They had just launched their fall/winter mother-of-the-bride collection. Honestly, Sarah was the kind of person who'd want a simple wedding with a few dozen friends and a plain satin dress.

But that wouldn't do for Jessie. She wanted to be mother of the bride at an event. She'd given birth too many times not to plan a fancy wedding. Since she was estranged from her other kids, Sarah was her only chance.

It looked like the popular colors for the season were wine and blush rose. Wine was too dark for her complexion, but the blush rose might work…

She heard Markus before she saw him.

"Keep digging." He entered the room, a delivery box tucked under his arm. He set the box on the table. "I know that he used to be a fed and is now a banker, but I want to make sure there's nothing we've missed before bringing him in deeper."

Obviously, he was talking about Sarah's new beau, Liam Hill. She understood that he had to be careful, but what would Sarah think if she knew that Markus was meddling in her love life? He nodded, listening to what the caller on the other end of the line said.

The computer froze, and a colorful wheel popped onto the screen. Markus had stolen all the internet in the room and the beach ball of death meant that her connection was lost. She still needed to send Sarah directions for tomorrow but had gotten sidetracked with shopping. Closing out the site, Jessie tossed the tablet onto the coffee table and sighed.

Markus ended the call and sat next to her on the sofa. He pulled her feet onto his lap. "What're you up to?"

She flicked her fingers toward the tablet computer. "I was shopping, but your call kicked me off the internet." She didn't care that her tone was filled with annoyance.

"I'm off the phone now," he said, rubbing the arch of one foot. "You can get back on."

She sighed and leaned into the pillow at her back. "There wasn't anything interesting to buy." She paused, knowing that there was more to her mood than no time on the internet. "Why are you so interested in Liam Hill?"

"I'm always careful about anyone who visits our compound, you know that."

She knew. "But he's with Sarah now. If she trusts him, so can you. Besides, I like him. I was just looking at mother-of-the-bride dresses. What do you think about me wearing blush rose?"

Ignoring her question, Markus said, "Your daughter might've spent time with his family a decade ago, but they haven't seen each other in years. I don't like the fact that he used to be with the FBI. I want to make sure he doesn't still have good friends in the Bureau. The kind of friends who could make my life difficult."

"What's that supposed to mean?" It felt like someone had just poured ice water down her back. Sitting up straight, she shivered. "Everything you do is legal, right?"

"Of course it's all legal." Markus dug his thumb into the arch of her foot.

"Ouch." Jessie pulled her leg away. "That hurts."

"You know I'd never hurt you and that I'd never break the law." His tone was petulant. "All this attitude from you and I just bought you a gift." He nodded toward the box.

"A present? It's not my birthday."

"It doesn't have to be a special day for me to get you something. Or maybe I should say, every day with you is special."

Like the sun coming through the clouds, Jessie's mood improved. She pressed her lips to his cheek. "You are good to me."

"Go on," he urged. "Open it."

She picked up the box. It was sealed shut with tape. "Just a minute. I'll grab scissors."

"I've got you covered." Markus stood and emptied his pocket onto the table. There was his money clip, filled with twenty-dollar bills. A phone charger. A utility knife. He opened the knife and sliced through the tape. After folding the blade into the metal scale, he handed her the box. "I hope you like it."

Inside the shipping box was another box. This one was from a designer she loved. Excited energy left her giddy. She was a kid at Christmas, if her parents could've afforded the best. She opened the store box. Tucked inside tissue paper was a beautiful cashmere sweater. She lifted it up, holding it against her shoulders. The fabric was long enough that it skimmed the top of her shoes. It was the exact sweater she'd seen online dozens of times. But it was so expensive that she knew enough not to ask. "I love it," she said, breathless. "I've wanted this coatigan for so long. How did you know?"

"Well, I noticed that you kept going to the same site and looking at this sweater. I figured you must like it a lot."

"How's that?" she asked, confused.

Markus frowned. "How's what?"

"How do you know what I look at on the internet?"

"Oh, that? I check your search history," he said.

"You what?" Now she was mad. No, not mad. Jessie was filled with venomous fury. "That's an invasion of my privacy. You have no right."

Markus was on his feet. "I have every right," he said, his voice booming. "This church belongs to me. Everything here is mine. You are mine." He pulled the sweater from her hands. "Remember what you were when I found you."

Of course she remembered. Sarah had just gone to college. Sure, it was only to Boise State, twenty minutes from their home. Yet her daughter had chosen to live on campus. She wanted the whole college experience, or so she said. But Jessie knew better. What Sarah wanted was to get away.

At the time, Nate was already working. His busy schedule didn't leave much room for his mother. It meant that Jessie was all alone. In those days, the guilt was too much. She was a woman who'd abandoned one set of children to give birth to another. Robert had left her, going back to Saint Jenny.

In a lot of ways, it seemed easier to end it all.

That's when she met Markus.

He offered her hope. A purpose. Love and a life of luxury.

"Do you remember how broken you were?" Markus asked, his voice softer.

Jessie nodded.

"Why give me grief if I'm interested in what you look at on the internet?" He chuckled. "Not that it's much. All you do is scroll through one designer's website after another. I don't even mind that you still conduct a search for the kids you had with your first husband." He paused. Markus wanted her to fill the silence with an explanation. She didn't. She wouldn't. He'd uncovered her secret. She still kept tabs on all her children, even though she hadn't been a mother to them in years. What he wanted was her motivation. Even if she knew why she always looked up her kids, she wouldn't tell him. Some things she would keep to herself.

After a moment, he held out the sweater. "Try it on. Let's see how it looks."

She took the garment. It was soft and warm, flowing over her hands like bathwater instead of wool. She slipped into the floor-length cardigan. Rubbing the fabric between her fingers, she sighed.

"You like it, then?"

"Like it? I love it," she said. "I think I'll wear it tomorrow."

"You know how much I like to spoil you." He picked up her computer from the table. "Let's take a picture. Then, you can send it to Sarah."

She knew that he was trying to make up for their earlier quarrel. Fluffing her hair, she moved to the front of the fireplace. "How do I look?"

"Cozy and chic," he said, before hitting the home button on the tablet. "Damn it. It looks like the battery died." He tsked. "I wish you would keep your devices charged."

"It had enough juice just a minute ago," she said, her teeth clenched. Jessie picked up the charger from the table and shoved it into her pocket. Once her computer was charged, she'd text directions to Sarah. But right now, it would do no good to point out that Markus had stolen more than the internet connection. He'd taken all the power, as well.

Chapter 12

Every table at the Tap Out Brewery was filled. The tangy scent of wing sauce mixed with the salty smell of deep-fried food and the crisp aroma of hops, barley and beer. The din of conversations mixed with a college hockey game that was on TV. Boise State versus Idaho State. Everyone at the restaurant had a favorite team—even Sarah.

Of course, she was rooting for Boise State. What's more, she was thrilled that they were ahead by 3 to 1 after the first period.

Thankfully, her group had been sat at a booth in the back corner, where they could hear each other talk. And Sarah could see a TV.

Sarah and Liam sat on one side of the booth. Frannie and Dante sat opposite. Malcolm pulled up a chair at the end of the table.

Picking up a menu, she scanned the entrée list. For months she'd wondered about her siblings. Now that she was with two of them, she couldn't find anything to say.

A female server with a long black ponytail approached the table. "Hi, I'm going to be taking care of you guys tonight. What can I get started for you?"

"Um," she said, not able to focus on anything listed. "What do you recommend?"

"Do you like pepperoni pizza?" Malcolm asked.

"Who doesn't?"

"Why don't we all get pizza and wings to share?" She could already tell that he had the same take-charge personality as her brother, Nate. But Malcolm's eyes were the exact green as her own. "And add in two pitchers of beer."

"Hey," Frannie protested, resting her hand on her baby bump. "The pregnant momma can't drink."

"Okay, make that one pitcher of beer and one pitcher of water," he corrected.

"I'll get that order in and be back with your drinks," said the server.

"So," he turned to her. "Frannie shared a little bit about you, Sarah. But it's not enough. Tell me about yourself."

She laughed nervously. "What do you want to know?"

"Favorite flavor of ice cream. Favorite holiday. Favorite Halloween costume." He lifted a finger as he counted off the questions.

She exhaled. "Favorite ice cream has to be cookie dough. Favorite holiday is Thanksgiving, because it's just about food, friends and family. Favorite Halloween costume as a kid." She paused, thinking. "In tenth grade, I dressed up like Jane Austen." She pointed to Liam. "And his sister was Amelia Earhart."

Liam shook his head and laughed. "I'd forgotten about those costumes. It's no wonder you and Allison were best friends."

"What's your sister do now?" Malcolm asked Liam.

"Actually, she's a fighter pilot in the air force."

"That's impressive," said Malcolm. "Sounds like you both knew what you wanted from life at an early age."

"I never thought about it that way," she said. "But I guess you're right."

Frannie asked, "Is she single? We need to find someone nice for Malcolm."

"I can find my own partner, thank you very much."

The server returned with two pitchers and a stack of plastic cups. Malcolm poured a glass of water and handed it to Frannie. "What would you like, Sarah?"

"Since I'm driving, I'll stick with water."

He filled the cup with water before passing it over. "I know Dante will have a beer with me. What about you, Liam?"

"You can't have wings and pizza without beer," he said.

Malcolm filled three glasses with beer. He handed one to Liam. "So, Frannie said that you're a banker from Washington, DC."

Liam took a sip of his beer and nodded. "I am."

"How's a DC banker end up in Owl Creek?" he asked. "I know I'm prying, but Sarah's my sister. Grilling her dates is part of my job."

Funny, to think that she shared a parent with both her brother and sister. It didn't take long to get a sense of her siblings. They were good people. Dependable. Hardworking. Honest.

True, Jessie and Robert hadn't been any of those things. But somehow, between them, they'd raised children who became decent adults.

"I'm looking for real estate in Boise," he said, using his lie. "I stopped by the library, ran into Sarah, and the rest is history. Now, here we are."

"If you're looking for real estate in Boise," Malcolm asked, "why are you in Owl Creek?"

"It's a chance for me to meet Sarah's mom. We met for brunch this morning at Hutch's Diner." He paused. While Frannie was the child of Sarah's dad, Malcolm was the son of her mother—Jessie. "I guess she's your mom, too."

"Yeah, I guess she is." He rolled a glass of beer between his palms. "So, Jessie was in town today."

"I'm sorry that she didn't stop by to see you," Sarah said. Still, her words weren't enough.

"Not a problem." Malcolm lifted the beer to his lips and took a long swallow. "I'm used to it by now."

Sarah doubted that was true. "You know," she said, "after my dad died and I found you all, I was furious with my mom. I really thought that we were the ones who were wronged." She paused. Maybe she shouldn't be so candid at a get-to-know-you dinner. But Malcolm looked so much like Nate. They had the same build and same unruly brown hair. She felt as if she were talking to the brother whom she'd known her whole life.

"But Nate and I were the lucky ones. Mom—as imperfect as she is—stayed with us. She left you all behind." She paused a beat. "I am so sorry."

Her brother nodded slowly. "It's not your fault. You never asked for any of this."

"Well, neither did you…"

"Sometimes I wonder, even now, if I did something and that's why she left."

It seemed like she wasn't the only person willing to be painfully honest.

She blinked hard. "It wasn't you. I haven't known you for long, but I can tell that you're great."

He smiled. "You're pretty great, yourself."

"Must run in the family," Frannie added. "Nate's a good guy, too."

Sarah was always proud of her brother. "Nate's the best."

"How's he doing?" Frannie asked.

Honestly, she'd been avoiding Nate. Not that she was upset with him, or anything. It's just that she'd have a hard time sticking to Liam's cover story. After all, Jessie was his mom, too. He had a right to know what was going on. Then again, Jessie was also Malcolm's mother. Did that mean she should confide in him? Sarah took a sip of water and answered Frannie's question. "Nate's good—like always."

Malcolm pulled his phone from his pocket and glanced at the device. The screen was illuminated with an incoming call. "I have to take this," he said, rising from the table. "Be back in a minute." He swiped the call open and spoke into the phone. "Give me a second to get out the door. I'm at Tap Out."

He wove his way through the crowd, toward the door. Once he was gone, she turned back to Frannie. "Did I scare him off?"

"I doubt it," said Dante. "He's made of pretty tough stuff."

"True," Frannie agreed. "He lives on the Colton family ranch, and there's always something happening there. Plus, he volunteers with a K-9 rescue unit. It could be anything and he definitely didn't make up an emergency to get away from you." She squeezed Sarah's arm and smiled. "Trust me."

Did she trust Frannie? As it turned out, everything she knew about her life and her family had been a lie. Even she'd gone down the rabbit hole of deceit. Now, she didn't know what to believe. "Tell me how you two met," she asked, changing the subject.

"Dante was my best customer," said Frannie, reaching for his hand. "Every time he'd walk into the store, I'd get butterflies. He always loved to talk books, so I knew he must be a good guy."

"I'm a lawyer by trade." Dante Santoro wore his dark brown hair and beard cut short. A bit of gray was starting to show on his cheeks and chin. Lacing his fingers through Frannie's, he continued, "You can't become an attorney without liking to read a lot. But usually, what I'd read was legal briefs and other boring stuff. My family has some unsavory connections, and I was trying to stay off the radar."

"By unsavory do you mean organized crime?" Liam asked.

"Unfortunately, I do," said Dante with a shrug. "I've always stayed out of the family business, though."

Dante picked up the thread of the story. "Once I saw how much Frannie loved books, I started reading everything, just to have something to talk about with her."

"That's the sweetest story I've ever heard," said Sarah.

"It's almost as sweet as you and Liam. Who'd have thought that you'd grow up together and then later, fall in love?" said Frannie.

"Agreed," said Dante. "That's a top-notch love story."

Sarah's cheeks got hot. What would they both say once they knew that her whole story had been bogus? Frannie obviously had no love for Jessie. Maybe she could trust her sister with the truth. Before she could say anything, Malcolm strode up to the table.

"The call I got is for a missing person from the Ever After Church." His jacket was draped over the back of his chair. After pulling the garment free, he shrugged into the coat. "The K-9 unit has been called in to search. It's going to get frigid tonight. Anyone who's out in those temperatures risks severe frostbite or worse."

"If they're from that church, they might not have gotten lost.

Maybe they tried to escape. Best to just let them get away," said Dante before taking a swig of beer.

"I don't care who's in the woods or why. It's my job to try and find them," said Malcolm.

"Take care of yourself." Frannie rose from her seat and pulled him in for a quick hug. "We don't want anything to happen to you."

"I'm always careful," he said, before turning to Sarah. He opened his arms. "Mind if I get a hug, too?"

"Listen to Frannie," she said, scooting to the edge of the booth. Standing, she pulled him into an embrace. "Be careful."

"It's good to know you. I'd like to stay in touch."

"Absolutely," she said. "I'll get your number from Frannie."

Frannie said, "I'll start a group chat and call it the Colton Crew."

"You call it that, then everyone will want to be a part of the text thread," said Malcolm.

"I don't mind." Sarah couldn't believe that things had changed so much for her over the course of a single day. This morning, she'd been terrified by the prospect of getting together with one of her siblings. Now, she had new affection for her brother and sister and the possibility of so much more. She gave Malcolm another tight squeeze before letting him go.

She slid back into the booth as he walked away.

"I don't mean to pry," said Liam. "But I have to ask about the Ever After Church. You said that the missing person didn't just wander off but perhaps tried to escape."

Dante lifted his glass of beer and took a sip. "I was just being glib. I shouldn't have said anything about someone who's missing."

"Anything you know about the Ever After Church would be helpful. I met Markus today. He's trying to get me to invest in a project." Since Liam knew all about the church leader, Sarah assumed that he was just trying to get more information.

"You want some expensive legal advice for free?" Dante asked.

Liam said, "I never turn down a bargain."

"Stay away from the Ever After Church."

This was the exact kind of information Liam needed. She asked, "Why's that?"

"I don't know anything for certain," Dante said. "It's just a vibe I get."

"That doesn't sound very lawyerly of you." Sarah smiled wide to show that she was teasing. Still, she wanted to know everything Dante knew or suspected. "Besides, if there are issues, I need to know. My mother's engaged to Markus." Sure, Sarah thought Markus was a pompous jerk from the first time they met. But her mother might be in real trouble.

"The reason nobody knows much of anything is because there's a lot of security around the church compound." Frannie glanced over her shoulder, looking at the door. "Too bad Malcolm left already. He's been in the area on other searches and turned away by security."

"That sounds expensive." She'd seen the images of the church members already and she knew how they lived. Still, she was interested in what Frannie and Dante would say. "The church must be really nice."

"With all the nice cars Jessie and Markus are driven around in, you'd think that the compound was like the Taj Mahal," said Frannie, an edge to her tone. "But a few members have come into town. They're all filthy and cold and hungry. I can't understand why they don't just leave. I mean, they aren't prisoners."

Dante gave her a side-eye. Letting go of his hand, she grabbed her glass. With her back ramrod straight, Frannie looked toward the TV. The air between them became muddy with irritation.

"What aren't you saying?" Sarah asked the couple.

Dante exhaled. "Let's just say that we have different ideas about what's happening at the Ever After Church."

"What do you think is going on?" Liam asked.

"I grew up with connections to the mob. I've seen how people can get sucked into an organization and brainwashed. That's not a church in those mountains. It's a cult. As far as people coming into town and being a nuisance." He sighed. "I think those people are desperate."

The photos from the compound were tattooed onto Sarah's

brain and into her soul. "It sounds like they're trapped without any hope."

"I guess if you think about it that way, they are." Frannie gave Dante a wan smile. He lifted her hand and grazed her knuckles with his lips.

The server approached the table, a large tray balanced on her shoulder. "I got pizzas and wings." She set two baskets of saucy wings on the table and then two large pizzas.

Sarah hadn't eaten anything since brunch. As the mellow scent of melted cheese surrounded her, her stomach contracted with a grumble. Pressing a hand to her belly, she said, "That all looks delicious."

Finally, the server placed four plates and four sets of silverware on the table. "Enjoy."

"I'm definitely going to get heartburn from all this, but it'll be worth it," said Frannie, reaching for a slice.

Sarah took her first bite of pizza. The sauce was the perfect blend of tangy and sweet. The pepperoni had the right amount of spice. The cheese was melty and mild. She chewed and swallowed. "This is great pizza. Too bad Malcolm had to leave before getting anything to eat."

"If there are leftovers, we can drop them off at the ranch on our way home." Dante plunged a buffalo wing into a dish filled with ranch dressing and took a bite.

Frannie had already finished one slice of pizza and reached for a second. "The first three months of my pregnancy, I had horrible morning sickness."

"She couldn't even look at food without feeling ill," said Dante. "Crackers and ginger ale were all she could keep down."

"Now, I'm making up for all the meals I missed," Frannie said before taking another bite.

"Tell me about the baby," said Sarah. "Is it a boy or girl? When are you due?"

"The due date's not for a while." Frannie placed a hand on her belly. "We don't know the gender yet but have an ultrasound appointment in a few weeks. If the baby cooperates, we'll find out then."

"Any guesses?" Liam asked.

"It's a girl," said Dante. "She'll be beautiful and brilliant, just like her mother."

"You are a keeper," said Frannie. She cupped Dante's cheek with her hand. Pulling him to her, she kissed him softly.

Sarah hadn't known Frannie for long. Yet, she was happy to see her sister so happy and in love. It was the kind of relationship that other people envied and Sarah had been wanting for years. Would she ever find someone? She glanced at Liam. He was watching her. He gave her a slow smile. For a moment, she could feel his lips on hers again. His mouth on her breasts. His hands on her thighs. Her cheeks warmed with the memories.

Soon, there were only three slices of pizza and five wings left. "That looks like enough for Malcolm. I'll get a to-go container." Dante lifted his hand, waving to the server.

"Looks like you all enjoyed your meal," she said, while approaching the table. "Can I get you anything else?"

"Just a to-go box and the check," said Dante.

The server was prepared. She set a black check presenter on the table. "I'll leave this with you and be back in a second with your box."

Dante looked at Liam. "Do you want to split the amount down the middle?"

Liam picked up the bill. "Better yet, I'll pay."

"You don't have to," Dante protested.

"Trust me, I'm on an expense account," he said, setting enough money onto the table to cover the tab and a tip. "Besides, you gave me some good insights on the Ever After Church. That's helped me out more than you know."

Sarah scooted out of the booth and glanced at the TV. There were only five minutes left in the third period of the hockey game. Boise State was still winning. The score was 4 to 1. She imagined the team could hold on to the lead until the end. *Go, Broncos!*

"Let's keep in touch," said Frannie, pulling Sarah into a hug. The one thing she was learning about her sister was that she liked to give hugs. She whispered, "You and Liam are a cute couple. I love the way he looks at you."

"I was thinking the same thing about you and Dante," said Sarah, giving her sister a final squeeze.

"Remember, we have to get a picture in our banned books shirts."

"It's a deal," she said, hoping there would be a next time.

Chapter 13

Snowflakes danced in the headlight beams as Sarah drove back to the hotel. She parked in the same spot, the ground already covered in white.

"I guess it won't be snowing in DC tonight," she said, joking about the weather.

He leaned forward and gazed out the windshield. "Probably no snow in Washington, but even a few inches will send everyone into a panic." He laughed. "Remember that weekend it snowed so much we were all stuck in the house and my mom had to stay at the hospital?"

"Of course I remember the blizzard of oh-eight." She put the gearshift into Park and turned off the ignition. "Your dad turned it into a party. We camped out in the living room and watched movies. He made pancakes for dinner. Those were good times."

He sat back in the seat but stared out the window. "I miss living in Idaho. I miss the weather. The people. Finger steaks." He gave a weak chuckle. "I just didn't realize how much I missed everything until coming back."

Sarah had friends. A job she loved. A family that might be growing, thanks to her trip to Owl Creek. From what she'd picked up, Liam didn't have any of those in Washington. "Sounds like you're pretty lonely in DC."

"It's hard to connect with anyone in a city that big. I work twelve, sometimes fourteen hours a day. Then the commute." He rolled his eyes. "Horrendous. It takes me an hour to drive fifteen miles. By the time I get home, I want to eat something— anything—drink a beer and maybe watch a little TV. Then, I call it a night. I get up the next morning and start over."

It sounded like his whole life was horrible, not just his commute. "What do you want?"

"I don't know," he said, with a shake of his head. "The irony is, if this case goes well, I'll be a shoo-in for the promotion. That will only mean longer hours, less time at home, less time to make a life."

"It's the modern paradox," she said.

"You're right, it is. I've been thinking that I'm the only one who works too much. But I'm not."

"The question is still the same," she asked, "what do you want to do?"

He turned to her. In the car's dim interior, everything was shades of gray. As if the world had been sketched with charcoal on paper. "Wise and beautiful," he said. "That might be the perfect combo."

"What about a burger and fries?" she teased. "Or peanut butter and jelly?"

"You are much better than a burger and fries." He smiled, his teeth bright in the darkness. Leaning onto the console between the seats, he said, "I guess we should talk about what happened in the room before we left."

They'd made love but Liam's rebuff from years earlier was a wound that had never completely healed. What's more, she wasn't ready to be rejected again. "It doesn't matter," she lied. "We're both adults."

"Oh." He was silent for a minute. "Well, if that's how you feel about it, then I guess we really don't have anything to discuss."

"For the record, I don't usually tumble into bed with any random guy after a few dates."

"I'd like to think I'm more than just some dude who took you out for finger steaks."

She smiled at the memory. At the time, she'd believed that Liam coming into her life was just luck. She didn't have an inkling that her world was about to change. Or maybe it was Sarah who was growing. "That date seems like it happened a million years ago."

He rubbed the back of his neck. "It's been a long week."

"It's going to be a long day tomorrow."

"I need to reach out to my boss and brief her on what happened today," he said.

"We should probably go, then." She opened the car's door and stepped outside. Cold bit through her jacket. Snow had already filled in the tracks left by her tires.

"Be careful." He reached for her to keep her from falling. "It's slick."

Truth was, she liked the feeling of his hand on her arm. She liked that he was worried about her safety. She liked having someone who cared. Could be that she liked it all a little too much.

Walking slowly, they made their way to the hotel's front entrance. Compared with the outside, the lobby was stifling. She unzipped her coat and followed Liam. He pushed the call button and the elevator doors slid open. She stepped into the car. Liam followed. Without speaking, they rode to the third floor and exited the car. After walking to their room, Liam swiped the keycard over the lock. It unlatched with a click. He opened the door. "After you."

Slipping inside, she flipped the light switch. The room was just as they'd left it. Sarah's suitcase sat on a luggage rack. One bed was made, the other was mussed. The musky scent of their lovemaking still hung in the air.

It was almost as if they'd never left.

Sarah hung her coat in the small closet. "Thank you for bringing me to Owl Creek. Without this investigation, I never would've run into Frannie."

Liam sat on the edge of the bed. Kicking off his shoes, he said, "You two would've found each other eventually."

Sarah imagined a golden thread tethering her to all her Colton siblings. Then again, the fact that she'd been lying to them all along would eventually come out. Would the truth cut that tie?

She sighed. "They're going to find out why we came to Owl

Creek in the first place. They're going to know it's all a scam."
She bit her bottom lip understanding what scared her the most.
"They're going to know I'm a liar and no better than Jessie."

"First, it's a federal investigation, not some swindle. Second,
you're doing this to save your mother from ending up in jail. Or
worse." He stepped closer and placed his hand on her arm. His
touch sent her pulse racing. "Trust me, your brother and sister
will understand. And they'll know that you're a good person."

Her whole life she'd tried to do the right thing. Get good
grades. Be a loyal friend. Be honest and helpful. What if she
was nothing but a fake?

He opened his arms. "You look like you need a hug."

Honestly, she didn't know what she needed. And yet, "A hug
would help," she said, stepping into his embrace. He wrapped
his arms around her, and she leaned into his chest. His scent,
sweat and healthy male, surrounded her. She inhaled deeply. It
did nothing to slow her racing heart. She took a step backward,
slipping out of his arms. "I feel better," she said, already digging
through her suitcase. She found her toiletry bag and pajamas.
"I'm going to get ready for bed. Do you need the bathroom?"

"I'm going to send my boss a text and fill her in about dinner. Take your time."

Once inside the bathroom, she turned on the light and closed
the door. After setting everything on the vanity, she studied her
refection. Sarah would never be a classic beauty, like her mom.
But she had bright eyes, an easy smile and, yes—she was happy
to be sweet. The world needed more sweetness.

So, what was a sweet girl like her doing in a hotel pretending to be an undercover FBI agent's girlfriend?

She cleansed her face, applied moisturizer and stripped out
of her clothes. Standing in her underwear, she looked at herself
again. She ran a finger over her curves. Her breasts were full,
her hips were round and her butt was muscular. Her beauty was
completely opposite her mother's. But that didn't make Sarah
any less attractive.

Her childhood memories were filled with moments of her
mom's disapproval. Most nights after dinner, Jessie would give
the kids a treat. Sarah would reach for a second cookie or the

larger slice of pie. Jessie never said anything, but it was impossible to miss the scowl that passed across her mother's face. A cloud blotting out the sun.

It's one of the reasons why Sarah constantly read. She could live a new life and learn about different worlds. In short, she'd go places that her mother couldn't follow.

It's also why she stayed with the Hill family so much.

But Sarah was no longer a child.

If she wanted to be an adult, she had to step away from her mother's shadow. For the first time, she'd walk in her own sun.

Her thoughts moved on to Liam. He was another enigma.

Sure, they were in a fake relationship. But she could still lose herself in his arms. Without another thought, she opened the bathroom door and stepped into the room. Liam had changed into his own version of pajamas—a white T-shirt and pair of gray sweatpants.

He looked up. For a moment, he just stared. Then, he stood straighter. "This is a nice surprise."

"I was thinking about what you said. I've been thinking about a lot of things, really. My mom. My siblings. You…" No, she wasn't doing it right. Sarah should think of something sexy and seductive to say. Instead, she was starting to ramble. Drawing in a deep breath, she tried again. "I'm not sure what will happen tomorrow—or the day after that. But right now, I want you."

He pulled her to him. She sighed as he slipped his tongue into her mouth. The future would bring its own troubles and joys. But for tonight she would just let go.

She ran her hands over Liam's chest. Even under the fabric, she could feel the hard muscles and planes of his body. She lifted the hem of his shirt. He had to duck down so she could pull it over his head.

Once his shirt was off, she traced his chest. Collarbone. Pectorals. Nipples. He hissed with ecstasy. She ran her tongue over his other nipple, her hand traveling lower. She slid her hand inside the waistband of his sweatpants and underwear. He was already hard. She ran her finger down his length.

"Jesus, Sarah," he moaned. "What're you trying to do? Drive me wild?"

"Basically," she said, feeling both playful and sexy.

Liam gripped her face in both his hands and kissed her hard. She didn't mind the pain. "I want you," he said, breathing into the kiss, "so bad."

"Not just yet."

"Not yet?" he echoed.

Before he could say anything else, she'd dropped to her knees. Liam let his pants fall to his knees. Honestly, Sarah had never done anything like this before. Oh sure, she'd occasionally taken a guy in her mouth. But never clad in only her bra and panties and in a hotel, no less.

Then again, today had been a day for firsts.

She ran her tongue around the tip, watching Liam through her lashes. Eyes closed, he let his head hang back. She took him in her mouth, and he moaned with pleasure. "Oh, Sarah."

She swirled her tongue over his length.

He massaged her shoulder as his breathing turned ragged. Liam pulled himself out. "You gotta stop doing that, or else I'm going to explode. Literally."

"That's kinda the idea," she said.

"I have a better idea. Get on the bed," he said while stepping out of his pants. Completely naked, he lay down on the bed.

Bending forward at the waist, she stretched out on top of him. She took him with her hand as he moved aside the strip of her panties. He slipped two fingers inside her before placing his mouth on her. Every part of her body was alive with sensations. The climax claimed her with a speed that was both exhilarating and frightening. She bit the inside of Liam's thigh as wave after wave of pleasure washed over her and through her and pushed her under until she couldn't breathe.

She panted. "Oh my God, I don't know where that came from."

"Roll onto your back," said Liam. "I want you."

"But you haven't come yet."

"I will," he said as she shifted to the mattress. "Besides, I don't think my leg can handle another one of your bites."

There, on his thigh, was a red ring of teeth marks. "Jeez, I'm sorry."

"Don't apologize," He rose from the bed. His wallet sat on the nightstand. Holding up a foil packet, he said, "This is my last one." After opening the condom, he rolled the rubber down his length. "If we need any more, we'll have to stop at a drugstore or something."

Would there be another time? Lying back, she opened her arms. "Come here."

Liam moved between her thighs. She watched as he slid inside her. The erotic vision was burned into her brain. He began to move inside her. She met him thrust for thrust. Neither spoke. The shifting of the bed and their heavy breaths were the only sounds in the room. Sarah could feel a new orgasm building. Reaching for the top of her sex, she rubbed the spot. Every part of her body began to tingle. Her feet. Her hands. Even her hair felt as if it was pulsing with an electric current.

Wrapping her legs around Liam's waist, she pulled him closer, driving him in deeper. Her hand was trapped between their bodies. It didn't matter, her climax was close. Liam reached for the headboard, using his arms to pump deeper inside her. It was all she needed.

She cried out as she came.

Liam was near, too. Funny how she'd learned to read his body after such a short time. Eyes closed, his brow was drawn together. A thin sheen of sweat glistened on his forehead and chest. A rumble of thunder began in his middle, and he groaned as he came. For a moment, they lay in silence as their heartbeats shared a rhythm. He kissed her slowly.

"The condom," she said. Sure, Sarah was willing to take a few risks and live dangerously. But she wasn't stupid. She wasn't ready to be a parent just yet.

"I'll be right back," he said, getting out of the bed.

She rose as he entered the bathroom and found her discarded panties on the floor. She removed her bra before slipping back under the blankets. Since her pajamas were still in the bathroom, she'd have to wait to get dressed.

Coming out of the bathroom, Liam stepped into his underwear. "It seems silly to sleep in the other bed," he said. "But I will, if that's what you want."

In a way, sharing a bed felt more intimate than having sex. If she wanted to create distance between them, now would be the time. But he was right—making him sleep in the adjoining bed bordered on ridiculous. Pulling back the cover, she joked, "I'll try not to snore too much."

He turned off the light before snuggling next to her. Her back was pressed against his chest. His breath washed over her shoulder. Bits of ice tapped against the window. She was warm and dry and sated from sex. But there were people living on the Ever After Church's compound who went to bed hungry and were sleeping in tents tonight. She was tired of wondering what her mother knew. Or wondering if Jessie even cared.

By helping Liam, she was doing the right thing. Would it be enough?

"What's going to happen tomorrow?" she asked, her words a whisper.

"Just getting onto the compound will be step one." Liam wrapped his arm around her middle and pulled her closer. "Next, I need to get into Markus's office. He has a computer that's never online. All his financial records are stored on the hard drive."

Rolling over, she faced him. "How're you supposed to do all that?"

"I'm not sure," he said. "I'll improvise."

"We," she corrected. "We'll have to improvise."

"I like having you on my team." She could sense more than see his smile.

"Once we get you into the office, how are you supposed to access the files you need?" she asked.

"I was given the password to the computer," he said. Before she could ask how he'd come across such sensitive information, he added, "A receptionist who worked for my mom's medical practice got sucked into the Ever After Church after a divorce. Because of her administrative background, she worked as Markus's secretary. When she realized what was happening, she contacted me. But she knew his password." His words disappeared into the darkness. "Cases like this can take years to develop, but you've helped me get close to Markus in just a few hours. If you ever want a change of career, you should consider the FBI."

Of course, he was teasing. "I'll leave all the clandestine operations up to you."

"You've sacrificed a lot for this case. I'd say 'thank you,' but it doesn't seem like enough."

"No need to thank me," she said. "Just get that evidence and put Markus Acker in jail."

Chapter 14

Sometime in the middle of the night, Jessie had texted Sarah directions to the church's compound. She had them on her phone first thing in the morning. For the day, she decided to wear a green cashmere sweater and tan slacks. Sure, she also had to wear snow boots, but the sweater was the nicest thing she owned.

Liam wore a flannel shirt, jeans and boots. When he'd shown up at the library he'd been in a pressed white shirt and loafers. Now he was much more casual. Was he getting comfortable being back in Idaho?

Since they were going to her mother's house for breakfast, neither bothered eating before they left the hotel. By 8:15 a.m., she was driving on a four-lane highway that led out of Owl Creek. Several miles outside town, they traded the interstate for a sparsely populated county route. That led to a two-lane road, which hugged the side of a mountain peak.

Liam sat in the passenger seat. Looking out the window, he said, "You never get views like this in DC. It's breathtaking."

She glanced out the window. Last night's storm had blanketed the mountains with six inches of new snow. Powder clung to branches, and it looked like the trees were covered in sparkling diamonds. In the distance, another mountain peak rose from the valley's cloud cover. Turning her attention back to the road, she said, "It is beautiful." But it was also secluded. She hadn't seen a house for miles. This far from civilization, would they be able to call for help if they needed it? "Do you have any cell coverage?"

Liam pulled his phone from his pocket and glanced at the screen. "Nope."

"Check and see if I have any bars." She nodded toward the cupholder where she'd tucked her device.

He picked up the cell and pressed the home button. "Nothing."

"My mom's internet is always spotty. But hopefully, there's a little coverage once we get closer to the church."

Liam glanced in her direction. "I hope you're right."

She didn't know what they were about to find, but without cell service, they were on their own. Sarah was so wrapped up in her own thoughts that she almost missed a wooden sign that was tucked into a copse of trees.

Property of Ever After Church had been stenciled in large, block letters.

Another note had been painted on by hand: Trespassers Will Be Shot.

Easing her foot onto the brake, she let the car idle next to the sign. "That doesn't seem very welcoming."

"Not like any church I've ever attended," Liam agreed.

She gripped the steering wheel tighter. "I guess there's nothing for us to do but see where this road leads." Pressing down on the gas, she turned onto the narrow track. Piles of snow lined the road. "At least they plowed this morning."

In the gully, a guard shack, made of plywood and painted tan, sat at the roadside. The road was blocked with a large iron gate, attached at both sides to a metal post. From each post, a metal fence stretched out as far as she could see in either direction. Loops of razor wire, the barbs glinting in the morning light, topped the fencing.

A dark-haired man, dressed all in black, stepped out of the guard shack. Standing in the middle of the road, he held up a hand for her to halt. She dropped her foot on the brake, stopping several feet from the man. The guard stepped up to the car and wound his hand in the universal sign to lower the window.

She pressed a button set into the armrest. The window lowered with a whirr. All the warm air in the car was sucked out into the cold morning.

"This is private property." The guard wore a gun at his hip. It was a fact she hadn't noticed until now. "You can't be here."

Dragging her gaze from the firearm to the man's face, she said, "I'm, uh, Jessie Colton's daughter. I'm here to see my mom."

"You got some kind of ID?"

"Yeah." Her purse was on the floorboard of the passenger side, next to Liam's feet. He handed her the bag. She dug through her pocketbook until she found her wallet. Her driver's license was stored in a pocket with a clear plastic window. "Here you go," she said, holding up her ID.

The guard took her wallet and examined the license. He shoved it through the window, giving it back. He pointed to Liam. "What about him?"

"My mom and Markus are expecting us," she said, projecting more courage than she felt.

Liam leaned past Sarah with his own license. "It's okay," he said. "I'm sure this guy is just doing his job."

The guard examined the ID for several seconds. With a grunt, he held it out to her. As she reached for the license, he said, "Go ahead."

"Is it easy to find my mom's house?" she asked.

The man nodded his head once. "Just follow this road."

"How am I supposed to know which house belongs to my mom and Markus?"

"Oh, you'll know," said the guard. "Trust me."

Without another word, he opened the gate and stepped aside. Sarah raised her window before easing her foot from the brake. She stepped onto the accelerator and the car slowly climbed farther into the woods. She glanced in her rearview mirror. The gate was once again closed. "My God, they are serious about security here. Did you see that fence?"

"Honestly, I've seen friendlier prisons," he said.

She understood that he was trying to be funny. In a different situation, she might've laughed. Now, she couldn't even manage a smile.

The tree line broke, opening to a muddy field. Like she'd seen in the photos, tents and shacks made of boards were haphazardly set up around the compound. There was a large metal building. With a single door and no windows, it almost looked like a warehouse. A sign hung above the door.

Cafeteria/Sanctuary.

Next to the cafeteria/sanctuary was a residential trailer.

Administrative Building.

A guard, another fit-looking man in dark clothes, stood outside the office door.

She kept her eyes on the road. "You see that building and the guard, right?"

"I see them both."

For a moment, neither spoke. Then, he said, "For what it's worth, you're doing a good job as an undercover agent. But we need to assume that we're always under surveillance while we're here. Just because we're alone doesn't mean Markus isn't listening."

"That's an unsettling thought, but I won't say anything that'll blow your cover." She corrected herself, "Our cover."

She glanced out the window. The Ever After compound was large. Several miles of forest had been cleared away on the hillside.

A dirt track wound through a slushy field. Either side of the single lane was lined with more tents and shacks. Several children, elementary school-aged by the looks of them, surrounded a muddy puddle. Using a stick, they slapped the water. Droplets flew into the air. The game stopped and thin faces with red-rimmed eyes regarded the car as they drove past. Despite the cold, none of them wore coats.

At the top of a rise stood the wooden frame of a large, rectangular building. The sound of hammer strikes rang out into the cold morning. Sitting next to the construction site was a beautiful A-frame house with a timber exterior and roof of green tin. She'd seen enough pictures to recognize her mother's home at once.

Even before Liam showed up in her life, her mom had sent several texts with photos of the property. But now that she was here, Sarah knew the truth. All the pictures had been carefully selected to only show what Jessie wanted her to see. It wasn't a mistake; her mother had seen the ugliness and chosen to look the other way.

A circular driveway, covered in gravel, looped in front of the house. After pulling up next to a set of steps, she placed the gearshift into Park and exhaled loudly.

"Are you ready for this?" he asked. "Because if you aren't..." He let his words unravel.

"There's no way we can go back now," she said, turning off the ignition. "Let's just get this over with."

The front door of the house opened. Jessie stepped onto the wide porch. She was clad in an ivory silk blouse and wool slacks. Atop it all was a long cashmere cardigan that almost swept the ground. Smiling brightly, she waved.

Sarah stepped from the car. Liam came up beside her and held out his hand. She took his palm in her own. How was she supposed to prepare for a moment like this? Yet she smiled at Liam, hoping the expression looked loving. "Showtime," she said quietly, before walking toward the house. Speaking to Jessie, she said, "Wow, Mom. You really do live in the mountains."

Her mother leaned on the railing. "Isn't the view breathtaking?"

She glanced over her shoulder. All Sarah could see was the tent city and children who needed coats and a hot meal. "There's a lot of people who live around here."

"Well, Markus is such an inspirational pastor, people just flock to his congregation," she said. "I hope you're hungry. I made your favorite."

"Apple cinnamon pancakes?" she asked.

"Apple cinnamon pancakes," her mother echoed.

A set of steps made to look like tree trunks led to a wide porch, complete with a set of Adirondack chairs. She climbed the stairs. Liam was right behind, his hand resting on the small of her back.

"Give me a hug," said Jessie, pulling Sarah in for a quick embrace. "Now, get inside. It's freezing out here."

Jessie held the front door as Sarah and Liam crossed the threshold. The walls at the front and back of the house were made up of floor-to-ceiling windows. A large stone fireplace bisected the room, separating the living room from the dining room.

The decor inside the house matched the rugged log cabin look, while also being tasteful and expensive. In the living room, a fur rug was spread out on the floor. A large green leather sofa filled the middle of the room. The table and the frame of a coordinating chair were made out of roughhewn logs. The adjacent dining room table was already set for four. There was a carafe of coffee, a pitcher of orange juice. Platters were filled with savory bacon, spicy sausage and sweet apple cinnamon pancakes.

"So?" her mom asked, "what do you think? It's a lot nicer than our old place in Boise."

"This place is lovely, Mom." She tried to smile.

"I'm glad you like it. Markus lets me do whatever I want with our house."

Markus came from a hallway to the right of the door. He wore jeans and a blue sweater with a collared shirt underneath. "I always let your mother do whatever she wants," he said. "She's such a persuasive minx."

Persuasive minx? Was this guy for real?

Jessie giggled.

Sarah thought she might barf.

Markus stepped forward and placed a dry kiss on Sarah's cheek. Reaching out his hand for Liam to shake, he said, "I'm glad we could finally get Sarah up here to visit."

Funny, she hadn't recalled ever being invited before.

Markus continued, "We should eat. I'm starved."

The choice of phrasing hit her like a punch to the face. For a moment, she saw stars. "*You're* starving?" she echoed.

"Yeah," said Markus, walking to the dining room table. "I skipped my early breakfast so I could eat with you all."

"What about all those people?" She pointed to the windows at the front of the house. "Who's supposed to feed them?"

"There's hunger all over the world," said Jessie, being willfully obtuse. "Our church sends money to ministries that feed the hungry."

"I'm not talking about anywhere else," she said, "there's hunger right here."

"Why don't you have a seat," said Markus as he sat. "The food's going to get cold, and we won't help anyone else by being miserable ourselves."

What did Markus know about misery?

Jessie slid into a seat next to Markus. He reached for her hand and pressed his lips to her knuckles. "This all looks delicious."

Liam caught Sarah's eye and shrugged. Obviously, he wasn't here to fight with her mom and Markus. What's more, her persistence could cause a rift that would jeopardize the investigation.

Still, an argument pressed against her chest until her ribs ached. She exhaled loudly before dropping into a chair. "Thanks for making the apple cinnamon pancakes, Mom. They really do look good."

Liam took a seat, as well.

Markus picked up a platter filled with bacon and stabbed four thick slices with a fork. Grease dripped from the ends as he transferred the food to his plate. "Here you go." He handed the platter to Liam. Aside from the meat and pancakes, Jessie had also set out dishes filled with berries, yogurt and granola.

There was little talking as everyone got their own food. Sarah took one pancake, one slice of bacon and a small dish of yogurt with granola on top.

"That's not a lot of food," said Jessie. "How are you feeling? Usually, you eat so much more."

It was just like her mom to wrap a criticism inside concern.

There was no way she was going to be able to eat while hungry children were playing in a mud puddle.

Markus took a large bite of pancake. Speaking as he chewed, he used his fork to point. "Everyone, eat something. I feel like a pig at the trough right now."

Sarah used the side of her fork to cut a wedge of pancake. She took a bite. The sweet apples and spicy cinnamon mixed perfectly with the fluffy batter. The food was more than delicious—it tasted like her childhood. All the best memories were of Sarah, Nate and their parents eating breakfast. "Thanks for making this for me."

"Of course," said her mother. "You know I'd do anything for you."

Was that true? Could she ask her mother to leave Markus? Even if there was nothing criminal happening with the church, he was still a bad man.

"Hey, what's this talk about doing anything for Sarah?" Markus asked, his tone jovial. "I'm going to get jealous."

Liam had eaten half of his pancake and two slices of bacon already. "Thanks for making us breakfast. You're a very good cook." The distant sound of hammers could be heard at the back of the house. "Looks like you have a lot of construction going on around here. What're you building?"

"I'm glad that you asked, Liam. Because this is the project that I want to discuss with you. Our community is always growing. What we need is a house of worship that's large enough for everyone. We have the labor on-site but what we need is materials."

Sarah tried to swallow another bite. It stuck in her throat. She washed it down with swig of orange juice. "House of worship?" she echoed. "What about plain old housing?"

"What do you mean?" her mom asked, her eyes wide.

Oh, she couldn't take the act anymore. "Don't play dumb with me, Mom. You must notice how poorly all these people live. It's freezing outside and you have people sleeping in tents. Why waste time and money building a church? People have to have their basic needs met."

Her mother said, "Everyone has come here because of Markus. They want to hear him preach. We need a church for all of us to gather."

"Then why spend all this time and money on *your home* when there are children living in shacks?" Sarah asked.

"I can see where you're confused." Markus chuckled as he

wiped his mouth with a cloth napkin. "The congregation named me as the pastor. Since I'm their leader, I need a home befitting my position. It's kind of like the US president living in the White House." Shaking his head, he chuckled again. "Could you imagine me in a shack? How would anyone respect me? Or your mother?"

Honestly, she hated his smug tone. She hated Markus's too-perfect appearance. She hated his views of the world. But mostly, she hated that her mother had fallen for his crap. "In Valley Forge, George Washington lived in a tent until quarters had been built for all of his men."

"What?" Markus asked, a slice of bacon halfway to his mouth.

"You said that because you were a leader that you needed the best house. During the winter of 1777, which was brutal by all accounts, Washington lived in a tent like a common soldier until the Continental Army built housing." She paused and took a bite of pancake. "I think George Washington is a pretty respected leader."

Markus's face turned scarlet. "You listen here, Missy…"

"You know," said Liam, interrupting whatever else was going to be said, "I'd like to hear more about the church. Since I'm here for my client, maybe they could give an endowment to help with costs." He paused. "That way, we can all go back to being a happy family."

Sarah bit her bottom lip. The pain eased away her anger. After a moment, she reached for Liam's hand. "Now you see why I love him."

"You were always a good kid, Liam." Her mother held up a platter. "More sausage?"

The conversation about the living conditions and the extreme poverty was forgotten. Markus spent the rest of the meal discussing his plans for the church and the grounds. Aside from a large sanctuary, which would welcome visitors, there would be a retreat center. Those who lived on the church property would each be given a home. He was careful to point out that families with children were a priority. The congregants would all have jobs—cooking, maintenance, teaching at a school that would be built. They planned to raise their own food and sell artisan goods at a store that needed to be constructed, as well.

"What my people want is an oasis of peace in the desert of chaos that is the modern world. They want to create a community where everyone is equal, useful and appreciated," said Markus. "I'm the leader because I was blessed with the vision for our own little slice of paradise."

If Sarah were being honest, all the plans sounded lovely. Too bad she knew that Markus was full of crap.

Chapter 15

"Eventually, we'll need a library." Breakfast had been eaten. A thin woman with gray eyes had cleared away the dishes and taken them to the kitchen to clean. Liam was with Markus in his home office. The pastor was eager to share all the plans the church had—assuming they could raise the capital. Sarah and her mother sat on a plush sofa in the living room. The view from the tall windows was a study in contrast. A mountain vista in the distance, with a collection of shacks and tents that looked like nothing more than a refugee camp. "That's something you could do, right, Sarah? We could work on that together. The library could be a mother-daughter project."

She held a mug of tea and squeezed the handle tighter. The porcelain bit into her flesh. "Yeah, Mom, it'd be great to start a new library."

"Like Markus said," her mother continued, "there are a lot of other things to address before we go worrying about books. But once everyone has a house, we can expand to schools and parks. I'll need your help. You'll be there for me, right?"

She hated lying to her mother. Taking a sip of tea, she swallowed all the facts she wanted to share. Then, she said, "I'm always here for you, Mom."

Inaudible voices came from the hallway a moment before Liam and Markus stepped into the room. "You two look as pretty as a picture," said Markus. "But I need to scoot for a few minutes. It's almost lunchtime and I say a few words before each meal. If you'd like, you can come with me, Liam. Then, you can see all the good we do."

Liam said, "That'd be great."

Then, like a light bulb moment from one of her favorite books, she knew how to get Liam into the office. Rising from the sofa, she said, "I'll go with you."

"I was hoping to keep chatting," said her mother. "I haven't even showed you around the house yet."

"You can show me once we get back. Right now, I want to see what you and Markus have done."

"Well." Markus inhaled, expanding his chest. "I'm happy that both Liam and Sarah have taken an interest in the church. Once you see how truly happy everyone is in this congregation, you'll feel better."

"That's what I'm hoping, too," she lied.

"Let me call my driver," Markus said.

"No!" *Damn.* She'd been a little too forceful. "I'd rather walk."

"You want to walk to the cafeteria? Are you kidding?" asked her mother. "That's almost a mile from here."

"A mile isn't that far," she said, setting her mug on a table. "Besides, Liam and I were looking at wedding dresses online last night. The ones I like are slinky. So, let's just say I could use a walk."

"Wedding dresses. Did you hear that, Markus?" Her mom's eyes glistened with unshed tears. "Oh, my baby's getting married."

"Well, it's not officially official." Sarah had lied to her mother so many times over the past few days, she shouldn't care about one more untruth. But for some reason, this fib mattered. "We're just talking."

"Doesn't this seem sudden?" asked Markus. "After all, you've only known each other for a few days."

Who'd have thought he'd be the reasonable one?

"Actually, we've known each other most of our lives. The

time wasn't right when we were kids." Liam reached for her hand. "But the minute we saw each other at the library, I knew."

"I think it's romantic," said Jessie. "Sarah used to have a horrible crush on Liam when she was younger. Remember that?"

Anything her mom said was always honey mixed with vinegar. "I remember." Leaning into Liam, she rested her head on his chest. "Looks like I had good taste, even as a kid."

"Well, if we're going to walk, we ought to get going," said Markus.

He strode to the front door and pulled it open. Cold seeped into the room. Damn. Picking up her coat from the back of the sofa, she made eye contact with Liam. She narrowed her gaze, while slipping her arms into the sleeves.

He regarded her for a moment and grabbed his own jacket. Was the look enough for him to know that something was up? Hopefully, he'd take advantage of the situation.

The group stepped onto the porch. Jessie hadn't bothered with another coat. Folding her arms across her chest, she pulled the long sweater tight around her body. "It's too cold out here," she grumbled.

"Get another jacket or something," she suggested.

"Everything I have is too short. It won't look right with my outfit." Jessie was only a few steps behind. Arms still folded, she mumbled, "And what about the hem of my pants? Nobody seems to notice that they'll get stained or ruined. Definitely, nobody cares." She sighed dramatically. "The things we mothers do for our children."

She slowed until her mom was next to her. Linking her arm through the crook of her mother's elbow, she said, "We'll walk together, and I'll keep you warm."

"Thanks, hon. It'd be better if we could drive."

"Getting out of the house is good, too."

"One day soon, this will be a lovely community. Right now…" Jessie let her words trail off. Liam and Markus had pulled ahead and were talking in hushed tones. Leaning close, her mother whispered, "Are you mad at me?"

"Why would I be mad?"

Her mom said, "What I said yesterday about my bag being worth more than your car. I guess it was rude."

"I don't care about your bag," she said, her jaw tight.

"To be honest, you sound pretty pissed right now."

Now, Sarah remembered why she never visited her mother—aside from Markus not allowing her to come to their house. She and her mom were oil and water. They never mixed, even when they were together. "Can we drop it, Mom?"

"If you were mad, I wanted to tell you that I'm sorry. I also wanted to tell you that I have a bag from the same designer. It's from last season. But if you want it, it's yours."

What was she supposed to do with a designer bag? If it was worth something, she could hold a raffle to raise money for the library. Then again, her mother was trying. The least she could do is accept the kindness. "Thanks, Mom. I'd love it."

"Oh, good." Jessie squeezed her arm tighter. She leaned in closer. "Now tell me all about those wedding dresses you saw."

"Markus might be right. This is a little too early to be talking about forever."

"Miracle of miracles—you agree with Markus," said Jessie with a giggle. "But he's wrong, you know. I've seen the way Liam looks at you. He's in love."

With a shake of her head, she chuckled. "I heard that before."

"From who? Margaret?"

The library in Boise seemed like it was a million miles away. "Actually, it was Frannie." Sarah cleared her throat. "Frannie Colton."

Jessie stiffened. "When did you see her?"

At least she didn't have to lie about seeing a few of her half siblings. "I ran into her yesterday."

"Oh?" Jessie let go of her arm. "Where was this?"

"At her store right after I had brunch with you and Markus."

"Imagine that," her mother snorted. "You ran into Frannie in her own store."

"You don't have to be sarcastic. I didn't know who owned the store when I walked through the doors."

"How could you not have known? Book Mark It is the only bookstore in all of Owl Creek." Her mother's voice was shrill.

"How was I supposed to know about anything in Owl Creek? You never talked to me about that place. Or the fact that Nate and I have ten half siblings." So much for not arguing with her mother.

Markus glanced over his shoulder. "You girls okay back there?"

"We're fine," her mother called out. "We are fine, aren't we?"

She exhaled. Her breath caught in a frozen cloud. "Sure, Mom. We're fine."

Sarah shoved her hands deeper into her pockets and trudged over the uneven ground. The tents and shacks they'd passed before were now empty. There was no longer the sound of construction ringing over the field. Even the children had abandoned their game at the puddle, leaving it eerily quiet. It was like they'd all disappeared. The only thing that remained was the scent of refuse that hung in the air.

"Where is everyone?" she asked. A gust of wind caught her question and whipped it away.

"They're in the cafeteria, which doubles as a sanctuary—at least for now," Markus called over his shoulder. He gave Liam an oily smile. "I give a sermon right before the meal. Everyone is waiting to be fed both spiritually and physically."

"What's your topic for today?" Honestly, Sarah didn't care. But she wanted everyone to be busy and talking.

"I'm not sure yet," said Markus. "I usually just let inspiration take over."

"Wait till you see him," her mom cooed. "He's so impressive."

The office was close. A guard still stood outside the door. Sarah inhaled. Icy air burned her lungs. Holding her breath, she counted. One. Two. Three. Then, she stumbled and hit the ground.

A white burst of pain exploded behind her eyes. Her fall had simply been meant as a diversion. Instead, she'd landed on a rock. Damn. She could already feel the bruise, blossoming like a flower, on her foot.

"Are you okay?" Her mom knelt at her side. Liam was right behind Jessie. Markus stood, looming behind them all.

Her ankle throbbed with each beat of her heart. "I was stupid and not paying attention."

"Here, let me help you." Liam gripped her elbow and pulled her to standing. "How's that feel?"

The man who'd been guarding the office jogged up the road. He called out, "Everything okay?"

"Looks like Sarah twisted her ankle," Markus sighed. Turning to her, he asked, "Can you make it to the cafeteria? You can sit in there and get some ice on your foot."

She placed her left foot on the ground. Okay, so maybe it wasn't that bad. But this was the exact distraction that she needed. "I don't think I can," she said, hoping to sound anxious and distraught. "I'd rather go to the house than have to limp through a bunch of strangers."

"Honey, Markus has to speak to the congregation," said her mom. "They're waiting for him."

"I don't want to hold him up. You can stay with me, right Mom?"

"How're you supposed to make it all the way back up the hill on a busted ankle? The cafeteria is right over there." Markus pointed to the large metal building. A few people stood near the door watching and waiting for the pastor.

The thing was, Markus had a point.

"I can run back to the house and get the SUV," the guard offered. "It won't take me a minute."

Markus waved the guard away. "Go, Roger. Hurry back."

The guard turned and sprinted up the hill.

"I'm already late," Markus huffed.

"You should go," her mother said. "Sarah has been clumsy her whole life. This isn't the first time I've taken care of a twisted ankle."

After placing a kiss on Jessie's cheek, he jogged down the hill.

"Start the music," he called out to the men waiting near the entrance. "I'm coming."

Markus entered the makeshift sanctuary. The doors closed, and the morning was filled with silence. Sarah wanted to smile, but she couldn't. She limped forward. "Maybe I should walk a little. That way my ankle won't get stiff."

Liam held on to her arm. "I've got a hold of you," he said. "You can lean on me."

Squeezing his wrist, she mouthed the word *Go*. It was all he needed.

Liam gave a slight nod and let his hand slip away.

"Hey, Mom," she said, turning to Jessie. "Remember when I slid down the driveway on my Rollerblades in middle school? I had road burn on my knee for a week."

"I remember you wanted those Rollerblades so bad for your birthday. Because of your fall, you used them once and never again."

Her mother kept talking about the incident. How her father, Robert, had been angry to waste money. How the Rollerblades had ended up going to Allison, a much more athletic kid, who could stay upright. Sarah listened but kept walking slowly toward the house. She didn't know how long Liam needed to be in the office, but she'd done all she could. The rest was up to him.

Liam scanned the hillside to make sure that he was alone. Sarah and her mother were already more than a dozen yards away. She was close enough that he could see the piping at the edge of Sarah's coat, tan on dark blue, but so far away that he couldn't hear what they said.

Other than the women, he was alone.

Slipping a hand into his pocket, he wrapped his fingers around the flash drive. It was cold and solid, a reminder of his determination to get the job done. He walked slowly to the office.

That was another rule from undercover training.

Those who look like they belong go unnoticed.

His footfalls clanged on the metal stairs, the sound ricocheting like a gunshot. He paused, waiting for someone to stop him. The hillside was empty. He gripped the handle and turned the knob. The door opened, swinging inside.

Since a guard had been posted outside, he wasn't surprised the building was left unlocked. Hopefully, everything else was just as easy. Stepping inside, he looked around the space. Light from a window filled a converted mobile home. What would have been a living room had been turned into workspace, complete with a sofa beneath the window and two metal desks. A row of filing cabinets filled the back wall. There was also a kitchen, complete with a round dining table and refrigerator and stove.

Two rooms, one at either end of the trailer, were closed. His intel didn't include which one Markus used as an office. For a moment, the indecision rooted him to the floor. There was no way to know which was the right one. But guessing wrong would waste time he didn't have.

The room to the right was closer. He strode through the outer office. The room was unlocked. Inside was another office. Desk. Chair. Filing cabinet in the corner. An open laptop sat in the middle of the desk. He knew one thing for certain: Markus wouldn't use a utilitarian and impersonal office.

Quickly, he walked to the other side of the trailer. He turned the handle of the second door. It didn't budge.

Kneeling, he examined the lock. It was typical of interior doors, meant to deter polite people from entering without warning. In fact, Liam could force his way inside with quick kick to the jamb or a shoulder to the flimsy fake wood. But that wouldn't do. He needed to be able to sneak out of the trailer, too.

This required a bit of finesse.

In the FBI Academy, agents were taught how to pick locks, especially simple ones like this. Sure, he hadn't had the need to use this particular skill but at least he knew how.

After rising to his feet, he hustled to the kitchen area. He opened several drawers before finding what he needed. A plastic caddy was filled with flatware. Spoons. Forks. Knives—both smooth luncheon knives and sharp steak knives. He grabbed a steak knife and returned to the room. He slipped the narrow end between lock and jamb. For a moment, metal grated against metal. Then, the lock released, with a soft click.

Standing, Liam set the knife on a nearby desk. He'd put it back once he was done. He turned the handle and opened the door. The floor was covered with an expensive-looking rug with a floral pattern in reds and golds. The single window was covered with velvet drapes, blocking out the sun. Yet, there was enough light for Liam to see.

A leather sofa sat at an angle in the corner. A matching chair was next to the sofa. A bar on wheels was tucked in the crook behind them both. In the middle of the room stood a large desk. The polished wood reflected the scant light. Sitting on the desk was a computer monitor and keyboard. The device was so old that the tower for the hard drive stood next to the desk.

Bingo.

It was the computer that Helena had seen Markus use.

Liam entered the room. The door closed behind him with a thud. Without the open door, there was no light. He didn't care, he'd seen enough to know the layout.

At the desk, he touched a key on the keyboard. The screen began to glow. A password field appeared. Helena had told him the password. It was Markus's birth date in reverse order. He had long ago memorized the numbers and didn't think while typing.

The password screen disappeared, and he held his breath.

It took a moment for the computer's menu to appear. He didn't have time to analyze all the data. Once he was back in DC, he'd have the luxury of time. Then, he could look at all the files. Placing the flash drive into the front of the tower, he entered a set of keystrokes.

A new message appeared. Copying hard drive. 10% complete.

25% complete.
45% complete.

Sweat snaked down his back. He didn't know how long it would take to copy the hard drive. But he only had a few minutes before someone noticed that he was missing.

Chapter 16

Jessie held tight to Sarah's arm as they walked up the hill. True, it was still cold outside, but she was now warmed by the fact that her daughter needed her. Truth be told, she hadn't been a good mother—not even to Sarah and Nate. But here Sarah was, still wanting her help.

"How're you feeling?" she asked.

"It hurts, but I think I'll be okay." Sarah hobbled forward, dragging her right foot. Funny, Jessie could've sworn she twisted her left ankle. A chill ran down her spine and it had nothing to do with the temperature.

"Do you remember the Christmas when you were eight years old?" she asked. "Your dad and I gave you and Nate sleds."

"We had gotten a foot of snow on Christmas Eve, so we both spent the morning sledding down the hill in the backyard." Sarah smiled before adding, "You made a homemade pumpkin pie and mashed potatoes. Dad roasted a turkey. When we came in—cold, wet and tired—the food was ready."

She recalled sitting around the table, as savory and sweet scents filled the small kitchen. Sarah and Nate were rosy cheeked with exertion and the cold. It was a nice memory. "I hope we can all be a family again. I know that you're making your own life, but I want us to always be close."

Sarah gave her arm a squeeze. "I know we don't always agree, Mom. But I do love you."

"And what about Markus?" Her fiancé didn't like to be discussed. More than once, a member of the church had questioned his authority. The punishment was always swift and severe. But outside, with nobody around, Jessie could ask.

Sarah snorted. "He does seem to love you. That counts for something."

"I know he's not your real father…" Jessie began.

Sarah stopped walking. "Mom, I'm a grown woman. I don't need a replacement dad. Besides, I'm not even sure that I knew my own father."

"You shouldn't say that," she chastised.

"Why not? It's true. You and Dad had a whole other life that we never knew about. You both had children from other marriages. What's worse, you never said a word to me or my brother. Or should I say, 'Nate,' because I have so many other brothers."

Sure, she deserved some of her daughter's wrath. It's just that Jessie didn't want to take it. "Can we please change the subject and talk about something pleasant?"

"Yeah, sure." There was a weariness to her tone that made Sarah sound older than her years.

"I have a confession to make." She held on to her daughter's arm tighter.

"A confession?" Sarah echoed. "That sounds serious."

"It's nothing too bad. It's just that I was looking at mother-of-the-bride dresses. I think I'd look good in dusty rose. If you're thinking about colors for the wedding, that is."

"I'm not sure that Liam and I are there yet."

Jessie looked over her shoulder. The camp was empty and quiet. "Where is Liam anyway?"

"He went with Markus."

"I don't think so…" Jessie brought back the moment that Sarah fell. The congregation was already assembled. Her daughter said she couldn't walk to the cafeteria. A guard had left his post at the office as Liam had helped Sarah to her feet. At the same time, Markus ran down the hill. She recalled him telling a man to start the music as he entered the building. What's more, he'd been alone. "Liam wasn't with Markus, I'm positive."

Keeping her eyes on the ground, she said, "Remember, he kissed me on the cheek and told me to be careful."

Jessie slowly shook her head. "That's not what happened."

"Yes, it is." Sarah's jaw flinched. The gesture was gone as quick as it came. But it was same tell she'd had all her life. Her daughter had just lied. But why?

Her heart started to race. The metallic taste of panic coated her tongue. She didn't know how Markus would react when he found out that Liam had wandered off. But she did know it wouldn't be good. He told her that all the security around the church compound was to keep nefarious characters out. But deep in her heart, she knew better. They were here to keep people in. She had to get Sarah and Liam off the mountain and back to Owl Creek. Or better yet, back to Boise. She gripped her daughter's arm tight. "Now, you listen to me."

"Ow," Sarah protested, trying to pull her arm away. Jessie only tightened her grip. A little pain now was better than what might happen later. "You're hurting me."

She leaned in close and whispered, "Markus is not a man to be trifled with. Here, he's not just God's representative on earth. For this community, he is God. His word is absolute."

She drew in a shaking breath. Her galloping pulse slowed. "You've got to come clean with me. What in the hell is going on here? Where's Liam?"

"Nothing's going on, Mom." But her daughter glanced at the office as she spoke.

"Is that where he went?" she asked. "The office? What does he want?"

With a defiant glint in her eyes, Sarah met her gaze but said nothing.

"We don't have much time. Be honest with me." She paused, waiting for her daughter to say something. Anything. Sarah remained mute. She tried again, "Keeping you safe is the only thing that matters to me. I know something's going on. But I can't help if you don't tell me the truth."

* * *

Funny thing, Sarah had wanted to be honest with her mother from the beginning. Now that her mom was begging for the truth, she hesitated.

She heard the revving of a motor a moment before she saw the black SUV. The vehicle was coming toward them fast, like a bird of prey. They didn't have much time now. Once the guard showed up, the conversation would be over.

It didn't matter what her mother had said, Sarah wasn't sure if she was to be trusted. Then again, what other choice did she have?

"Markus is a crook," she said, starting with the obvious. "He's been stealing money from his congregation. Using his money to buy nice things." She didn't add that many of those nice things had gone to Jessie. She didn't need to. They both knew the truth. "He's embezzled millions of dollars. The FBI is investigating him. You have to leave him before it's too late."

"Liam's still with the FBI, isn't he?" her mom asked.

"He is."

"And he's the one investigating Markus. Is he in the office looking for evidence?"

There was no reason to lie to her mother anymore. "He is."

Her mother asked, "You two aren't really a couple, are you?"

"Let's just say that it's complicated."

A tear ran down her mother's cheek. She wiped it away with the heel of her hand. "Why didn't you come to me from the beginning? Or is that complicated, as well?"

"Mom, there's a lot for us to discuss," she began.

Her mother waved a hand, as if wiping away Sarah's words from a whit board. It was almost like she'd never spoken. "There's only one thing to worry about right now. Liam has to get out of that office. If Markus ever finds out that he's been fooled, there'll be hell to pay."

She turned and looked at the trailer. From where she stood on the hill, the building looked smaller, like a child's toy. They'd walked too far to get Liam out now. Had Sarah been wrong to have kept her mother in the dark? Questions jumbled together in a big pile until she couldn't parse one from the next. But there was only one question that really mattered. "What kind of hell is happening here, Mom?"

Before her mother could answer, the black SUV stopped in the middle of the road. The guard, she remembered his name was Roger, put the vehicle into Park. He opened the driver's side door. "Where's the other guy?"

Her mom looked Sarah in the eye. "I sent him to the office." Slipping her hand into her pocket, she turned to Roger and smiled. "Markus brought my phone's charger with him to the office yesterday and forgot to bring it back. When I remembered, I sent Liam to grab it for me."

"Nobody's supposed to be inside that building without permission," said Roger. "That's why I'm posted outside all day."

"Then we won't tell Markus that you left your post."

The man opened his mouth, ready to argue with Jessie. He seemed to think better of it and gave a single nod. "Let's find your charging cable and get you all back to the house. Like you said, I've been away from my post for too long." He opened the back passenger door—a sure sign that they were supposed to get into the SUV.

Jessie slid into the back seat. Sarah limped toward the open door and got into the back seat, as well. The SUV had three rows of seats. In the front, there were two captain's chairs. The middle row was also made up of two captain's chairs. TV monitors were set in the back of the front headrests. The back seat was a long bench.

She ran her hand over the buttery-soft seat. "This is like a very fancy spaceship," she said, making a bad joke.

Nobody laughed.

The guard slid behind the steering wheel. He put the gearshift into Drive, and they rolled down the hill. He slowed in front of the office. "You both relax. I'll get the other guy and your phone's cord."

Jessie opened the door before Roger put the vehicle into Park. "I can do it myself. It'll just take me a second."

Obviously, everything her mom told the guard had been a lie. And honestly, she didn't know what was going to happen next. But she wasn't about to let her mother go alone. Opening her own door, Sarah dropped down to the ground.

"Hey," Roger called out. "I thought you twisted your ankle. Doesn't look like it hurts you now."

"It doesn't," she agreed. "Must be a miracle."

The office was dark, save for the light coming from the monitor. In the middle of the screen, a line marked off the percentage of files that had been copied and transferred to Liam's flash drive. The machine was a relic, as far as computers were concerned. The slow download had worn even his patience thin. But he'd come too far to leave without his evidence.

"C'mon," he said, as if his urging could get the computer to process faster. "What's the freaking holdup?"

The line filled in another inch.

Download 79% complete.
84% complete.
99% complete.
100% complete.

"Thank you," he said, entering the keystrokes that erased any trace that he'd been on the computer at all. Once the computer was shut down, he removed the flash drive. He stuck the stick into his sock. It wasn't an ideal hiding place, but it was better than his pocket.

Then, he heard it. The crunch of wheels on gravel and the idling of an engine. At the window, he pulled back the curtain an inch. One of the black SUVs sat next to the building, a cloud of exhaust surrounding the vehicle in a haze. Jessie Colton exited the vehicle and hustled toward the office. He hoped to get into and out of the building without any witnesses. Obviously, that wasn't going to happen now.

He needed to think. Yet, he couldn't hear his own thoughts over his pulse slamming into his skull.

The door to the trailer opened, hitting the wall with a crack.

"Where is he?" He recognized Jessie's voice.

"He's in Markus's office," said Sarah.

Had he been double-crossed by mother and daughter?

The door handle jiggled. Then, someone knocked. "Liam, we have to go," said Jessie, before adding, "Now."

He didn't know what to believe or whom to trust. But staying in the office wasn't an option. He opened the door and stepped into the reception area. The door closed behind him. Jessie stood on the threshold. Sarah was behind her mother. Without saying a word, Jessie pulled a thin white cord from the pocket of her sweater and shoved it into his hands.

The outer door opened again. One of black-clad guards followed—to him, they all looked the same. He pointed a finger at Jessie. "I told you to wait in the SUV."

"And I told you that I could handle this myself," said Jessie. "And see, he has my phone cord."

There were too many moving pieces in this game for his liking. But his training kicked in. Another rule from undercover agent's training. *Always stay in character.* He held up the plastic cord, letting it dangle from his fingers like a dead snake. "Found it."

"Thank you." Smiling, Jessie took the cord and shoved it back into her pocket. She patted the guard's arm as she passed him at the door. "Lock the door behind you and take us up to the house."

Sarah reached for his hand and pulled him into her mother's wake. The flash drive in his sock snagged on his pants. He stepped outside. The air had the icy bite that promised more snow. The back door of the SUV was still open. Jessie slid into the back seat. Sarah squeezed his hand once and followed her mother. Liam got into the front seat of the passenger side. The driver rounded in front of the bumper and slid behind the steering wheel.

Roger slammed the door and shoved the gearshift into Drive. The air in the SUV was rank with anxious energy, like the moment before a bomb was set to explode. He watched Roger from his periphery. The other man gripped the steering wheel. His knuckles were white. The ride to Jessie's house took only minutes. Yet in the silence of the SUV, it felt like hours.

The guard slowed next to the steps that led to the porch.

Jessie leaned between the two front seats, "Roger, I think it best if we don't mention that Liam was in the admin building. You know that Markus won't be happy that you neglected to lock the door."

"Yes, ma'am," he said. "Thank you."

Liam opened the door. He drew in a deep breath and exhaled. Sarah and Jessie stood beside him. They waited as the SUV drove away. He turned to the women. "What in the hell is going on?"

"I should be the one asking you that," snapped Jessie. "How dare you put my daughter in danger."

He wasn't about to break cover. Looking at Sarah's mom, he said, "I don't know what you're talking about."

"Yes, you do," said Sarah. "I told her."

The three words hit him like a fist to the face. For a moment, he saw stars. "You what?"

"I had no choice. Roger had just shown up with SUV. If you tried to sneak out, he would've seen you. My mom helped, face it." The steel in Sarah's words surprised him.

True, he knew that she much was more than the kid with a bad case of hero worship. The wind caught her hair, blowing it around her face. She gripped her locks and held them in her fist. Snowflakes danced, swirling and swooping, in another gust. She reminded him of a Nordic warrior, and he admired her even more.

"Let's go inside," she suggested. "There's a lot we all need to discuss."

"No," said Jessie. "We don't have time for a tête-à-tête. You both need to leave."

"What're you talking about, Mom?" Sarah asked.

"You know how I said that Markus rules this community?" She exhaled. "There's no telling what he'll do to either of you. Please, just go."

Liam had never seen the serious and intense side of Jessie before. To him, she'd always been flighty and dramatic. For the first time, he wondered if he'd underestimated her.

"If it's so dangerous that I have to leave, then you're coming with me," said Sarah.

"I can't leave," said Jessie. "He'll come looking for me."

"The FBI has ways to keep you hidden," he said. "You'll be safe."

"What about Sarah? Or Nate? Or Malcolm? Or any of my other kids? Can you shelter them all?"

He knew the FBI wouldn't bring all the Coltons into protective custody. "I'll do what I can."

"That's not enough," she said with a mirthless laugh. "Now, you both need to go."

For Liam, leaving now would be perfect. He had the evidence he needed. But he didn't like leaving Jessie behind. Markus sounded like more than just a crook, but a sociopath, as well.

"Won't that seem suspicious?" Sarah asked. "What will you say to Markus?"

Jessie gave a small shrug. "I'll tell him that you and I got into a fight or something. And that's what you have to say at the guard shack. They won't worry about letting you leave."

"Mom, listen to what you're saying," The pain in Sarah's voice cut deep into his chest. "You cannot stay. Who cares about your nice house and your fancy purses. They aren't what make you the person I love. They don't make you who you are—my mother."

Jessie said, "To keep you safe, I need to stay, at least for now."

"I'm not leaving without you," said Sarah.

The sound of music, faint but unmistakable, rolled up the hill. The congregation had been released. Liam's time was up.

Chapter 17

Roger stood in front of the crappy converted mobile home that was being used as the church's administrative building. The cold seeped in through the soles of his shoes. Shoving his hands into the pockets of his coat, he watched as the people, skinny and sad, shuffled by. They all sang, like they were happy. He'd heard all their stories. Lost souls, who finally found a place in the world. People who couldn't find a direction now had a leader to follow.

He he'd been let go from the Bingham County Sheriff's Office six months earlier. One late night, another deputy had swiped a baggie of weed from the evidence locker. They'd all toked up. In the morning, the sheriff figured it out. Everyone was questioned. Roger was the only one who confessed. By noon, he'd been fired.

In the small eastern Idaho county where he lived, his misconduct was a scandal. Roger became a pariah in his family. With no other options, he'd answered the online ad for security personnel. Markus hired him after a single interview.

When he thought about it that way, he was like all the hollow-eyed people who shuffled past.

But in a lot of other ways, he was different. After six months on the job, he hated the Ever After Church. He hated standing around sweating in the summer and freezing his balls off in the winter. To him, everyone on this compound was a bleating sheep. Except for Markus, that is.

He was a wolf.

And speak of the devil—literally.

Striding up the road, Markus watched Roger.

Shifting from one foot to the other, he lifted his chin in greeting. "The sermon go well today, sir?"

"My sermons always go well."

"Glad to hear it," he said.

Roger had never been the churchy type. He didn't believe all the mumbo-jumbo about heaven or hell. You lived your life. Good happened when you worked hard. Bad happened when you screwed up. In fact, he was a prime example of that belief system.

"Did you get Jessie and the others back to the house?" Markus asked.

He didn't want to find out what would happen if he lied to the pastor. So thankfully, his answer was the truth. "I did, sir."

"How did Jessie's daughter seem? Will she need a doctor?"

"Actually, I think the injury wasn't as bad as we first thought."

"Good. Good." Markus walked up the set of stairs to the office building. He reached for the handle and pulled on the door. Neither budged. "Why's the door locked?"

"Since I wasn't on guard, I figured..." He reached into his pants pocket and removed a heavy ring of keys. He climbed the steps and stood next to Markus. Now would be the time to confess that Liam had been in the office unattended. He didn't believe Jessie's story about needing her phone charger. Then again, he'd learned a tough lesson about telling the truth. Sliding the key into the lock, he opened the door and stepped aside. "There you go, sir."

"You can come inside," the pastor said. "We can chat while I collect some of my things."

That's how it started last time. An invitation for a friendly conversation. Roger wasn't a brainiac or anything. But he was smart enough to not piss in the same well twice. "I really should be outside."

"Nonsense," said Markus with a laugh. "You're here to protect me. Besides, the office is better than standing out in the cold."

"Well," he chuckled. "I can't argue with that thinking, sir."

Markus touched his temple. "I'm the smart one. That's why I'm in charge."

The pastor entered the trailer. Roger followed. The room was warm and smelled of coffee. He'd grown up in a mobile home like this one. He hadn't talked to his mother in months. If he called now, would his mom invite him to come home?

"I won't be a minute," said Markus, pulling him from his thoughts. He pointed to a sofa. "Have a seat."

Roger dropped onto the soft cushion. The ache in his back was eased. His feet warmed up a little. That's when he saw it. A knife sat on the edge of a desk, the blade glinting in the light. His chest tightened, making it impossible to breathe. It was proof that Liam, that son of a bitch, hadn't just been in the office for Jessie's phone cord. But worse than that, it was evidence that Roger had failed at his job. What's more, he'd lied to the pastor.

Now, all he could do was hope the cutlery was overlooked.

Markus walked to his office door. From his pocket, he produced a key that worked into the lock. After turning the handle, he pushed the door open.

His pulse slowed as he made a plan. Once the pastor closed his office door, he could put the knife away.

Markus turned. "I forgot to ask…" His question unraveled as his gaze dropped to the desk. And the knife. He looked up at Roger, his eyes narrowed. "What the hell is going on?"

Roger's mouth was dry. He swallowed. "Um."

"Um?" Markus echoed. "Is that all you have to say?" He picked up the blade and pointed it at Roger. "I think there's a lot you know and you better start talking."

Sarah wasn't going to leave without her mother. But what was she supposed to do if Jessie refused to go?

She tried a new argument. "If you want to keep me safe, get

in the car. Because I'm not leaving without you. So, if you're staying, then I'm staying, as well."

Liam said, "Listen to your daughter. If you don't, I'll forcibly move you to the car."

"You are the most stubborn people I know," her mother said, pointing. "Both of you."

Sarah's purse was still in the house, but her car keys were in the pocket of her coat. Using the fob, she started the engine and unlocked the doors. "Let's get out of here."

Her mom opened the rear passenger door. Sarah reached for the handle on the driver's side. Liam held out his hand. "Let me drive."

She placed the keys in his palm. He wrapped his fingers around her hand. Their gazes met and held. There was so much she wanted to say. But every second was precious. "Let's get out of here."

Her hand slipped from his grasp, and she opened the passenger side door. Sliding into the seat, she put on her seat belt. From the driver's seat, he held out the flash drive. "Tuck this under the floor mat," he said. "Or someplace nobody will see."

Did he really think that the car would be searched? Well, until they'd left the compound, Sarah didn't know what to expect. She took the stick and pulled back the carpeted mat. There was a groove in the flooring. She tucked the flash drive into the recess and replaced the mat. "It's hidden for now."

He started the ignition and put the car into Drive. Snow had collected on the windshield, leaving them in a cocoon of white. Liam turned on the wipers and eased around the circular drive. He slammed his foot on the break. Sarah rocked forward, bracing herself on the dashboard. When she looked up, she saw it.

A black SUV was right in front of them.

Liam eased the car to the right, trying to pass the vehicle. The SUV nosed forward, taking up the whole road and blocking their path. Both front doors opened. Markus exited the vehicle first. Roger followed.

Liam rolled down the window as the two men stepped up to the car.

"Where are you going?" Markus asked, leaning an elbow on the car's cowl.

Liam said, "Sarah and her mom started talking. Well, Jessie wants to reach out to Malcolm. None of us have cell service, so we figured we'd drive to the road."

Honestly, she was impressed. Liam was a convincing liar. No wonder she'd bought his story about being a banker.

Markus turned his gaze to the back seat. "That true, Jessie?"

"I'm not sure that I'll reconcile with all of my kids." Her mother's voice was thin and reedy. She cleared her throat. "But Sarah convinced me to give it a try."

"You know what I think?" Markus asked. "I think you all are lying to me."

"Don't be ridiculous," said Jessie. "Why would anyone lie to you?"

"You're right, I am being silly." He shoved a hand into his pocket and pulled out a knife. "Except for this." Holding up the blade, he asked, "You recognize this?"

Liam gunned the engine, swerving around the rear bumper of the car. The force shoved Sarah back. Her station wagon jostled over the side of berm. There was a crack. The back windshield exploded as a bullet punched a hole into the dashboard. Smoke snaked out of the vents. Sarah looked over her shoulder. Roger stood in the middle of the road with a gun in his hand.

"Get down." Liam shoved the back of her head toward the floor.

Another gunshot rang out. The car bucked to the side.

Holding the steering wheel with both hands, Liam cursed. "He got the tire."

Then, time splintered into a thousand different shards.

Another bullet was fired. Another tire was struck. The car skidded across the road before hitting a snowbank. The world turned upside down as the vehicle flipped onto its roof. Her stomach lurched as the car tumbled end over end.

Hanging upside down, she was pinned in place by the seat belt.

There was the drip, drip, drip of blood landing on the roof of the car.

Everything was stark. Bright white snow. Blood so dark, it looked black. The sides of her vision were hazy, like a photograph that had started to fade.

In the distance, she heard her mother's cries.

Liam's voice came from everywhere, echoing in her head. "Sarah. Are you okay? Can you hear me?"

She wanted to answer but didn't know how to speak. And then, there was nothing.

Liam stood on the uneven ground. Cold bit into a cut on his face. The back of his head throbbed. Running his fingers over his hairline, he found a knot already forming. Markus and the guard with the gun had dragged him from the wreckage. They'd pulled Sarah and Jessie out of the car, as well.

Jessie sobbed. "What just happened, Markus? You shot at us. You shot at me. And for no reason!"

"Shut up," Markus snapped. "I'll deal with you later."

Jessie's makeup was smeared, but she seemed uninjured. Sarah was a different story. The accident left her unconscious. A cut ran along her forehead. Red ran down her cheeks, making it look like she was crying blood.

"Let's go," said Markus. He'd traded the knife for a gun. Using the barrel, he pointed toward the house.

Roger carried Sarah. Liam's fingers itched with the need to hold her. He wanted to kiss her and whisper that everything would be okay. But if he told her that now, it would be a lie. They were trapped.

His training as an undercover agent had covered a lot of topics. They'd discussed how to behave if captured, but they never discussed what to do if hostages were taken. Had he been on his own, Liam might've tried to run—the evidence in the car be damned. But there was no way he was going to leave the compound without Sarah.

The walk to the house took only a minute. Markus opened the front door and stepped aside. "Both of you," he ordered to Jessie and Liam, "get inside."

He hated to obey but there was no sense in getting shot for

bravado. Without a word, he crossed the threshold. The faint scent of cinnamon and apples still lingered in the air.

Pointing to the sofa, Markus said to Roger, "Put her down there. Then call everyone else on your team. I want all the congregants gathered in the cafeteria. After that, get all the security personnel up here."

"I'm on it, sir," said Roger, before setting Sarah on the couch and leaving through the front door.

Jessie stroked her daughter's hair. "Can you hear me, hon?"

Sarah moaned and her eyelids fluttered. That had to be a good sign.

Markus lifted the gun. "I'm only going to ask you this once. How'd the knife end up on the desk in the admin building?"

A million answers came to him in a downpour of ideas. But he wasn't about to break cover. "What knife?"

"You think I'm stupid?" He pulled a chair out from the dining room table. "Have a seat."

He wasn't going to let the other guy get the upper hand. "Thanks, I'm fine standing."

"You need to get in that chair, or else I'm going to put you there." He leveled his gun at Liam, aiming for the chest.

"You know what I think? I think you're not going to shoot me. Assault with a deadly weapon is quite a crime." Especially when the victim is a federal agent. "I don't think you're stupid. In fact, I think you're smart enough not to get your hands too dirty."

He smirked. "I like you, Liam. I really do. But you see, I can't have people here that I don't trust. I know you were in the admin building. What's more, you used the knife to pick the lock on my office door. But I need to know why." He paused. "Tell me now. Are you still with the FBI?"

Truth be told, Jessie's story about the phone charger wasn't the best. But it was all he had. Besides, there was no reason to deny that he'd been in the office. Obviously, the security guy had ratted them all out. Then there was the problem of the knife on the desk. "Jessie asked me to get something for her, which I did. I might've poked around a little. But if you don't trust me, why should I trust you? Just remember, it's you who wants a lot of money from my client."

Markus rocked back on his heels at the mention of cash. "Why'd you drive away?"

"You used an SUV to block the road. You threatened us with a knife. What kind of man would I be if I didn't get Sarah and her mom somewhere safe?"

"Your story is convincing," Markus agreed. "But it's a little *too* convincing for me to think it's true."

"Stop it," Jessie yelled. "Leave Liam alone. He's answered all your questions. And why is nobody worried that my baby girl is hurt?"

"I told you," Markus said through gritted teeth, "that I would deal with you later."

The front door opened. Four guards, all dressed in black, entered the house. The large room became smaller. Markus smiled and handed the gun back to Roger. The other man slipped the firearm into a holster he wore at his side. Looking at Liam, he said, "I'm only going to tell you once more. Sit in the damn chair. Because if you don't take a seat now, you'll be begging for it later."

Sure, Markus wasn't asking for much. But he wasn't about to give in. "I'll pass."

"Take care of him, Roger."

Roger stepped forward. His gaze locked with Liam's, the security guard drove his hand into Liam's gut. The pain was instantaneous and drove the air from his lung. The first punch was followed by another. This one connected with his chin. For a moment, Liam saw stars.

It didn't matter that he was supposed to be a banker. He wasn't about to get beaten up and not fight back. He swung out wide, catching Roger in the side of the head. That's when the other guards started fighting dirty. All three came at him at once. One guy grabbed his arm, while another landed a blow to his side.

Breakfast threatened to come up. But he'd be damned before he puked in front of these bastards.

Jessie started pleading with Markus. "Tell them to stop."

"See what you've made me do? Did you really send him into the office for your phone charger? What were you thinking?"

"I'm so sorry. He's family."

"That's enough, boys," said Markus. The beating stopped, but the pain remained. "Sit him in the chair."

He was dragged across the floor and propped up in the seat. He was exhausted and would've preferred they'd left him on the ground to pass out.

Hands on his knees, Markus looked him in the eye. "Now that I've got your attention, I need to know why you were in my office. Are you still with the FBI?"

"Just trying to find out about you for my client," he said, shocked by the conviction in his voice. "But I gotta be honest. I won't be recommending your project."

"You keep saying that, but the thing is, I don't believe you." He paused. "Roger, go to the kitchen and get me a glass of water."

"Yes, sir," he said, before disappearing into the kitchen. A moment later Roger returned with a glass filled with water. He held it out to Markus. "Here you go."

Markus rose to his feet and took the glass. He walked to the sofa and let the liquid trickle onto Sarah.

She coughed as the water ran over her face. Rubbing her eyes, she sat up. "What the hell?"

"It's time for you to wake up," said Markus. "Because your boyfriend won't tell me the truth. But you are all the motivation I need."

"Leave her out of this," said Liam. His lips were thick, and it hurt to speak. Holding on to his ribs, he tried to stand. A guard pushed him back into the chair, knocking the wind out of him.

"Give me your gun," said Markus, holding out his hand to Roger.

The guard placed his hand on his holster but didn't hand the firearm over. "You don't want to do this."

"Oh, don't I?" Markus turned to another guard. "Gun?"

The man removed a pistol from his holster and handed it to Markus. For a moment, the pastor held the firearm in his palm.

Then, he pointed it in Liam's direction. "Now, tell me the truth. Who are you and what do you want?"

It was a risky move to call Markus's bluff. After all, he'd ordered a group of thugs to beat the crap out of Liam. But roughing someone up and shooting them were two different things. "You know who I am and what I do. Don't believe me, look on the internet."

"Wrong answer."

Pivoting, he aimed at Sarah and pulled the trigger.

Chapter 18

Sarah didn't have time to think, only react. She tensed, bracing for the bullet's impact.

"No!" her mother screamed, shoving her to the floor.

A flash of fire erupted from the gun's muzzle. There was a blast that left her ears buzzing. The acrid scent of gunpowder filled the room.

But the pain never came.

Jessie was slumped over on the sofa. Her long blond hair fell over her face. Her breaths came in a wet wheeze.

She looked at her mother and fear gripped her throat. "Mom?" Sarah rose to her knees, kneeling next to her mother. "Are you okay?" She pushed back her hair, and saw bloody foam clinging to Jessie's lips. "Mom?"

Jessie slumped to the side. Her ivory outfit was dark red with blood and gore. That's when she understood it all. In pushing Sarah to the floor, Jessie had caught the bullet.

"Mom!" Rising to her feet, she lifted her mother's sweater. The bullet had torn a hole between her breasts. The wound wept blood. Sarah struggled out of her own coat. Wadding the fabric, she pressed it to the gash. "Mom, can you hear me?"

Jessie opened her eyes. "Are you okay, Sarah?"

"I'm fine, Mom." Her eyes burned. "The important thing is that you'll be fine, too." She looked over her shoulder. The room was filled with men—Markus, Liam and four guards—staring at her. "Damn you all. Help."

"I shot her? I shot Jessie?" Markus was pale. The gun slipped from his hand, clattering to the floor.

Liam rose from the chair. "There has to be a first aid kit around here somewhere."

Roger said, "There's one in the admin building."

"Go get it," said Liam. "And use the phone to call 9-1-1. Tell them to send an ambulance." He stood and scooped up the gun. While slipping the firearm into the waistband of his jeans, he pointed to the remaining security guards. "You gather up all the towels you can find. We have to stop the bleeding."

They all rushed from the room.

One guard emerged from the kitchen with a stack of clean dishrags. He handed them to Liam.

Holding the towels, Liam knelt next to Sarah. "You need to pull your coat away when I tell you. Got it?"

She nodded.

"Now."

Sarah lifted her jacket, now soaked with blood, as Liam pressed the towels onto Jessie's wound. Blood pooled on the leather sofa and leaked to the floor. Her mother's lips were blue. She reached for Sarah's hand; her skin was cool.

Scooting next to her mother, she stroked the hair from her forehead. "Roger went to call an ambulance and get a first aid kit. We'll get you fixed up in no time." The towels Liam pressed to the wound were stained crimson. Her mom had lost a lot of blood. How much more could she lose before…? No. She wouldn't think that way.

Looking back at her mother, she tried to smile. "You just hang in there."

"You were always an easy child, Sarah. I'm sorry I wasn't a better mother."

"Don't say that. You were a great mom. The best."

"I tried." Her mom swallowed and grimaced with the pain. "I need you to do something for me."

A guard helped Liam switch the gore-stained kitchen towels for a large bath towel. To Sarah, it seemed like the blood wasn't soaking the fabric as quickly as before. It meant something important. But was it good or bad?

"Anything," said Sarah.

"I want you to talk to your brothers and sisters—not just Nate—but everyone. Let them know that I made bad choices and they suffered. Tell them that I'm sorry. But make sure they know, I'm proud to be their mom. And Jenny's kids, too. I'm proud that I was their aunt."

The burning in her eyes was too much. Tears leaked down her cheeks. She wiped them away with her shoulder. "I'm going to let you tell them yourself, Mom. Once we get you to the hospital, I'll call them all. They'll come and see you, I'm sure of that."

"Oh, Sarah," said her mom. "I hate to leave you. But I won't make it to the hospital."

"Don't say that, Mom. Please."

"I'm sorry that I won't see you get married. Or have children of your own. But I know that you'll be a beautiful bride and great mother."

"You're going to be okay," she said. But her mother's lips had turned gray, and her hand was like a block of ice.

"He's here," said her mother, into the distance. "Your father's come for me."

"Mom. Mom. Mom. Don't go. I need you."

Jessie smiled and closed her eyes. She exhaled, and then she was no more.

Markus stood in the corner, his hands trembling. A keening wail echoed off the walls. For a moment, he couldn't find the source. Then he realized, he was the one crying. "Ohmigod. Ohmigod. She's dead. I can't believe it. She's dead." There was empty space in his soul now, one that only Jessie could fill.

"She's dead because of you, sick bastard." Sarah stood. Her sweater and hands were covered in Jessie's blood.

"I didn't," he began. But, of course, he had. "I didn't mean to." He'd aimed at Sarah. "If she hadn't shoved you out of the way, she wouldn't be dead."

Even after everything he'd given to her, Jessie still loved her kids more than she loved him. Someone had to pay for his pain.

He might've pulled the trigger, but it was all Sarah's fault. Balling his hands into fists, he lunged forward.

"I wouldn't do that if I were you." Liam aimed the gun at Markus.

He froze, arm lifted and ready to strike. Three of his guards stood to the side. They all had guns. "One of you," Markus barked. "Do something."

Two of the men backed away. They opened the door and sprinted from the house.

That left a single guard. "You," he ordered. "Shoot him."

"I can't do that," the young man said. "You need to leave. Roger went to call an ambulance. Because it's a shooting, the cops are going to show up, too. You don't want to be here when they arrive."

"Like I said." Liam lifted the gun. "Don't move."

A sour taste filled his mouth, but he wasn't about to submit. Turning, he ran around the fireplace and toward the kitchen.

"Stop or I'll shoot," Liam warned.

Markus ran faster.

Pop. The air sizzled as a bullet whizzed by his ear.

Pop. Pop. Pop. Pop. Liam fired at him as he ran. The bullets slammed into the wall, sending splinters flying through the air.

He skidded to the back door and turned the handle. Before he could pull the door open, Liam ran into the kitchen. "Step away from the door."

Markus pulled the door open.

Leveling the gun, Liam pulled the trigger.

Click.

Markus didn't have time to gloat. He ran outside. Cold air bit his hands and face. He glanced over his shoulder. Liam came up from behind but was slowed by a limp.

Running down the back stairs two at a time, Markus skidded on the fresh snow. Somehow, he kept on his feet. Heart pumping and legs burning with exertion, he sprinted toward the tree line.

He didn't know how far he'd gone when he realized that the only sound in the woods was his own breathing. He slowed, then stopped. Fat snowflakes fell from sky, lazily twirling in and around the bare branches. Leaning on a tree trunk, he looked back the way he'd come. His shoeprints were filling with snow, and soon they'd be gone. It'd be like he vanished.

No, that wasn't true.

His old computer was still in the administrative building. On it was his entire financial life. If anyone ever saw his bookkeeping, he'd be a wanted man. It wouldn't just be the authorities who would hunt him down.

Hidden in the forest, he trudged through the trees, always keeping the compound to his left. The hammer strikes that usually filled the day were silent. Good, he was glad that all the members of his church were waiting in the cafeteria. Honestly, he didn't care what they thought. He didn't need them anymore.

It took only a few minutes to circle around to the administrative building. There was no guard outside. The door was unlocked. He still had the key to his office, and he opened that door, too. He didn't bother to download the files or destroy the hard drive. Markus picked up the tower and left the same way he'd come.

As he trudged back to the woods, a pang of grief stabbed him in the chest. Jessie's loss would haunt him for the rest of his life, he knew. But he had a new reason for living—to avenge the death of his beloved and make every one of her children pay dearly.

Sarah sat on the floor and held her mother's cold hand. Liam had found a sheet somewhere in the house and draped it over Jessie's body.

He knelt at her side and held out a steaming mug. "Green tea with honey," he said. "Sorry, I couldn't find a lemon."

How could she even think about something as simple as tea? Her mother was gone—dead because of Sarah—and her world was shattered. "I'm not thirsty."

"Drink," he said. "It'll help you feel better."

Right now, her emotions were a blank canvas and she felt nothing. Her whole life, she'd been Jessie Colton's daughter. Sure, her mom could be exasperating. But without her mother, Sarah didn't know who she was.

"Drink," he insisted.

She reached for the mug because she didn't have the energy to argue. She took a sip. The tea warmed her from the inside out. Yet, now she could feel the grief. It was a black shadow that closed in on her from all sides. The dark so complete that she might never see the light again. "My dad is dead. My mom is dead." Her voice cracked on the last word. "At twenty-six, I'm an orphan. Too young to lose both my parents. Too old to have anyone care for me. It means that I'm all alone."

"You aren't alone," Liam began.

She wasn't in the mood to be pacified. "Don't," she said. "Just don't." And then, "What's going to happen now with Markus?"

"He ran into the woods. Because of the snow, I lost his trail. A warrant will be issued for his arrest. Once everyone gets organized, a search party will start to look for him."

"Will they find him?" she asked, taking another sip of tea. "Will that bastard ever be made to pay?"

"They'll find him," said Liam.

"Soon?"

"I can't really say for sure. But a lot of resources will go into bringing Markus Acker to justice."

It wasn't exactly what she wanted to hear, but she knew it was the truth.

"She really loved me," she said, as the first tears started to fall. She drew in a shaking breath, trying to control her crying. It was no use.

"She really did love you," Liam agreed. He took the mug from her hand and set it on the floor. Then, he reached for her shoulders and pulled her into his chest. He was solid and warm and comforting. The black shadow of grief swallowed her whole. Leaning into the embrace, she let the tears come. In the distance was the lonesome wail of a siren. The ambulance, meant to save her mother, was on the way. Yet, it was too late for them all.

There was no reason for Liam to maintain his cover any longer. Official vehicles—ambulances and police cruisers—lined the rutted lane that ran through the Ever After Church compound. Lights atop cars strobed, turning the constantly falling snow red and blue. Standing in front of the house, he briefed a contingent of local law enforcement.

Fletcher Colton was a detective for the Owl Creek PD and one of Sarah's half siblings. At first glance, it was obvious that Fletcher and Sarah were related. They had the same brown hair and green eyes. There was also Archer Mackenzie, a forensic analyst, and Ajay Wright, part of the search and rescue team with the Idaho State Police. Pumpkin, a yellow Lab, sat next to Ajay's feet. She regarded Liam with her head cocked, as if she, too, were listening to what he had to say. Both Archer and Ajay were romantically involved with two members of the Colton crew—Hannah and Lizzy.

He'd begun by telling them about the undercover operation, meant to retrieve the data from Markus's computer. He ended with the events of the past few hours. "After the car wreck, Markus took us all to the house to be questioned. He knew something was off because I screwed up. I used a knife to pick the lock to his personal office but didn't put the blade back. Once he saw it, he ordered his goons to rough me up."

"Looks like you got more than a little roughed up," said Ajay. Ajay kept his brown hair short. He wore a heavy coat. The words *Idaho State Police Search and Rescue K-9 Officer* were emblazoned across the back.

Liam hadn't taken the time to look in a mirror. But he could tell that he'd been beaten badly. Pain seared through his chest with each breath. His lips were swollen, and one tooth was loose. He shrugged. Pain stabbed him in the side. "I'll survive."

"And then what happened?" Archer coaxed. Where Ajay was clean cut, Archer was scruffy. His dark brown hair fell past the collar of his coat. His cheeks and chin were covered in stubble, like he hadn't bothered to shave in days.

"Markus turned the gun on Sarah, but Jessie pushed her out of the way. She caught the bullet instead." Liam pointed to his own breastbone. "She bled out in minutes. I chased Markus but he got into the trees before I caught him. I'm not prepared for this weather." He held out a hand. Several snowflakes landed on his palm, melting instantly. "I figured that it'd be better to let the professionals find him."

Fletcher sighed. "We all know my mom didn't approve of how Jessie took off, leaving her kids behind. Then, there was the whole episode of Jessie trying to get a portion of my dad's life insurance. Still, it's a tragic way to die." He paused. "Where's Sarah?"

Liam pointed to one of the ambulances. "She's getting checked out by the EMTs."

"We need to search this entire area. Aside from the financial crimes, there are some murders linked to this church. Who knows what evidence we're going to find," said Fletcher. "Before we get started, I'd like to speak to Sarah."

"I think she'd like that," he said, walking toward the vehicle.

Ajay, Archer and Pumpkin hung back.

The ambulance's rear doors were closed. Using the side of his fist, Liam banged on an inset window. The impact sent a bolt of pain rocketing from his hand to his teeth.

A female EMT opened the back door. A lanyard with an ID card hung around her neck. Her name was Zoey. "Can I help you?"

"Yeah," said Liam. "Detective Colton would like to talk to his sister. Is Sarah up for visitors?"

From inside the ambulance, Sarah called out, "I'm up for a visit."

Zoey jumped to the ground. "You fellas have a few minutes before we head back to town." She pointed at Liam. "And you should come with us."

"I'm fine." He wasn't going to let a few scratches and bruises take him away from the investigation.

"Everyone is always fine until they aren't," said Zoey. "But my recommendation is that you get checked out, too."

Eventually, he'd see a doctor. Right now, he wanted to see Sarah. Holding on to the handles on either side of the doors, he hefted himself into the back of the ambulance. Sarah lay on a stretcher. Her bloody clothes had been traded for an Owl Creek EMT sweatshirt and pair of dark gray sweatpants. A bag of fluids hung on a hook. Clear tubing led from the bag to a needle that was taped to the back of her hand.

"They put you on meds?" Panic raced like a raging river through his bones. "Is anything seriously wrong?"

"This?" She touched the gauze pad that covered the needle. "It's just a saline drip. The EMT wants to make sure I stay hydrated."

A jump seat was pulled down next to the stretcher. He dropped into the seat, suddenly weary. "That's good news."

Fletcher pulled himself into the back of the ambulance, as well. "Hey, Sarah," he said.

She smiled weakly. "What're you doing here?"

"Well, I'm a detective in Owl Creek," he said before adding, "I'm sorry about Jessie."

"Thanks," said Sarah. "I still can't believe she's gone. I keep hoping this is the worst dream of my life and I'll wake up at home." She paused. "What happens now?"

She'd asked Liam the same question. He didn't blame her for being concerned and wanting answers.

"Right now, there are several teams getting ready to get to work. One team will search the compound. The other team will start searching the woods for signs of Markus. There are also officers on hand to question members of the church."

Liam was looking for evidence of financial crimes. "I'll process the admin building. I'm looking for records associated with fraud. Whatever I find will have to go back to the Hoover Building with me."

"I'm going to help you," said Sarah, swinging her legs to the side of the bed. "I can't sit here, alone. Besides, I'm a librarian. It makes me an expert at organizing lots of information."

"If you're up to it," said Fletcher, "you can join the team. You and Liam can take the admin building. I'm going to bring everyone together for a final briefing. Then, we can get started. See you in a minute." Fletcher climbed out the ambulance, leaving them alone.

"Do you mind if we chat for a minute?" he began. But he didn't look like he knew exactly know where to begin. "I'm sorry about your mom."

"Like Fletcher said, it's tragic."

"No, it's more than that. I was the one who got you involved in this case. If it weren't for me…"

"We aren't going to play what-if," she said, interrupting. "Neither of us will win that game. I'm devastated that my mom is gone. But the only person I blame for what happened is Markus."

Liam reached for her hand. Having his palm next to hers felt like coming home. "Markus won't get away. I promise," he said. But there were other things that he wouldn't say. He was the one who let Markus Acker escape, which meant that it was Liam's job to find him.

Chapter 19

Zoey, the EMT, returned to the ambulance. "Ready to take a trip back to Owl Creek?" she asked Sarah. "There's only a medical clinic in town. If any of your injuries are serious, you'll get sent to Conners." Conners was a town located more than thirty miles away. "But I think you'll be released as soon as the nurse practitioner gives you an exam."

"Change of plans," said Sarah. "I'm staying. Can you get the IV out of my hand?"

"I'd advise against it," Zoey warned.

Sarah appreciated the advice, but her mind was made up. "I'm staying."

The EMT removed the needle and placed a bandage over the puncture mark.

"Are you sure that you're up to this?" Liam asked.

The bruise at the back of her head throbbed. Her eyes were gritty from crying. What's worse, she felt like a rag that had been wrung out and then thrown in a corner to rot. But she couldn't rest while Markus Acker was at large. "I'm fine," she said. "Lead the way."

Liam didn't bother with the short ladder attached to the back of the ambulance. He dropped down and landed with a curse. "Damn it."

Sarah backed out, climbing the rungs to the ground. "Are *you* sure that *you're* up to this?" she asked, copying his question.

"I'm fine."

To her, he didn't look fine. Both of his eyes were blackened. There was a bruise on his cheek. A cut to his chin. And his lips were swollen. But she knew that he wasn't about to leave without completing his job. So, Sarah didn't argue.

Liam said, "Looks like the briefing is over there." A group of people were gathered on the driveway in front of Jessie's house.

"The Statie is with Lizzy, right? The other guy dates your sister Hannah." He paused as they both walked slowly toward the group. "Ajay. Archer," said Liam.

"Hi, Sarah," Ajay said.

"Hey," said Archer. "I'm sorry about your mom."

Ajay added, "We'll find the bastard who shot her. Don't worry."

"Thanks," she said. A yellow Lab nudged her hand. She scratched the dog's scruff. "Both of you. Or should I say, all three of you."

"This is Pumpkin," said Ajay. "She works with Search and Rescue."

Before she could add anything else, Fletcher whistled. "I need you all to gather around."

A group formed around her brother. Some of the people wore Owl Creek PD uniforms. Others were clad in street clothes. Sarah and Liam approached. The wall of bodies separated, making room for them in the circle.

"Now that we're all here," said Fletcher, "let me introduce everyone. Archer Mackenzie will process the house, collecting evidence associated with the shooting. Ajay will take a team from Search and Rescue into the woods to look for Markus. Hopefully, he hasn't gotten too far, and we can wrap this up tonight. Liam Hill is with the FBI. He's going to go through the records in the admin building. Sarah's going to help organize everything for transport back to Washington, D.C. The uniformed officers, Muriel and Kate, will lead a team from the PD to talk to all the church members. Hopefully, someone knows where Markus might go or who might help him." He paused. "Any questions? Comments?"

There were none and the group dispersed.

Sarah paused, looking at the house. Her mother had been so proud to own a nice home. But it had come at the ultimate price. Turning her back, she walked through the snow. The drifts were over her ankles and there was no sign that the storm was done.

Her car, a twisted hunk of metal now, lay on its roof. The SUV that blocked their escape was in the middle of the road.

"Hold up a minute," Liam said.

She stopped.

He crawled through one of the broken windows of her car. The vehicle teetered. Without question, today had been the worst day of her life. It would only be fitting for some other horrible thing to happen—like Liam getting crushed by the wrecked station wagon. She couldn't take a second loss today. "Be careful," she said, bending at the waist to be heard through the open window. It didn't seem like enough. "What's so important that you can't wait for the car to be taken to impound?"

Liam backed out the same way he entered the car. Rising to his feet, he dusted snow from his knees. "I needed this." He held up a slim piece of black plastic.

"The flash drive." Her mother had lost her life for that information. "I hope it's worth it."

"Me, too." He shoved the device into his pocket.

They walked in silence to the admin trailer. Liam held the door open and Sarah crossed the threshold. Her eyes were drawn to one of the desks and the landline phone. "Do you think that phone works?"

"Roger called 9-1-1 from here, so yeah. It works."

Roger. She hadn't had time to think about the burly guard— or any of the other security personnel Markus employed. They had all seemed to disappear along with their boss.

"If you need to make some calls, I can give you a minute," Liam offered.

"You can stay…"

He waved away her offer. "I'll just be outside." He opened the door and stepped onto the landing. "If you need me, just yell."

"Thanks." She dropped into a seat. As the door closed, she lifted the receiver from the cradle. Holding the phone to her ear, she entered a set of numbers that had been memorized long ago.

Her brother answered after the third ring. "This is Nate."

Sarah's chest constricted. She tried to find the right words. But how was she supposed to tell him that their mother was gone?

"Hello?" he said again, annoyance evident in his tone. "Is someone there?"

"Hey, Nate," she croaked. Tears gathered in her lashes. She wiped them away with the back of her hand.

"Sarah, is that you?"

She cleared her throat. "Yeah, it's me. Listen, I've got bad news. We need to talk."

"Hold on a minute. Let me close my office door." On the other end of the line, she heard the soft click of a latch engaging. "What's up?"

"It's Mom," she began.

Nate groaned. "What'd she do this time?"

"You don't understand," said Sarah. "She was shot."

"Shot?" he echoed. "By whom? Although I bet that I can guess. It was that piece of crap. Markus." He cursed. "Hopefully, now she'll kick him to the curb with the rest of the garbage."

"Nate," she said. "She can't do that."

The line went silent. Had the connection been lost?

After a moment, he asked, "How is she?"

The question stretched out, filling the miles between the two siblings. But more than that, it filled the years. Memories—both good and bad—washed over Sarah in a tidal wave. And then came the knowledge that death was another word for *never again*. Never again would Sarah receive a text from her mother, excited with a new purchase. Never again would she eat her mother's apple cinnamon pancakes. Never again would she tell her mother about her day. Never again would she hear her mother say, *I love you*.

Nate's question had gone too long unanswered. "She's not good. In fact, she didn't make it."

"What happened?"

She spent a few minutes giving him the barest details about the past week. Sometime soon, she'd tell him everything. Finishing her story, she said, "She lost her life saving mine."

"First of all, I don't want you to feel any guilt," said Nate. "None of this is your fault. The bastard who shot Mom is the one to blame."

"If it weren't for me, she would still be here."

"You can't carry that baggage. You were a good daughter. I cut Mom out of my life years ago. You always tried to maintain a relationship." His voice was hoarse, thick with emotion. "I guess I always figured there'd be time for us to reconcile. But now, it's too late." He paused. "What do you want to do for a funeral?"

"Honestly, I haven't had time to think about anything."

"I'm going to take a few days off. I'll come to Owl Creek. Not sure if I'll leave later today or first thing tomorrow. A lot will depend on Vivian's schedule." Vivian Maylor was Nate's new girlfriend. Always classy and kind, she was the one person who made Nate happy.

"It'd be great to see you both. I'm staying at the Inn on the Lake," she said.

"Once I have plans, I'll check in with you," he said before ending the call.

Nate was lucky to have found Vivian. At least he wouldn't be alone while dealing with the loss of another parent. Her mind wandered to Liam. Like a switch being flipped, their charade was over. Too bad her feelings for him couldn't be turned off in the same way.

There was a light rapping on the door before it opened. Liam stepped inside. "It sounded like your call ended, so I figured I'd check on you."

She tried to smile. Her cheeks were tight. "I reached out to Nate. He needed to know what happened." She paused. "He asked about a funeral. I don't know where to begin."

"I hate to tell you this, but it might be several days before the authorities release your mom. They need time to collect evidence from the body."

Was she supposed to stay in Owl Creek until her mom could

be buried? Sarah had a job. A cat. Not to mention that a room at the Inn on the Lake was more than she could afford. There was too much to think about and she was suddenly exhausted.

"Hey." Liam patted her shoulder. "You've been through a lot. I can get you a ride back to the hotel so you can rest."

The word *ride* brought up a whole new set of problems. "My car's totaled. That's another thing to worry about."

"I'm sure the FBI will work something out with you." He paused. "But what about now? Do you want to go back to town?"

Sarah didn't want to sit in a hotel room, alone, without any company. "I'll stay," she said, thankful for at least one decision made. She stood. "Having something to do will help—especially if it puts Markus in jail." Drawing in a deep breath, she asked, "Where do we start?"

After several hours of searching the admin building, Liam had to admit that the paperwork kept by the Ever After Church was surprisingly organized. A forensic audit would have to wait, but everything he found looked legit. Soon, he'd box up the documents and have them shipped to the Hoover Building. There, a team of financial analysts would comb through every sheet of paper.

Then again, he knew that there wasn't anything incriminating to find in the filing cabinets. That's why he'd come to Owl Creek, to see what Markus kept on his personal computer. And sure, someone had taken the actual processor. But it didn't matter. Liam had the memory stick with a copy of the hard drive. Or so he hoped.

Taking the flash drive out of his pocket, he held it in the palm of his hand.

Sarah stood next to him. She'd been right when she claimed to be good at organizing documents. If it wasn't for her help, Liam wouldn't have made as much progress.

He held up the memory stick. "I hope I got enough evidence."

His ribs and side ached with each breath. The pain made it hard to concentrate. In fact, all he wanted to do was rest. Yet too much had been sacrificed for him to leave before the job was done.

"We should find out." Sarah sat behind one of the two work-stations in the reception area. An open laptop was on the desk. The password was written on a sticky note, taped to the base panel. She entered the keystrokes and held out her hand.

Liam hesitated for a moment, before handing her the flash drive.

She inserted the drive into the port on the side of the computer. A menu appeared and she opened a document. Liam stood behind Sarah and watched over her shoulder as she opened a spreadsheet.

Suddenly awake, he scanned the lines and columns. As it turns out, Markus was an exacting bookkeeper all the time. "I'll be damned."

"What'd we find?" Sarah's cheeks turned rosy.

Liam leaned forward, pointing at the screen. His arm brushed her shoulder. He remembered the moments after they made love. He held her in his arms, placing a kiss on the same spot he now touched. But he couldn't get sucked into the memories. Now, more than ever, he needed to focus. "See that? It looks like Markus has been receiving large amounts of money from an account in Colombia. Then, they get listed as a donation to the church. He doesn't spend any of the money, just sends the funds to an account in Delaware."

"That's illegal?"

"It depends on who sent the money in the first place. Colombia makes me wonder if he wasn't working with one of the drug cartels." Had Liam just gotten the evidence that Dubois needed? He continued, "Delaware is a banking-friendly state. But like with everything, criminals can take advantage. Now, we have account numbers. Once I get a subpoena, we can unravel this accounting mess."

"Is this what you needed?" she asked. "Will it be worth all the sacrifices in the end?"

"Nothing will ever be worth the loss of your mom. But what we have here will help to put Markus in jail for a long time to come."

"Good," she said. "That'll be a start."

She was so near that her breath washed over him and mingled with his own. The look in her eyes was so sad. Liam was the one who'd caused all her heartache. He wanted to ease the sorrow. He also wanted to feel her lips on his, despite the fact that his mouth still throbbed.

Even though the relationship had been phony, he knew that his feelings for Sarah went beyond friendship or even their shared history. But their weeklong affair was about to end.

In an instant, he saw their future. And he knew it was bleak.

With the evidence needed to build a case against Markus Acker in hand, Liam would be called back to DC. He'd be given the promotion, but then all his time would be spent at work. Sure, he could suggest a long-distance relationship. Sarah could come to Washington for a visit. But with her, it wouldn't be enough. They'd get frustrated with the separation until finally one of them called it quits.

Better to avoid the heartache before it started.

"Thanks for all your help." The need to touch her again was like a hunger. "There's nothing else for us to do here." He checked his phone. He didn't have any coverage, but the cell still gave him the time. It was 3:26 p.m. "Let's get back to Owl Creek. I need to call my office and we should get something to eat."

"I'm not hungry." Sarah closed the computer and removed the flash drive. She held it out to him. His fingers grazed hers. He ignored the electric current that ran up his arm and shoved the memory stick into his pants pocket. "But I agree we should get out of here."

Sarah stood and walked across the room. She opened the door. Thick gray clouds hung low in the sky. Fat white flakes drifted slowly to the ground. Snow covered the bottom two stairs of the steps.

His coat sat on the sofa. He picked it up and held it out to Sarah. "You want this?"

"I can't," she began.

"I'm not going to let you go out with just a sweatshirt," he said.

"Let me?" she echoed.

"Okay, that came out wrong. You've been through a lot and the last thing you need is to get sick or something."

She reached for the jacket. Standing on the stoop, she shrugged into the coat. She pushed the sleeves up to her wrists, but the coat hung down to her knees. "Not very stylish," she joked. "But at least it's warm."

He was glad that she still had a sense of humor. It'd help her get through the next few months. Finding Markus, assuming that the pastor was found, would only be the beginning. After he was taken into custody, there'd be a trial. Appeals would follow. Through it all, there would be media attention.

He'd do what he could to shield Sarah, but he could never give her back her quiet life.

Fletcher Colton strode through the snow toward the admin building. "I was just coming to check on you. What'd you find?"

"We've got everything we need," he said, patting his pants pocket. The flash drive was still there. "Once Markus has been captured, there's enough damning evidence to put him away for years. Any chance we can get a ride back to Owl Creek?"

"I'll get you a ride with one of the uniformed officers," he said.

A female officer, Juliette, gave them a ride back to the Inn on the Lake. By the time they arrived, it was after 4:00 p.m. Liam hadn't eaten since breakfast. Despite Sarah saying she wasn't hungry, he was ready for a meal.

Housekeeping had visited the room while they were gone. The beds were made, and the towels had been refreshed. Everything was the same and, yet, different. "Want to grab something to eat? Or there's a restaurant downstairs. I can get room service to deliver," he asked.

Sarah took off his coat and laid it on a bed. "I need a shower, and then I'll do whatever you want. Just don't ask me to make a choice. I'm done with decisions for the day."

A menu for the hotel's restaurant was tucked into the drawer of the bedside table. He scanned the pub fare. Burgers. Soups. Chicken wraps. Finger steaks.

He should get his fill of finger steaks now. In a few days, Idaho would be a memory.

Before ordering food, he had to get in touch with his office. Enabling the encryption app on his phone, he placed a call to Constance at the Hoover Building.

"I was wondering when I'd hear from you," she said. "How'd it go?"

"I was able to download the hard drive. There's a lot of information we need to go through. But I'm confident we have what we need for an arrest, indictment and conviction. But it came at a high price."

"How high?" she asked.

"Jessie Colton was shot and killed by Markus. He ran into the woods. The local and state police are looking for him. It's been snowing all day, so I don't know what kind of trail they'll find."

"Hey, don't be so down," she said. "In the eyes of the federal government, your operation was a success."

Funny. With the loss of life, he didn't feel successful. "I'm going to send you all the data taken from the computer."

"I'm sure Dubois will need a debrief, but that can wait until you get home."

Home was something Washington, DC, would never be for Liam. "I'll see you when I get back."

"You know, the promotion will be yours. Honestly, you deserve it," Constance said before ending the call.

How was it that Liam ended up with everything he wanted, and nothing that he wanted at all? He picked up the coat Sarah had left on the bed. He brought the collar to his nose and inhaled deeply. It smelled like her, like flowers and sunshine. He couldn't help but wonder how long the fabric would hold her scent.

Chapter 20

Five days later
Washington, DC
Hoover Building

Liam was in the same conference room where it all started. This time, every seat around the long table was filled. Beyond A-DIC Dubois and her entourage, Nadia Starkey, assistant director, was also in attendance.

Much of the information copied from the computer's hard drive had been analyzed. It looked like Markus Acker was laundering money from some very bad people. He had cleaned money for a drug cartel from South America as well as a group in North Carolina that bombed a day care center. For funneling the money through his church, Markus was given a commission. Over the last five years, he'd made over six million dollars.

He and Constance were giving the briefing. This time, they'd compared notes and even practiced what they were going to say. So far, everything had gone well. Liam clicked a remote he held in his palm. The final image for the briefing filled the screen. In it, Markus and Jessie embraced as they admired their new home. In the foreground, a thin and dirty child cried. It was the same picture he'd shown Sarah—back when he needed her to help him get onto the compound. He and Sarah had spoken on the phone several times since he left. She'd returned to Boise when he left for Washington, DC. The Bureau had provided her with a rental car until her station wagon could be replaced. She'd been planning Jessie's funeral. It would be held in Owl Creek the next day.

Obviously, Liam wouldn't be attending.

Refocusing his attention on the meeting, he said, "The facts prove that Markus Acker was a rich man. A man who claimed to also serve humanity. Why did he steal money from those who couldn't afford it? Markus is still at large, presumably in the woods near Owl Creek, Idaho. If he's found—when he's found—that's the question I will ask. After I arrest him for his other crimes, of course." His joke earned him a few chuckles. "Any questions?"

"I have one," said Assistant Director Starkey. "What's being done to find Acker?"

Constance answered the question. "The Idaho State Police has taken the lead on the search. So far, there hasn't been any hard evidence for his location. There are three theories. First, is that he's found an abandoned cabin and is holed up there. The second is that he's gotten help from one of the criminal groups he's worked with in the past."

"And what's the final theory?" asked Dubois.

"Well," said Liam, "Markus could've died in the woods. Hypothermia. Animal attack. A minor injury in that climate could be deadly. If that happened, we may never find him."

"That's not good enough for me," said Starkey. "I want to set up a task force in Owl Creek. The FBI needs a full-time presence to work with state and local authorities until this Acker character is caught." She turned to Dubois. "Make that happen."

"Yes, ma'am," said the A-DIC as she scribbled a note on a pad of paper.

Starkey turned her attention back to Liam and Constance. "I heard that a supervisor position has opened in your unit and both of you are the top candidates. The career board met and made a decision. Both of you are well-qualified, but Special Agent Hill will be given the job."

"Congratulations, Liam," said Constance with a smile. "You'll be a great supervisor."

Liam's gut twisted into knots. Yet, he smiled and tried to look proud. "Thank you, all, for your confidence. But Constance did an amazing job organizing things here. All I did was get beat up."

"Talk about taking one for the team," Starkey joked. When he'd gotten back to DC, he'd been seen by a doctor. Thankfully, none of his injuries required treatment. "You really did go above and beyond for the investigation and the Bureau. I like that you recognize everyone on your team. The FBI is lucky to have you in management." She rose from her seat and stepped forward. Her palm was outstretched. "Congratulations again," she said, shaking his hand. She also shook hands with Constance. "Don't worry about your career. Good things are coming your way."

"Yes, ma'am," said Constance.

The room emptied.

A-DIC Dubois was the last person to leave. "Good job, both of you," she said on her way out the door.

"So, what's first on the agenda, boss?" Constance asked.

Liam knew what he wanted to do. But the question remained, was he willing to abandon his life plan? Then again, a life is exactly what he wanted. "Hold on a minute," he said to his colleague. "I need to grab Dubois."

He jogged down the corridor, catching up with the A-DIC. "I have a suggestion for who could run the federal task force out of Owl Creek."

Dubois raised her eyebrows. "You do? I'd love a recommendation."

He laid out his plan, much of it coming to him as he spoke. As it turned out, he had a knack for improvising.

When he finished, she asked, "You're sure? You know how this will affect the decisions that have already been made."

"I know," he said. In the end, it would all be worthwhile.

"Alright," she sighed. "I'll make it happen."

He turned, walking slowly back to the conference room. For the first time in years, Liam knew exactly what he wanted.

The following day
Owl Creek, Idaho
Abel's Funeral Parlor

The funeral director, a Black woman named Letitia Abel with her braids coiled into a bun, had deposited Sarah in a sitting room to wait for the funeral to start. The room was filled with a sofa and two wingback chairs, all upholstered in blue velvet. A wooden table stood in the middle of the seating arrangement. The top was polished until it gleamed with the glow of the overhead lights.

As Letitia had explained, the room was meant for the family to wait before the services began. But aside from Nate, she didn't expect any other family to attend. He was already here, along with Vivian. They were both seated in the small chapel, which meant that Sarah was alone. Again.

The thing was, she didn't know who else might show up. It was no secret that her mother had burned many bridges. She hated the idea that nobody would come to the funeral. But she was prepared to deliver her eulogy to only Nate, Vivian and Letitia.

She glanced at the wall clock: 9:58 a.m. It was almost time. Leaning forward, Sarah reached for a cup of water. The papers on her lap scattered to the floor.

"Damn it," she cursed, before pressing her lips tightly together. Was cussing in a funeral home as taboo as swearing in church? She didn't know. Placing the cup back onto the table, she dropped to her knees. She sorted the pages, placing them in order.

"I think those who plan to attend the services have gathered." Letitia stood on the threshold. She was dressed in a pantsuit of silver and white that coordinated perfectly with the room.

"I didn't hear you come in," said Sarah while standing. For her mother's funeral, she'd had borrowed a black sheath dress from Margaret. On her friend, the dress came to the knees. On her, the hem stopped at midcalf. She dusted off the front of her outfit. Was anyone ever prepared to say a final goodbye to a person they loved? Yet, she couldn't put off the inevitable. "I'm ready," she said.

She followed the woman into the chapel, where the funeral was to be held. At the front of the room was Jessie's casket, closed now, with a spray of roses draped across the top. There was also a photograph of her mother on a stand. Next to the casket stood a lectern with a microphone. Pews filled the room. None of the seats were empty.

As expected, Nate and Vivian were in the front row. Next to them were Frannie and Dante. Malcolm was there. Fletcher Colton was also in attendance, along with his girlfriend. She thought her name might be Kiki. Archer Mackenzie was with Lizzy. Ajay and Hannah were there, as well.

In the middle of them all sat Jenny Colton.

Sure, Sarah knew that Jenny and Jessie were identical twins. But looking into the crowd and seeing her mother's double stole her breath. She inhaled and searched for the one face she knew she wouldn't see. It was ridiculous to think that Liam might come. Yet she had secretly hoped that he'd find a way to make the trip.

Rolling back her shoulders, she stepped up to the lectern. Setting her notes on the upper tray, she leaned toward the microphone. "My mother wasn't a perfect person," she said, beginning with the truth. "Then again, none of us are perfect, either. I know that I'm not. My mom was fiercely proud. She loved to laugh and loved to love. She was passionate and never did anything halfway. And when it came down to it, she laid down her own life so that mine would be spared."

The door at the back of the chapel opened. She paused and looked up. Light shone from behind, cloaking the new arrival in shadow. But the shoulders were familiar. She recognized the tilt of the head, the way he moved. Her heart skipped a beat as the door closed softly.

So, Liam had come after all.

The bruise under his eye had faded from violet to gray. Stubble covered his cheeks and chin. His hair was mussed, and he wore a sweater and jeans. She imagined that he'd taken an overnight flight to Boise and driven directly to Owl Creek. And he was still the most handsome man in the world.

She looked down at her written eulogy. The words she worked hard to perfect were no longer sufficient. Holding tightly to the sides of the lectern, she let out a long breath. "I knew my mother better than anyone else. Sure, she could be maddening. But I was with her when she died. Those last few moments as I held my mother's hand will always be the most precious and painful of my life." She paused, swallowed and wished that she'd thought to bring her glass of water. "But at the end, when she knew that she wasn't going to make it, my mom had one thought. And it was of all of you. She asked me to deliver a message to everyone. She knew she had been in the wrong. She was sorry for all the hurt she caused. Because of that pain, she didn't know how to start over. But do not doubt how she felt. Jessie Colton loved you all." She drew in a deep breath. "Thank you for coming today. It would've meant the world to my mom, and it means the world to me."

Soft music began to play. As instructed by the funeral director, Sarah walked down the middle aisle. She was followed by Nate and Vivian. There was a reception area at the back of the chapel, where the siblings could greet their guests.

The first person in line was Jenny Colton. From a distance, the sisters had looked identical. But now that her aunt was closer, she could see differences between the two women. Jenny's profile was softer. Her hair was shorter. There was a light in her eyes that Jessie never had. "Hi, Sarah," she said, opening her arms for a hug. "You gave a lovely eulogy. Your mom would've been proud."

She let her aunt embrace her. It was almost like being hugged by her mother. "Thank you for coming. I know you two were estranged," she began.

"But she was my sister, and I never would've stayed away. I only wish that things had worked out different between the two of us." A dark-haired man stood next to Jenny. She reached for his arm. "This is your uncle Buck."

Buck Colton was taller than her father had been. But the brothers shared the same green eyes—the same ones that Sarah had inherited herself. "If you ever need anything," said Buck, giving her a quick hug, "don't hesitate to call."

"Thank you," she said. "It's nice to finally meet you."

"I know all of this—losing your dad, finding this whole family you never knew about and then losing your mom, too—is overwhelming. But as far as I'm concerned, you're a Colton." He included Nate in his words. "Both of you are family."

"We're both leaving in the morning," said Nate.

"Well, stop by tonight. Heck, I'll invite everyone. We can raise a glass to the memory of Jessie."

She looked at her brother. Nate shrugged. "Obviously, we don't have any other plans."

Sarah said, "We'd love to stop by. What can we bring?"

"Just yourselves," said Buck, patting her shoulder. "I'll be happy to get to know you better."

Jenny gave her another hug. It seemed like Frannie had picked up her affinity for hugs from her mother. "I know I can't replace your mom. But I'm here for anything. Good news. Bad news. I'm only a phone call away."

Sarah's chest ached from the kindness shown by her aunt and uncle. She gripped Jenny's hands. "Thank you both, so much."

The next people in line were Frannie and Dante. Frannie pulled Sarah into a tight hug. "I'm so sorry for what happened. I'd love to chat with you more. Do you have time to grab a cup of coffee—or should I say, tea?"

"Buck wants to have everyone over for dinner tonight," said Nate as he shook hands with Dante.

"Great." Frannie gave her another hug. "I'll talk to you then."

The line of Coltons seemed endless. Malcolm gave her a hug. There was Ruby and her boyfriend, Sebastian. Wade and his girlfriend, Harlow. Chase and Sloane. Greg and Briony. They were all kind with their condolences and warm with their welcomes into the family. Jenny had been right, nothing and nobody could make up for the loss of her mother. But maybe time with her newfound family would help ease the ache from her loss.

Then, the receiving line was down to only one person. Liam.

Nate shook hands with him. "Vivian, his younger sister was Sarah's best friend when we were all kids. He's with the FBI."

"Nice to meet you," said Vivian.

Nate said, "I guess we should go outside and get some air."

Then, it was just Sarah and Liam. Her chest was tight with grief and loss. But in seeing him, there was also happiness and hope.

"You came," she said.

"There's no place else I'd rather be." He reached for her hand, lacing his fingers through hers. She liked the way they knitted together, fitting perfectly.

She hadn't spoken to Liam in two days. True, they'd both been busy. Yet, she hoped it wasn't a sign of things to come when they neglected to call the other. "How was your presentation?" No, the FBI didn't call it a presentation. "Brief," she corrected. "How was your briefing?"

"It was good. The career board met. I was offered the supervisor's position."

She wanted to be happy for him. But once Liam got sucked back into working long hours, they'd never have time to speak to each other. "Congratulations," she said. "I know that's what you wanted."

"I *did* want the job. That is, until I realized what's important. I want a home and a family. I want someone in my life that I love and like and respect. I want more than a spouse. I want someone who can be a true partner. My job's important, but I want more." He paused. "I turned down the promotion."

"Why did you do that?"

"Because I finally know what I want in my life. It's you." He pulled her close and wrapped her in his embrace. Her cheek was pressed to his chest. She felt as well as heard everything he said. "I love you, Sarah."

"I love you, too." Still, she wasn't sure what came next. "Don't tell me you left the FBI. I won't believe that story again."

He laughed quietly. "I'm still with the Bureau. But my job's changed a little. I'm going to oversee a federal task force, coordinating with other law enforcement agencies, to find Markus Acker. I'll be in Owl Creek most of the time. But it's a hell of a lot closer to Boise than Washington, DC."

Sarah wasn't sure of the rules about kissing in a funeral

home. Yet, she rose to her tiptoes and brushed her lips over his. "Welcome home, Liam."

Hand in hand, they walked out of the funeral home and onto Main Street. The sun, a white ball, hung in a sky of robin's egg blue. A breeze blew past Sarah, ruffling her hair. It held the first kiss of spring and the promise of something new.

Chapter 21

The Colton Ranch was located outside Owl Creek and surrounded by acres of farmland. Nate had driven, and Vivian sat in the passenger seat. Sarah and Liam were in the back seat. Cars, trucks and SUVs already lined the long driveway that led to the Colton family home. The focal point of the structure was the red barn, but rooms spread out from the main building and looked to be more functional than for aesthetics.

Sarah leaned forward, poking her head between the two front seats. "I think it's kinda charming," she said. "But Mom would've hated living in a place like this." She bit her lip. How long would it be before she stopped worrying about her mother's opinions?

"Agreed," said Nate. He blew out a long breath. "Let's go."

He turned off the ignition and opened the driver's side door. Vivian followed. Sarah remained, rooted in the back seat. Sure, the Coltons had been nothing but kind. But by now they all knew that Sarah had been working with the FBI from the beginning.

Liam reached for her fingertips. "It'll be okay," he said. "I'm with you."

She squeezed his hand. His touch was all the assurance she needed.

She opened her door and stepped out of the car. Liam followed. Nate and Vivian stood only a few feet away. As a group, they all walked toward the front door. The sun was dropping below the hills, but there was a lingering warmth in the air. "Looks like spring finally decided to make an appearance," she said, not really speaking to anyone but not able to stay silent, either. "How are the cherry blossoms? They must be at their peak now."

"They started to bloom, then we got a horrible storm. The wind and rain stripped the trees bare." Liam huffed out a breath.

Nate stepped up to the front door and knocked.

The door was opened by Hannah's daughter, Lucy. If she remembered correctly, the little girl who stood before them was five years old.

"Hello." Lucy's diction was clear. "Aunt Sarah. Uncle Nate. I haven't seen you since the wedding."

Well, she might look like a five-year-old with her pigtails, but she sounded more like she was fifty. Sarah crouched in front of the child. "I'm happy to see you again."

"It's nice to see you, too. Come in," Lucy opened the door wider. Sarah and the rest stepped into the large room. It was filled with lights, voices, laughter—and people. Every one of them was related to Sarah. Could they also become her family? Lucy continued, "How have you been?"

Nate nudged Sarah in the ribs. "Look, another brilliant Colton. I bet Lucy likes books, too."

"I love books. I'll go and get some of my favorites. They're in the back bedroom." Lucy ran toward what must've been the back bedroom, her pigtails bouncing with each step.

From across the room, Frannie waved. She was wearing another T-shirt with a quote. *I'm with the banned.* Images of famously banned books were also on the shirt. *A Wrinkle in Time. Of Mice and Men. To Kill a Mockingbird.* Among others. The fabric was tighter across her stomach, making it obvious that Frannie was pregnant.

Arms opened for a hug, Frannie pulled her into an embrace. "I've been looking for you. There's something I want to talk about with you in private."

Sarah's heart sank. So, it was going to happen now. Frannie

was going to yell at her for being a bad daughter. At least she was classy enough to want some discretion. Fletcher was talking to Nate and Liam. Lucy had returned with her books and was showing them to Vivian. But there were still too many people around to chat in private. "Let's step outside."

Back on the stoop with the door closed, Frannie asked, "How are you feeling?"

"Sad," said Sarah. "Guilty."

Her sister shook her head. "I can't imagine what you've been through. But for what it's worth, don't feel guilty. You were a good daughter. If Jessie hadn't gotten involved with Markus, then none of this would've happened. I won't speak ill of the dead, but don't give up because of your mom's choices."

"That should become my mantra," she joked. "Don't give up."

"Never give up. And you have all of us here to support you."

Sarah inhaled. She could breathe a little easier. "Thanks for the pep talk. It helped. We should get back inside."

"Can I get another minute?" Frannie didn't wait for an answer, and said, "I know you've dealt with a lot recently, but I have a favor to ask."

This wasn't how Sarah expected the conversation to go. "Sure," she said. "If I can help at all, I will."

"You know how I told you that we had an ultrasound appointment coming up? Well, there are some complications. Nothing too serious now, but the doctor wants to keep it that way and suggests bed rest."

Sarah reached for Frannie's arm, suddenly protective of her sister and the child she hadn't met. "Should you be standing here? Let's get you back inside."

"I'll put my feet up in a minute. But I wanted to talk to you first." She paused. "Would you consider running Book Mark It? I know you have a job, but I wouldn't trust my store to anybody else."

For a moment, Sarah said nothing. And then, "You aren't mad at me for lying to you? After all, Liam and I were faking our relationship."

Frannie shook her head. "Neither of you were faking anything. And besides, you ended up together. So, the only person you lied to was yourself."

"I never thought about it that way."

"Well, think about my offer. Besides, it'd be nice to have you here, with family."

"Let's get you back inside," said Sarah, opening the door. "And I promise to let you know my decision soon."

Inside, Liam approached. "There you are," he said. "I was wondering where you'd gone."

"Think about it," said Frannie before wandering to the sofa.

"What's all that about?" he asked.

She said, "Frannie wants me to run Book Mark It. She's having issues with her pregnancy and needs some time off."

"What are your thoughts?"

Honestly, Sarah hadn't had time to consider the offer. There was a lot she'd be leaving behind in Boise. Her friends. Her job.

But something about moving to Owl Creek felt right. She said, "If I came here, I'd get to know all my siblings better."

She scanned the room. Was this her place? Honestly, she would love to share her favorite children's books with Lucy. Talk about popular fiction with Dante. Visit Frannie for tea and a chat. Go to Tap Out Brewery with Malcolm for wing night and a hockey game. Plus, Liam was going to be in town.

Well, when she thought about it that way, there wasn't really a decision to make.

"If I moved here," she asked, "what would you think?"

Liam answered her by placing his lips on hers.

Were all of Sarah's dreams finally coming true? Then again, her mother wasn't around to share in her joy.

"There you are." She recognized the voice but knew it wasn't Jessie who'd spoken. She broke away from the embrace to see Jenny approaching. She pulled Sarah into a hug. "I'm so happy to see you."

"I hope you like the looks of me," said Sarah. "You'll be seeing me a whole lot more."

"Oh?"

"I've decided to help Frannie out by running Book Mark It."

"Oh good." Jenny hugged her again. "Frannie needs help, and we all want you here."

Buck approached with a bottle of beer in his hand. "Good to see you both," he said, shaking hands with Liam.

"Did you hear the news?" Jenny asked. "Sarah just decided to move to Owl Creek."

"Well, how could I know if she just decided?" Buck reasoned. Jenny swatted his arm playfully.

"But it's the best news I've heard in a long while. We'll be happy to have you around more." Buck kissed Sarah's cheek. "And I heard that you were coming to town, Liam. I suppose you are going to be needing a place. We've got lots of nice places listed with Colton Properties."

"We haven't really talked about where we'd live," said Sarah. Moving in together after only a few weeks seemed sudden. Then again, if she'd learned anything this month, it was to take risks. "We can stop by in the morning and see what's available."

"You want to talk to Chase." Buck pointed to another brother with brown hair and green eyes. And then, he pointed to a long table that ran through the center of the adjacent kitchen. It was covered with platters and bowls that were filled with food. There were several kinds of salads, steaks, grilled chicken, steaming baked potatoes and green beans. "Go grab a plate. The steaks are from our own cattle and the rest of the produce is from our own farms. I can't have you leave here hungry."

Jenny squeezed her shoulder once more, before walking away with Buck.

"They're nice people," said Liam. And then, "What do you think? Should we move in together?"

Sarah was definitely thinking *yes*. But she still needed some time. She slipped her hand into his. She loved the way they fit together. Would they always be perfect for each other? "Let's see what's available tomorrow, and then we can decide."

Hand in hand, they walked toward the buffet. Sarah felt like she was walking into a dream. But really, it was the life she'd always wanted.

Ten days later
Owl Creek, Idaho

The gray light of a new day filtered around the drawn curtains. Liam eased onto the corner of the bed, careful not to make too much noise. He worked his foot into a sock as Tolstoy slinked across the comforter. The cat butted his head against his forearm. One sock on, he scratched the cat under the chin.

From the other side of the bed, Sarah rubbed her eyes. "What time is it?"

"It's too early for you to be awake," he said, leaning over to kiss her cheek. It was 5:32 a.m. A call had come into the task force hotline. A man who owned a cabin ten miles outside town had stopped by his property before dawn. One of the windows had been broken and the glass was covered with a piece of wood. The man was worried that Acker had been—or was—on the premises. That's when the cottage owner called. Liam was on the way to check out the lead. "Go back to sleep."

"I'll get up and make you breakfast," she said, her voice hoarse.

"I don't have time to eat anything right now," he said. "Besides, you have a big day."

Tolstoy sauntered over to where Sarah lay and curled up behind the bend in her knees. By the time Liam put on his other sock, they were asleep once again. For now, he and Sarah had rented a house three blocks off Main Street. The two-bedroom house was owned by Colton Properties, and while it was small, it was perfect for them.

In his sock feet, he walked quickly and quietly down the hall, through the living room and to the front door. A pair of work boots sat on a mat next to a table in the entryway. Liam picked up a set of keys and his cell phone from the table and shoved them into his pocket. Next, he worked his feet into his boots. He opened the closet door and removed a blue windbreaker. FBI was stenciled in large yellow letters on the back and smaller white ones on the left front. Also in the closet was a gun safe. Liam pressed his thumb onto a sensor and the latch opened with a *click*. He removed his Sig Sauer and the magazine. After loading his firearm, he placed it into a holster at his hip.

Opening the door, he stepped into a new day.

His official Bureau car was parked in the driveway. He unlocked the door and slipped behind the wheel. As he started the engine, his phone rang, connecting to the in-car audio. Caller ID flashed on the dashboard.

Fletcher Colton.

Using controls on the steering wheel, Liam answered. "I'm shocked to hear from you so early," he said, not surprised at all. If Liam had gotten a call for the task force, then so had Fletcher. "You on your way to the cabin?"

"I am," he said with a yawn. "What're the odds that this is another goose chase?"

He understood Fletcher's skepticism. Over the past week, the task force had received more than thirty calls. Residents had heard something or seen something or had a feeling that Markus was close. It wasn't up to the task force to decide if the lead was credible or not—they investigated them all.

In fact, the night before, they'd been called by a hysterical woman who heard someone trying to break into her garage. As it turned out, nobody was trying to get in. But a raccoon had gotten stuck and was trying to get out.

"I'll tell you this. Even if a raccoon broke that window, he didn't repair it with a piece of wood."

"I guess you're right," Fletcher grunted. And then, "Is it weird that last night I dreamt that I had rabies?"

"I'll see you up there," said Liam before ending the call.

It seemed like the search for Markus was driving everyone a little bit bonkers. Although he didn't blame Fletcher for his odd dream. The raccoon in the garage had been mad. And who knew that the chubby trash pandas had such sharp-looking teeth.

Soon, he pulled onto a lawn that surrounded the cabin. Driving a police cruiser, Fletcher parked next to him a moment later.

Liam exited the car. The sky was a clear, soft blue. The ground was frozen, the brittle grass crunching under his feet.

Fletcher exited his car, as well. He held a printout from the task force's call center. "Looks like this property belongs to Gus and Amanda Ferguson. It was Gus who came up early this morning to turn on the water and to start getting the house ready for summer. He noticed the broken window that had been covered with a board. With all the media coverage about Markus, he got spooked. That's when he left and called us."

There were two windows on the front of the house. Curtains were drawn, but both were intact. "Let's check it out," said Liam. They walked around the side of the house. One window was covered with a piece of plywood. "Bingo," said Liam.

"What're the chances that Gus broke the window last winter and patched it up, but forgot?" Fletcher asked.

"That seems unlikely. But you never know." They walked the perimeter, checking to see if anything else looked suspicious. Nothing was amiss. Standing next to the front door, Liam asked, "Did Gus give us permission to search his property?"

Fletcher held up the printout. He pointed to the page. "He did. Says so, right here."

That's all he needed to enter the building. Still, Liam knocked on the door. "This is the FBI. We're coming in. Put your hands up." It was standard procedure to knock before entering. He turned the handle. To his shock, the door was unlocked.

Wide-eyed, he looked at Fletcher. The detective reached for a gun he carried on his hip. Liam removed his firearm, as well. He nudged the door open with his toe. From the entryway, he could see the whole cabin.

There was a living room/kitchen combo. To the left was a fireplace. Along the back wall, two bedrooms straddled a bathroom. At one time the furniture had been covered in cloth. But now, the sheets were piled in a corner. Empty cans and boxes of food sat on the kitchen table. The remnants of a fire filled the grate.

"Someone's been here," said Liam. "And I don't think it's a raccoon."

"We need to get someone here to collect evidence. And then, get the K-9 units out and looking for a trail." Fletcher reholstered his gun and then pulled a phone from his pocket. He placed a call. "Hey, Archer. Sorry to bother you so early but we found something…"

Sarah stood at the counter of Book Mark It. It was her first day on the job and she hadn't been sure what to expect. The store had only been open for thirty minutes and already half a dozen customers had come through. Of course, one of them had been Aunt Jenny, who stopped in to say hello.

As the last customer paid for their purchase, the door opened. Liam entered the store. She couldn't help it, just looking at him made her heart race.

"Hey," she said. "You were up and out early."

"I was. But first, how's your day so far?"

"Well, I was able to walk to work, which was nice. Aunt Jenny stopped by already and Frannie will come in after lunch." She opened the front of her loose cardigan to show Liam her T-shirt underneath.

"Read banned books," he said. "Nice."

"Dante's going to take a picture." She pointed to a spot on the wall behind the cash register. "Then, we'll put the photo right there."

"Sounds like you're having a good day."

She was. "You know what would make it better?" She came around from behind the cash register. Reaching for Liam, she answered her own question. "If you kissed me."

He placed his lips on hers. Sarah was exactly where she needed to be.

"So," she began, "what happened with your early-morning call?"

"It was him," said Liam. "Or at least, I think it was Markus. Archer collected fingerprints. We'll run those later today. If it's a match with him, we'll know. Ajay and Malcolm have taken out a team of K-9s. If there's a trail to follow, they'll find it."

Sarah started to shiver, even though she wasn't cold. If Markus was still in the area, then none of them were safe. Especially her. "What happens now?"

"I will continue to love and protect you," said Liam. "Not just until Markus is arrested, but always."

Sarah sank into his embrace. It wasn't like all the books that she'd read over the years. This wasn't The End.

It was the beginning of a whole new life with the man she loved.

* * * * *

Don't miss the stories in this mini series!

THE COLTONS
OF OWL CREEK

Colton Undercover
JENNIFER D. BOKAL
October 2024

Colton's K-9 Rescue
COLLEEN THOMPSON
November 2024

MILLS & BOON

Second-Chance Bodyguard
Patricia Sargeant

MILLS & BOON

Dear Reader,

I'm so glad you've joined me for our final Touré Security Group story. This is Zeke and Celeste's romance.

When you first met Celeste Jarrett in *Her Private Security Detail*, did you suspect Zeke *wanted* Celeste to work with him and his brothers on the case more than he actually *needed* her help? So did I. Pretty smooth, Zeke. But we have to admit Celeste brought her own specific set of skills to the investigation that helped the Touré brothers solve the case faster than they would have on their own. She's so much more than just a sparkling personality.

But Zeke and Celeste still have a lot to learn and a lot to teach each other. The next lessons for each of them involve three little words. Zeke must learn to say "I need help." And Celeste desperately needs to hear "I love you."

I hope you enjoy Zeke and Celeste's story at least as much as I loved writing it.

Warm regards,

Patricia Sargeant

Nationally bestselling author **Patricia Sargeant** was drawn to write romance because she believes love is the greatest motivation. Her romantic suspense novels put ordinary people in extraordinary situations to have them find the "hero inside." Her work has been reviewed in national publications such as *Publishers Weekly*, *USA TODAY*, *Kirkus Reviews*, *Suspense Magazine*, *Mystery Scene Magazine*, *Library Journal* and *RT Book Reviews*. For more information about Patricia and her work, visit patriciasargeant.com.

Books by Patricia Sargeant

Harlequin Romantic Suspense

The Touré Security Group

Down to the Wire
Her Private Security Detail
Second-Chance Bodyguard

Visit the Author Profile page at millsandboon.com.au.

To My Dream Team:
My sister, Bernadette, for giving me the dream.
My husband, Michael, for supporting the dream.
My brother Richard for believing in the dream.
My brother Gideon for encouraging the dream.
And to Mom and Dad, always with love.

Chapter 1

"Ms. Archer, I'm Hezekiah Touré of Touré Security Group." Hezekiah spoke gently, leaning toward the grieving widow. "My brothers and I are so very sorry for your loss."

Jayne Archer huddled on a scarlet-cushioned dark wood chair in the front row of the large Elizabethan-style salon at Eternal Wings Funeral Home Friday evening. The carpet was an abstract navy-and-scarlet pattern. The cloud-white walls were framed in dark wood trim. Family and friends who cared about the middle-aged woman surrounded her in the stuffy room, holding her hand, rubbing her back, patting her arm. A hymn, "Blessed Assurance," played softly on the funeral home's sound system. The comforting scent of lavender floated around him.

The wake for Jayne's deceased husband, Dean Archer, had just ended. Hezekiah had found it emotional but inspiring and at times joyful. Random descriptives from family members' and friends' remembrances echoed in his mind: honorable, caring, professional and corny. The few times Hezekiah had met with the older man, Dean had struck him as being all those things, as well as having a quick, if corny, wit.

"Thank you." Jayne raised her head. Her voice was raw from crying. Her large brown eyes were pink. Fat teardrops rained down her round chestnut cheeks. "Touré Security." She frowned as though searching for a memory. "Dean mentioned he'd hired your agency to provide security for the company. He'd been looking forward to working with you."

He smiled at her kind words. "My brothers and I had been looking forward to working with him, too."

Hezekiah's two younger brothers—Malachi and Jeremiah—were his equal partners in the family-owned security company their deceased parents had founded more than thirty years ago in Ohio's capital city of Columbus. They'd been shocked and saddened to learn of their newest client's sudden death a week earlier. Hezekiah had offered to attend the wake to represent their company and family.

None of them had attended a funeral since their mother had died two years earlier, three months after their father. He'd appreciated the expressions of sympathy from vendors and industry colleagues, as well as from friends, neighbors and their security contractors. He hoped to provide the same comfort to Dean Archer's widow.

Hezekiah pulled a business card from his black faux-leather wallet. "Ms. Archer, please call us if there's anything we can do to help you."

She accepted his card. Her smile trembled at the edges. "Thank you."

Hezekiah returned his wallet to the front pocket of his black suit pants. With a final goodbye and condolences, he turned to leave the stuffy salon. It was crowded with other mourners waiting patiently to express their sympathy. Many were drying tears, giving comfort, receiving comfort or all three. The scene brought back painful memories of his parents' funerals. Straightening his shoulders, he maneuvered his way out of the room and toward the business's exit.

"It was decent of you to come." The voice originated from somewhere behind him in the funeral parlor's lobby. Detective Eriq Duster, a forty-plus-year veteran of the Columbus Division of Police, approached him. Like Hezekiah, the homicide detective wore a tailored black suit with a bright white shirt. But instead of a broad black tie like Hezekiah's, Eriq wore a simple black bolo. The bronze slide clip was shaped like a trout.

Hezekiah retraced his steps to meet the older man halfway.

"I'd hoped to get a chance to speak with you privately. I'm so sorry for your loss, Eriq. Dean told us you'd been friends for decades."

"Since high school." The wrinkles creasing the sixty-something's dark features seemed a little deeper. "He was like a brother. We were both only children. My late wife introduced him to Jayne. I wouldn't have made it through losing my Addie without them."

Hezekiah felt Eriq's sorrow like an expanding balloon, pressing against his chest. He searched his mind for words of comfort. "He spoke highly of you. I could tell he valued your friendship. Thank you again for recommending my brothers and me to his company. We appreciate your referral."

Having a veteran homicide detective recommend their security consulting company was a tremendous honor.

Eriq's smile didn't quite lift the clouds of sorrow from his jaded brown eyes. "You guys have earned it. Your parents would be proud of the way you've built on their legacy."

"Thank you." Hezekiah felt like a fraud accepting the compliment. How could his parents be proud of him when he'd dragged the business they'd created to the brink of financial ruin?

Eriq reached out to pat Hezekiah's shoulder. The detective's throat muscles worked as he swallowed. "You're welcome." His voice was husky. He dropped his arm. "I'm going to check on Jayne. Thanks again for coming." He turned toward the large salon.

Hezekiah stopped him. "Eriq, let us know if there's anything we can do to help. If you want to talk or anything, please call us."

Eriq's smile was a little more natural. "Will do."

Hezekiah watched him disappear into the salon before he turned toward the funeral home's exit. He'd left his black SUV in the adjacent parking lot. Pushing his way through the glass-and-metal door, he paused at the top of the five-step entrance. He closed his eyes and pulled in a deep breath, catching the scents of lilacs, fresh-cut grass and automotive fuel. He needed to break the bonds of grief that had shackled him since he'd walked into Dean Archer's wake. It had brought back the pain of his parents' deaths, which he'd shared only with his brothers.

His eyes snapped open. A prickly sensation crawled down his spine. Someone was watching him. He was sure of it. It was an unsettling feeling. From his vantage point at the top of the steps, he scanned both sides of the street. He stared at the dozen or so pedestrians on the sidewalk below. No one looked back. Most strode past at a brisk pace. A few meandered in groups, deep in conversation. He tracked the cars rolling down the avenue. Maybe the feeling was from an incidental encounter, a casual glance from a passerby. But it had felt like more than that. Hezekiah took another deep breath. The tightness in his back and shoulders had burrowed in. His black cap-toe oxfords tapped gently on the concrete as he jogged down the steps.

He strode the short distance over the sidewalk before turning left into the funeral home's black asphalt parking lot. The disturbing sensation of being watched continued. He glanced over his shoulder and around the nearby perimeter. Nothing. Hezekiah frowned. His father had often quoted to him a line from Joseph Heller's *Catch-22*: "Just because you're paranoid doesn't mean they're not after you." So true.

Hezekiah pulled his keyless car entry device from his right pants pocket and pointed it toward his SUV. Nothing happened. *Curious.* He continued forward and pressed the button again. No reaction. He knew he'd activated his car alarm before leaving the parking lot. Even if he hadn't, his alarm was set to automatically activate. Had his keyless-entry battery died?

He stopped beside his car and tested the driver-side door handle. It was unlocked.

What the...

His body chilled. He circled his vehicle, scanning every inch of it—body, windows, tires, muffler. Everything. He stopped beside the passenger door. A large manila envelope sat on the front passenger seat. He grabbed it, looking around the lot again. A few people were trickling out of the funeral parlor, but no one paid attention to him.

He opened the envelope and saw two eight-and-a-half-by-eleven sheets of paper. He pulled them out. The first was a plain white sheet. Two words were written in black marker. "You're next." The second sheet was a printout of a black-and-white image of him getting into his car that morning. His blood went cold. His father had been right: he may be paranoid, *and* someone was out to get him.

"Earth to Celeste. Come in, Celeste."

Celeste Jarrett dragged her eyes from her laptop Friday evening. Anything to encourage her business partner to get to the point. Her attention settled on the other woman seated at her office's conversation table across the midsize square room. "What?"

Nanette Nichols, part owner of Jarrett & Nichols Investigations, rolled her big brown eyes. Beneath her shimmery silver shell blouse, her chest rose and fell in a sigh of disappointment. "I've been calling you for five minutes."

"No, you haven't." Celeste's tone was as dry as dust.

Nanette continued as though Celeste hadn't spoken. "If *I'm* the one planning my wedding, why are *you* the one having bride brain?"

Celeste sent a pointed look to the stacks of champagne-colored envelopes spread across her conversation table's blondwood surface. "Why are you filling out your wedding invitations in my office?"

Nanette shrugged. "So we can keep each other company."

"Hmm." Celeste didn't recall saying she needed company. She returned her attention to her computer screen. "My brain hasn't checked out. I'm doing research for my case."

Nanette continued shuffling through the invitations. The event was less than three months away. Nanette's boyfriend of two years, Warren Collingsworth, worked in the marketing department of one of the top health insurance companies in the country. With Nanette's blessing, he'd applied for a promotion, which would mean relocating from Columbus, Ohio, to San Diego. As soon as he'd been offered the position, he'd proposed, and Nanette had been in her element, planning their San Diego destination wedding.

Celeste was happy for Nanette. Warren was perfect for her. But she was going to miss the other woman. They'd been patrol officers and then homicide detectives together with the Columbus Division of Police for a little more than a year. They'd taken a year to plan their investigations agency, which had opened almost three years ago. Nanette insisted Celeste could visit the couple in San Diego whenever she wanted, but it wouldn't be the same.

"Is this the case with the widow of the security-company owner who doesn't believe her husband committed suicide?" Nanette tapped her professionally manicured ebony-tipped nails on the table. It was a tell that she was biding her time before changing the subject. Nanette could only go so long without being the center of attention. That was probably one of the reasons they got along. Celeste preferred being in the background.

"Uh-huh." Celeste only half listened as she scrolled through her internet search result links. "Meryl Bailey, Arthur Bailey's widow. He'd founded Buckeye Bailey Security." She'd agreed to take the case after meeting the grieving widow yesterday morning.

"So? What do you think? Did he kill himself—or did someone do him in?" Nanette had wrapped up her final case two weeks ago yesterday. She continued to come into the office, allegedly so they could keep each other company while Warren was at work. But after nine years of friendship, Celeste knew the truth. Nanette needed attention. Celeste liked Nanette, but her business partner was high maintenance.

Celeste lifted her eyes from her screen again. She folded her arms under her chest and contemplated Nanette. The other woman looked photo-session ready. Her perfect makeup emphasized her wide, light brown eyes in her warm brown face. A wealth of long, shiny raven tresses framed her oblong face and pooled on her shoulders. Celeste was doing well when she remembered her lipstick.

"I don't know. He was under a lot of stress." Celeste counted some of the reasons for his tension on her fingers. "His business wasn't doing well. He'd lost another big account. And he was behind on his loan payments."

Nanette affixed a clear mailing label to another envelope. "Despite all those strikes against him, his widow doesn't think he committed suicide because he's Catholic?"

Celeste shrugged. Her job was to gather the facts, *not* debate her clients. "She said her husband had been afraid of losing his immortal soul. She claims he would've declared bankruptcy before he'd commit suicide. And she's adamant he wouldn't have wanted her to find his dead body. He wouldn't have wanted to upset her."

Meryl had indeed been very agitated when she'd found her husband in his car, locked in the garage, with the engine still running.

"Then who does she think killed him?" Nanette held an envelope in one hand and a stamp in the other.

Celeste reached for a sheet from her writing tablet. She flipped it so Nanette could see both sides. "It's a long list... mostly competitor companies, employees, clients, vendors and a few relatives."

Nanette gaped. "It's sad that she thinks so many people would want her husband dead. Just sad."

"I know." Celeste set the list aside. Her internet searches focused on queries for connections that might reveal a common link. She was starting with Buckeye Bailey Security's competitor companies.

"So, have you decided who you're bringing as your plus-one to my wedding yet?" Nanette made it sound like an idle question.

Celeste knew that with Nanette, there were no idle questions. "For the half a billionth time, I'm not bringing anyone to your wedding. I'm traveling on my own. I will entertain myself on my own. Then I will leave on my own. I'm a capable, responsible person who can fend for herself, as you well know from our long and illustrious association. Don't worry about me."

Nanette gave another long-suffering sigh. "What about that hot security consultant you've been dating?"

Celeste gave her a second look. "How do you know he's hot?"

Nanette rolled her eyes. "I was curious about the man who finally convinced you to break your vow of celibacy, so I looked him up. His photo on his company website is H-O-T *hot*."

Celeste returned to her research. "We're not dating." And she was still celibate. "We had coffee and lunch."

She'd invited him to coffee on a Sunday, after which he'd

asked her to lunch later that week. Both times, she'd remembered her lipstick. And she'd enjoyed his company. He'd been interesting, intelligent, charming and surprisingly funny. Apparently, she hadn't impressed him the same way.

He'd called her after their lunch date. It was as though he'd known the exact moment she'd return to her office and settle behind her desk. Her heart had skipped a beat when she'd recognized his number. And then he'd explained why he was calling.

"Celeste, I don't think we're compatible. I enjoyed working with you during The Bishop Foundation case, but I don't think our personalities are the right fit for anything more. I wish you all the best."

She'd been too stunned to ask him what was wrong with her. That had been seven weeks ago today. It was still a sore spot.

Nanette tsked. "Why are the good-looking ones so hard to nail down?"

Celeste blinked. "What are you talking about? Warren's very handsome and he's been yours since the day you met two years ago. You're both lucky."

"Yes, we are." Nanette sighed. Celeste could almost see the stars in her eyes. "I'm excited about our future together, even though I know it'll be hard work starting an investigative agency on my own."

There she goes again. The lingering sentence. The side-eye. It was emotional extortion.

"You'll get plenty of references from past clients—and me. And you won't have to worry about money. You've got savings, and I'll be sending you regular payments for your share of Jarrett and Nichols."

Nanette set aside another completed invitation. "Or we could relocate Jarrett and Nichols to San Diego. Have you given that any more thought?"

Celeste sighed. "I've already said I don't want to move to San Diego. I've lived in Columbus for more than thirteen years. I don't want to uproot and start over in a new city where I won't know anyone."

"You'll know me and Warren."

"And I'm sure Warren would love to have me over every night for dinner and just to hang out."

Nanette shook her head as she sealed another envelope with tape. "All I'm saying is that you don't have anything to keep you here. What do you have to lose if you come with us?"

"That's not the compelling argument you think—" Celeste's hand froze on her touch pad. Her lips parted in surprise.

The headline for one of her search results triggered alarm bells in her head. "Owner of Archer Family Realty Remembered." Quickly scanning the article, Celeste learned Dean Archer had died unexpectedly of a heart attack in his office two weeks after Meryl Bailey's husband allegedly committed suicide.

And that had been less than two months after losing Dean Archer's contract—to Touré Security Group. She caught her breath.

Could that be their missing link?

"Earth to Celeste. Come in, Celeste," Nanette's voice sang out.

Celeste slowly rose from her seat. She held tenuously to the dots she was just starting to link. "I may have found our connection."

Nanette's brown eyes widened. "Did you find a motive for Arthur Bailey's murder?"

"Possibly." She looked down at her computer. "But I'll have to speak with Zeke Touré."

Her heart flipped with nerves—or perhaps nervous excitement?

"How was the wake?" Kevin Apple greeted Hezekiah from his seat behind his U-shaped gray-laminate reception desk Friday evening.

In the three months the twentysomething had been the Touré Security Group's administrative assistant, he'd proven himself to be an asset to the agency. He was professional, intelligent, motivated and personable. Kevin had been up front about his goal of becoming a personal security consultant. Jerry had put him on a training schedule. They'd have to find a new admin soon. In the meantime, Hezekiah was enjoying the organization and efficiencies Kevin brought to the agency.

Kevin also had a bit of hero worship for Jerry. He'd recently gotten a similar haircut, and Hezekiah could swear his youngest brother also had the same bronze pullover and charcoal slacks that clothed the admin's gangly frame. He and Malachi had bets on when the two men would come to work wearing the same outfit.

"It was nice. Thanks." Hezekiah's fingers flexed on the manila envelope. He loosened his tie.

A movement in his peripheral vision brought his attention to the hallway that led to the agency's offices and conference rooms.

"Zeke." Malachi came to an abrupt stop beside Jeremiah in the reception area. He'd loosened his tie and rolled the sleeves of his ice-blue shirt midway up his forearms. "We thought you were going home after the service."

Hezekiah glanced at Kevin before responding. "I want to check on a couple of things before the weekend."

Malachi and Jeremiah exchanged a look. Hezekiah's tension eased. The gesture showed his brothers understood his subtle message. They sank into two of the four overstuffed slate gray armchairs that followed the reception area's perimeter. Malachi set his black briefcase on the floor beside his armchair and laid his steel gray jacket, a match to his pants, over its arm. Jeremiah dropped his tan satchel between his feet.

Kevin's dark brown eyes twinkled with humor. A wry smile creased his thin brown face. "That's my cue to leave." He tugged his own tan satchel—a match to Jeremiah's—onto his shoulder. "I'm meeting my girlfriend for dinner. Have a good weekend." He waved over his left shoulder as he pushed through the Plexiglas doors with his right hand.

"You, too." Hezekiah echoed his brothers' farewell as he watched the younger man disappear down the staircase.

"What's up, Number One?" Jeremiah set his right ankle on his left knee. He was slim and fit, in a cobalt blue polo shirt and smoke gray slacks. "You've got that Houston-We-Have-a-Problem look."

Hezekiah offered the envelope to Malachi, who was closest to him, as he lowered himself onto the third armchair. "I found this on the front passenger seat of my car after Dean's wake."

Malachi pulled the two sheets of paper from the envelope, holding them so Jeremiah could also see them. They skimmed the first page, then the second. Their heads snapped up. Their nearly identical dark eyes widened with shock, then narrowed with fury.

Jeremiah exploded out of his chair. "You found this *in* your car? How is that possible?"

"The perp must have used a key jammer." Malachi's voice was low and controlled. His eyes scanned the printout of the image of Hezekiah climbing into his car that morning. "It blocks the signal from your key fob, preventing your door from locking and your alarm from activating."

Hezekiah gestured toward the papers in Malachi's hands. "How close does someone have to be for the device to work?"

"A few feet." Malachi moved his shoulders beneath his shirt. It was more of a flex to ease tension than a shrug.

Hezekiah looked between Malachi and Jeremiah. "Have either of you received any threats or suspicious packages or phone calls? Anything?"

"No." They shook their heads, echoing each other.

"We would've told you." Malachi lowered the printouts.

Hezekiah's tension eased a bit more. The furrows across his brow disappeared. His brothers hadn't been threatened. At least, not yet.

Jeremiah dragged both hands over his tight dark brown curls. He marched across the plush dark gray carpet to Kevin's desk, then back to his armchair. His movements were stiff. "How could they have known you were going to Dean's wake?"

"They couldn't have." Malachi sat back against the armchair. "They must've followed you from your house to our office and then to the wake. But how did they know where you lived? And what time you left for work?"

Jeremiah bit off a curse as he crossed back to Kevin's desk. "They've been following you for a while." He turned, pinning

Hezekiah with an intense look. "Have you noticed a car or any vehicle hanging around?"

Hezekiah unfolded from his armchair. He shoved his hands into his front pants pockets and considered the carpet as he paced to the wall on the other side of Kevin's desk. "No, I haven't noticed any tails."

"They must be good." Jeremiah completed another round trip to his vacated armchair. "You would've noticed if someone had been following you."

Pausing with his back to his brothers, Hezekiah pinched the bridge of his nose with the thumb, and index and second fingers of his right hand. The office suite had seemed comfortably cool when he'd first entered. It had quickly become stuffy and oppressive. The tension blanketing the room added to his anxiety. There were too many unanswered questions. His mind had tried to fill in the blanks during the half hour commute back to the office from the funeral parlor. Who was targeting him? Since when? Why? What was their next move?

Are my brothers in danger?

Hezekiah lowered his arm. "I haven't noticed any tails, but I did sense someone watching me as I left the funeral parlor." He turned to face his siblings. "I didn't see anyone looking back at me, but I couldn't shake the feeling I was being surveilled."

Jeremiah folded his arms across his chest. "That's it. You're staying with me until we figure this out."

Malachi narrowed his eyes at his younger brother. "He should stay with me. My house has the most secure system."

Jeremiah leaned toward Malachi. "*I'm* the one who's a trained personal security guard. I can better protect him if he's in physical danger."

Hezekiah reared back at the idea of his younger brothers coming to his rescue. He was the eldest. He was supposed to protect them.

Are they in danger?

"Hold on." He raised his arms. "First, Mal, your security system may be more advanced than ours because you're into the techy gadgets, but we all have high-quality systems. Second, we're all well trained in self-defense, thanks to Mom and Dad. I'll be fine on my own."

"That's crap, Zeke." Malachi's measured tone was misleading. Hezekiah could feel Malachi's temper emanating from him like a force field. "If this had happened to me or Jer, you'd relocate us to another country for our safety. Why are you any different?"

Because I'm the oldest.

Hezekiah dragged his hand over his clean-shaven head. "If I were to stay with you, I'd be putting you in danger. I'm not doing that."

Jeremiah set his hands on his lean hips. "So you think you can handle this on your own? I'm sick of your lone-wolf act, Zeke. There are three of us. Let us help you."

Malachi swept his arm out. "We don't even know where the threat's coming from."

"I may be able to help with that." Celeste Jarrett's voice came out of his dreams and into his agency.

The ground shifted beneath Hezekiah's feet. He turned toward the suite's entrance. His eyes swept her lithe figure. She stood in the threshold, wearing her usual black slacks and T-shirt. Her wide hazel eyes pinned him in place. A cool smile curved her full, heart-shaped lips. "Hi, Zeke. Long time, no speak."

He swallowed, easing his dry throat. *Ouch.*

Chapter 2

Celeste called on her better angels as she let the Touré brothers escort her to their conference room Friday evening. She needed them to keep her grounded. Every time she thought of Hezekiah Touré's final phone call, she wanted to go off.

She crossed into the conference room toward the rear of their office suite. Jerry held the black-cushioned chair on the right side of the large, rectangular glass-and-sterling-silver table for her. He took the seat beside her. Mal settled into the chair opposite Jerry, which left Zeke sitting right in front of her. Perfect. She schooled her features to keep even a hint of irritation from her expression.

The Touré brothers were ridiculously handsome, tall and athletic, with chiseled sienna features softened by full, sensual lips. Their dark, deep-set eyes could make you forget your inhibitions. Celeste had an out-of-body experience every time Zeke's almond-shaped coal-black eyes connected with hers.

The brothers had very different personalities, though. Zeke, the de facto head of the company, was in charge of corporate security. He projected an unmistakable air of strength and authority. Mal led the agency's cybersecurity division. He was the contemplative one who considered everything—what you wanted him to see and things you didn't want him to notice—before deciding on a course of action. Jerry oversaw the agency's personal security services. He gave the impression of being in constant motion, even when he was sitting still. He was impetuous and impatient, which tended to catch people off guard.

The conference room's chalk-white walls were decorated with beautiful oil paintings displayed in black metal frames. The subjects were well-known Ohio landmarks, including the Ohio Statehouse, the Cincinnati Observatory, the Paul Laurence Dunbar House, the Rock & Roll Hall of Fame and The Ohio State University Oval. Celeste remembered that they'd all been painted by Zeke.

The back of the room was a floor-to-ceiling window offering a portal for a wealth of sunlight. It overlooked the front parking lot and framed the treetops and a distant view of the city's outer belt, Interstate 270.

Celeste's eyes dipped to the manila envelope lying on the table in front of Zeke before returning to him. She ignored the way her heart vaulted into her throat. "May I see the contents?"

He slid the envelope across the table to her. Celeste withdrew the two sheets of paper. Her heart stopped. This was worse than she'd thought. She masked her battle to restore her composure by taking her time examining the printouts. Finally, she returned them to the envelope, then nudged the packet back to Zeke. Did he notice her hand shaking?

She swallowed the lump of fear in her throat and addressed Mal and Jerry. "Arthur Bailey died three weeks ago."

Mal nodded. "We were sorry to hear that. We sent a card and flowers to his family."

Of course they did. The considerate gesture, even toward a competitor, was in keeping with the Tourés' reputation in the community. "His death was determined to be suicide—"

"How did he die?" Zeke's deep, bluesy voice caused her heartbeat to skip.

Celeste steeled herself to meet his eyes again. "Meryl found his body in his car. Their garage was locked, and the engine was running. According to the ME's report, his blood alcohol level was .12, legally drunk."

Zeke briefly closed his eyes. "I'm so sorry. I didn't know."

His brothers echoed his sentiment.

Returning her attention to Mal and Jerry, Celeste continued. "Meryl doesn't believe Arthur committed suicide. He'd been under a lot of stress, but he wasn't depressed. Most importantly, she's adamant he wouldn't have wanted her to find him like that. She's hired me to look into his death."

Jerry gestured toward Zeke. "What does that have to do with the threats against Zeke?"

Impatient as always. Celeste had noticed that about Jerry when she'd worked with the Tourés on The Bishop Foundation case. She could relate. She didn't like wasting time, either. "Arthur died less than two months after losing the Archer Family Realty account to TSG."

"Wait a minute." Zeke lifted his hand, palm out. "Do you think he committed suicide because we got the Archer account?"

Celeste looked at his large palm and long fingers. She could almost feel their warmth on her skin. She dropped her eyes to the table. "I don't think Arthur committed suicide. As I was saying, a little more than a month after losing the account, Arthur dies. Two weeks later, Dean Archer dies. Today, you received a threatening message." She inclined her head toward the envelope between them. It gave her the shivers.

Zeke's thick black eyebrows knitted together, and his eyes narrowed in a sexy frown. "You think Arthur's and Dean's deaths are connected to this message?"

Celeste spread her hands. "I don't think these are coincidences."

"Neither do I." Mal's tone was sharp, cutting off any possible denials.

Jerry's dark eyes hardened with determination. "At least now we have a possible motive for the threat. That will help us identify the killer."

Zeke arched an eyebrow. "Alleged killer." He pinned Celeste with a skeptical look. "Dean died of a heart attack. And I empathize with Ms. Bailey, but does she have concrete evidence that Arthur didn't kill himself? Did it look like a break-in? Were there signs of a struggle in their home or garage? Did he have defensive wounds from a fight?"

Celeste shook her head. "All she has is a gut feeling—and their forty-year marriage. I believe her suspicions should be taken seriously."

Mal rotated his swivel chair to face Zeke. "So do I. But if she's right, then the killer—or killers—was able to get close to the victims."

Zeke met Mal's eyes. "What about Dean's heart attack?"

Jerry tossed a hand toward his brother. "Come on, Zeke. You know as well as we do that there are poisons that can mimic a heart attack. We need to get you someplace safe while we look for the person threatening you."

"I'm not going to let someone send me running for cover." Zeke leaned into the glass-and-sterling-silver table. The shift brought him closer to Celeste. "We're a security company. How would that look?"

"Like we can take our own advice," Mal responded.

Zeke held his brother's eyes. "We're going to find the person behind this threat."

"We'll combine our resources." Celeste looked around the table. Working together, surely they would be able to keep the stubbornest Touré safe.

Zeke shifted his attention back to her. "With all due respect, Celeste, I'm not convinced our two situations are connected. My brothers and I will do some investigating of our own to see whether the deaths are suspicious."

Celeste blinked. Was he being cautious? Or was he trying to avoid her? The answer was ridiculously obvious to her.

"All right." With a mental shrug, she stood. The brothers rose with her. "I've got to get back to work. I have to catch a killer—and save your life."

Celeste wasn't certain how long her legs would support her. She turned to lead the men from their conference room without waiting to witness Zeke's reaction to her provocative claim. Yes, she'd made the statement to irritate him, but it was also true. Someone was targeting the people involved in the Archer Family Realty account. Zeke might not think the threat was serious, but she wasn't willing to bet his life on that.

* * *

"We should work with Celeste." Jerry had a habit of repeating himself.

He and Mal followed Zeke back to his office after they'd said goodbye to Celeste Friday evening.

"We will, *if* Arthur's and Dean's deaths turn out to be suspicious." Zeke circled his heavy oak-wood desk and settled into his black-cloth executive chair. His brothers took the two visitors' seats in front of him.

Mal balanced his elbows on the arms of the black-cushioned chair and steepled his fingers. "Are you letting your past experiences with Celeste block your common sense?"

"I'd like an answer to that, too." Jerry looked from Mal to Zeke. "Didn't you guys go out a couple of times? What happened?"

"Nothing happened." Zeke tried to appear unfazed. He had the sense he wasn't fooling Mal. "This just isn't the right time for me to be in a relationship."

Jerry's face wrinkled with confusion. "Why not?"

Zeke pinched the bridge of his nose. "It's just not."

"The agency's doing better, Zeke." Mal's tone was low and somber. "Pretty soon, we'll be caught up on our debt and able to pay ourselves instead of living off our personal savings. And with Kevin's help, we're getting organized and processing new accounts faster."

Jerry gestured toward Mal. "He's right, Number One. Either way, you're allowed to have a life."

Zeke's lips curved in a half smile. "Thanks, Number Three, but I do have a life. A rather nice life."

Which could be even nicer if he spent more of it with Celeste. He might be able to pretend with his brothers, but he wouldn't lie to himself. He'd enjoyed their time together. Too much. She was smart, interesting, easy to talk with and sexy as hell. But he was wary of the distance he sensed her keeping between them. He wanted a relationship. But he suspected she was just after a casual fling.

"Nice?" Jerry spat out the word like it was rotten meat. "Listen, Zeke, I've been where you are right now, worrying about

the agency and the two of you. But now that I'm with Symone, I feel better, not just because of her but because I have balance in my life."

Zeke knew his brothers were happier now that they were in relationships with people they cared about and who cared about them. Grace and Symone were wonderful. Both men had met their significant others while on assignments. Mal had been reunited with his ex-girlfriend, Dr. Grace Blackwell, when a serial killer was trying to steal one of her formulations. Jerry had met Symone Bishop when she'd hired Touré Security Group to protect her stepfather.

Zeke breathed past a pinch of envy toward his brothers. "I'm happy for you. I hope to be where you are one day, but this isn't that day."

Mal nodded, seemingly willing to change the subject. For now. "What's our next step?"

Zeke gestured toward his laptop. "I'll email Eriq. He and Dean had been friends since high school. He should know whether Dean or anyone in his family had a history of heart disease. I'll also ask him whether the ME found anything suspicious during his examination of Dean's body."

"Good idea." Jerry stood to pace the office. "Do you want to talk with Jayne?"

Zeke considered the question. "Not yet. She'd be devastated by the theory that someone took her husband's life. I'd rather not tell her unless we're sure Dean was killed and we know why."

"Good point." Mal lowered his hands. "But I meant what's our next step in keeping you safe. You should stay with one of us."

Jerry turned to Zeke. "Stay with me."

Zeke lifted his hands, palms out. "For the last time, I'm not bringing this danger to either of your doors. I have a security system and self-defense training, just like the two of you."

Mal crossed his arms over his chest. "There's safety in numbers."

"There's danger, too." Zeke gave them both a pointed look. "Suppose something happens and the danger spills out and touches Grace? Or Symone? That's not a chance I'm willing to take. Are you?"

Mal arched a thick black eyebrow. "Nice try, Zeke."

Jerry applauded. "Yeah. That was award worthy. But you know Mal and I would make sure Grace and Symone weren't involved with this. We'd keep them safe."

Zeke did know that was true. "Let's regroup after I hear from Eriq. Then we'll talk about a plan for how to handle this."

Another inquiry. Maybe they should ask for Celeste's help. Investigations were her specialty.

No. One distraction at a time.

Jerry spread his arms. "Regardless of whether your situation is connected in some way with either Dean's death or Arthur's suicide—or both—you received a death threat. You can't pretend that didn't happen."

Mal stood. "We're going to protect you, whether you want us to or not."

He spun on his heels and strode from Zeke's office. His anger was disconcerting, especially since he never raised his voice or slammed anything. Zeke exchanged a look with Jerry.

His youngest brother jerked a thumb over his shoulder in the direction Mal had taken. "What he said." Then he disappeared through Zeke's office door.

Zeke couldn't blame his brothers for their reaction to the packet he'd received. As Mal said, if the situation had been reversed, he'd be acting the same way. Or worse.

But the situation wasn't reversed. Zeke clenched his teeth as his frustration tried to boil over. He was the one who'd received the threatening note. He'd do his best to protect the people he loved. An image of Celeste floated across his mind. He'd do his best to protect all of them.

"What are you doing?" Zeke spoke through the driver-side window of Mal's black SUV early Saturday morning.

He'd awakened about a half hour ago, shortly before dawn. From his bedroom window, he'd immediately spotted the vehicle nestled between two other cars a short distance from his house on the other side of the street. He should've known his younger brothers would pull something like this. Zeke had changed into his running clothes and shoes before rushing out to confront them.

Mal's almond-shaped ebony eyes were defiant. "Jerry and I are staking out your house."

Jerry leaned forward from the front passenger seat. His midnight eyes challenged Zeke to oppose them. "We haven't seen anyone or anything suspicious. Yet."

Zeke looked up and down his residential street. He didn't sense anyone looking back.

This early on a Saturday morning, there weren't many lights on in his neighbors' homes. A handful of cars had parked on either side of the blacktop. A few sat on concrete driveways. The sky was a soft gray as night eased into morning. The sun was only just starting to peek over the horizon. Birdsong intruded on the stillness of daybreak. The air was swollen with dew. Zeke smelled the moisture in the soil, on the grass and on the late-summer-turning-toward-early-autumn leaves.

His eyebrows met. "You spent the entire night out here?"

Good grief. While he'd been reviewing business reports, reading industry magazines, preparing for bed, both of his younger siblings had been guarding him and he hadn't known. That irritated him.

Mal gave a curt nod. "Right."

"We took turns sleeping." Jerry shrugged. "I don't need much, though. I feel pretty good now, like I can go another couple of hours. But I'll probably burn off that energy during our run. Don't worry, we packed our jogging clothes to save time."

Judging by his chatter, Jerry was probably more tired than he realized.

"I asked you not to get involved." Zeke's anger was stirring again. "You deliberately ignored me. I don't want you—"

"Fall back, Number One." Jerry cut him off. "Stop talking to us like we're your children. Mal's only two years younger than you, and I'm two years younger than him."

Mal leaned closer to Zeke, his head and shoulders partially emerging from the SUV's driver-side window. "We're a security firm, Zeke. If we can't protect our own, what good are we?" The fire in his ebony eyes was like a mini inferno, telegraphing the temper he was controlling. "More than that, we're brothers. If we don't take care of each other, who will?"

The confrontation sparked a memory of a conversation he'd had with their mother a little more than a year before her death. The recollection played like an old black-and-white film across his mind.

"Zeke, give your brothers a chance to lead once in a while. You love them. That's why you're so eager to help them. But they love you, too. Give them a chance to show you by letting *them* help *you*."

All these years later, he was still struggling with that lesson. *It's a lot easier said than done, Mom.*

Drawing a deep breath of the dew-laden morning air, Zeke straightened from the car. "Come in and get dressed. We need to hurry if we're going to meet Eriq by ten at Cakes and Caffeine."

Jerry jumped out of the SUV. "You've heard from him?"

Zeke led them to his home. "Yes, but the news isn't good."

Chapter 3

"Thanks again for letting me search your husband's offices here and at your home." Celeste sat on the navy-vinyl-and-silver-metal swivel chair behind Arthur Bailey's ash-blond-laminate desk late Saturday morning.

She pulled her denim jacket against her. The midsize room was cool and smelled like dirt. It wasn't surprising, considering a transparent layer of dust covered everything, including his desk, file cabinets and the bookcase on the far wall.

She and Meryl wore clear plastic gloves. Celeste had suggested the precaution in case they found evidence in Arthur's office that could support Meryl's belief her deceased husband hadn't killed himself. That he'd in fact been murdered. They'd taken the same approach when they'd searched Arthur's home office earlier. They hadn't found anything there, and it looked like they were about to strike out here as well.

Celeste sat back against Arthur's desk chair and surveyed his office again. The space was an organized mess. Folders were scattered across the desk and his ash-blond, faux-wood conversation table. Books and folders grew in messy piles from the table's two matching chairs.

"Anything to help learn the truth about what happened to Art." Meryl searched the bookshelves, shaking the books and binders stored there. The widow was a curvy sixtysomething with an unruly mass of salt-and-pepper curls. "It would help to know what we were looking for."

Celeste had gone through his desk and all the files in his drawers. She'd searched each folder in his cabinet. Some of the files had been sticky. A small bowl of individually wrapped hard candies gave a hint of how that could've happened. Celeste had even pulled out every drawer in the cabinet and desk in case he'd taped something to them.

She watched her client give a thick reference manual a rough shake, then replace it on the shelf before choosing another target. The older woman was dressed all in black, with a button-down blouse tucked into a narrow skirt and topped by a knit cardigan. Her black flats seemed to have a lot of mileage on them.

An image of the threatening note Zeke had received flashed across her mind. *You're next.*

"I'm not sure." Celeste stood, circling Arthur's desk on the way to the small conversation table. "Anything that seems suspicious or raises questions."

She didn't want to scare the other woman the way the note sent to Zeke had scared her. After finding her husband's dead body, the new widow was probably having nightmares, if she was sleeping at all. Celeste didn't want to add another frightening element to any of her dreams.

"What do you mean by *anything suspicious*?" Meryl returned a book to the shelf. Setting her hands on her full hips, she turned to Celeste. "We already know he wasn't shot or stabbed, so we're not looking for a gun or a knife. Are we looking for a bottle of poison? But if someone had drugged him, they would've done that at the house." She gasped. Her voice became thin, breathless. "Are we looking for a note? A threat?"

"Sit with me for a minute." Celeste removed a stack of folders from one of the chairs and placed it on the small table. She put the books from the second chair beside the folders. They'd already searched these items. Celeste sat while she waited for Meryl to join her.

The older woman pressed a small, chubby hand against her chest as she seated herself. She stared at Celeste with wide gray eyes. Her thin pink lips were parted as though she wanted to say more but words wouldn't come. The color had been leached from her white face.

"You think someone threatened my husband before killing him and that the threat is somewhere in this office or in our home." Her words were a statement.

"Meryl, if Arthur was murdered, I may have identified a motive. What did he tell you about the events that occurred before and after Archer Family Realty pulled their contract from Buckeye Bailey Security?"

The widow clenched her hands on her lap. "We talked about everything." She closed her eyes briefly. "Art was so upset. He was devastated after losing Dean Archer's contract. It was a big contract, and he'd provided their security for almost a decade."

"Why did Dean leave Art's company?" Celeste prompted.

Meryl pulled a dainty white-and-pink handkerchief from her cardigan pocket and dried her eyes. "It wasn't due to costs. I'm sure about that. Art's contracts were very competitive. Dean dropped him because the security guards assigned to their offices weren't professional. They arrived late. They left early." She briefly closed her eyes. "They even *slept* on the job. Can you imagine that?"

Celeste's eyebrows shot up her forehead. "Oh no."

"Oh yes." Anger flashed in Meryl's stormy gray eyes. "Dean complained to Art several times. Art tried talking to the guards, incentivizing them, reprimanding them. Nothing worked. They wouldn't listen." Her fist tightened on the handkerchief.

"Why didn't he fire them or assign different guards to Dean's account?" Celeste watched the other woman's body language and paid attention to her words. Meryl was holding back.

She dropped her eyes to the thin tan carpet. "Good guards are hard to find."

Especially when you were rumored to pay as poorly as Buckeye Bailey.

"So Archer Family Realty left Buckeye Bailey Security and contracted with Touré Security Group." Celeste sat back. Her eyes flicked around the office without focusing on anything. "How did Art react to Dean's decision?"

"He was angry, of course." Meryl's voice rose several octaves.

"With whom?" Celeste suspected the protective wife had been angry, too. "The guards? Dean? The Tourés? All of the above?"

Meryl shook her head. Her short curls bounced around her face in a frenzy. "No, no. Art didn't like Dean's decision, but he understood it. He wasn't happy that Touré Security got his contract, but he would've done the same thing in their position."

"Then he was angry with the guards." Which made sense. If they'd been more conscientious of their responsibilities, Art wouldn't have lost the Archer Family Realty account.

"Of course." There was a faraway look in Meryl's eyes. Celeste sensed the other woman had stepped back into her memories. "We took a big hit to our finances when we lost the Archer account. We had to find ways to shrink our monthly expenses. And Art had to let go of some of his contractors. It wasn't an easy decision, but in fairness, those guards had cost us the account. They had to go."

Yes, they did.

As a small-business owner, Celeste understood that, for the sake of his bottom line and his reputation, Art couldn't afford to keep those contractors on his books.

Celeste stood to walk the large room. Her suspicions that Art Bailey's and Dean Archer's deaths were linked and that they were suspicious grew. And she was even more afraid that Zeke's threat was connected, too. But she needed proof. Tangible evidence to support her gut instinct and to convince one very stubborn Touré. She lingered beside Art's desk. What had she missed?

"How many guards did you let go?" Celeste looked at her client from over her shoulder.

"Four." Meryl answered without hesitation. She knew a lot about her husband's company. "There were three eight-hour shifts each weekday. Then the guards rotated the four weekend shifts, but they couldn't work more than forty hours in a week." She searched Celeste's features with wide, tear-filled eyes. "Do you think one of them killed Art?"

Celeste turned away. She needed to clear her mind, and she couldn't do that staring into Meryl's grief-stricken eyes. What did she have so far? A grieving widow's assertions, a dead Realtor and a threat against a security expert. If she was still a homicide detective, would she launch an investigation with that?

No.

Her eyes landed on the shelf above Art's computer. From this angle, she could see something lying beneath the row of dusty framed family photos and aging knickknacks. She went back to the conversation table, then carried her chair to Art's desk. It was more stable than the swivel chair he'd used.

"What is it?" Meryl's words broke on a sob.

"There's something on the shelf. I think it's an envelope." Celeste toed off her black loafers and climbed onto the chair.

"Careful you don't fall." Meryl sounded steadier. "That's a strange place for an envelope."

Celeste agreed. She leaned forward, collecting the knickknacks standing on the shelf. She placed the treasures carefully on Art's desk. They didn't appeal to her, but the fanciful porcelain replicas of woodland animals probably meant a lot to Meryl.

She gathered the half dozen photos from the shelf. There were images of children, grandchildren, and a recent photo of Art and Meryl, which was different from the one beside his computer. They stood cheek to cheek, beaming at the photographer. Art had been a tall, handsome man. He was clean shaven. His gray hair was conservatively cut and thinning on the top. His ruddy cheeks and sparkling blue eyes suggested a good nature.

Finally, Celeste was able to grab the envelope. It was a nine-by-twelve manila carrier with the opening at the top. Its eerie similarity to the one Zeke had received yesterday gave her chills. She flipped it over. It was blank on both sides. Its metal clasp was sealed, but someone had ripped open the top. Celeste touched its jagged edges with a gloved finger. She glanced again at the shelf. A flood of investigative questions echoed in her ears.

How long had the packet been on the shelf?

Why had Art put it there?

Who'd sent it?

Hopefully, the envelope's contents would answer at least some of those questions. Celeste climbed off the chair and carried it and the packet back to Meryl.

"What is that?" Meryl gestured toward the envelope with the handkerchief clutched in her right fist.

"Let's see." Celeste sat before peeking inside. The contents confirmed her suspicions of what they were about to see. "Are you ready?" She held Meryl's eyes, searching for the answer before the other woman spoke.

Meryl filled her lungs with air, exhaled and straightened her shoulders. She nodded. Celeste pulled out two sheets of paper and laid them side by side on the table between them.

"Oh my—" Meryl gasped, covering her mouth with both hands.

Celeste studied the printouts. The first was a color image of Art getting into a red pickup truck. The second was a note, a single sentence, two words: *You're dead.*

Eriq Duster was waiting when Zeke, Mal and Jerry arrived at Cakes and Caffeine Coffee Shop on Old Henderson. The burly older man was wearing a gray Ohio State basketball T-shirt and shorts, and was nursing a large coffee. His casual dress was in keeping with Zeke's and his brothers'. They each wore dark shorts—navy blue, black and gray—with metal-hued pullovers—silver, bronze and rust.

The coffee shop was crowded with couples, families and friends enjoying a late-Saturday morning snack. Sunlight streamed in through its lightly tinted windows set into the stark, chalk-white walls. A stone fireplace stood in the center of the dark hardwood flooring. A handful of retirees and students were curled up on fluffy armchairs beside it, reading books or newspapers while sipping hot drinks. Scarlet-and-gray booth seating lined the café's perimeter. Cushioned gray armchairs and cozy dark wood tables were positioned around the room. Several customers occupying those booths and tables were working on laptops. Some were alone. A few collaborated in groups.

The veteran detective had taken a booth for four toward the back of the shop. The brothers joined him after buying their coffees.

Eriq lifted his tan disposable cup. "I could use something

stronger." He offered the faintest of smiles. Grief had replaced the cynicism in his dark brown eyes.

"I think we all could." Zeke sat on the other side of the gray-laminate table from Eriq. Jerry was beside him.

"Dean didn't have hypertension." Eriq stared at the white plastic lid topping his cup as though it could provide the answers to his most pressing questions: Who'd killed his friend, and why? "His family didn't have a history of heart disease."

"You're sure?" Mal was seated beside Eriq.

Eriq looked up, nodding. "We grew up across the street from each other. Our families were more like extended relatives than neighbors. His family has a history of diabetes but not hypertension. Jayne verified that. During his last annual physical, Dean's numbers were fine."

Jerry spread his hands on either side of his coffee cup. "If his death certificate read *heart attack*, who signed off on it?"

"Dean's staff found him unconscious at his desk after lunch." Eriq leaned into the table as though it could hold him up. "The EMTs thought he was having a heart attack. That's what the attending physician told Jayne. That Dean had died of a heart attack. I didn't question it. Some homicide detective I am."

Zeke looked at his friend's clenched fist on the table. "You reacted as a friend first."

Mal cradled his cup between his palms. "Dean could've been poisoned with a toxin that mimics heart attacks."

Zeke nodded. "Like digoxin. It's highly lethal and difficult to trace."

Eriq frowned. "Since he was found at work, one of his staff must have poisoned him."

Zeke narrowed his eyes, calculating the possibilities of foul play. "Not necessarily. Digoxin could take up to two hours to kill someone, which gives us a wide window of opportunity."

"How do you know so much about this poison?" Jerry arched a thick black eyebrow. "Should we sleep with one eye open?"

"It was used in a James Bond movie." Zeke's tone was dry. He turned back to Eriq. "You know we need to ask. How were Jayne and Dean?"

Eriq nodded. "They were good. Solid. I spent a lot of time with them. They were happy."

Zeke nodded. The detective and the victim had been friends for decades. He would know if the couple was having marital problems. Dean would have told him. "We need to know all Dean's movements on that day. Does Jayne have any theories on who might have wanted to harm him?"

"I haven't told her about our concerns. Not yet." Eriq held Zeke's gaze. "First I want to know what made you question Dean's cause of death."

Zeke gathered his thoughts. "Did you know Arthur Bailey died?"

Eriq blew a breath. "Yeah. Suicide. I was sorry to hear it. He was a nice guy."

Zeke inclined his head. "His widow doesn't believe he killed himself. She's hired Celeste Jarrett to prove it."

"CJ?" Eriq raised his eyebrows. "If anyone can get to the truth, she can. She's as tenacious as a bulldog."

Zeke knew that to be true—although he wasn't convinced Celeste would appreciate the bulldog comparison. "Celeste began to suspect Meryl Bailey might be right when she read about Dean's sudden death. She became even more convinced when she found out about the threat against me."

Eriq's expression went blank with shock. "What threat?"

Zeke looked around the table at his brothers. They returned his regard with similar levels of deep concern. He addressed Eriq. "Someone got into my car yesterday while it was parked at the funeral parlor. They put a note on the front passenger seat. It just read *You're next.*"

"There also was an image of Zeke getting into his car yesterday morning," Jerry added.

Eriq's eyes widened. "So CJ thinks there's a connection between you, Dean and—"

A strident bell interrupted their meeting. Zeke pulled his gray cell phone from the right-front pocket of his navy shorts. He bit off a curse. "My house is on fire."

Mal and Jerry shot out of the booth. Zeke rushed after them. He was already calling emergency services.

Celeste wasn't the only one who didn't believe in coincidences. Between the threats against him, and Dean's and Arthur's suspicious deaths, Zeke doubted this fire was an accident.

By the time they arrived at Zeke's home and had climbed out of Mal's car, firefighters had extinguished the fire and were securing the area. Before they left, the crew chief told Zeke it had been a grease fire. They'd been contacted in time. There wasn't much damage, and it was safe to enter the home. The chief also admonished Zeke not to leave his house when the stove was on in the future.

But Zeke hadn't used his stove that morning. After their run, he and his brothers had returned to his house. Since they only had an hour to change before meeting Eriq, he'd loaned Mal and Jerry clothes, and they'd agreed to eat at the coffee shop. He didn't bother to correct the firefighter, but his findings had confirmed Zeke's suspicion. The event hadn't been an accident. Someone had deliberately set his home on fire.

The flames had left a trail in the kitchen from the front-right burner, across the stove and over the counter. The window curtain above the sink was in tatters. His counters were scorched, and his flooring was damaged. Ignoring the sour stench of burnt wood, tiling and linoleum, Zeke packed a bag. He couldn't stay here tonight. He had to concentrate, and he needed to think. He led his brothers out of his home and locked the door.

"Could you take me to a hotel?" Zeke followed Mal across the street to his car. "I'll come back for my car later or tomorrow."

"A hotel?" Jerry's surprised question came from behind him. "That's a bad idea, and you know it. A hotel is the least safe place."

Zeke turned to face his youngest brother, who'd paused on the curb. "Someone tried to burn my house down, probably hoping I was still inside. I'm not bringing that to your doorstep."

Jerry thrust his arm behind him. "The fact that someone tried to burn you alive is exactly the reason you need to stay with either me or Mal. Not in some all-access hotel where this killer could walk right up to you."

The sound of a revving engine competed with Jerry's voice.

Zeke turned toward the noise. Before he could focus, Jerry had body-slammed him, sending him flying across the street and into Mal, protecting him from harm. But Jerry couldn't protect himself.

As if in slow motion, Zeke watched as the black sedan plowed into his youngest brother. Jerry became airborne, his arms and legs flailing like a discarded rag doll. His body spun up and over the car in a macabre somersault. Jerry landed on the asphalt with a sickening thud.

Zeke sprinted to him. "Jerry!"

"How's Jerry?" Celeste came to a stop less than an arm's length from Zeke. She was breathless from running up three flights of steps and down the hall. She'd been too upset to wait for the elevator.

Zeke was hunched over on one of the hard plastic gray chairs in the OhioHealth Riverside Methodist Hospital's waiting room Saturday afternoon. He looked up, frowning his confusion at her. "Celeste? What are you doing here?"

Celeste took another step toward him. She pulled the black denim jacket she'd shrugged on over her black T-shirt closer around her. It was cool in the hospital. "Eriq texted me. How's Jerry?"

Zeke stood. His navy knee-length shorts hugged his slim hips and exposed his long, powerful calves. His copper short-sleeved shirt stretched across his broad chest. "He has a mild concussion. His arm's broken, but the doctor said it's a clean break. Thank goodness. She also said the hospital will keep him a day, two at the most, to monitor his concussion. Symone, Mal and Grace are with him now."

Celeste glanced over her shoulder, wondering where Jerry's room was. She turned back to Zeke. "Then why are you out here?"

He shoved his hands into his pockets and flexed his shoulders restlessly. "I—He..." Zeke dropped into his chair. "I saw that car hit him. Jerry went flying. I thought I'd lost him." He turned his head and scrubbed his hands over his face. He bit off a curse. "That was supposed to be me. He pushed me out of the way. He risked his life to save mine. If I'd lost him, it would've destroyed me."

Celeste didn't know her half siblings, but she didn't need to to feel Zeke's pain. It was like a knife in her chest. It stole her breath. She sat in the matching chair beside him. Lifting her right hand, she stared at the broad expanse of his back in front of her. His muscles were taut beneath his shirt. Was it okay for her to touch him?

Unsure, she let her hand fall onto her lap on top of her black cotton shorts. Celeste spoke to his shoulder blades. "You didn't lose him. Stop thinking about what could've been and focus on what is. The doctor said Jerry will be fine. Believe her. You need to support him during his recovery. You also have to find the person who hurt him and tried to kill you."

Zeke straightened his back and squared his shoulders. "You're right." He shifted to face her. "I owe you an apology. I should have at least considered your theory that the threat I received was connected to Art's and Dean's deaths. I'm sorry."

He was close enough for Celeste to get a whiff of his soap-and-sandalwood scent. It had haunted her dreams night and day for weeks. She inhaled, and the fragrance brought her back to their lunch together. His sexy smile, quick wit and charming manners made her feel warm all over again. She'd accepted that he didn't want things to go any further between them, but she'd treasure the memories of their time together.

Celeste stood, shoving her hands in the front pockets of her shorts. "Even if you had listened to me, I don't know if it would've changed anything."

"I would've been more cautious. Will you help me?" He caught and held her eyes. "Please?"

At that moment, staring into his deep-set coal-black eyes, she thought she'd do anything for him. "Of course." The words left her on a sigh.

"Thank you." His broad chest expanded as he drew a breath. "Have you learned anything more about Art's case?"

"He'd received an anonymous threat similar to yours." Celeste pulled out her black cell phone and swiped through it, searching for the photos she'd taken of the sheets of paper. Sitting, she handed the phone to Zeke so he could see them. Their fingers brushed as he took the device. Zeke glanced at her before looking at the photos.

His face tightened. "Art's photo is almost identical to mine. I was getting into my car in the picture they'd taken of me."

"I remember." Celeste reclaimed her phone, shifting to face him. "I think Art was always meant to be the first victim."

Zeke frowned at her. "What makes you think that?"

She swiped back to the image of the note. "His message reads, 'You're dead.' Your message reads, 'You're next.'"

Zeke narrowed his eyes. "Why is that significant?"

"It suggests the killer has a stronger connection to Art than either you or Dean. Art seems to be the trigger. Meryl told me Art had fired four security guards after he lost the Archer Family Realty contract to you."

Zeke pinched the bridge of his nose with the thumb and two fingers of his right hand. "I can't believe my brother was almost killed because of a vendor contract."

Celeste didn't care whether it was okay for her to touch him. She put her right hand over his left forearm. Beneath her palm, his muscles jumped, then relaxed. "*Almost*. That's key. He's going to be fine. And I'm sorry about your house." She squeezed his arm, then dropped her hand. "Meryl's pulling the personnel files of those four fired guards so I can research their backgrounds."

"We'll help." Mal's voice came from behind them.

Celeste and Zeke rose to face him. Mal's girlfriend, Grace, was with him. They exchanged nods of greeting. Celeste didn't know much about Dr. Grace Blackwell. She was a biomedical scientist with Midwest Area Research Systems. She was brilliant, tall and beautiful, with striking cinnamon eyes and long dark brown hair.

Zeke's tension stirred around him. "Jer's still okay?"

Mal nodded. "He has a whopper of a headache. He finally gave in and asked the nurse for painkillers. Symone's going to stay with him a while longer."

Jerry and Symone Bishop, chair of The Bishop Foundation, had met a little more than nine weeks ago when Symone had hired the Touré Security Group to protect her stepfather from a stalker. That was the first case on which Celeste had collaborated with the brothers.

Grace chuckled. "I don't know whether either of them noticed we'd left."

Celeste smiled her appreciation of Grace's attempt to lighten the mood.

Some of Zeke's tension dissipated like fog. "I'm glad she'll be with him."

"Me, too." Mal switched his attention to Celeste. "When will you get those personnel files from your client? I'd like to help you go through them."

Celeste checked her black smartwatch. It was a little past noon. Meryl had just started compiling the records when Celeste had left her less than an hour ago. That had been right after Eriq had texted her about Jerry's accident and Zeke's home. "It'll take Meryl at least an hour to download those records onto a thumb drive. Maybe two o'clock? I'll text both of you when I hear from her."

"Great. Thank you." Mal arched an eyebrow, addressing Zeke. "How are we going to get you out of here? I'm sure the stalker followed you to the hospital."

"Mal's right." Grace scanned the lobby as though searching for the criminal in question. "They're probably waiting outside, watching for when you leave."

Zeke dragged his right hand over his clean-shaven head. "So what do we do?"

A light bulb came on in Celeste's head. "I have an idea."

Chapter 4

"I'm so sorry, Jerry." Zeke stood at the foot of Jerry's hospital bed late Saturday afternoon. Guilt and regret were heavy burdens on his shoulders.

Why had he been so pigheaded? Why hadn't he listened to his brothers? If he hadn't insisted on handling the situation on his own, Jerry wouldn't be in the hospital with bruised ribs and his right arm in a cast. He squeezed his eyes shut and bit back a string of curses.

You have to learn to accept help, Zeke. His mother's chastising words echoed in his ears. She'd always been after him for rushing in to fix other people's problems but not accepting help with his own. Because of his stubbornness, his youngest brother could've been killed.

"Knock it off, Number One." Jerry's voice was strained. His features were tight with the effort to handle his pain. "Or I'll get out of this bed and shake some sense into you."

Symone stood on Jerry's left, closest to the window. She rested a gentle hand on his shoulder. "No, you won't, tough guy. I'll do whatever I have to to keep you in that bed."

Her tone was playful, but Zeke saw the remnants of fear in her large chocolate eyes behind her black-framed glasses.

Jerry's lips curved into a faint smile as he looked at her. *"Whatever* you have to?"

Symone's blush almost matched the color of her floral knee-length dress with three-quarter-length sleeves. The heat the couple generated made it clear the two had forgotten Mal, Zeke and Celeste were also in the room.

Zeke caught and held Symone's gaze. "I'm sorry for not doing a better job protecting Jerry."

Anger flashed in the back of Symone's eyes. She adjusted her glasses. "Were you the one driving the car that hit him?"

Zeke's eyebrows knitted in confusion. "You know that I wasn't."

"Then how is this your fault?" She paused as her breath hitched. Jerry took her hand. "I don't want your apology, Zeke. Don't you dare absolve this monster. Find them and have them thrown in jail."

Mal's words were quiet. "Symone's right, Zeke. Our focus is on finding the person responsible for hurting Jerry."

A bit of Zeke's tension eased with the knowledge his family didn't blame him even as he continued to blame himself.

"Come on." Celeste put a hand on Zeke's shoulder to push him from Jerry's room. "You've got your marching orders. You, too, Mal. Symone's got Jerry covered. We need to get Zeke out of here without being seen."

"I'm still on this case." Jerry's words carried a hint of panic.

"We haven't forgotten, Jer." Mal's tone was dry.

Zeke stopped to look back at him. "We're a team, Jer. I'm sorry I didn't act like it."

Celeste's hazel eyes twinkled with approval. "You can make up for it now. But first, we need a nurse."

Zeke gave her a quick look. "For what?"

Her grin didn't reassure him.

"Meryl and I found the threat Art had received," Celeste said, addressing Zeke and Mal. They were seated on the other side of her desk at Jarrett & Nichols Investigations late Saturday afternoon. "It's similar to Zeke's. There's a note and a photo of Art, taken as he was leaving for work one morning."

Zeke accepted the printouts of the photos Celeste had taken of a manila envelope and its contents. He'd seen these images on her cell phone earlier, but that wasn't the reason he was distracted. His thoughts were still on the machinations Celeste had put into play so she and Mal could secret him out of the hospital.

Celeste had somehow convinced a nurse and an orderly to help them. The pair had gotten a wheelchair, blue surgical shoe covers and a sky blue robe for Zeke. He'd refused to change into the powder blue polka-dot cloth gown that tied in the back. Instead, he'd compromised by wearing the gown and robe over his street clothes. He'd had no problem slipping the pale blue disposable shoe covers over his white sneakers and rolling up his pant legs, but he'd had to be nudged into the wheelchair. He'd thought Mal had gotten off easy with the soft blue doctor's scrubs, complete with matching cap.

Once Celeste was confident their disguises would work, she'd wheeled Zeke to her car. She'd borrowed a bright blue nurse's uniform. It was the first time Zeke had seen her in anything other than black.

Dressed as a surgeon, Mal had exited the hospital several minutes later with the orderly. After dropping the orderly off at a local sandwich shop to be picked up by the nurse, Mal had met Celeste and Zeke at her office. The scheme had been complicated, but Zeke understood it had also been necessary. Lives were at stake—and not just his own. Despite the seriousness of their situation, he had the impression Celeste and Mal had enjoyed themselves. To be honest, so had he. It felt like going undercover.

Zeke brought his attention back to the case. A wave of sadness rolled over him as he reviewed the printouts. He and his brothers had liked Arthur Bailey. Whenever they'd run into the older man at industry events, they'd gotten along well. He couldn't imagine Art doing anything that would make someone want to kill him. Neither could he imagine the jovial security expert taking his own life.

The color printout was framed to show Art in profile as he climbed into his ruby-red pickup truck. The sixtysomething father of four had loved that truck like a fifth child. He was wearing black denims and one of his many scarlet-and-gray Ohio State Buckeyes jerseys. The second sheet carried a two-word typewritten message that read *You're dead*. Both the image and the note had been printed on plain white copy paper.

Zeke's skin chilled. He passed the papers and envelope to Mal on his left. "His wife hadn't been aware of this threat?"

Celeste shook her head. "No, Art hadn't shown it to her. We found it buried on a shelf above his desk."

This was the first time Zeke had been to Jarrett & Nichols Investigations. Celeste's cozy office carried a trace of her vanilla-and-citrus scent. He settled back onto the sterling-silver-and-black-vinyl visitor's chair and took a deep breath. His eyes swept his surroundings a second time. He was searching for something that would give him insight into the mystery that was Celeste Jarrett. It would be a challenge. She didn't have any personal items in the room.

On her L-shaped faux-maple-wood desk, everything appeared to be in its place. She seemed to have a penchant for black metal office supplies. Her pen-and-pencil holder stood beside her stapler. A fresh notepad lay beside it. The metal inbox on the corner of her desk sheltered a single glossy sheet of paper that looked like it had been torn from a magazine. A photo of a woman, posing in a pale lavender off-the-shoulder, low-cut gown with a full skirt, dominated the layout. He had a few questions about that. Beside it, the matching outbox contained several envelopes, topped by a utility bill. The shelf above her laptop on her left was empty, as were the surfaces of the file cabinets to her right. No photos. No trinkets. No hints about the woman behind the desk.

"Based on the angle of this photo, it wasn't taken from a car." Mal had changed out of his scrubs. He sat on Zeke's right with his left ankle on his right knee. His attention was glued to the printout. "The killer must have been standing down the block, waiting for Art. They must've been studying his routine for at least a couple of days."

Celeste frowned. "What makes you think that?"

Mal continued his scrutiny of the image. "It takes seconds for a person to get behind the wheel of their car. But this picture isn't rushed. It's sharp and almost perfectly framed. The photographer was ready. This wasn't their first attempt at taking Art's photo. They'd taken several practice ones beforehand."

Celeste's straight dark eyebrows stretched toward her hairline. "That's pretty impressive, Mal. Thanks."

Zeke fought back a proud smile. "We should ask Art's neighbors if they've noticed anyone new in the area."

"Either a new walker or jogger, with or without a dog." Mal placed his copy of the printouts into his black faux-leather portfolio, which he balanced on his left thigh.

"Great." Celeste added a note to her manila folder on her desk marked *Buckeye Bailey Security Case*. "While we're doing that, we can research our primary suspects. Meryl gave me a copy of the personnel files of the four security guards Art recently fired. I'll make copies of the files before you leave." She rested her right hand on the folders beside her.

Zeke's eyes drifted to the sterling silver ring she wore on her right thumb. Black infinity symbols encircled the band. Who'd given it to her, and why? Was that person still in her life?

"That'll be helpful." Mal looked up from his notes. "I'll do some additional background searches."

Celeste's eyes gleamed with determination "I'll help."

"So will I." Zeke looked from Celeste to Mal. "We should look into Meryl and Jayne Archer as well to see if they have any connections or suspicious people in their backgrounds."

"You're right." Celeste's sigh was distracting. "And we will, but I doubt either of them has anything shady in their pasts."

Mal's eyes narrowed on Zeke. His tone was firm. "You can't stay at your home."

"Especially since it's the scene of an arson investigation." Celeste's tone was dry. "We need to get you somewhere safe."

Zeke stood to pace Celeste's tiny office. Long strides carried him past her bookcase stuffed with law enforcement publications—industry magazines, legal reference books and technology manuals. A book on social media marketing barely visible among the business journals gave him pause. He couldn't imagine the cagey private investigator having a social media presence. She was as reticent as Mal.

Turning, he gestured toward his brother. "I can't stay with you or Jerry. I'd be putting you in danger. We don't know for certain the killer's only targeting me. Why would they?"

"If the killer's targeting all of us, that's even more of a reason for us to stick together." Mal's frown was familiar. It was an indication that his brother was immovable from his position. Zeke couldn't fault him. If their situations were reversed, his expression would be the same.

Celeste's grin seemed incongruous. "Stick together for what? To make it easier for the unknown assassin to hit all three of you at once? That's ridiculous, and if you were thinking straight, you'd see it yourself. Good thing I'm here. Zeke's right, Mal. He can't stay with either you or Jerry. Even if Zeke's the sole target, the killer probably has both of you on their radar."

Having Celeste on his side eased some of the strain from Zeke's shoulders. "We don't know whether or when Dean received a threat. I found mine at Dean's wake. That fact, plus the wording—*you're next*—makes me think the killer wants to take us out one at a time."

"In which case, we won't know whether Mal and Jerry are in danger until the killer gets to you." Celeste's voice was brittle with concern. Zeke's eyes held hers.

Anger shook Mal's words. "Another reason to make sure they don't get to you."

"No." Zeke's voice was sharper than he'd intended. "Just because you haven't received a threat *yet* doesn't mean the killer's not looking for you."

Mal's frown returned. "My house has state-of-the-art, cutting-edge security systems."

Zeke matched his brother's expression. "I said—"

"Guys." Celeste extended her arms, palms out. "I have the perfect solution to this problem. The killer doesn't know about your connection to me." She pinned him with a challenging, taunting look. "You'll be safer staying at my place."

Zeke narrowed his eyes. That depended on her definition of *safer.*

"It's not much, but it's mine." Celeste stepped aside to welcome Zeke into her home Saturday evening. She didn't have any reason to feel defensive. So why did she?

Celeste loved her little cottage in Worthington, a northern

suburb of Columbus. The area was quiet. Most of her neighbors had either retired or were about to. Here, she was safe. She was accepted. It was her sanctuary. And she'd trusted Zeke enough to invite him to stay indefinitely, unlike her reaction to her previous boyfriend.

In the six months she'd dated He Who Would *Never* Be Named, Celeste hadn't even invited him over for coffee. The fact her subconscious had blocked her from making that gesture should have served as a warning. Maybe it would have if she hadn't been so desperate for affection. Celeste turned her back on that thought.

She dropped her house key into one of the small compartments of the yellow-and-black knapsack she used as a purse and waited for his reaction to her home. She was just curious. It wasn't as though she wanted his approval.

Did she?

The minute Zeke crossed her threshold, her thirteen-hundred-square-foot two-bedroom, one-and-a-half-bath residence felt like a one-bedroom condo. It wasn't just his six-foot-plus, two-hundred-thirty-some pound build. It was his commanding presence that filled the room and wrapped itself around her. That, and his soap-and-sandalwood scent. Not that she was complaining.

Zeke's eyes seemed to inhale their surroundings, taking in everything at once. "I like it. A lot."

The warm glow inside her grew a little bigger, a little warmer. "Thank you. So do I."

Zeke walked farther into her home. "It's so bright and welcoming."

Celeste followed him, trying to evaluate the open floor plan with the dispassionate eyes of a stranger. They'd entered through her attached one-car garage into a short, narrow hallway with white-paneled walls. To their left was the Honeywood staircase that led to the second floor. Behind them, overlooking the front of the house, was a cozy sitting room. She spent a lot of time curled up on its white-and-seafoam-green armchair and matching ottoman. The space was filled with leafy green plants that basked in the room's abundance of natural light.

Stepping past Zeke into the slate gray-tiled hallway, Celeste gestured to her left away from the sitting room. "This is the living room."

The hallway led to a modest room with maple-wood flooring. Its thick, cream faux-leather sofa and love seat surrounded a rectangular sofa table made of powder-coated iron and engineered wood. It stood on a tan-and-brown area rug in the center of the room. Potted plants congregated at the base of the two generous arched windows on the far wall. A large black flat-screen TV mounted beside the white stone fireplace dominated the space.

Celeste took him through an archway to the right of the TV. "This is the kitchen. You're in luck. I just went to the grocery store, so the fridge and cupboards are fully stocked."

"Thank you, Celeste." Zeke's words were sincere, but his tone was distracted. His eyes swept the cream cupboards, black appliances and slate gray tiling.

"Sure." Celeste hesitated. Zeke seemed dazed. What was he thinking? She shrugged off the awkward feeling and pulled her cell phone from the front-right pocket of her shorts to check the time. "I'll take you upstairs. The courier should be here with your luggage soon."

Zeke followed her up the staircase. "I'd only packed one bag, but I don't know how long I'll be imposing on you."

Celeste spoke over her shoulder. "You're not imposing. And you're welcome to use my washer and dryer, if it comes to that."

"You have a beautiful home." He sounded almost surprised. "It must be such a pleasure to return to it at the end of the day."

He got it. He understood what her sanctuary meant to her. Celeste's heart felt full. "Yes, it is. I love my job. I enjoy doing investigations whether it's corporate, government or personal cases. But my home is my favorite place on earth."

"I can tell." Zeke's tone was pensive.

Celeste reached the top landing and stepped into the room toward the back of her house. "This is my home office."

The cozy space had been designed as a second bedroom. Like the rest of her home, it was flooded with natural light. But she'd covered it with somber paint and filled it with darker furniture. She'd omitted the little calming touches like fluffy throw pillows, soft afghans and leafy plants. This space was meant to keep her focused on her work. Her small dark wood desk faced the lone rectangular window overlooking her backyard. The black faux-leather chair was similar to the one in her office at the agency. To the right of her desk, a black printer-cum-copier sat on top of a dark-wood-and-black-metal cabinet. Beside it was a smaller desk on which she assembled reports and spread out evidence. Above it was a poster board she used to track timelines and suspects. The maple-wood folding door to the wardrobe on the left was closed. It stored her treasure trove of undercover disguises.

Celeste looked up at Zeke beside her. He had about six inches on her. "You're welcome to work in here, if you'd like. I can bring up one of the chairs from the dining room."

Zeke's dark eyes sparkled with curiosity and interest. "Thank you. I'd appreciate that."

"No problem." She didn't have much experience hosting guests. She hoped she was doing okay.

Get a grip, Celeste.

This wasn't a sleepover or a staycation. It was a homicide investigation. They were after a serial killer who'd already murdered two people. Zeke Touré looked like he'd walked out of her wet dream and into her home office. But he was their sole surviving target, and his life was in her hands.

Get it together.

Besides, seven weeks ago, he'd told her he wasn't romantically interested in her. She stole a glimpse of him standing beside her. His shorts revealed his lean, well-muscled legs. His broad shoulders strained against his T-shirt. She'd have to box up those sexy fantasies in the farthest corner of her mind. At least for the time being. It wouldn't be easy, but she was a professional.

Swallowing a sigh, she looked away. "I have a treadmill, weight machine and other exercise equipment in the basement." She crossed to the closet. "But if you want to jog outside, I have a ton of disguises you can choose from." She opened the deep closet with an unintentional flourish.

Zeke stepped forward, stopping close enough for her to share his body heat. His eyes were wide as he scanned the contents. Celeste had acquired a variety of items for both women and men, including scarves, hats, wigs, eyeglasses, eye patches, jewelry, ascots and neckties. The wardrobe ranged from expensive-looking clothing and shoes to tattered attire. She also stocked materials to create sideburns, mustaches, beards, thinning hair and scars.

"Why do you have all of this?" Zeke sounded puzzled and awestruck.

"It's for undercover work and surveillance. If I always look the same, my target might become suspicious." Celeste took a clear silicon hair cap from a box on one of the shelves. "This is great. I use it to cover my hair, then apply a skin-toned latex mask. With a suit and mustache, I look like a man."

Zeke's eyes held hers. "Impossible."

A blush pricked her cheeks. Celeste made herself look away. "I'll show you the rest of the house."

Nearing the end of the short hallway, Celeste gestured toward a blond-wood door on their left without stopping. "The bathroom. I'll get you some towels." She pushed open the last door on the upper level. "This is the bedroom."

Celeste loved this space. It was one of the biggest rooms in her home. The white-paneled walls reflected the natural light flooding in from the two large windows in both the east and west walls. Gossamer-thin white drapes framed each window, stopping inches from the maple-wood flooring. Cream ceramic planters of pothos ivy were centered at the top of the four windows. A trace of lavender from the plug-in she'd attached to the outlet between the west-facing windows scented the air.

A white marble vanity table and natural white grain chair were partially visible beyond the half wall to the left behind the simple blond-wood chest of drawers.

A matching blond-wood dresser sat at the center of the front wall to her right. Matching nightstands stood on either side of the king-size bed in front of them. It dominated the room. Soft white coverlets and fluffy pillows in soft blues and greens swallowed the mattress. The pillows echoed the colors of the thick area rugs that surrounded the bed.

Celeste didn't mind silence. She'd been raised by her paternal grandmother, Dionne Eve Jarrett, who hadn't spoken much, at least not to her. But Zeke had had plenty of time to survey the room. Why wasn't he saying anything?

She glanced at him. "Is something wrong?"

"This could be a problem." He was hesitant.

"What?" Celeste scanned her bedroom.

Zeke turned to her as though in slow motion. "There's only one bed. Where do you want me to sleep?"

Celeste looked at her king-size bed. Those fantasies escaped her box and inflamed her body. She swallowed.

Chapter 5

Celeste's bed was giving Zeke an erection. It was the definition of decadence. A mountain of thick pastel pillows crowned it. A coverlet as soft and fluffy as summer clouds spread across its vast expanse, beckoning to him. Images of them naked beneath that cover, wrapped in each other's arms, were burned onto his mind. As he stood at the foot of her bed Saturday evening, Zeke could smell her all around him. He clenched his hands into fists and gritted his teeth, trying to focus on their life-and-death situation and not his body's reaction to her nearness. It was a losing battle.

"Where do you think you'll sleep?" Celeste seemed puzzled. She gestured toward the erotic fantasy masquerading as bedroom furniture. "On the bed. I'll take the sofa."

Zeke stiffened. "Excuse me?" He hadn't been raised by wolves. "I'll take the sofa. I'm not going to displace you from your bed."

Celeste gave him a once-over that made his knees shake. "You won't be comfortable on my sofa. You're too tall and too broad. I've fallen asleep on my sofa a bunch of times. I'll be fine."

Zeke became even more obstinate. "I can sleep anywhere. I've slept in my car when my brothers and I have done stakeouts."

"And how did you feel the next morning?" Celeste continued

when Zeke remained stubbornly mute. "Please. Take the bed. You've made your point that chivalry is alive and well among the Touré brothers, but this is a matter of practicality."

"What about your office?" He swung his arm toward the room at the other end of the hall.

Celeste's lips twitched as she struggled against a smile. "I suppose you could put your head under the worktable, then angle your feet to fit beneath my desk."

She had a point.

Zeke surveyed her room again. An argument could be made that Celeste was even tidier than he was. It looked like she made her bed before she left for work, just like him. Her kitchen was spotless, without so much as a teaspoon in her sink. In her living room, her television remote controls had been neatly lined up in the center of her coffee table. Her throw cushions had been fluffed and strategically placed on her sofa and love seat. Every nook and cranny had been well organized.

The only thing left to work out was their sleeping arrangements.

Closing his eyes, Zeke pinched the bridge of his nose with his right hand. "What have you done in the past when you've had houseguests?" He lowered his hand and looked at her.

Celeste gave him a blank look, as though he'd spoken to her in an unknown language.

Zeke scanned her room again. As with other rooms in her house, her bedroom walls were decorated with mounted photographs of seascapes and mountain trails, and shelves of wood carvings and clay sculptures. But she didn't display photos of family, friends, coworkers or even herself in her house. Why was that?

He frowned at her. "Have you ever had friends or family come for a visit?"

Faint color darkened her high cheekbones. Her voice was cool and perhaps a bit defensive. "You're the first houseguest I've ever had."

Zeke was gaining the first bit of insight into his host. "I'm not taking your bed."

"You're not sleeping on my sofa." Celeste was firm. "We'll

share the bed. In deference to your chivalry, I'll roll a blanket down the middle."

Out of the frying pan, into the fire.

If he were a kettle, his body would be whistling. Zeke swallowed, easing the dryness of his throat. Thinking of being that close to her in a bed—even with a rolled blanket between them—made his heart jackhammer against his chest. "I'll sleep on the floor."

"Seriously?" Celeste planted her hands on her slender hips. "Do you see that hardwood flooring? You wouldn't be comfortable sleeping on that. If it makes you feel better, I'll add pillows to the blanket barrier. I have plenty of them."

That was an understatement.

Celeste checked the time on her cell phone. "Your suitcase should be here soon. I'll start dinner. I was planning on jerk-chicken stir-fry. Is that okay?"

"It sounds great. Thank you. I'll help."

Celeste turned to lead the way from her bedroom. "Great. There's still plenty we need to discuss. We can do that while you give me a hand in the kitchen."

"Of course." Anything to distract him from what was bound to be a restless night.

"If I didn't know you were a private investigator, I'd think you were the chef of a four-star restaurant." Zeke's crooked smile trapped Celeste's breath in her throat.

He continued to shrink the size of her home. Standing beside him at the kitchen counter Saturday evening, Celeste could feel him all around her.

The scents of jerk chicken and sautéed vegetables lingered in her kitchen as Zeke helped her clean up after dinner. He'd complimented Celeste on their meal several times. Either he'd been really hungry or she was a better cook than she'd thought.

"Thanks. Again." The warmth that rolled over her didn't come only from his praise. Celeste worked a little harder to push her attraction for the corporate-security executive to the back of her mind. "I hadn't realized how much fun cooking with someone else could be."

Or cooking *for* someone. Cooking and baking were more interests than hobbies. Culinary programs were her guilty pleasures. But the only other people she'd cooked for were Nanette and He Who Would *Never* Be Named, the first man she'd stupidly given her heart to. She'd cooked both meals in her old apartment. Neither of them had been to her sanctuary.

Zeke nodded as though he was mentally filing her statement away. "I'd like to interview Meryl. Can we meet with her in the morning?"

She nodded as an image of the security company owner's widow popped into her mind. "I get it. You have your own questions and want to get your own read on her and her marriage to Art. No problem. I'll arrange a time with her. In the meantime, I've got a few questions for you. You know the drill, hotshot. Anyone new come into your life in, let's say, the last six months?"

Like a love interest you met maybe seven weeks ago?

"The only new relationships I've had in the past year are professional." Zeke stacked his dishes on top of hers in the sink. "You know what it's like to run your own company."

"So the only new people you've met are related to your work?" Celeste loaded the dishwasher. She hoped she sounded more nonchalant than nosy.

"That's right." Zeke disappeared into the dining room, then returned with the pitcher of fresh lemonade. "Our company's starting to grow."

"I've noticed. Congratulations."

"Thank you." Zeke tossed her a smile that conveyed his relief. "We just hired an administrative assistant, Kevin Apple. We did a thorough background check on him. And you and I have just started collaborating on cases, but we've known each other for years."

With her peripheral vision, Celeste watched Zeke find space for the pitcher in her refrigerator. There wasn't another woman in the picture. She just wasn't good enough. Again. Celeste's mood nose-dived.

She continued packing their dishes into the dishwasher. There were twice as many place settings as she was used to having.

"Tell me about your new clients. Who are they? Do you have any concerns or suspicions about them?"

"Why are you asking me these questions?" Zeke circled Celeste where she stood at the sink, prewashing the dishes. "You said Art was the trigger for these threats and murders."

Celeste shoved aside the fresh hurt from the reminder that Zeke didn't think she was good enough. "That's my theory. But we can't overlook the possibility—slim though it may be—that I'm wrong and something else triggered the attacks."

Zeke chuckled. "All right." He began transferring the pots from the stove to the sink. "Mal does a complete background check on all our new clients and their principals. It's part of our client-onboarding process. He hasn't turned up anything suspicious on any of them. If he had, we wouldn't work with them."

She recalled Mal's background reports. "Mal's incredibly thorough."

"Yes, he is. He flags anything even remotely questionable about our clients."

Celeste heard the pride in Zeke's voice. What was it like to be part of such a close-knit family? She could only imagine it would be wonderful to have people to lean on when you were in trouble, celebrate with when you achieved success, comfort you when you were down. Someone to just be with when you didn't want to be alone. Celeste shrugged off her regrets. She couldn't do anything about her past, but she was happy with her present. And although she was losing her business partner, her future still looked bright.

She started the dishwasher, then turned to watch Zeke scrub her pots and pans. She ignored the way his T-shirt wrapped around his biceps, which flexed and relaxed with his every move. "The new person in your orbit may not have made direct contact with *you*. They may have connected with someone close to you."

"That's a good point." Zeke's thick, dark eyebrows knitted over his broad nose.

"I'm more than just a sparkling personality." Celeste rolled her eyes. "Who's managed to breach your inner circle?" She took the dish towel from the rack beside the refrigerator and used it to dry the newly scrubbed pots and pans as Zeke set them on the drainboard.

Zeke's chuckle was a low rumble that played on her stomach muscles like pebbles skipping across a pond. "You mean, besides you?" Celeste arched an eyebrow at him. Undaunted, Zeke continued. "As you know, Mal reunited with Grace a little more than five months ago. And Jerry started dating Symone about two months ago. But they were both clients first, so we did thorough checks on them."

"You've checked out Grace, Symone, Kevin and all of your clients." Celeste straightened from putting the final pot in a lower cupboard. "Are you sure there isn't someone who could've slipped through the cracks? A vendor? A new tenant in your office building or new neighbors on your block?"

Zeke shook his head at every suggestion, but Celeste sensed him combing through his thoughts. She led him into her living room and settled onto her soft white faux-leather love seat.

"Kevin has a new girlfriend." Zeke dropped onto the matching sofa to Celeste's left.

Celeste mulled that over. "Have you and your brothers met her?"

Zeke shook his head again. "They've only been dating a few weeks, a little more than a month. But I'd better let Mal and Jerry know about our suspicions." He pulled his cell phone from his front-right shorts pocket and typed into it.

Celeste's attention drifted to the cold, stone fireplace across the room. Votive candles and framed scenic photos were arranged on the simple blond-wood mantel. She gave them only a cursory look as her thoughts tumbled around in her mind. "So to your knowledge, she's never been to your agency. Would Kevin give her a tour without telling you?"

"No." Zeke's cell phone buzzed, claiming his attention. He checked the device, then returned it to his pocket.

She waited for Zeke to expand on that. Her lips trembled with amusement when he didn't. For Zeke, the matter was closed. "How can you be so sure?"

"We're a security agency." Zeke spread his arms. "We use the same procedures and protocols we recommend to our clients.

Our offices have surveillance cameras and alarm systems. If Kevin was giving tours of our agency, we'd know."

"That's a little creepy."

Zeke gave her another crooked smile. "The cameras aren't everywhere, just the common areas—reception, kitchen, supply closet. Not in our offices or the conference room. We keep sensitive information about our clients and their businesses. We have to take precautions to keep them safe."

"Hmm." She considered her own client files. "Maybe I should take those precautions, too."

"I'd be happy to set up a system for you."

Zeke was willing to work cases with her. He'd asked her to help Touré Security Group with Symone's investigation. He'd accepted her help with this matter. And now he'd offered to install a surveillance system for her. But as far as a personal relationship, well, Zeke just wasn't into her. Until that moment, she hadn't realized how much she'd looked forward to getting to know him better. Disappointment was a bitter taste in her mouth.

Did her smile look as unnatural as it felt? "Thank you. I'd appreciate that." Celeste pushed herself to her feet and locked her knees. She spoke over her shoulder as she circled the love seat on her way to the stairs. "I'm going to work for a few hours before bed. Do you need anything?"

"No, thank you." He sounded as though he'd been caught off guard. "I'll bring my suitcase upstairs. Is it all right if I store it in your closet?"

"Of course." Without a backward glance, she mounted the stairs. "I'll clear some drawers and closet space for you."

"I don't want to inconvenience you." His voice was tentative.

"It's no trouble," she called over her shoulder.

At least one mystery had been solved. Zeke would never consider her anything more than a colleague. Knowing that, she could concentrate on catching the serial killer and stop thinking about her broken heart.

"I still think I should sleep on the floor." Hezekiah Touré could test even the patience of a saint.

Celeste wasn't a saint.

Zeke had emerged from the bathroom, where he'd changed into baggy navy shorts and a gray Ohio State Buckeyes T-shirt that hugged his torso like a lover's arms.

She sat up in bed, tucking the sheet under her arms to provide an extra cover over her chest in addition to her short-sleeved, scoop-necked sapphire pajama top. "I promise you'll be perfectly safe sharing this room with me."

A smile brushed across his lips. "And I promise the same."

"I know." Pity.

She sensed he wanted to say something more. His eyes lingered on her, but then he shifted his attention to the space between the bed and the vanity.

Zeke gave a decisive nod. "I'll be fine on the floor."

Celeste glanced down to her right. She'd spent at least half an hour changing her bed sets, including the six pillowcases, making sure the pillows and covers were evenly distributed, and rolling the comforter into a narrow border, perfectly centered on the king-size mattress. She'd placed the makeshift divider beneath the bedsheets. She'd even added the pillows. The barrier ran the length of the bed, starting from between the two sets of pillows. But still, the arrangements weren't good enough for him. Fine. It was late Saturday night. She needed to get some rest before they met with Meryl Sunday morning.

With a mental shrug, she pulled the comforter from beneath the sheets and pushed it to the right side of the mattress. "Suit yourself. There are extra sheets and blankets in the linen closet. You can have those three pillows." With that, she lay back down.

"Thank you." Zeke crossed to the bed. After taking the comforter, he spread it on the floor, close to the chest of drawers. He set the pillows in place on top of it before leaving the room.

Celeste folded her arms behind her head and watched him stride down the narrow hallway, presumably to the linen closet to collect those sheets and blankets she'd mentioned. Seconds later, the light came on in the passageway, spilling into her bedroom. The closet's folding door opened with a soft swoosh. There was a faint rustle of cloth as Zeke searched for the items he needed. Celeste frowned. Was he messing up her storage system? No, she could relax. He was too tidy and respectful to do that.

She was tempted to roll over and pretend to be asleep. It was late. She was an early riser. But what was the point? They'd both know she was faking. No one would be able to sleep while someone was building a nest on the floor beside them. The linen-closet door closed with a muted snick. Seconds later, Zeke came into view.

He glanced at her before kneeling on the floor to arrange the sheets and blankets. "I'm sorry to keep you up."

She freed her arms from behind her head and curled onto her right side. "Did you get enough blankets?"

"Yes, thank you." He reached across the comforter to spread a seafoam green sheet over it. His movements were stiff and awkward. Was he deliberately avoiding looking at her?

She stared at the back of his head. "And pillows? Will three be enough?"

"I'm sure they will be." There was a smile in his voice. That was better. "I'm sorry to deprive you of your usual half dozen fluffy pillows."

She feigned a sigh of disappointment. "I'm glad you recognize my sacrifice."

"Thank you." He finally looked at her. His dark eyes twinkled with amusement. "I usually get up at four forty-five a.m."

"That's fine." Celeste shrugged beneath the sheets. "I'm an early riser, too."

"Thanks." Zeke stood to turn off the overhead light. "Ready?"

Celeste stretched to turn on the lamp on her right nightstand. "Ready."

Zeke turned off the top light, plunging the room into shadows and seduction. Celeste watched his silhouette walk to his makeshift bed, then disappear from her line of sight. She turned off the lamp.

"Perfect." His sigh floated up from the floor, pulling another smile from her.

Celeste loved that about Zeke. With him, her smiles were spontaneous. Her laughter was real. She felt almost playful. Years of loneliness evaporated when she was with him, and she was happier. She wanted to hold on to this feeling and this moment. But that wasn't a good idea. She and Zeke wanted different things from their relationship. He wanted a colleague. She wanted so much more.

"Why didn't you want to share the bed with me?" *OMG!* Had she actually said that out loud? Judging by the funereal stillness coming from the other side of the room, she had. "Never mind. Forget it. I didn't—"

"It wouldn't have been a good idea." Tension was palpable in his voice.

Celeste rolled onto her back and scowled at the ceiling. Moonlight and streetlamps eased the dark shadows across the white spackle. What did he mean by that? She'd placed a blanket down the center of the mattress, for pity's sake. Their platonic relationship would have survived the night.

Her eyes widened. Did he know how she felt about him? She was mortified.

Celeste forced herself to draw a slow, calming breath. "Zeke, why did you decide to stop going out with me?"

The silence was long and impenetrable. Celeste squeezed her eyes shut. She clenched her hands into fists at her sides.

Please just tell me. Just tell me.

Her eyes popped open when he finally spoke.

"I wanted to get to know you, Celeste." His words were like foreplay, stoking a fire within her. "But you wouldn't let me."

"What do you mean?" Memories from their coffee and lunch dates played across her mind like a movie trailer. What was she missing? "We talked."

"Yes, but it was always about *me*." He'd managed the perfect note of frustration. "I wanted to get to know *you*. I wanted our dates to be a give-and-take. But I was doing all the giving, and you were doing all the taking."

Celeste's lips parted with shock. That wasn't what she was doing. She rose up on her right elbow and turned to his silhouette in the dark. "Men like talking about themselves." He Who Would *Never* Be Named certainly did.

"You're doing it again." This time, his sigh was a soft note of disappointment. It pierced her heart. "Instead of telling me why you don't talk about yourself, you're turning our conversation back to me. Do you even realize you're doing that?"

Celeste fell back onto her pillows. No one had ever accused her of not talking about herself. Now she was the one who didn't know what to say. She'd expected Zeke to break her heart. She hadn't expected him to also make her head spin. "You know everything about me. I'm from Chicago—"

"Why did you leave?"

"I was a homicide detective—"

"Why homicide?"

"I co-own a private investigation agency."

"Why didn't you return to the department? I know they wanted you back." A rustle of cloth gave the impression Zeke had turned onto his side. "I've asked you these questions before. Remember? If you don't want to tell me, I'll respect that. But I'm looking for a relationship, Celeste, not casual encounters."

"I'm not interested in casual encounters, either." Her mind was still reeling.

"But you don't seem to want me to get to know you." He sighed when she didn't respond. "Good night, Celeste." Zeke's makeshift bed rustled again as he settled in to sleep.

Celeste curled onto her side. "Night."

He was asking her to let him in. She wanted to, but how did she even begin to take down her protective walls? There were so many of them.

And the scariest thought of all, the one that was going to keep her up all night: What if she opened herself up to him and he didn't like what he found?

Chapter 6

Zeke's alarm went off at 4:45 a.m. on Sunday. His room was still dark.

Wait. It wasn't his room. It was Celeste's. His arm shot out to slap his alarm into silence. He didn't want to disturb her. He sat up and looked over toward her mattress. Although his eyes were still adjusting to the dark, he was pretty sure there wasn't a body in that bed.

He whispered her name. "Celeste." Silence. A beat later, he tried again, louder this time: "Celeste?" Still nothing.

Zeke tossed off the bedding and stood to cross the room. His body was stiff from sleeping on the floor despite the nest of blankets and pillows he'd used for his makeshift mattress. Turning on the overhead light, he looked to Celeste's bed. It was empty. It was also made. His lips parted in shock. If he hadn't seen her before they'd fallen asleep, he would've thought she hadn't gone to bed last night.

What?

How?

His eyes swept the room. A plain sheet of paper was taped to the door. He pulled it free to read it. *Good morning, sleepyhead! Gone for a run. Back around 5 AM. Make yourself at home.—C*

He read it again. She'd gone for a run and would be *back* in fifteen minutes? How long had she been up? And how had she managed to make her bed, get dressed and leave the house without his hearing her? He was a light sleeper and a security professional. He was trained to react to every out-of-place sound. How had he slept through her movements? He laid the note on the nearby dressing table. Apparently, he'd have to wait fifteen minutes for his answers.

Zeke pulled black running shorts and a brown wicking T-shirt from a drawer Celeste had cleared for him. He collected his black running shoes from her closet and added a gray baseball cap to help mask his face. He dressed, then hurried downstairs with minutes to spare. The front door opened as he reached the entryway. Celeste was early.

She locked the door before turning to him. Her beauty froze Zeke in place. Her face glowed with energy and enthusiasm. Sweat dampened her brown skin. Her cheeks were flushed with exertion. Her hazel eyes twinkled up at him like sunlight on the river.

"Good morning! How'd you sleep?" She grinned, and Zeke's knees went weak.

He grabbed the staircase railing to steady himself. It took a moment to register her words. "I must have slept very well. I didn't hear you moving around at all."

Celeste wiped her upper lip with the back of her hand. "Inquiring minds want to know. Do I snore?"

"Not that I heard." Zeke gave her an answering smile.

Celeste pumped her fist as she strode past him. "Yes!"

Zeke stepped off the stairs and followed her. "Do *I* snore?"

Before today, he'd considered himself to be a morning person. He had nothing on Celeste. Who would've thought the cynical private investigator with the Johnny Cash wardrobe would greet the morning with so much vigor and excitement?

Celeste spoke over her shoulder. Long strides carried her into her kitchen. "More like a deep breather."

Zeke chuckled. "I'll take that. You must be a morning person."

She stopped beside the pass-through window. Her lips parted, and her eyes widened as she feigned surprise. "You're not?"

"It's not even five. Give me a moment." Zeke smelled the sharp, salty tang of her perspiration. "What time did you leave?"

"About four." She pulled a glass from the cupboard. Her limbs were long and slender in knee-length black biker pants. She wore a sleeveless orange-and-silver reflective jacket over her black wicking T-shirt, which was heavy with sweat. "I did a little more than six miles. Would you like a glass of water?"

"Yes, please. You left the house at four?" Zeke shrugged his eyebrows. "But you didn't set an alarm. Did you have trouble sleeping?"

"Slept like a baby." She offered him a glass of water, nodding when he thanked her. "It occurred to me that we should ask the guards if they've received threatening messages or if anyone new has come into their lives. If the motive is revenge for the murderer being fired, wouldn't they be upset with the people who came in late or slept during their shifts? They're the ones responsible for the killer being out of a job. Right?"

"That's a good point." Zeke was impressed. "In fact, if the killer is one of the guards, I'm surprised they wouldn't have already taken their revenge on their ex-coworkers."

Celeste gave him a considering look as she took another deep drink of cold water. "Are you going for a run?"

Zeke drained his water before answering, giving himself time to think. Once again, she'd changed the subject each time he'd asked something personal. She was a master at deflection. He tried a more direct approach. "Do you always wake up before 4:00 a.m.?"

Celeste started to answer, then paused. Her expression shifted. Her bright hazel eyes darkened with caution. "I've been waking around three fifteen, three twenty for as long as I can remember. That's why I don't need an alarm clock. I just get up when my body tells me to."

Zeke was like a sponge, eager to soak up as much as she was willing to share about herself. But he had to move slowly. Her tense voice and jerky movements let him know she was uncomfortable talking about herself.

He approached Celeste, putting his empty glass in the dishwasher beside her. "And that's usually three fifteen? Why so early?"

"I don't know." She shifted her stance. "I grew up with my paternal grandmother. It drove her crazy that I'd get up and start moving around so early. She'd make me go back to bed, but I couldn't sleep. I taught myself to move quietly so I wouldn't bother her. At college, I kept up the habit so I wouldn't bother my roommates. As a police officer, moving quietly was a valuable skill."

"I can believe that." Zeke had dozens of other questions, but the strain in Celeste's eyes urged him to wrap up his interview. "Thank you for telling me about yourself."

She rewarded him with a relieved smile. "Sure."

"And to answer your question, yes, I'm going for a run. I don't think the killer has any idea I'm here. And the cap masks my features." He tipped his brim.

"Hmm." Celeste finished her drink. "It does, but you should still wear one of my fake mustaches. You can never be too careful."

Zeke arched an eyebrow. She must enjoy playing dress-up. She also had a good point about being careful. "Do you have a particular one in mind?"

"Yes, I do." Celeste's smile gave Zeke an uncomfortable sense of foreboding.

"Why do I have the feeling I'm not going to like your choice?"

Once again, Celeste strode past him, this time on her way upstairs. "Maybe you have trust issues. I hear that's going around."

Zeke arched an eyebrow behind her back. He was entrusting his life to someone with trust issues. That suspicious nature made Celeste an ideal person to keep him safe. But it was an impediment to having a personal relationship with her.

Fortunately, all he needed was a bodyguard. That's what he kept telling himself. The problem was, he wanted so much more.

"I've been trying to understand why Art hadn't told me about the threat he'd received." Tension orbited Meryl as she sat on the overstuffed warm-gold-cloth sofa in her living room late Sunday morning. Anger entered her voice. "I've been going round and round about it in my head, and still I can't understand it. I was his *wife*. Why would he withhold that information from me? If he'd told me, maybe I wouldn't be his widow now."

Her voice choked on her last sentence. Meryl's eldest child, Katie Bailey-Smith, was on her left. She put her right arm around her mother's shoulders to hold her close.

"I'm so sorry, Meryl." Celeste's voice was husky with empathy. "The most logical explanation is that Art hadn't wanted to worry you."

Zeke sat beside Celeste on the lumpy matching love seat on their host's right. The scent of the herbal tea Katie had served them floated up to him from the large blue ceramic mug cradled in his hands.

Meryl's wide gray eyes were pink with tears as she looked to Celeste. "You can see how that further supports my conviction that Art didn't kill himself. Can't you?"

In her voice, Zeke heard the unspoken pain of not being able to remove the image of her loved one's dead body from her mind.

"Of course they can, Mom." Katie's voice was firm. Her eyes, identical to her mother's, were dark with anger and frustration. "Why would my father kill himself if he didn't want to worry my mother? That makes absolutely no sense."

Katie looked like her mother, just twenty-plus years younger. Both women were dressed in almost identical simple black long-sleeved dresses. It was clear to Zeke that the Baileys' first child was their protector. Katie's younger siblings remained in the kitchen. Low, somber voices occasionally drifted out to him. He couldn't make out what they were discussing, but the clang of steel pots and pans and the clatter of porcelain indicated they were making lunch.

Meryl's eyes were stormy as she pinned Zeke with a look. "I know what I must sound like—a hysterical woman who's in complete denial. But when you've been together for as long as Art and I, and when you love each other as completely as we did, you know each other inside and out. You know what the other would and wouldn't do and why. You know the other's intentions regardless of the results. Art and I were together since we were kids. Now our children have children. That's a long time,

Mr. Touré. That's why you'll never be able to convince me that my Art killed himself. Someone murdered him."

"Please, call me Zeke." He shared a look between mother and daughter. "And I believe Art was murdered, too. It's too much of a coincidence that Art would kill himself after receiving a message threatening his life."

Zeke's words seemed to take Meryl's and Katie's tempers down a notch or two.

Meryl's sturdy shoulders lowered on a sigh of relief. "So you'll find whoever killed my husband?"

Zeke glanced at Celeste before returning his attention to Meryl. "Yes, we will. We believe Art wasn't the killer's only target. Dean Archer's death was also suspicious. And I was threatened as well."

"Oh, no." Meryl's words were muffled behind her hand. "I'm so sorry."

Katie gasped. "Oh, my gosh."

"You were right to be concerned, Meryl." Celeste's tone was somber. "Art is the first victim we're aware of, but his killer has a bigger agenda."

Katie addressed Zeke. "If the police had listened to my mother, Dean Archer would still be alive, and you wouldn't have been threatened."

"We don't know that." Zeke was certain the killer wouldn't be that easy to find.

Katie and Meryl stared at him as though he was a dead man walking. Their fatalism wasn't helpful. Zeke looked away, taking a visual tour of the living room. The walls were a dingy cream. They were a few shades lighter than the worn, wall-to-wall carpet that extended past the archway and into the dining room. A simple, scarred dark wood coffee table stood in front of the sofa. A thick warm-gold armchair was off to the side.

Warm-gold curtains were open, framing the narrow windows on either side of a redbrick fireplace. Part of a train set and several colorful building blocks had been abandoned beside them. The dark wood fireplace mantel was teeming with family photos. Zeke set his mug on the coaster Katie had provided, then crossed to the fireplace for a closer look. Images included

Meryl and Art alone and together, and pictures of their children and grandchildren through various stages of their lives: births, baptisms, graduations and weddings.

More murmurings carried from the kitchen, joined by the scrapes of chairs across linoleum and the whir of a blender. He recalled a comment he'd made to Celeste. *I didn't know Art well. We only saw each other at business functions. But he always seemed happy.* Zeke realized now that joy came from his family.

"The logical place to start is the connection between Art, Dean and Zeke." Celeste's usual gruff manner was on a break. Her gentle tone and manner as she spoke with Art's grieving family impressed Zeke. "Dean canceled his contract with Buckeye Bailey Security and hired Touré Security Group. According to the time stamp on the photo of Art entering his car, it was a few weeks later that he received the threat."

Zeke turned away from the fireplace. "After Dean's wake Friday afternoon, I found a note in my car that stated 'You're next.' Based on the connection between Art, Dean and me, and the fact Art fired the guards assigned to Archer Family Realty, we're investigating the guards first. Can you offer any insights into them?"

Meryl and Katie exchanged a look. Zeke could feel their tension, as well as their desperation to find the person who'd taken their loved one from them.

"I didn't know Art's employees well." Meryl spread her arms. Her right fist clutched a used facial tissue. "I have my own job and didn't spend much time at his company. All I knew about his employees is what he told me, which wasn't much." She gestured toward Celeste. "I gave you the employee files on the guards who'd been assigned to Dean's company."

"We were hoping for more personal impressions." Celeste set her blue ceramic mug on a coaster beside Zeke's. She pulled her notepad from her knapsack. "Had Art complained about one of them in particular? Did he argue with any of them? How were his relationships with them before Dean canceled the contract?"

"Even a seemingly minor argument." Zeke resumed his seat and retrieved his portfolio from his attaché case.

Meryl frowned at the carpet as though searching her memories. "No, he didn't blame one above the others. He blamed them all equally—as well as himself."

"Dad blamed himself?" Katie let her arm slide from her mother's shoulders. "Why?"

Meryl used the tissue she clutched to wipe her nose. "Your father said he should have acted sooner and taken more drastic steps to address Dean's concerns about the guards. I remember him saying if he'd removed one of the guards, he'd still have the Archer account."

"'One of them'?" Zeke and Celeste asked in unison.

"Do you remember which one?" Zeke continued.

Meryl shook her head. "But I can still hear his voice. 'If I'd just removed that guard, I'd still have the bleeping account.' Except he didn't say 'bleeping.' Art had been very upset. Losing Archer had been a devastating blow to his company. It was a big account, and he'd had it on contract for years."

"I'm sorry." Having just signed the contract with Archer Family Realty, Zeke was aware that it was a significant account. They requested guards stationed at their company office as well as their holdings. Plus, Touré Security Group was providing cybersecurity services.

"There's nothing for you to be sorry for." Meryl looked at him with wide, startled eyes. "My husband understood you didn't take Archer from him. He lost the account. He never blamed you or your brothers. He liked and respected your family."

Meryl had removed a weight Zeke hadn't realized had been on his shoulders. "Thank you for telling me that. Had anyone new come into Art's life? Guards, clients, colleagues?"

Meryl began shaking her head even before Zeke finished his question. "No, no one new. He couldn't afford to hire new guards, even after firing those four. And there weren't any new clients, although he was hopeful he'd find someone to replace Archer." She stretched her shoulders. "And he didn't mention new colleagues."

"What about you, Meryl?" Celeste searched the widow's face as though trying to read her mind. "Have you met anyone new? Perhaps in the neighborhood, at work or church?"

"Or through a friend?" Zeke added.

"No, no one." Even as Meryl said the words, Zeke sensed her struggling to draw even a crumb of a clue from her memory. "I've known most of my friends since the kids were young. We don't have any new hires at work—at least, none that come to mind."

"What about me?" Katie leaned forward, catching Zeke's eyes. "Would it be significant if someone came into my life?"

"It could be." Celeste's pen was poised over her notepad, ready to record anything her client's daughter shared.

Katie switched her attention to Celeste. "I met a woman at the gym. She seemed a little strange. She made me uncomfortable. And now she's gone. It's like one day she makes herself part of the group of people I hang out with at the gym, then a week or so later, she drops off the face of the earth."

Zeke exchanged a look with Celeste. She seemed to have the same reaction he was having. That was textbook suspicious behavior.

Celeste sat back, studying Katie. "What made her seem strange?"

Katie spread her hands. "Well, first, she invited herself into our group like some kind of parasite. She ignored every clue we gave her—subtle and not so subtle—that she wasn't welcome. She asked a bunch of nosy questions, then she vanished without a trace. Doesn't that seem strange to you?"

"Very." Celeste nodded. "What's her name?"

"That's the thing." Katie exhaled a heavy sigh. "I wasn't paying attention. Heida or Gretchen or Hannah. Something like that. I'll ask my friends if they remember." She retrieved her cell phone from the coffee table.

"Where's your gym?" Zeke asked.

"A few blocks from my house." Katie typed a quick message into her phone before returning it to the table. "I live in Delaware." She named a city north of Columbus.

"What do you remember about her?" Zeke hoped she recalled something helpful. Anything.

Katie looked at her mother. "Now that I think about it, she asked a lot of questions about our family." Her cell phone beeped. She took it from the table to read the screen. "One of my friends from the gym thinks her name is something like Annie or Allie or Alex. Sorry." She sent a reply, then set the device on the table again.

"No problem." Celeste shook her head. "It's probably an alias. If she was involved in your father's death, she wouldn't have given her real name. But even an alias gives us a start."

Celeste was right. For that reason, Zeke recorded the six possible names on the writing pad in his portfolio. "What kinds of questions did she ask about your family?"

"She wanted to know if my parents lived nearby. Whether we spent a lot of time together and where we liked to go." Katie's memories seemed to stoke her temper. "She always looked like she was about to work out, which was really strange. I mean, she had her hair in a ponytail, and she always wore shorts and T-shirts. But she never did anything. She was never sweaty or anything. Who goes to a gym if they're not going to exercise? I've heard of people joining a gym but not going. I've never met anyone who gets up early, goes to the gym, but doesn't work out."

"Could you describe her for me?" Zeke turned to a blank page in his writing tablet. "Was her face thin or was it rounder like yours?"

"I wish I'd taken a picture of her with my phone." Katie frowned at the redbrick fireplace across the room. "Her face was fuller, but it wasn't quite round. She was about my height, five foot ten, and stocky. Her hair was light brown or a dark blond. She wore it in a ponytail, but she had bangs that covered her forehead and her eyebrows."

"What about her eyes?" As he spoke, Zeke sketched a round face fringed by heavy bangs, with hair swept back as though in a ponytail. "Was there anything special about them? Were they close together? Wide? Small?"

"Her eyes were unremarkable. I can't remember if they were blue or green." Katie shrugged helplessly. "They might have been brown. And she had a small, thin nose and thin lips."

"That's *really* good." Celeste's voice was low. She'd leaned closer to watch him work. "You're *really* talented."

Zeke could feel her warmth seeping into his clothing, getting under his skin. "Thank you." He looked at her, and their eyes locked. He didn't want to break their connection, but he had to. Summoning all his willpower, he pushed himself to his feet and crossed to Meryl and Katie on the sofa. He held out his portfolio to show them the sketch. "Is this what she looked like?"

Meryl's lips parted in surprise. "This is wonderful. Celeste's right. You're *very* talented."

"Yes, you are." Katie spoke the words on a breath. "I think her eyes are a little farther apart. And her bottom lip was fuller. And her cheekbones… I think her face is shaped more like a heart."

Zeke made the alterations to the sketch. He caught Celeste's vanilla-and-citrus scent as she came to stand beside him. He wanted to wrap an arm around her waist and pull her closer. Instead, he focused on moving Katie's Mystery Woman's eyes farther to the sides and making her bottom lip fuller and her cheekbones more prominent.

He turned the notepad back to Katie and her mother. "What do you think?"

Katie's jaw dropped. "Oh my gosh. That's her!" She jabbed her index finger toward the sketch. "That's her!"

Meryl looked from Katie to the notepad and back. "Are you sure?"

"I'm positive." Katie's voice hitched. She looked up at him. Her gray eyes were wide and dark with pain. "Do you think she killed my father?"

Zeke exchanged a look with Celeste. The caution he felt was reflected in her eyes. "There may not be a link between her and your father's death. The only way to know is to find her."

Katie's eyes returned to the sketch. "You've given me hope that my father's murderer will be caught."

Zeke tried to share her optimism. There was a lot at stake: his life, and his brothers' and Celeste's lives. He had to find the killer for all their sakes.

"Jerry's appetite's back." Mal's image appeared in the center of the camera during the videoconference Sunday afternoon. "But then, how long did we really expect his appetite to be gone?"

Zeke's responding quicksilver smile eased the tension from his features and captivated Celeste. He'd carried his clean laptop from her home office to her dining room. The table there provided enough space for them to sit together.

Zeke turned his smile to her. "Jerry's like a human garbage disposal."

Celeste didn't think the youngest Touré would appreciate their description of his eating habits, but she enjoyed being clued in on the joke. "But he's so fit."

"For now." Mal snorted. "Symone will bring him home from the hospital. Fill me in on your meeting with Meryl Bailey. Did she give you any insights on the guards?"

Zeke tapped his pen against his portfolio. "Meryl and her daughter, Katie Bailey-Smith, couldn't tell us anything about the guards—"

Celeste interrupted. "It sounded like Art didn't tell Meryl much about his employees."

Zeke nodded. "We'll have to rely on the personnel files she gave us."

Mal rested his right hand on a small stack of manila folders beside him. "I've started going through them. Art was very thorough."

"Good." Zeke turned to the page with the sketch of the Mystery Woman he'd redrawn and cleaned up. "Katie mentioned meeting someone recently at the gym she belongs to. Did you get the sketch I emailed earlier?"

Mal tapped a few keys on his computer. "You think this woman from Katie's gym could be involved? She doesn't match any of our four suspects, not even if they wore a disguise."

"That's true." Celeste leaned closer to Zeke, ostensibly to get a closer look at his sketch. She breathed in his soap-and-sandalwood scent. "But Katie said this woman had attached herself to her and her gym friends, and asked several questions about her family, then disappeared. She described her as 'creepy.'" Using both hands, Celeste made air quotes for "creepy."

Mal grunted. "I'd describe that as 'creepy,' too."

Zeke frowned at his illustration. "The woman's about five

ten and average build. Katie couldn't remember the color of her eyes but said her hair was either brown or dark blond."

Celeste leaned back against her chair. "Neither Katie nor her friends could remember the woman's name. If she's the killer, she would've given them a fake one anyway."

Zeke looked up at his computer monitor. "If I send you a more detailed sketch on unlined paper, do you think you can run it through your fancy facial-recognition program?"

Still seemingly looking at the photo file of the sketch, Mal arched an eyebrow. "*Our* facial-recognition program isn't that fancy. It's a basic trial membership. It'll recognize photos, but I'm not sure it'll recognize the photo of a sketch. It's worth a try. Send me the new image as soon as you have it."

Zeke nodded. "I'll get on that once we're done here. Also, I gave Meryl and Katie your business card and told them to contact you if they think of or hear anything else that could help identify the killer or an accomplice."

Mal switched his attention from the file to Zeke. "So you definitely think we're looking for more than one person? An accomplice?"

Zeke's shrug was a restless flex of his broad shoulders. Tension pulsed like an invisible force field around him. "If she were planning to kill Art, why did the Mystery Woman make contact with his daughter in Delaware? She must have known Art lives and works in Columbus. What purpose would it serve to connect with Katie?"

Mal rested his forearms on the table in front of the computer. "Maybe she was hoping Katie would tell her parents, making her contact with their daughter seem like a subtle threat. 'I can reach your family anywhere.'"

"I don't think that's it." Celeste's thoughts raced. Zeke was onto something. "Katie didn't tell her parents. Even if she had, why would they give the encounter a second thought? But if one of the guards wants revenge for being fired, why didn't they make both deaths look like either a suicide like Art's or a heart attack like Dean's? The killer wouldn't have reason to suspect the police would have questioned those deaths. Such elaborate staging makes it seem as though more than one person's involved, which begs the question: do we have the right motive."

Mal spread his hands. "If not revenge, then what?"

"I don't know. Yet." Celeste sighed. "But in case our killer isn't one of the guards—or if one of the guards is working with an accomplice—we need to cast a wider net. We're asking everyone about new acquaintances they've made within the last six months. So, Mal, besides Grace and Symone, have you made any new friends?"

Mal narrowed his eyes in thought. "I haven't but Kevin has. I'll do a background check on his new girlfriend."

"Great." Celeste loved action-oriented people like the Tourés. She pushed her chair back from her desk. "You do that. In the meantime, Zeke and I will chat with Jayne Archer."

She pulled her cell phone from the front pocket of her black jeans and used it to check the time. The widow of the recently deceased Realtor Dean Archer was expecting them in just over an hour. Would she or members of her family also have had an encounter with Katie's Mystery Woman? If so, the connection would elevate the Mystery Woman from creepy gym stalker to a certified suspect for murder. Celeste slipped her cell back into her pocket and glanced at Zeke. The urgency of their situation was like a punch to her chest. They needed to find this Mystery Woman before she found him.

Chapter 7

"Eriq said you think my husband was murdered." Jayne Archer sat across from Zeke and Celeste at her rectangular blond-wood kitchen table late Sunday afternoon. She looked and sounded as though she'd been crying for days. Her voice was raw. Behind her small, rimless glasses, her dark brown eyes were pink and puffy. "That would explain this letter."

She pushed a simple manila envelope across the table toward Zeke, handling it gingerly, as though it was hazardous waste. Seated beside him, Celeste squeezed his forearm before he could accept the packet. Reaching for her knapsack on the hardwood floor beside her chair, she pulled two pairs of disposable gloves from one of its many zippered compartments. Celeste gave one set to Zeke. She donned the other.

He tugged on the gloves, grateful she'd thought to bring them with her. Dean's full name was written in cursive across the front. "Do you recognize the handwriting?"

"No." Jayne's voice quivered, breaking the word into multiple syllables.

Zeke hadn't thought so, but he had to ask. His eyes dropped to the used tissue Jayne clutched in her right fist. He wished they didn't have to put her through this interview while her grief was still so fresh. He regretted having to question both mourning families. But in criminal investigations, time was of the essence.

He returned his attention to the envelope. He had a sick fore-boding about what they'd find inside. Zeke glanced at Celeste before pulling out the two plain white pages. He laid the papers on the table between them. The first sheet contained a two-word threat: *You're next.* The second was a full-color image of Dean getting into a gleaming bronze sedan.

Celeste stiffened. "Where did you find this?"

"In Dean's home office." Jayne removed her glasses before using her tattered tissue to dry her eyes.

"Did you ask him about it?" Reaching out, Celeste slid the box of facial tissues closer to their hostess. Jayne murmured her thanks.

"Of course." Her scowl was furious. Her brown cheeks were flushed. "He claimed it was a joke. I pushed him on it. I mean, who keeps a *joke* made in such poor taste? But he wouldn't change his story. He must've thought I was as dumb as a rock."

"No, ma'am." Zeke's response was firm. "He didn't think you were stupid. He was desperate to protect you."

"Zeke's right." Celeste drew the letter closer to her. "Never forget that Dean loved you very much. A love like that is rare."

Celeste sounded wistful, as though she was grieving a lost lover. Zeke frowned. Was he the one who gave her the ring she always wore on her thumb? Was that the reason she was reluctant to get involved with him? His heart tore a little.

He took a breath, then addressed Jayne. "Does Eriq know about this threat?"

"I'm giving it to him tonight." Jayne put her glasses back on. "He's joining my family and me for dinner. Would you two like to join us?"

Celeste blinked as though surprised. "Oh, no. But thank you." She pointed at the papers and envelope. "May I photograph these?"

Jayne glared at the items. "Of course."

As Celeste used her cell phone to capture the evidence, Zeke surveyed the kitchen. Thin white curtains were closed over both windows, blocking some of the sunlight and casting the cheery room into shadows. Pot holders along the stove, hand towels beside the refrigerator, and place mats on the table added colorful accents that eased the sterile backdrop of stainless steel appliances and snow-white walls. Half a dozen mugs, cups and partially filled glasses seemed forgotten on the white-and-yellow marble counter.

Zeke sipped the coffee Jayne had given them when they'd arrived. It had cooled. He set the white porcelain cup on its matching saucer. "Had Dean mentioned being worried about anything, or had he seemed preoccupied?"

"Yes." Jayne removed her glasses again and used a fresh tissue to dry her tears. "He had trouble sleeping. He was barely eating. He'd lost a lot of weight that he didn't need to lose. That's why I didn't question his having a heart attack. He'd been under so much stress."

"I understand." Celeste put the threat and the printed image into the envelope before sliding them across the table. "Had he given you any idea what was bothering him?"

Jayne shook her head, glaring at the packet. "He'd become so secretive. Maybe even paranoid."

"Paranoid?" Celeste glanced at Zeke.

"What makes you say that?" Zeke asked.

Jayne's frustration swept across the table like a gathering storm. "He'd stopped jogging outside and used the treadmill instead. He said he'd switched because of the heat. But it hadn't been that hot, and he *loved* running outdoors. He'd also started working from home more often and wouldn't tell me why." Her words came faster until they were almost running together. "Since he was being so mysterious, I decided to search his home office." She stabbed her finger toward the manila envelope. "That's when I found that vile message."

Zeke frowned, considering the package. If Dean's reclusiveness had been in reaction to that threat, why hadn't he brought it to Eriq? He wished the older man were still alive so he could ask him. Eriq might have been able to prevent Dean's death.

Celeste's voice refocused Zeke's wayward thoughts. "Had you or Dean made any new acquaintances in the past six months or so?"

Jayne's still-smooth brow furrowed. She dropped her eyes to the table. "None that I can think of at the moment." She rubbed her arms as though she'd felt a chill. She was wearing an oversize red T-shirt and loose-fitting navy shorts. Were they her husband's?

Celeste rotated the ring on her right thumb. "How about your children? Have they met anyone new?"

"I'll ask them." Jayne split a look between Celeste and Zeke. "Do you think the threat could be from someone we've recently met?"

"It's possible." Zeke pulled one of Mal's business cards and a manila folder from his briefcase. "If you think of anyone who's recently been introduced to you or if you learn of someone new in your children's lives, you can call my brother, Mal." He gave Mal's card to Jayne, then opened the folder to reveal the sketch of Katie Bailey-Smith's Mystery Woman. "Do you recognize this person?" He slid the sketch across the table to Jayne.

Jayne slipped her glasses back on and drew the image closer. "Oh, this is very good. Whoever drew it is very talented."

Celeste looked at Zeke. "Yes, he is."

The admiration in her eyes made Zeke's cheeks warm. He tugged his gaze away. "Thank you. Does the woman in the sketch look familiar?"

"Nooo." Jayne drew the syllable out with uncertainty. "Wait." She laid the sketch back on the table and placed her long, slender left hand over the top of the head. It sounded as though her words were being pulled from her. "She might, but I'm not sure. About a week before…his death, I went to Dean's office. He'd been so depressed. I wanted to surprise him with a lunch date. I'd styled my hair and took extra time with my makeup. And I wore my favorite dress with heels." She smiled softly at the memory. "When I arrived, he was talking with a young woman who claimed to want to list her house with him. But she had short red hair—too short for a ponytail."

"Why did you say she *claimed* to want to list her house with Dean?" Celeste asked.

Jayne glanced at the sketch again before raising her eyes to Celeste. "The woman was in her mid- to late twenties. I would have expected her to fill out the agency's online form rather than coming into the office. For someone in that age group, that seemed odd to me."

"That does seem weird." Celeste glanced toward Zeke before returning her attention to Jayne.

"Why are you covering the top half of the sketch?" Zeke inclined his head toward Jayne's hand. She seemed to have forgotten it still lay on the paper.

"There was something else that was odd about her." Jayne lifted her left hand and turned the sketch toward Celeste and Zeke. "She wore very large dark sunglasses that she kept on the whole time she was meeting with Dean. Who does that?"

"You were in Dean's office during the entire meeting?" Celeste asked.

"They weren't discussing state secrets." Jayne shrugged one shoulder. "And I used to help Dean at the agency when he first opened it. Anyway, I remember thinking the sunglasses were too big for her and that they drew attention to the lower half of her face. She had a small, pointed chin, and her lower lip was fuller than her upper lip, just like in your sketch. I can't swear it's the same person, but it's quite a coincidence."

Zeke reached for the sketch at the same time Celeste did. He positioned it between them.

Celeste looked up at Jayne. "Your attention to detail is amazing. I can't believe you caught that."

Jayne smiled at Zeke. "The praise belongs to the artist. You're very talented, Zeke. You put so much detail into the image it looks almost lifelike."

"Thank you." Zeke returned his attention to the drawing. There was now a possible connection between this Mystery Woman and both of their victims, despite her obvious efforts to conceal her identity. Who was she, and what was her connection to Archer Family Realty, Buckeye Bailey Security and Touré Security Group?

"If Jayne's right, Katie's Mystery Woman is another connection between Art and Dean." Celeste felt Zeke's energy beside her at the dining table Sunday evening. They were videoconferencing with Mal. Fresh from the hospital, Jerry had also joined them. "Which supports our theory that the connection between

Archer Family Realty, Buckeye Bailey and TSG is the Archer contract, and that the motive is revenge."

"That makes the most sense." Jerry looked uncomfortable in what appeared to be his home office. The cast on his left arm was too prominent to ignore. The scarlet T-shirt beneath the gray hooded sweat jacket emphasized the pallor of his tense, chiseled features. When they'd asked, he'd said he felt fine. Obviously, he was lying.

Mal had rolled up the sleeves of his lightweight smoke gray sweater. "While we're on the subject of the Mystery Woman, Kevin's girlfriend broke up with him. She told him she was going home to Toronto."

"Well, that's not suspicious much." Jerry's response was as dry as dust. "Another person who mysteriously enters, then mysteriously disappears from the life of someone connected to a target in this case."

Mal grunted his agreement. "I'll show him the sketch tomorrow. I didn't want to text it to him in case his ex cloned his phone—"

Jerry interrupted. "Good thinking."

Zeke nodded. "Yes. Thanks for taking care of that."

Mal moved some files around on his desk. "Unfortunately, the facial-recognition program we have isn't able to work with the sketch."

"Thanks for trying." Celeste rotated the sterling silver ring she wore on her right thumb.

"Yeah, nerd. It was worth the effort." Jerry's attempt at humor was strained. "Mata Hari keeps showing up all over our case, but we don't know how she could be connected. Is there another angle with the contract?"

"Or for a second killer?" Mal's voice was tight, as though he was struggling under the pressure of having his brothers in danger.

Zeke rubbed the back of his neck. "Do you think there could be two killers with two different motives for murder?"

Celeste looked to Zeke, trying not to get lost in his coal-black eyes. "It's a solid theory and would explain why she's partnering with one or more of the guards, *if* that's what she's doing."

Zeke turned back to his brothers. "Are there possible connections between our Mystery Woman and the fired guards?"

Mal tapped on his laptop's keyboard. "Two of the four guards assigned to the Archer account were women. Agnes Letby, sixty-two, and May Ramirez, sixty."

"Jayne said our Mystery Woman is in her twenties." Jerry's tone was pensive. "I'm doing the background check on Ramirez now. She has three daughters. All in their thirties. None of them live in Ohio."

Celeste didn't see that as an obstacle. "They don't have to *live* in Ohio. One of them could be visiting. And maybe they're in their thirties but look like they're in their twenties."

"So we're searching for two killers." Zeke pinched the bridge of his nose. "Right now I can't think of an alternative motive that connects our three companies."

"Unless it's a case of hell having no fury like a woman scorned." Jerry raised his uninjured right hand, palm out. "Hear me out. Are we sure one of the widows isn't involved? Maybe Meryl killed Dean for canceling his contract with Art, then killed her husband because his failing business was putting a strain on their finances."

Celeste folded her hands on the desk in front of her. "That's an interesting theory. But why would Meryl hire me to find her husband's killer? That's like hiring me to find herself. Why wouldn't she just confess?"

Zeke's soft laughter stirred the butterflies in Celeste's abdomen. "Don't go soft on him just because he's injured. Even in pain, Jerry can dish insults as well as take them. Don't let him fool you."

"Thanks for letting me know." Celeste flashed him a grin and watched the light spark in his eyes.

"Whatever, man." Jerry gave them a crooked smile. "What about Jayne?"

Zeke spread his hands. "Victims' spouses are usually the top suspects, but we don't have a motive for Jayne. Eriq said they were happy and had a strong marriage."

Jerry ran his right hand over his tight curls. "I had to ask."

Zeke closed his portfolio. "In the morning, Celeste and I

will start our interviews of Art's former guards with Damien Rockwell. We'll try to find out if he's connected to this woman without pushing her farther underground."

Celeste gave Zeke a warning look. "We also don't want to give away too much about our investigation and lose our edge."

Mal sat back against his chair, shrinking his image on the computer screen. "You'll have the background report on Rockwell within the hour."

"That'll be great. Thank you." Zeke shared a look between Mal and Jerry. "I wish we knew for certain neither of you were targets. Are you sure you haven't received threatening messages, either written or recorded?"

Mal arched a thick black eyebrow. "We'd know if we'd received one of those. I haven't."

"Neither have I," Jerry said.

Celeste crossed her arms under her chest. The answer seemed obvious to her. "You're in charge of TSG's Corporate Security Division. You worked on the contract with Dean. That's the reason the killer's identified *you*, not your brothers." She turned to Mal's and Jerry's images on the screen. "But that doesn't mean you guys are in the clear. Stay sharp. Zeke's the primary target, but the killer could come after *you* to get to *him*."

If Meryl hadn't asked her to investigate Art's suspicious death, Celeste wouldn't have realized Zeke was the target of serial killers. She hadn't believed Art had been murdered—not at first. But now she knew Meryl had been right. Someone had killed her husband and made it look like suicide. The same person—or people—appeared to have killed Jayne's husband. Now they were targeting the man she... What? All right, she had feelings for Zeke. Very strong feelings. Celeste wanted justice for both widows and their murdered spouses. But her sense of urgency was focused on Zeke. She had to keep him safe. She had to find the people who were threatening him. At any cost.

If he reached out, his fingertips would almost touch Celeste's mattress. Zeke's palms tingled with that thought late Sunday night. His makeshift bed lay between Celeste and her chest of drawers. He turned his head against the pillow and stared at the ceiling. An image of Celeste as she'd looked before he'd turned off the light was superimposed over its shadows. She'd pulled her fluffy white coverlets over her chest. Thin cream ribbons of material wrapped her slender shoulders. Curiosity and desire had branded a question on his mind: What did Celeste Jarrett wear to bed?

After reading Mal's report on Damien Rockwell, the former Buckeye Bailey Security guard whom he and Celeste would interview in the morning, Zeke had needed a mental break. He'd wanted to clear his mind so he could approach the case from a fresh perspective. But filling his thoughts with Celeste would not help him get a good night's sleep.

"Are you worried about your brothers?" Celeste's soft whisper was like a jolt of electricity.

Zeke started. He turned his head toward her voice. His eyes had adjusted to the dark. He could make out the bed, but from this angle, he couldn't see her lying on it. That was for the best.

Trails of light from the moon and nearby porch lamps slipped into the room from the edges of the window's curtains. The constant chirp of crickets from her yard and the occasional swoosh of cars rolling down her street created their background music. The faint scent of Celeste's vanilla-and-citrus perfume was everywhere.

Zeke frowned. "How did you know I was awake?"

"Are you kidding?" Her low chuckle caused the muscles in his gut to tighten. "I can feel your tension way over here."

He rolled onto his left side. "You can sense my tension, but in the mornings, I can't hear you make your bed or leave your house."

Her sheets rustled as though she was shifting on her mattress. Was she deliberately being noisy to pile onto his confusion?

"I'm a trained investigator." She kept her voice low, as though she didn't want to be overheard by...whom? "I'm adept at being undetected."

"Well, lady, you've got mad skills. Not even my parents were as talented."

Her low laughter tied his abdominal muscles in knots. "I'm flattered. Your parents are still highly regarded in the security and law enforcement communities."

He forced himself to breathe. "I mean it."

"So do I." Celeste hesitated. "I know you wouldn't say something like that if you didn't mean it. So thank you."

"You're welcome." Zeke rolled onto his back, searching for a way to fill the awkward silence.

Celeste threw him a lifeline. "I understand your concern for your brothers' safety. But, Zeke, they can take care of themselves. That's their job, taking care of themselves and other people."

"I know. But I don't even have the words to describe how scared I was when that car struck Jerry." He rubbed his eyes with the heels of his hands as though he could erase the memory. "Standing there, all I could do was watch his body roll over the car, then fall onto the street. I never want to feel that afraid or useless again."

"I understand." Her words were soft sympathy. "You and your brothers are so close. And you're used to being in control. That attack took that security from you. Thankfully, Jerry will be all right."

"Thank God for that." Why did she think he was controlling? His brothers often accused him of the same thing. "And thank you, for listening."

"Of course." Her sheets rustled again, almost as though she was making a big performance of rolling back over on the bed. A trace of amusement entered her voice. "Will you be able to sleep now? If not, I'm happy to switch places with you. Maybe you'd sleep better on a real mattress."

Zeke chuckled. "My father's ghost would haunt me for the rest of my life if I were to toss a woman out of her own bed." He lay still and let her laughter caress him.

"If you're sure." Celeste's voice rolled with amusement. "You need your rest."

"As do you." He was reluctant to bring their conversation to an end, but it was getting late. "Good night, Celeste. Sleep well."

"See you in the morning, Zeke." Her sheets rustled again.

Yes, you will. Bright and early.

Zeke smiled at the ceiling. She wasn't going to leave her home undetected for a second morning in a row. His pride was on the line.

Chapter 8

"Thanks for meeting me so early." Damien Rockwell glanced at his silver Timex Monday morning. His thin dark brown features were tight with tension. "My shift starts soon, and I don't want to mess up this job, especially after what happened at Buckeye Bailey."

Zeke and Celeste stood with Damien near the parking lot behind the glass-and-metal building that housed the offices of Damien's new employer. According to Mal's background report, it had taken Damien six weeks to find a new job. The post with the investment company appeared to be a step up for him.

"The appointment time is fine. We're morning people." Zeke gave Celeste on his left a pointed look.

Hours later, it still stung that, for the second morning in a row, Celeste had made her bed, gotten dressed, and left her home for a predawn jog and he hadn't heard her. How did she do it?

"I don't know if I can really help." Damien's almond-shaped dark brown eyes shifted between Zeke and Celeste. Beneath his security guard uniform—white shirt with a black tie, blazer, pants and loafers—he had the long, wiry build of an avid runner. "You really think someone killed Art? That's cray. Who would do that?"

"We think his death is connected to the Archer Family Realty account." Zeke wondered about the twentysomething's agitation. Was it all due to his need to get to work on time? Or was something more behind it?

Damien frowned his confusion. "Why would Dean Archer off Art?"

Celeste shook her head. "Dean Archer was also killed. We're looking into both murders."

"But you two aren't cops?" Damien waved a hand between Zeke and Celeste.

Celeste shrugged her knapsack off her left shoulder and set it on the sidewalk between her black loafers. "We're investigators, but we're working with the police."

Damien looked around, then lowered his voice. "To be honest, I don't like talking about the past, you know? I'm still embarrassed about getting fired. I didn't really know what I was doing, all right?"

"What does that mean?" Celeste frowned up at the guard. He was a few inches shorter than Zeke but several inches taller than Celeste. "You didn't know you were sleeping on the job?"

"Shh! Keep your voice down." Damien's cheeks flushed pink. He tossed furtive glances behind both narrow shoulders before continuing. "That's not what I meant. I'd just, you know, graduated from college. I was still kind of transitioning from student to, you know, responsible adult. But I've got my act together now. Being unemployed has a way of forcing you to get serious and really grow up."

It wasn't yet seven o'clock, but already more than half a dozen employees had arrived at the investment firm. The company followed the same procedures Touré Security Group recommended to its clients. Zeke observed the staff using identification cards to access its secure entrance. He'd seen two guards at an identification-screening station in the center of the lobby.

"At least you landed on your feet." Celeste gestured toward him. "And you must be making more money here than you'd made with Buckeye Bailey." She surveyed their surroundings.

A dozen or so vehicles—dark SUVs, bright compact sedans, and dark gray or silver hatchbacks—stood in the asphalt parking lot. Black mulch beds nurtured young burning bushes and small evergreen shrubs. In the distance, rush hour traffic congested US Route 23. The scents of moist earth, cut grass and engine exhaust surrounded them. Zeke focused on Celeste's vanilla-and-citrus perfume.

Damien stiffened. His eyes narrowed with suspicion. "Yeah. New job, new company, more money. There's nothing wrong with that."

Zeke frowned. "No, there's not." Then why was the younger man defensive? "As we explained when we contacted you yesterday, we just have a few questions about your time with Buckeye Bailey Security and Archer Family Realty. Was there tension between any of the guards and management?"

Damien hesitated. "I don't know if I'm comfortable talking about other people."

"This is a homicide investigation." Celeste shoved her hands into the front pockets of her black slacks. She wore them with a black button-down shirt and black jacket. "If you've seen or heard anything that could help our investigation, you're compelled to share it."

"So how about it, Damien?" Zeke shrugged, trying to cut some of the building tension. "Were there any conflicts between Art and your colleagues?"

Damien's expression eased from wariness to resignation. "All right. I did overhear Art arguing with a couple of people about their payroll deposits. But you didn't hear it here."

"What about their deposits?" Zeke prompted to get Damien talking again.

"They were late." Damien's eyes stretched wide with horror. "You know, I think Art was having cash flow problems. One guy said his pay had been late *twice*." He held up two fingers as though emphasizing the gravity of the situation. "Yeah, Art must've *really* been having *a lot* of money trouble."

Zeke made a mental note to fact-check Damien's theory about Art's money. If his competitor were having financial challenges, what was the source? "Which guard had more than one late payroll deposit?"

Damien's expression conveyed his reluctance to give up the name. Zeke sensed Celeste's impatience. "Cooper. Chad Cooper. That's one guy I wouldn't want to cross. Dude looks like he's straight out of Rikers."

Chad Cooper was also on their suspect list. But according to Mal's preliminary report, Chad was in prison for aggravated assault and robbery. His sentence had started days before Art's murder. That was an airtight alibi.

Unless Chad was working with someone on the outside. Katie's Mystery Woman, perhaps?

"Did you ever hear Chad threaten Art?" A cool breeze played with Celeste's wavy dark brown tresses. She brushed the hair from her eyes.

"Nah." Damien shook his head. "He was furious, but he never really took it *that* far. The closest he got to a threat was saying something like, 'This better never happen again.' You know? I mean, you can't blame the guy for being angry that Art stiffed him. Everyone's got bills. And if you do the work, you need to be paid."

"What about you?" Celeste watched Damien closely. "Did you ever get stiffed?"

"Nope." Damien's chest puffed out with pride. "Not once."

"Really?" Celeste's straight black eyebrows flew up her forehead. "If everyone else's checks were bouncing, why didn't yours?"

"Not *everyone's*. Just a couple of people." Damien's response carried a thread of irritation. Annoyance glittered in his dark eyes. "Or maybe it was just Chad's. I don't remember."

Celeste glanced at Zeke before addressing Damien. "If your memory comes back, please call us. The payroll issues could be an important point."

Zeke shared Celeste's frustration, but he wouldn't pile on to Damien. Instead, he took a calming breath before asking something else. "Where were you August 22?"

Damien's expression went blank. Zeke sensed him sifting through his memories. "I don't know. Wait. That was a Friday. The Guardians were playing." The guard referenced Cleveland's Major League Baseball team. "I was at a sports bar, watching the game with friends."

They could ask Eriq to confirm that later, if necessary. Zeke pulled the sketch of their Mystery Woman from his inside jacket pocket. "Do you recognize her?"

Damien took the sketch from him. He frowned as he studied the drawing before giving it back. "No. Sorry. She's cute, though. Who is she?"

"That's what we're trying to find out." Zeke folded the sheet and returned it to his pocket.

Celeste gave Damien a considering look. "You don't seem overly concerned that Art was murdered."

"Art was okay, even though he fired me." Damien crossed his arms over his narrow chest. "We weren't friends, but I didn't have anything to do with his death, if that's what you're getting at."

"And how was your relationship with Dean Archer?" Zeke asked.

Damien shook his head and spread his arms. "I don't think I ever spoke two words to Mr. Archer."

"Have you received any threatening messages?" Celeste's abrupt change of topic surprised the younger man.

Damien rocked back on his heels. "No." He glanced at Zeke before turning back to Celeste. "Do you think I will? Should I be worried?"

"If you get a note, yes." Celeste looked at Zeke. "Do you have any other questions?"

Zeke understood Celeste's tough approach, but the surprise on Damien's face got to him. He couldn't walk away when the younger man looked so unsettled. He pulled a generic Touré Security Group business card from the same inside jacket pocket that secured the sketch of their Mystery Woman. He didn't want to leave his or his brothers' information all over Franklin County. "We don't believe the killer is targeting you, but if you have any concerns—or if you think of anything else—call us."

He and Celeste thanked Damien for his time, then strode back to her car. "Do you want me to drive?"

She frowned at him. "It's my car, control freak."

He heard Jerry's voice in the uncomplimentary nickname. Shaking off the memory, he veered toward the passenger door of Celeste's black four-door sedan. "Maybe you could go a little easier on the next suspect."

She paused, meeting his eyes across the hood of her car. "We get more information when one of us plays tough and the other is empathetic. If you'd like, next time you can be the empathetic one."

She must be kidding.

Zeke gave her a skeptical look. "You're not as gruff as you pretend to be."

She arched an eyebrow as though challenging him. "You don't think so?"

"No, I don't."

"I'd hate to disappoint you." Celeste disappeared through her driver-side door.

Zeke folded himself onto the passenger seat. "Tough as nails or soft like bread, you could never disappoint me."

Something in Celeste's expression shifted. She blinked and the moment was gone. "I'll hold you to that."

Why did he have the sense she was only half joking? Celeste navigated her car out of the parking lot, leaving him with another mystery to solve.

"Kevin recognized the woman in Zeke's sketch." Mal made the announcement during their videoconference. He and Jerry were in the Touré Security Group conference room Monday morning.

Celeste didn't know why she was surprised, but she was. She'd suspected the serial killer had found a way into Zeke's inner circle the same way she'd made contact with Art's daughter.

"Who is she?" Zeke sat beside Celeste at her dining room table.

"His ex." Mal flexed his shoulders. "She told him her name was Anne Castle. It's probably an alias."

"Kevin said she's a green-eyed brunette." Jerry seemed to be getting used to the cast on his left arm, which was fortunate. His doctor had told him he'd have to wear it for at least six weeks, until the end of October. "She must have been wearing a disguise for at least one of these identities."

Celeste rotated the ring on her right thumb as she shifted through her memories. "She was a blonde with Katie, a redhead with Dean and Jayne, and a brunette with Kevin."

Mal crossed his arms over the ice blue shirt that stretched across his broad chest. He wore it with a navy tie. "Kevin said she was curious about TSG. She told him she wanted to be a police officer, but if that didn't work out, her fallback was security—"

Jerry grunted. "That's hurtful."

Mal ignored the interruption. "Fortunately, Kevin didn't tell her anything. It's against policy to share processes and procedures."

Celeste shivered with a sudden chill. She found and held Zeke's eyes. "That rule saved your life." She tore her eyes from his. "Did she give him a number, email, address?"

Jerry ran a hand over his tight dark brown curls. "Kev tried her cell. The number's no longer in service. And the address she gave him is a furniture store on the east side."

"What about a photo?" Zeke's voice was starting to reveal his frustration. Celeste understood.

"Nothing usable." Mal rubbed the back of his neck. "She didn't like having her picture taken. In the few images Kevin has, she's covering her face."

"If I were a serial killer, I wouldn't want anyone taking my photo, either." Jerry's deep sigh expanded his chest and lifted his shoulders. "Poor Kev."

Celeste winced at the painful memory of her own love-stricken mistake. That had been five years ago. She'd been older than Kevin appeared to be. All things considered, Kevin's situation had turned out well. His circumspection had prevented real harm from coming to the Touré family. Celeste hadn't been as lucky.

Zeke's right shoulder brushed Celeste as he sat back against his dining room chair. Heat spread across her chest, and up and down her arm. "Kevin may know more than he thinks. She may have let some comment slip that could tell us where she likes to hang out or where she's really from or even where she went to school."

Jerry jumped on that. "I'll follow up with him."

"Thank you." Zeke's impatience once again seemed under control. "In the meantime, Damien Rockwell thinks Art was having financial trouble. Mal, could you dig around to see if that's true? If it is, we need to know what was straining his accounts. Did he owe someone money?"

"I'm on it." Mal typed something into his electronic tablet in front of him.

Celeste shifted to face Zeke. "Meryl didn't say anything about money being tight."

Jerry drummed the fingers of his right hand on the conference table. "Are we sure she's not a suspect?"

Celeste turned to Jerry's computer image. "Didn't we have this conversation yesterday?"

"Hear me out." Jerry raised his right hand, palm out. "What if she and Jayne agreed to kill each other's husband?"

Zeke's thick black eyebrows knitted. "You mean, like the plot of *Strangers on a Train*?"

Jerry jabbed his index finger toward Zeke. "Exactly."

"No." Zeke's tone was final. "Seriously, Jer. Let this one go. There's no *there* there."

Celeste said a prayer that Jerry listened to his brother. "Damien should stay on our suspect list."

"I agree." Zeke finally looked away from her as he considered his brothers' images on the monitor. "Why was he the only guard whose pay was never late?"

Jerry shrugged his uninjured right shoulder. "Maybe he's lying about Art having cash flow issues."

"Or about his deposits never being late," Mal suggested.

Celeste felt a rush of adrenaline. Brainstorming investigations with the Tourés was like running mental sprints. She enjoyed the way the brothers worked their cases together and advanced—or dismissed—ideas and suggestions. She also appreciated being treated as though she'd always been part of their team.

With Nanette, she often felt as though she was doing the heavy lifting on her cases as well as her partner's. Another confirmation that she was making the right decision by remaining in Columbus. As much as she liked her business partner, she didn't want to start fresh with Nanette in San Diego just to continue the same pattern of behavior. She'd rather continue their agency on her own.

"We need to set up our next interview." Zeke's statement was a call to wrap their meeting.

Jerry tapped a command into the laptop with Mal's help. "Next up is May Ramirez. I've just sent both of you a copy of the background report on her. Mal and I have already gone over it. May's close to retirement. She's divorced. She has four children, two grandchildren and perfect credit. After being fired from BBS, she took a job as a security guard at the Deep Discount Mart in Dublin. Her work contact information's in the report."

Zeke was already uploading the file onto his smart tablet. "Great work. Thanks."

"And with one arm. Thank you." Celeste exchanged a teasing smile with Jerry before printing the file from her laptop. She heard the faint hum of the printer in her office upstairs.

Jerry grinned. "Don't mention it."

Mal's fingers danced across his tablet. "Jer and I are working on the final two guards: Agnes Short and Chad Cooper. Agnes is retired and remarried. She and her new husband recently moved to North Carolina. You can take her, Jer."

Jerry leaned closer to Mal's tablet. "Her being out of town doesn't clear her, though. She could be working with Kev's ex, Anne Castle."

Mal inclined his head toward his screen. "So could Chad Cooper. His prison sentence started in June, two months *before* Art's murder."

Zeke stared across the dining room, as though the resolution to their case was written on the far wall. "They'd both have perfect alibis if we hadn't stumbled across the Mystery Woman."

"We didn't stumble. That was solid investigative work." Celeste rolled her eyes. "I'm more than just a sparkling personality."

Zeke's grin banished the lines of fatigue from his chiseled

features—and dazzled Celeste. "You're right, of course. Please forgive me."

Celeste was pretty sure he was mocking her. She ignored him. "To your point, the Mystery Woman could be working with any of our suspects. Or all of them."

Jerry shook his head in disbelief. "So instead of reducing our list of suspects, we've actually added to it?"

"It seems like it." Celeste shrugged. "We'll interview Agnes and Chad but prioritize the two suspects who are local and not in jail." She stood. "I'll ask May if we could meet with her this afternoon. We need to keep up the momentum of our interviews."

The sooner they completed these interviews, the sooner they could solve this case. Hopefully. Then Zeke would be safe—and so would her heart.

"Lunch is ready." Celeste spoke from the doorway of her home office Monday afternoon. "I also got a hold of May Ramirez. We're meeting her at four."

Her words pulled Zeke from the draft of his business plan. He'd been building out charts, notes and calculations since he and Celeste had ended their videoconference with Mal and Jerry almost two hours ago.

He stood and stretched, finally registering the aromas of spicy chicken soup with fresh vegetables, including onions, tomatoes and peppers. "I'm sorry. I meant to help cook. I lost track of time."

Celeste waved a hand toward the stacks of printouts beside his laptop. "What are you working on?"

He flexed his shoulders to ease their stiffness. "Updates to TSG's business plan."

Celeste turned to lead him downstairs. "It looks like you're struggling with it."

Zeke followed her into the dining room. She'd set the blond-wood dining table. Lunch was served on matching brown-and-white cotton crocheted table mats. Both settings contained a medium-sized cream porcelain bowl filled with chicken-vegetable soup, a smaller matching bowl of garden salad and a clear acrylic glass of lemonade.

"I *am* struggling." Zeke held her chair before circling the table to his seat. "This looks and smells wonderful. Thank you so much. If you don't mind my using your kitchen, I can cook dinner. It's not fair that you do all the cooking."

On the center of the table, three vanilla votive candles stood to the right and three more to the left of a large, round brown-tinted glass bowl filled with vanilla potpourri. The bowl was centered on another brown-and-white cotton crocheted table mat.

"I don't mind your using my kitchen at all. I'd like to try your cooking." Celeste tossed him a teasing smile as she spread a brown napkin on her lap. "What's your specialty dish?"

"That would be my blackened chicken with asparagus spears." Zeke dug into his salad. It was a meal by itself. Celeste had filled it with baby spinach, cucumbers, celery, carrots, raisins, mushrooms, onions, and cheddar and mozzarella cheeses. He appreciated a salad that was more than a bowl of lonely iceberg lettuce.

They talked about the entrees they enjoyed cooking, their comfort foods, favorite restaurants and go-to desserts. Time flew. Zeke felt himself relaxing, as he always did in her company. And this time she didn't dodge his questions. If they'd talked about cooking during their coffee date, could they have worked up to more personal questions over lunch? He'd never know. Anyway, that was in the past. Whether they had a future was up to Celeste.

Collecting her place setting, Celeste turned toward the kitchen. "I understand what you're going through with your business plan. Those things are the worst."

Zeke stacked his dishes and followed her. "It would be easier if I weren't worried about these threats against my family."

"It also would be easier if you weren't doing it on your own." Celeste looked at him over her shoulder. "There *are* three of you, you know. Why don't you let your brothers help?"

He set his dishes on the counter near the dishwasher, then returned to the dining room to continue clearing the table. "We're equal partners, but I've been the de facto director since our parents died."

Celeste was silent for a beat or two. "You and your brothers expanded your marketing beyond the small companies that have been your agency's bread and butter. You're reaching out to medium and large businesses."

"That's right." Zeke shrugged his shoulders, trying to ease his sudden tension. He carried the pitcher of lemonade to the fridge. "I'm worried about industry trends. We need to be proactive, anticipating changes, instead of reactive."

Celeste's expression was thoughtful as she loaded the dishwasher. What was she thinking? "You've been getting a lot of press lately, too, because of the high-profile cases you've been involved in." Her grin was sheepish. "I've been a little jealous."

A smile replaced his frown. "Is that right?"

"A little bit." She lifted her left hand, measuring perhaps half an inch with her index finger and thumb. "But my point is, aren't the marketing changes you've made and the press you've been getting enough? At least for now? Do you think it's a good idea to add a lot of new services at the same time?"

"We've got to try something." Zeke closed the refrigerator door and clenched his fist around its handle.

"What does that mean?" She straightened to look at him. Her voice was brittle with concern. "What's going on, Zeke?"

Zeke released his grip on the refrigerator. He pinched the bridge of his nose. "I told you I took the lead on the operating decisions for TSG."

"And?" She finished packing the dishwasher.

Shame swamped him. "My decisions haven't always been strategic. In fact, a couple of them have been pretty stupid and have hurt the company."

"Hurt the company?" Celeste stilled, frowning at him in disbelief. "What are you talking about? TSG is solid. It has a great reputation, not just in the security industry but in the business community as a whole."

"Maybe from the outside looking in." Zeke blew out a breath. "We're running the agency. We're paying our bills on time. We're making payroll for our contractors. But we haven't paid ourselves in months." He risked a look at Celeste. Her expression of surprise made him clench his teeth.

"Well, that won't continue for much longer." Celeste spread her hands. "You've been getting so many calls you've had to hire an office assistant for the first time in TSG's history."

Zeke moved the soup pot from the stove to the sink and filled it with water. "How did you know that was the reason we hired Kevin?"

"I'm an investigator, remember?" She arched an eyebrow and looked at him from under her long, thick eyelashes. "I can add two and two and get to four. Why else would you hire an admin when your thirty-year-old agency has never had one before?"

Her indignant tone made him smile. "I apologize. I didn't mean to offend you."

"Apology accepted." Celeste inclined her head.

Zeke finished scrubbing the pot, then rinsed it. Steam rose from the faucet. "Do you really think I'm a control freak?" He braced himself for her answer.

"You're with me because you don't want your brothers taking care of you." She leaned against the kitchen counter and crossed her arms under her chest. "You're beating yourself up over business decisions your brothers must have approved. So yes, I think you're a control freak. You think so, too, otherwise you wouldn't be asking."

Zeke couldn't deny a word of what she'd said. "What's wrong with my wanting to keep my brothers safe?" He placed the pot on the drainboard.

Celeste straightened from the counter and circled him. She took the pot from the drainboard and dried it with a dish towel she'd taken from a hook near the stove. "I'm confident things will get better soon for you and your brothers."

"I hope so." He dried his hands with a paper towel from the roll suspended above the counter. "I've been thinking about what Damien Rockwell said about Art and Buckeye Bailey. TSG's finances are on shaky ground. I can see myself in Art's position. One bad decision, one lost client could damage our company. I've got to find a way to stabilize our finances."

"You can't compare TSG to Buckeye Bailey." Celeste bent to return the pot to the lower cupboard. "Your agencies are very different. You provide annual training to your contractors and hold them to a higher standard. I don't mean to speak ill of the dead, but Art was well-known for cutting corners."

Zeke wanted to hold on to her encouraging words with both fists. But she didn't have the full picture. "We're still paying off debt from the cabin construction. It was originally intended as a secluded vacation spot for high-profile clients who wanted their privacy. We aren't getting as much use out of it as I'd hoped."

"At least you're able to pay it off." Celeste propped herself against the refrigerator. "You and your brothers will figure it out. Take a breath and step back. The answer's probably right in front of you. Right now you're just too busy to see it."

The tension in his neck and shoulders untangled. The way she listened to his concerns soothed him. Her reassurances encouraged him. But it was the expression in her wide hazel eyes that drew him to her. She believed in him even as he doubted himself. Before he realized it, he'd drawn Celeste into his arms and lowered his lips to hers.

Chapter 9

Celeste's breath caught in her throat. She'd seen the light in Zeke's coal-black eyes shift. She'd felt the air between them sizzle. Yet his kiss surprised her. In a good way. A very good way, like waking from a wonderful dream and realizing you hadn't been asleep.

She leaned into him, deepening their kiss. Zeke's arms wrapped around her waist, drawing her even closer. Her muscles trembled. Her mind blanked. She parted her lips on a sigh. Zeke's tongue pressed against them, urging her to open wider, then swooping in. He teased and caressed her, tasting her and allowing her to sample him. Celeste mimicked his actions. Zeke groaned in response. His large hands slid down her back and cupped her hips to his. Celeste melted. Her blood heated. She raised up on her toes to fit herself more closely to him. She wanted more. She wanted now.

She wanted him.

Her cell phone screamed. Celeste flinched. Her eyes sprang open. They locked with Zeke's. The heat in their dark depths set her body on fire. Her cell sounded again. Its vibration was trapped between her right derriere and Zeke's left hand.

"You should get that." The pulse pounding in her ears muffled Zeke's voice. He released her hips. His warm, rough palms moved over her arms, drawing her hands from his shoulders. "It could be related to the case."

Before she could stop him, he'd turned from her and strode out of the kitchen.

Darn it.

Celeste pulled her phone from the back pocket of her black jeans. She checked the caller ID. It was Nanette, the human prophylactic. "What's going on?"

"I thought you were ignoring me." Her partner sounded confused.

"I couldn't even if I'd wanted to." *And I had.*

"You don't sound happy to hear from me." Her voice betrayed her pout.

If only you knew. Her abdominal muscles tightened with residual yearning. "It's this case. I've got a lot on my mind." *Like the way Zeke tasted on my tongue.*

"Oh. How's it going?" Nanette seemed distracted.

Was she counting the RSVPs to her wedding reception? Reviewing the menu options? Checking her seating plan? Whatever Nanette was doing, Celeste knew her partner wasn't interested in her murder investigation, so why had she called?

"We're checking leads, but what do you need?" Celeste stopped in front of the bay window in her living room.

She scanned her surroundings through its sheer curtains. Her neighborhood didn't have sidewalks, and the narrow two-way street in front of her home didn't invite cars to linger. In other words, it wasn't a hospitable surveillance environment for serial killers. But she wasn't taking any of that for granted with Zeke's safety at stake. She craned her neck west and east. Any pedestrians nearby? Cars moving slowly? Items displaced on her walkway? No, no and no. The tension in her shoulders eased a bit. Celeste refocused on Nanette's voice.

"Have you reconsidered moving to San Diego with me?" Beneath Nanette's voice, papers rustled and tape dispensers screeched.

"You mean you *and* Warren?" Celeste spun on her bare heel and strode through her living room, dining room and foyer.

"Of course that's what I mean. We're getting married."

Celeste's patience was straining. "And I've already told you I'm not moving to San Diego."

Earlier, she'd opened the venetian blinds over the tinted glass of the French doors that led onto her rear deck. Both her ten-by-six-foot oak deck and her yard, which stretched beyond the structure, were empty. *Good.*

"But I'd really like you with me." Nanette's voice bordered on a whine. "We make a good team. Won't you reconsider?"

Celeste scanned as far as she could see beyond her yard. "Nanette, I'm investigating a serial killer, remember? The person I'm protecting is another target. I don't have time to think about anything else, including your wedding." *Or the way Zeke's body felt pressed against mine.*

Nanette's heavy sigh trudged down the satellite connection. "I know you're on a case, CeCe—"

"Please don't call me that." Celeste had been making the same request for six years. Another example of her partner not listening to her.

Nanette continued. "You're always on a case, but my whole life is on hold until you make your decision. I won't know what I'm going to do until you know what you're going to do."

Celeste tucked her left thumb into her front jeans pocket and drummed her fingers against her hip. How was Nanette's life on hold? She was on the cusp of a new journey with someone she loved to distraction. They were planning their wedding and relocation. If anything, her life was moving at warp speed.

"I've already made my decision. You don't want to accept it." Satisfied that her backyard was secure, Celeste paced back to her living room.

Nanette exhaled. The frustration in the sound was thick enough to cut with a knife. "How could you not want to move to San Diego? It's a bigger market than Columbus. We could be even more successful there."

"I don't want to start over." Irritation tightened Celeste's grip on her phone. "Take me off your to-do list. You have enough going on with your wedding and your move."

Nanette was still talking. "I do have a lot going on, including worrying about launching another investigative agency all by myself. It would really be a big help if I knew I could count on you."

And there it was: the real reason Nanette wanted her to move to San Diego. She wanted Celeste to do the heavy lifting with the business launch the same way she'd done the bulk of the work opening Jarrett & Nichols Investigations in Columbus.

Celeste stilled. She wasn't alone in the living room any longer. Zeke was behind her. His steps were almost silent on the stairs. She turned. Zeke had changed into a lightweight gunmetal-gray suit, pale blue shirt and dark blue tie. In a moment of insecurity, Celeste wondered whether she should change her jeans and blouse. She decided against it.

Holding Zeke's eyes, Celeste responded to Nanette. "You'll be fine. I have confidence in you. You should have confidence in yourself."

"But, CeCe—"

"*Please* don't call me that." Celeste checked her watch. She and Zeke needed to leave now if they were going to meet May Ramirez at the Deep Discount Mart on time.

"—how can I concentrate on my wedding or relocation or new house when I don't know what's going to happen to me?"

She turned her back to Zeke to clear her mind. "Nanette, you and Warren are going to live happily ever after in San Diego. It doesn't matter whether I join you. I've got to go. I have a meeting."

"I really, really want you with me in San Diego." Nanette sounded like an overtired child. "It's not as though you have anything or anyone keeping you here."

That may be true, but it still hurt to hear. "Goodbye, Nanette."

Her business partner tsked. "When will your case be over?"

Celeste started. "Are you serious right now? As soon as the *serial killer* gives us their timeline, I'll share it with you. Bye." She ended their call and turned back to Zeke where he stood on the stairs. His shoulder was propped against the wall. "Sorry about that. Are you ready to go?"

Zeke straightened. "Are you leaving Columbus?" His voice was quiet and devoid of inflection.

Why did she want to hide from his question? Celeste briefly

closed her eyes. Because that question made her remember she didn't have a home. She had a house she loved, a business she was proud of and a community she wanted to serve. But where was home for her? Where was the community that stood with her when she was in trouble? Where were the people who didn't want anything more than friendship from her? She'd been asking those questions her entire life.

Celeste grabbed her knapsack from the closet beside her front door. Her movements were impatient, like her mood. She spoke with her back to Zeke. "My business partner, Nanette Nichols, is getting married."

Zeke interrupted. "Are you in the wedding?"

Celeste frowned at him over her shoulder. "Why are you asking?"

A ghost of a smile played around his lips. "I noticed a torn page from a magazine in your inbox. It had a picture of a purple bridesmaid dress."

"Yeah." Celeste shivered and turned away to close the closet door. "Nanette asked me to be a bridesmaid. I declined. I'm pretty sure she was trying to fix me up with another one of Warren's friends."

"Warren's her fiancé?"

"Yes." Celeste dug out her car keys from a compartment in her knapsack. "He accepted a promotion to a position in San Diego. Nanette wants our business to relocate there."

"What do *you* want?" Zeke's deep, bluesy voice soothed her fraying nerves. His seemingly sincere interest in her answer eased her tension.

"I'm staying in Columbus." She lifted her knapsack onto her left shoulder. "Nanette's having trouble accepting that."

Zeke descended the stairs. "What's preventing you from moving to San Diego?"

Celeste stilled. It was weird—in a good way—to have someone ask her that question, as opposed to hearing Nanette's repeated assertion that she didn't have anything keeping her here. She hadn't realized before how lonely and alone hearing that made her feel.

She took a moment to consider her response. "I suppose it's

the lesser of two evils. I'm not looking forward to running the agency by myself. But I don't want to uproot my life and move across the country, either."

"I wouldn't want to do that, either." Zeke stopped at the base of the staircase. "Are there other reasons you've decided to stay here?"

Was it her imagination, or was he fishing for something? She searched his eyes for the answer to that question. Either Zeke Touré had a really good poker face or his question didn't have any hidden agenda. "Like what?"

"That's what I was wondering." Zeke crossed his arms. "Where does your family live?"

Celeste stiffened. "I told you. I'm from Chicago."

Zeke inclined his head. "I remember. But what about your family?"

This confiding thing was even harder than she'd thought. "My paternal grandmother raised me. She and her family are in Chicago. We aren't close." He could probably hear that in her voice. "My mother died in childbirth."

"I'm so sorry." Zeke's tone was thick with empathy.

"Thank you. I'm named after her." She'd never confided that to anyone before. She shoved her fists into the front pockets of her jeans.

He broke the short, tense silence. "Thank you for sharing that with me."

Celeste stretched her shoulders to release some of her tension. "I've lived in Columbus for more than a decade. I don't have family here, but I have a home I love, places I enjoy visiting and professional networks that help me with my business."

"And there are plenty of people who'd miss you if you left."

Celeste realized her snort of disbelief was less than gracious. "Like who?" *You?* Her toes curled in her loafers as she remembered their kiss.

Zeke held her eyes, raising her body's temperature. "Plenty of people. Eriq, for one. You're like a daughter to him. My brothers, Symone, Grace and I enjoyed working with you on The Bishop Foundation case."

He enjoyed working with her. Seriously? She so wanted to

challenge him on that. *What about that kiss, Zeke? Do you remember sliding your tongue into my mouth? I sure do.*

But she couldn't summon the nerve. "I enjoyed working with you, too." She checked her watch again. "We'd better get going. We don't want to keep Ms. Ramirez waiting."

"It helped me to talk with you about TSG's business plan." Zeke crossed to the door that led to Celeste's attached two-car garage and held it open for her. "I'm happy to be your sounding board about your future plans for your agency."

"I may take you up on that." Celeste entered the garage, breathing in Zeke's soap-and-sandalwood scent as she passed him.

She didn't have the courage to admit it—not even to herself—but Zeke was one of the reasons she was staying in Columbus. As pathetic as it might sound, she wanted to be part of his life. A colleague in their adjacent industries. A partner on future cases.

And after that kiss...well, perhaps the door hadn't been completely closed on something more.

"I have *never* been late to work. Not a single day in my *life*." May Ramirez shook a small, angry finger at Zeke and Celeste. Her petite body trembled in her gray-and-orange Deep Discount Mart security uniform. "And I've *never, ever* slept on the job. But I was fired because *other* people did. How is that fair?"

"It's not." Zeke's response was reflexive. He hadn't meant to say anything. But the tiny woman was an imposing figure.

He cradled a disposable cup of coffee between his palms as he sat with Celeste and May in the discount store's mini coffee shop late Monday afternoon. The three matching small, circular blond-wood tables near them were empty. That, and the cacophony of sounds from the customers, clerks and pop music playing over the audio system provided cover for their meeting.

Zeke had offered to buy the refreshments. He and Celeste had chosen small coffees. May was on her lunch break. She'd ordered a sandwich combo with chips and an allegedly fresh apple turnover for dessert. According to their background check, May was in her midsixties, but she looked much younger. Her tan features were smooth, and her thick, simple bob was still a glossy dark brown.

As he lowered his coffee to the table, Zeke's right arm brushed against Celeste's where it rested on the table beside him. She scooted her chair farther away, giving him more room. "You're still angry about being let go from Buckeye Bailey Security even though the separation occurred almost two months ago."

A blush darkened May's cheeks. She straightened on the hard plastic cream chair as though trying to appear taller than her five foot one-or-two inches. "Of course I'm still angry. I'll be angry for the rest of my *life*. I was fired because the guards on other shifts were unprofessional. Why was *I* punished for *their* bad behavior?" The older woman took another bite of her roast beef sandwich.

Celeste sipped her coffee. "You think Art Bailey fired *you* because of what other guards did?"

"I don't *think* it. I *know* it." May's cherubic features were strained. Even her hair seemed to vibrate with tension. "Art told me I should've told him the other guards were coming in late, leaving early and sleeping on the job. Why would I do that? I'm not their supervisor. We didn't even work the same shift."

Zeke frowned. Had he heard correctly? "Art only assigned one guard to each shift? Since when?" The security industry's general rule of thumb called for one guard for every one hundred people. Archer Family Realty employed between one hundred and fifty to two hundred people.

May's bowed lips tightened. "That's right. It was another one of his brilliant cost-saving ideas." Her sarcasm was hard to miss.

A memory played across Zeke's mind like a movie trailer. Years ago, Buckeye Bailey Security had surprised the corporate-security industry by reducing his staff to one guard per shift at each of their contracted locations. This had occurred while Zeke's parents had still been alive. They'd commented to him and his brothers that they thought this was a bad idea. And it had been. Art had laid off a number of guards, and several more had quit. His company also had lost a few clients. Those were the reasons his parents had believed Art had gone back to staffing two guards per shift. Now one of his former guards was telling them that Art had once again reduced his shift staff. How much financial trouble had the other business owner been in, and why?

Zeke tried digging a little deeper. "We understand Buckeye Bailey had trouble making payroll. Did you have that experience or know anyone who did?"

May snorted. "No. Art paid garbage to begin with. If he'd stiffed me even once, I would've left. The job wasn't that great. I mean, the hours were good, and the work wasn't demanding. But I could've gotten another job." She spread her arms, indicating the discount store. "I got this one."

Zeke exchanged a curious look with Celeste. Damien Rockwell, the first guard they'd spoken with, made the payroll problem seem like a regular thing, although he admitted he'd never had a problem with his paycheck. According to May, there weren't any payroll issues at all. Why would either guard lie?

May gestured toward Zeke. "You know, I considered applying for a job with TSG. You guys have a good rep, and you pay well."

"Why didn't you?" He genuinely wanted to know.

May wrinkled her nose and shook her head. "You have that physical fitness test, and your contractors have to know CPR and basic first aid. That's too much."

Celeste gestured toward May with her paper coffee cup. "Do you keep in touch with any of the other guards from Buckeye Bailey?"

May's eyes widened with surprise. "No. Why would I?"

Celeste shrugged her slender shoulders under her scoop-necked black cotton blouse. "Curiosity. Spite."

"I like you." May's features relaxed into a smile that transformed her appearance. She looked younger and more approachable. Celeste blinked at the other woman's response. May split a look between Zeke and Celeste before continuing. "I did hear Chad Cooper's in prison. I could've predicted that. He had the weekend hours and filled in during the week when other guards called off. I don't know how he got a job in security in the first place."

Celeste's straight eyebrows knitted. "Why do you say that?"

May shook her head and expelled another breath. "He's one

scary guy, and he hangs out with scary people. I mean, is that the kind of person you want representing you to your clients? What was Art thinking?"

Zeke recalled the mug shot Mal had provided with his preliminary file on Chad. He could understand why May would describe him as "scary." His Buckeye Bailey personnel file indicated he was in his early twenties, but his scowl made him look much older. He had a bony, square face framed by a wealth of dirty-blond tresses that grew past his shoulders. But his ice blue eyes, with their dead, flat stare, had left the strongest impression on Zeke.

"Do you know why he was arrested?" Zeke finished his coffee.

May checked the time on her cell phone. "I heard he got drunk and got into a fight. I told you, he and his friends are really scary, like they'd kill you as soon as look at you."

Celeste moved her coffee cup aside and folded her forearms on the table. Her shoulder brushed Zeke's upper arm. She shifted her chair farther away. "What was Chad like to work with?"

"Angry and lazy." May looked uneasy, as though the memory of Chad was disturbing. "Like I said, I didn't see him often. He was a floater and a weekender. But I remember he acted like he was untouchable, like he could do whatever and would never lose his job." She snorted. "Once he had the nerve to ask me for money. Can you believe it? Of course, I said no."

Zeke's eyebrows lifted. He was equal parts surprised and impressed. "You weren't afraid of him?"

May scowled. "Of course I was afraid, but I know people like that. You give them money one time, they'll keep coming. It's like a slow death. If he was going to kill me over money, it would be better for him to do it quickly and get it over with."

His surprise faded, leaving him only impressed. May seemed to be more courageous than she thought.

"Do you remember where you were August 22?" Celeste's question cut through the brief silence. Had she meant for it to be jarring?

May's thin eyebrows stretched toward her bangs. "That was three weeks ago. Do you remember where *you* were?"

Celeste spread her hands. "Zeke and I are working with the police to investigate Art Bailey's and Dean Archer's murders."

"What?" May jumped as though her exclamation startled even her. She looked around the mini dining area. They were still the only customers. She lowered her voice to a stage whisper. "*Murdered?* I'd heard Art committed suicide at the end of August and Dean Archer died of a heart attack. What was it? Two weeks ago?"

"It's been ten days." Zeke mentally shrugged. Whether it had been fourteen days or ten, the family wouldn't have closure until the killer was brought to justice. "Where were you Friday, August 22, May?" He considered the petite woman as he waited for her answer. How could she have forced Art into his car? Did she own a weapon?

"I was here." May waved a hand around the store. "I work noon to nine, remember? And I didn't know where Art lived until I read his obituary."

Zeke looked at Celeste. He could tell they were thinking the same thing. They'd need to verify May's alibi with her supervisor. He'd ask Eriq and his partner, Taylor Stenhardt, to follow up on that. But based on this interview, May Ramirez had moved to the bottom of their suspect list.

He turned back to the former guard. "May, have you received any anonymous messages—either letters, emails or phone calls?"

"No, I don't think so." May shook her head, still seeming to search her memories. She stiffened. Her eyes leaped between Zeke and Celeste. "Wait. Are you saying *I* could be in danger? Why would anyone kill me? What have *I* done?"

Celeste waved her hands in front of her. "If you haven't received any messages yet, you're probably in the clear—"

May scowled. "That doesn't sound as encouraging as you seem to think."

Celeste held the other woman's eyes. "You're probably in the clear, but stay vigilant."

Crossing her arms under her chest, May leaned back against her chair. "Well, thank you for letting me know there might be a threat out there with my name on it."

Zeke unzipped his black faux-leather portfolio. He pulled out the sketch of their Mystery Woman and turned it toward May. "Do you recognize this person?"

May leaned into the table for a closer look at the image. Her hands were flat on the table, as though she didn't want to get her prints on the paper. After a few seconds of silent scrutiny, she responded, drawing out each word. "No, I don't think I've seen her before." She pulled her eyes from the sketch and pinned Zeke with a look. "Is she the killer?"

Zeke returned the sketch to his portfolio. "We believe she's connected to Art's and Dean's murders." *And the threat against me and, possibly, my brothers.* He drew out a generic Touré Security Group business card and gave it to May. "If you think of anything else that could help identify Art's and Dean's killer, or if you have any concerns about your safety, please call us." He stood, holding the back of Celeste's chair as she rose to stand with him. "Thank you again for your time and insights, May."

"Thanks." Celeste nodded at May before turning toward the store's exit.

Zeke matched his pace to her shorter but fast steps. He lowered his voice. "We need to find the source of Art's financial problems and how they're connected to Dean and TSG."

And they needed the answer sooner rather than later. His brothers' safety depended on it.

Chapter 10

"I'll ask Eriq to verify May's alibi with her supervisor." Zeke shifted on the smoke gray passenger seat of Celeste's older black sedan to look at her as they drove out of Deep Discount Mart's parking lot Monday evening.

"May doesn't seem like a strong suspect, but we need to look under the surface." Celeste braked at the parking lot exit to check traffic.

Zeke leaned forward to get a better look at the congestion. Rush hour was in full swing. Time seemed to stand still before they were able to exit onto the street.

Zeke relaxed against the cushioned bucket seating. Like his SUV, Celeste's sedan was spotless. The carpeting was vacuumed. The dashboard and console were dusted. The windows were clear. And the interior smelled like vanilla and citrus. He drew a deeper breath.

Zeke's eyes traced the clean line of Celeste's elegant profile. "I think it's time to interview Chad Cooper and Agnes Letby. We've agreed either or both could be working with the Mystery Woman, which means they could be part of these murders even though she's out of state and he's in prison."

"That's true." Celeste checked her rearview and side mirrors. Her words came slowly, as though she was considering her response. "One or both of them could have planned the murders, then told the Mystery Woman what to do—who to make contact with, how to kill Art and Dean, and when. You know, I'm really getting tired of referring to her as the 'Mystery Woman.' I hope we get an ID on her soon."

Had Chad or Agnes also told their Mystery Woman who to get close to in his world, and how and when to kill him and his brothers? No matter how many times Celeste, Mal and Jerry told him his brothers weren't the target, Zeke couldn't get past the fact that TSG was a family-owned company. The three of them were a unit.

He forced those dark thoughts from his mind. "Both May and Damien said they'd seen Chad's temper. And we know he has financial troubles because he asked May for money."

"His money issues must be pretty bad if he's asking coworkers like May for a loan." Celeste brought her car to a stop at the traffic light before the Ohio State Route 315 North on-ramp. "May said they barely knew each other. He must have been pretty desperate to ask her for money."

Celeste studied her side and rearview mirrors again before returning her attention to the traffic light. Was she avoiding making eye contact with him? "If his situation was already desperate, Chad could have lost his temper over being fired."

Imprisonment during the time of the murders was usually an airtight alibi for homicide suspects. But the addition of this unknown person and her connection to the murders raised doubts about Chad's and Agnes's alibis. Based on information from Damien and May, Chad's motive could be money. And both former guards referenced Chad's temper. But the fact she'd retired and remarried seemed to indicate Agnes had moved on with her life. Was that her attempt at misdirection? Could she still be harboring a grudge against Dean and Art?

"He has a history of striking out when he's angry." The traffic light turned green. Celeste eased the car forward toward the state route on-ramp. "His arrest record shows a pattern of assaults, but we don't have any examples of his being involved in homicides."

"Point taken." Zeke inclined his head. "I still don't think we should rule him out. And despite his repeated arrests, he hasn't learned to control his temper. It's not hard to imagine his crimes escalating."

Celeste checked her blind spot before merging onto the state route. "I'm not ruling him out. It's just Chad's record shows he's an impulse guy. I can see him more as the kind to beat up Art when Art fired him. I don't see him as taking a year to plot multiple elaborate murders. Do you?"

Zeke considered her words. Her arguments were solid, but he couldn't give up on his theory of Chad as a viable suspect.

"You've made good points. Here are a few of mine." He counted each on his fingers. "Chad is our only suspect with a criminal record. His financial problems give him the strongest motive. He has a temper. And, according to May, he has 'scary' associates."

"All right. I'll arrange a meeting with Chad." Celeste retrieved a pair of large sunglasses from the compartment above her rearview mirror. She put them on without taking her eyes from the road, then once again changed lanes. She positioned her sun visor to cover the top half of her side window.

The sunlight wasn't that bright.

She sped past two cars before working her way back into the middle lane. She studied her rearview and side mirrors again. This time, her scrutiny was even longer. She was staring at those mirrors like they were crystal balls and she needed to read her future. Straightening on his seat, Zeke faced forward. He searched his passenger-side mirror.

"We're being followed?" He already knew the answer. There was no other explanation for her erratic driving and the tension snapping in the space between them.

"Yes." Celeste was grim.

Zeke clenched his teeth. "Our cover's been blown."

Our cover's been blown.

Celeste sat straighter in her seat. She'd come to that same conclusion. The navy blue SUV had pulled in behind them from a side street several blocks before the entrance to Ohio State Route 315. Maybe it was a coincidence that it had merged onto the route also. But the hairs on the back of her neck disagreed. And they were never wrong.

The driver wasn't trying to be inconspicuous. Either they wanted her to notice them shadowing her in the middle lane or this was their first tail. Celeste didn't believe the driver had firearms. This wasn't a John Wick movie. It was more likely that they were driving close because they wanted to get a good look at her. She hoped her sunglasses and sun visor would prevent that.

"What's the plan?" Zeke's voice was deep and tense.

Adrenaline pumped into her system. The pulse at the base of her throat was leading the stampede. Most people had a fight-or-flight response to danger. Her response had always been fight-or-fight-harder.

Celeste tightened her grip on the steering wheel. "Text Eriq. Have him and Taylor meet us at the substation on Red River Road. That's where we'll lead our stalker."

Zeke started texting before Celeste had finished speaking. "Done."

"Great. Now I'll describe the car for you. We'll give the description to Eriq and Taylor. Tell me when you're ready." She waited for Zeke to launch a clean page on his smart phone's Notepad app.

"Ready," he prompted her.

Celeste squinted at her rearview mirror. "Navy blue Ford Expedition. Older than 2020. And the license plate is H-R-S, maybe eight, one, maybe three, four. No distinguishing stickers or marks." *Darn!* "But it has the name of the rental company on the plate's frame." She gave it to him.

"Eriq and Taylor are on their way to the substation." Zeke tapped his cell phone screen. "You must really know cars to be able to estimate their model years."

Celeste looked over her shoulder to make sure the right lane was clear before moving into it. "No, but I'm familiar with the Ohio law that states after 2020, cars no longer need front license plates. Since it has a front plate, it must be 2020 or older. Our stalker just switched lanes."

From the corner of her eye, she noticed Zeke clench both fists.

As someone used to being in control, it must be frustrating to be a passenger while they were being tailed.

"Can you make out the driver?" His voice was tight.

Celeste was glad he wasn't turning around to look himself. She didn't want the tail to see him or have further confirmation Zeke was her passenger.

In reflex, Celeste glanced at the rearview mirror. "I can't make out the driver. He or she is wearing a ballcap and sunglasses. It could be our Mystery Woman. Or it could be someone I ticked off in traffic and this is a road rage incident."

"I think you'd be able to tell the difference." His tone was dry.

Celeste took the Henderson Road exit off the 315 North and turned toward the substation a few miles away. "The driver couldn't possibly think we haven't spotted them."

Zeke grunted. "I think they want us to see them. They're probably trying to intimidate us."

"Why?" Celeste glanced at him before returning her attention to the traffic. "So we could stop trying to identify them and instead wait docilely for them to kill you? As if." A rush of fear formed a lump in her throat.

Frequent glances in her rearview mirror assured her the SUV continued to shadow them as they wound their way through the northeast Columbus neighborhoods. Traffic was snarled with commuters impatient to make their way home. The SUV stayed with them through every stop light, intersection and turn until they got to the substation.

Celeste turned into the asphalt parking lot in front of the police substation, then glanced in her rearview mirror. "The SUV's moved on." She pulled into a space on the left side of the visitor's lot close to the substation's entrance, then put the car in Park. Spaces for law enforcement vehicles were in the rear. "Let's wait for Eriq and Taylor inside. Hurry."

Zeke climbed out of the vehicle and waited for her. "We're going to have to leave your car behind since they've identified it. I can't figure out how, though."

Celeste walked with him to the substation. She had no trouble ditching her car if it would help ensure Zeke's safety. "Our stalker knows we're investigating the case. The question is, how did they know we'd be interviewing May this afternoon?"

The police substation was a square, three-story redbrick-and-tinted-glass building. It smelled of old carpeting, burnt coffee and stale doughnuts. It had taken years for Celeste to enter a police building—any police building—without being triggered by memories of the betrayals that had caused her to give up her career in law enforcement.

She'd loved being a police officer and then a detective. Her role allowed her to ensure justice for neighbors who'd been wronged. Her childhood experiences gave her a greater dedication to protect her community from bullies and other threats to their safety. But those dreams ended in heartbreak when He Who Would *Never* Be Named had used her, framing her for his corruption and turning the department—her found family—against her.

Those memories shook her, causing Celeste to stumble on the stairs as though someone had once again pulled the rug from beneath her feet.

Zeke caught her arm with catlike reflexes, keeping her from stumbling. "Are you all right?"

Celeste was mesmerized by the concern darkening his eyes. She blinked, breaking her trance. "Yes. Thank you." She offered him a weak smile, hoping to dispel the doubts she read in his expression.

She strode through the substation's glass door as Zeke held it open for her. Celeste squared her shoulders as she shoved the poisonous memories of the past back into the far corners of her mind. At the desk, she gave their names to the officer on duty and explained they were waiting for Eriq and Taylor. While they waited, Zeke updated Mal and Jerry via text. Based on the way his cell lit up, it was safe to say his brothers were more than a little concerned.

Zeke pinched the bridge of his nose. "*This* is the reason I hesitated to update them. Even though I told them we're meeting with Eriq and Taylor, they act like I can't handle myself."

Celeste gave a bark of startled laughter. "Look who's talking. You're the dictionary definition of an overprotective older brother."

Was that a blush of embarrassment darkening his chiseled cheeks? Celeste's heart melted a little.

Fortunately for Zeke, Eriq and Taylor strode into the substation in time to save the eldest Touré from coming up with a defense.

"CJ!" Eriq wrapped her in a bear hug that eased her final knots of tension and lifted her from the floor. "It's been way too long."

Celeste laughed as she hugged him back. "We had lunch last week, crazy man."

The older detective was a father figure to her. That was the reason he was the only person in her life allowed to give her a nickname.

"You work too hard." Eriq stepped back and turned to Zeke. He gave the younger man a firm handshake and squeezed his shoulder. "It's good to see you, Zeke."

Taylor's greeting was warm, though more subdued. "It's good to see both of you are safe. We hope it stays that way."

"Absolutely." Eriq turned to lead them into the bullpen. "Let's get a meeting room. We've checked up on Jerry a couple of times. Sounds like he's on the mend. Thank goodness." He stood aside near the doorway of a closet-sized conference room toward the front of the bullpen.

Taylor led Celeste, Zeke and Eriq into the cramped space. The scent of burnt coffee and stale pastries followed them in. A midsize rectangular table dominated the room. The dark gray conference phone in the center of its smooth blond-wood surface reminded Celeste of a Star Wars Wing Fighter. Six matching chairs surrounded it, two on each side and one at each end. Thin pale gray wall-to-wall carpeting—the same carpeting that ran through the bullpen—muted their footsteps. Black-framed photos of the mayor of Columbus, division of police leadership and police headquarters downtown seemed intended to bring color and dignity to the dingy surroundings. They didn't.

Circling the table, Taylor took one of the two chairs on the right. "Zeke, you texted us about the tail."

Zeke sat beside Celeste on the left side of the room and pulled out his cell phone. "Celeste gave me a partial description of the SUV." He read from his notes.

Taylor jotted down the characteristics of the navy blue Ford Expedition, including the estimated year and partial license plate. "Good job, Celeste." She stood and crossed to the door. "I'll run this through the system and see what we get. Be right back."

Celeste watched Taylor disappear beyond the threshold, leaving the door open. She wanted to will the detective to come back with good news. The sooner they found the stalker, the sooner Zeke would be safe. But it didn't work that way. She forced her muscles to relax. While they waited for Taylor, Celeste and Zeke filled Eriq in on their impressions of their first two security guard suspects, Damien Rockwell and May Ramirez.

After listening to their summaries and observations, Eriq sat back on his blond-wood chair. "Do you think one of them could have been tailing you?"

Zeke crossed his arms over his chest. "I don't know how. May went back to work after she met with us. And how could Damien have known where we'd be this afternoon? Celeste made the appointment with May only a few hours ago."

Reading the question in Zeke's dark eyes, Celeste shook her head. "We weren't followed to Deep Discount Mart. But if someone knew we were investigating the case, they'd know we were going to interview May. They just wouldn't know when."

Eriq nodded. "And our Mystery Woman is unaccounted for. She could have had May under surveillance, waiting for the two of you to show up."

Taylor returned in time to hear Eriq's response. "She's not a mystery anymore." She set two printouts on the conference table. The first was a copy of a driver's license. The other was Zeke's sketch of the anonymous woman. "Look familiar?"

Zeke leaned forward, brushing his right arm against Celeste's left shoulder. She was beginning to think he was doing such things on purpose.

He drew both printouts closer. "She's a definite match." He looked at Celeste. "What do you think?"

She nodded. "Absolutely."

Taylor glowed with satisfaction. "Meet Monica Ward. She rented the Expedition when she came into town from North Carolina."

"North Carolina?" A memory stirred in the back of Celeste's mind. "Isn't that where the retired guard, Agnes Letby, lives?"

Eriq grumbled. "Along with about eleven million other people, but it's a good start."

"A very good start." Celeste picked up the sheet of paper and studied the driver's license image. "Who are you working with, Monica, and what's your connection to this case?"

"Our Mystery Woman has a name—Monica Ward." Zeke felt a surge of satisfaction in being able to share that information with his brothers. They were one step closer to keeping his family and Celeste safe. "Taylor was able to identify her using Celeste's description of her rental car."

Zeke, Celeste, Eriq and Taylor had called the Touré Security Group from the police substation's meeting room early Monday evening.

"Impressive." Jerry's praise was stuffed with excitement. "And, Celeste, quick thinking taking Zeke to the substation. We knew you were the right person to watch our brother's back."

Mal's response was less enthusiastic. "This feels like a trap."

"And there's Mr. Buzzkill." Jerry's tone was dry.

Mal continued as though Jerry hadn't interrupted him. "Why would Monica Ward get close enough to be identified?"

Zeke glanced around the table. Across from him, Eriq and Taylor frowned at the phone, deep in thought. Beside him, Celeste returned his regard as though waiting for his response. Zeke felt himself being pulled into her hazel eyes. He broke their contact.

"Mal has a point." Zeke focused on the phone, imagining his brothers sitting together in their company's conference room. "Celeste noticed Monica wasn't trying to remain undetected."

Celeste leaned closer to the conference phone. "It was obvious from the beginning she was following us."

"That just means she doesn't have experience tailing someone." Jerry's response was a verbal shrug.

Celeste looked at Eriq seated across the table from her and shook her head. "It was more than that, Jerry. She wanted us to know she was there."

"She's taunting you." Mal's voice was grim. "She's tired of trying to flush you out. She wants you to come after her instead."

Zeke's eyes widened. "You may be onto something."

"Well, you two aren't going to do that." Taylor inclined her head toward her partner seated beside her. "Eriq and I will track down Monica Ward. I've already put out a BOLO for her and her car. We'll let you know when we bring her in for questioning."

Be On the Look Out. Celeste nodded, folding her arms on the table in front of her. "Hopefully soon. The sooner we bring her in, the sooner Zeke will be safe."

Zeke looked at her in surprise. It felt strange having someone other than family voice their concern for his safety. Usually, people expected him to take care of them as well as himself. It felt odd—in a good way—to have someone so invested in his well-being.

He swallowed to ease the dryness in his throat. "I'm not the only one in danger. Let us—Eriq, Taylor, my brothers and me—handle the case from here. The threat level has surged. I don't want you caught in the middle of this. *We* don't want you in the middle of this."

Zeke ignored Eriq's snort of derision, Taylor's sigh and the snickers coming through the phone.

"Excuse me?" Celeste's eyebrows jumped up her forehead.

Zeke glanced at Eriq and Taylor. They seemed almost pitying of the situation he'd created for himself. No help there. He returned his attention to Celeste. "Celeste, I've put not only my family but you in danger. I'd feel better if you left us to investigate this case without you."

Celeste shifted on her chair to better face him. She tapped her right index finger with her left one. "First, I've been in law enforcement for almost ten years. I was a homicide detective before becoming a private investigator." She tapped her right middle finger. "Second, this is *my* case. Meryl Bailey hired *me* to find her husband's killer. I'm not walking away." She tapped her ring finger. "And third, *I* invited *you* to this questionable party to keep you safe when *I* deduced that you were the killer's next target. You're welcome."

Zeke started to argue, but the expression in her eyes gave him second thoughts. "All right. Points taken. And thank you."

Celeste still seemed to be bristling. "Besides, Monica Ward already knows about me. Just as I was taking down her license plate, I'm sure she was taking mine. If she has my plate, she has my address."

"We need to move you." Mal's voice came over the phone. "Both of you."

"We'll go to the safe house." The idea of staying alone in the secluded cabin in the middle of the woodland resorts with Celeste Jarrett put his body on a slow burn.

"Good." Mal's approval was short and to the point. "Jerry and I will get a couple of burner cells and clean laptops to you. They'll be waiting for you at the resort's main office."

"That's a good idea," Jerry said. "The system will alert you if you're being tracked."

"It's going to be tricky getting you to this safe house." Taylor jerked her head toward Zeke and Celeste on the other side of the table. "Monica could be waiting for you to leave the substation."

"I've got a plan for that." Celeste's words sparked a battle between hope and dread in Zeke.

He shifted on his seat to face her. "What are you thinking?"

Celeste gave him one of her rare smiles, the one that touched her eyes. "I'm putting out a call for disguises."

Zeke sighed. Dread overpowered hope.

Chapter 11

"Should I put your Halloween costumes back in the storage closet?" Nanette steered her BMW coupe into the left-turn lane onto Morse Road. She was taking Celeste to the car-rental center Monday evening.

"They're not Halloween costumes. They're disguises." This wasn't the first or even fifth time she'd explained that to Nanette. The fact she'd bought most of these outfits from Halloween costume stores notwithstanding. "And no, thanks. I'll take the trunk with me."

In response to Celeste's call, Nanette had paused her wedding planning to deliver Celeste's second-hand green-and-brown trunk to the substation. The oversize luggage was outfitted with wheels and a handle and was stuffed with a myriad of disguises. Not costumes. Despite the variety, Zeke had proven to be a difficult customer. Most of the outfits were sized for Celeste's smaller frame. Zeke was built like a professional football tight end. In addition, he didn't have any imagination when it came to undercover disguises.

Zeke hadn't even entertained her "wealthy Texan" idea. He'd responded with a flat stare when she'd explained a successful disguise was both subtle and unexpected. His preference had been a fedora, fake sideburns and mirrored sunglasses. *Boring!*

He'd borrowed Eriq's tan blazer to distract from his clothing.

Celeste shook off her exasperation. In the end, all that mattered was that Zeke's appearance was sufficiently altered to enable them to move him to safety. His outfit—although unimaginative—had accomplished that.

Celeste had used the "wealthy Texan" disguise herself. Why waste a good idea? She'd changed into a man's wine red shirt, black bolo tie and gray suit coat. She'd stuffed her hair under a silver Stetson, added lifts to her oversize black boots and hid behind silver-rimmed sunglasses. Presto chango, she hoped. Celeste had walked out of the substation's front entrance with Nanette. She wore the Stetson and sunglasses even in her partner's bright red Beemer. Zeke and Taylor had exited through the rear, where Taylor's police-issued vehicle was waiting. The detective was taking Zeke to the car-rental company, where Celeste would meet him.

Touré Security Group had had a corporate account with the rental company for years. An account with a rental-car company, a safe house at a cabin resort... Those were things she hadn't even considered aspiring to for her business. She couldn't fathom why Zeke would think his family's agency wasn't doing well.

Nanette kept her eyes on the traffic signal, waiting for the left-turn arrow. "What are you going to do about your car? It's still at the substation's visitors' parking lot, right?"

"Eriq's taking it back to headquarters." Celeste knew Nanette understood she was referring to the police headquarters off Marconi Street in downtown Columbus.

Nanette snorted. "I wonder what Monica Ward will make of that."

"*If* she's still waiting for Zeke and me." Celeste abruptly shifted topics. "Could you lend me some clothes to wear while I'm at the safe house?" She studied the passenger-side mirror. She didn't think they were being followed.

It wouldn't be hard to tail Nanette. Celeste was half convinced she could do it on foot. Her partner's bright red BMW stuck out in traffic. She also drove like a snail. Celeste glanced at her from the corner of her eyes. She suspected Nanette drove slowly so people could admire the way she looked behind the wheel. In fairness, she looked great, but they were on the clock. Celeste checked her watch. It was already after six.

"Of course." Nanette bounced with excitement. "You know I don't wear black, right? I embrace *all* the bright colors. But no problem. I'll have the suitcase delivered to the safe house." Nanette pulled forward as the turn light activated. "Where is it?"

"You know I can't tell you that." Celeste knew her business partner didn't have any black items in her wardrobe other than the obligatory little black dress. But then, beggars couldn't be choosers. She adjusted her Stetson and sunglasses. "The fewer people who know where we are, the safer we'll be. Have the courier take it to TSG. And thank you. I promise to be careful with your belongings."

"I know you will." Nanette turned left onto High Street. "But come on, now. Do you think the killer will track me down and torture me to find out where you are or something?"

"This is serious, Nanette." Celeste shifted on the soft silver-and-black leather seat to face her partner's profile. "We aren't keeping tabs on an unfaithful spouse or tracking leads in some white-collar crime. Two people have already died under suspicious circumstances, and a third has been threatened." Celeste faced forward. "If you have an emergency, call or email me. But only in an emergency, Nanette. Please don't call me to talk about your wedding or your move. Okay?"

Nanette's sigh was sharp with impatience. "Celeste, I wouldn't have to call you if you'd hurry up and answer my questions."

"What questions?" Celeste was equally impatient.

"For example, what about your plus-one for my wedding?" Nanette stopped at a red traffic light. She gave Celeste a sly smile. "Are you and Zeke back on?"

Celeste unclenched her teeth. "I told you, I'm coming alone."

She checked the side mirror again. She didn't detect any suspicious activity. The killer probably wouldn't expect her to be traveling in a flashy bright red car.

"Urgh! You're so stubborn." The traffic signal turned green. Nanette guided her car across the intersection. Slowly. "What about San Diego?" The words seemed to have been dragged from her, as though she worried they would trigger Celeste.

They did.

"Really, Nanette?" She shifted on the passenger seat again. "Now? I just told you a serial killer followed Zeke and me to the substation. But you want me to set that aside and plan the rest of my life for you? Right now?"

Nanette scowled. "I know, Celeste. And I'm sorry. But I'm worried about my financial future. I love Warren and I'm so proud of him. He earned this promotion. But what about *me*? What am *I* supposed to do?"

Celeste took a deep breath, then exhaled. She heard the panic in Nanette's voice. She could almost taste her fear. "Nanette, you and I started our own private investigation agency. You can do it again on your own in San Diego. You're a good business-person and a great investigator. You'll be fine."

"But I want you to start the agency with me." A slight whine entered her voice.

Translation: *Nanette wants me to handle all the paperwork and promotion needed to launch the business, just as I did in Columbus.*

"And I told you, I'm happy here in Columbus."

"But there's nothing keeping you here."

An image of Zeke slipped into her mind, but Celeste remained silent. Fortunately, Nanette didn't push the issue.

Pulling into the turn lane, her partner waited for a break in traffic before guiding her BMW into the car-rental company's parking lot. Celeste surveyed their surroundings for anything suspicious or seemingly out of place. Nanette snagged a space near the nondescript building and put her vehicle in Park.

Celeste looked at her in surprise. "What are you doing?"

Nanette's thin eyebrows knitted. "I want the man you'll be staying with for heaven knows how long to meet me. That way, he'll think twice if he has any ideas of foul play because he'll know at least one person will be coming after him."

Celeste paused. That was kind of sweet. With a mental shrug, she climbed out of the coupe and crossed briskly into the one-story smoke-glass-and-silver-metal structure. She sensed Nanette following close behind her. Celeste pushed through the glass entrance and spotted Zeke waiting for her toward the back of the customer service waiting area. He was still wearing the fedora and fake sideburns, but he no longer had Eriq's tan blazer. He must have given it to Taylor to return to her partner.

She stilled as Zeke removed his mirrored sunglasses. His eyes swept over her as though making sure she was unharmed. Celeste nervously adjusted the Stetson and pushed her dark sunglasses higher up the bridge of her nose.

Zeke's attention shifted to Nanette behind her before he recaptured her eyes. "Everything all right?" His deep, bluesy voice wrapped around her.

"Yes, everything's fine." She sounded breathless. Celeste stopped a little more than an arm's length from him. "Nanette Nichols, Hezekiah Touré."

Nanette offered him her right hand. "You're even more attractive in real life. Why did you and Celeste stop dating?"

Oh. My. Goodness.

Celeste froze. She could feel the blood rushing into her cheeks. She tapped the floor with her left foot, hoping it would trigger the ground to open up and swallow her. It didn't.

She pivoted to her partner. "Thank you for your help, Nanette. You can leave now."

Nanette held on to Zeke's hand. "Are you free the first Saturday in December?"

Zeke glanced at Celeste before turning back to Nanette. "What's happening the first Saturday in December?"

Nanette beamed at him, still holding his hand hostage. "I'm getting married. You—"

"Nanette." Celeste's voice was a low hiss. "There's a serial killer after us. Please leave. *Now.* We'll talk later."

Her partner scowled at her. "I'm going to hold you to that." She released Zeke's hand and stepped back. "Take good care of my girl." She turned on her heels and disappeared through the front door.

Celeste saw the car fob in Zeke's large right hand. "Let's go. And this time, you can drive."

She marched toward the rear exit without looking at him. As she pushed through the door that led to the rental-car parking lot, she sensed Zeke's confusion but gave thanks for his silence.

If she expended a bit more effort, she might be able to forget the humiliation her soon-to-be former partner had visited upon her and focus on keeping Zeke alive.

The safe house rose from a fantasy. Celeste's eyes widened as she took in the two-story log cabin. The dark-pine-and-red-cedar post-and-beam structure glowed in the waning sun as Zeke approached its attached garage Monday evening. It stood among the evergreen pines and ancient oak trees toward the back of the sprawling resort owned by one of Touré Security Group's long-time clients.

Celeste had first learned of it when she'd helped the Touré brothers on The Bishop Foundation case a couple of months ago. She'd heard the notes of relief and pride that they'd had the facility in which to secure Symone Bishop, the nonprofit organization's chair.

Touré Security Group guards protected the resort's buildings and grounds. To the west and south, sturdy, old oak and evergreen trees sheltered the cabin from a distance. Craning her neck, Celeste thought she spied a hiking trail in the distance. Ah, it would be such a pleasure to jog that trail. A healthy, active river provided additional protection to the east. The nearest cabin was perhaps five miles north of them.

Zeke activated the garage door opener he'd received from the front desk—along with one set of keys, she'd noticed. What was that about? Was it his way of making sure they never left each other's side? He didn't have to worry about that. Until she was convinced he was safe, she was going to stick to him like gum on his shoe.

The heavy red-cedar door rose slowly as Zeke crept the car forward. He put the dark gray sedan in Park and pulled the emergency brake before giving her a wry half smile. "I haven't been here since Jerry and Symone used it. But I've been told it's in good shape."

That was intriguing. What had he expected? "Are you saying one of the Touré men isn't perfect?"

Zeke gave a startled bark of laughter. "We're all far from perfect."

Celeste's eyes moved over Zeke's shoulders, back and hips as he climbed out of the sedan.

There was at least one Touré who was pretty close to perfect in her book.

Zeke unlocked the breezeway door that connected the garage to the cabin. To the left was the dark pine entry door and straight ahead was the cabin's great room. The space was decorated in muted tones: warm tan, soft brown and moss green. A stone fireplace stood in the front of the room. The pine flooring gleamed. Beneath the cedar-wood coffee table, an area rug picked up the room's accent colors. A matching overstuffed brown sofa and two chairs with ottomans surrounded the table. A dining room was set at the edge of the great room with a kitchenette beyond it. Both areas continued the great room's colors. The whole cabin smelled of cedar pine.

Symone had mentioned during more than one videoconference how beautiful the cabin was. Seeing it for herself was something else. Celeste felt her tension ebbing. She sensed Zeke relaxing little by little as well. This would be a great spot for a long weekend vacation. For now, with a killer after them, there was only so much relaxing they could do. It helped to have a space in which she could take a breath and think clearly, though.

Zeke's voice broke into her thoughts. "Which would you prefer to do first: make dinner or take the tour?"

She continuing to admire her surroundings. "The tour."

Zeke nodded, crossing to the stairs. "Hopefully, our clothes will arrive soon."

He'd asked Mal to lend him clothes just as Celeste had asked Nanette to pack her a bag. They weren't willing to take the chance that Monica Ward hadn't found Celeste's home address yet. The delay in receiving luggage was a small price to pay for safety.

Celeste mounted the staircase behind Zeke, momentarily distracted by the sight of his flexing glutes. She clenched her hands to keep from reaching out. Squaring her shoulders, she took a deep breath and inhaled his warm soap-and-sandalwood scent. It was going to be a long stay at the resort.

"This cabin is basically one big panic room," Zeke said over his shoulder. Celeste heard pride as well as wariness in his tone. "We set up security cameras around the cabin's perimeter and in the trees closest to the grounds. All the windows are covered with a tint sheet. We can see out, but if anyone's skulking outside, they can't see in. Of course, we shouldn't go outside. And Mal will include a clean laptop and cell phone for both of us when he sends over our luggage." He stopped at the top step and turned to face her. "You know the rules. No personal devices while we're in hiding at the safe house."

Celeste looked up and felt herself being drawn into his coal-black eyes. She forced herself to blink, turning her attention away. "I've got it." The sooner they located Monica Ward and identified whoever she was working with, the sooner they could leave the safe house and get back to normal life. That's what she wanted.

Wasn't it?

At the top-floor landing, Celeste counted four rooms.

Zeke turned to his right. "We use this room as the operations office. The computers here manage the security systems. I'll show you how it works later." He stepped toward the next room. "I'll sleep here. It's closest to the stairs."

Celeste crossed the room's threshold. It wasn't a big space, but it was clean and comfortable. It had the same soothing decor as the rooms downstairs. A patterned coverlet in moss green and soft brown covered the queen-size bed. It matched the area rugs that surrounded it. An ornate cedar carving of a landscape had been placed on the snow-white wall behind the bed above the headboard. The bed frame, nightstand and dressing table were made of the same wood. Celeste changed direction and wandered to the bed across the room. She trailed her fingertips over the coverlet. The cotton material was soft.

She stopped in front of one of the tinted windows and assessed the cabin's layout in relation to this room. It was closest to the stairs, meaning it was closest to any potential danger. In operational terms, this was the space in which the protector would set up in the interest of shielding the protectee. Zeke appeared to have forgotten which one of them held which role.

She turned to confront him. "Since you're the killer's target, I should take this room."

Zeke stepped back into the hallway as though distancing himself from her words. He must know she was right. "No, I'll show you to your room."

Okay. Enough was enough.

Celeste straightened to her full height, which was six inches shorter than his. She squared her shoulders and pushed her fists into the front pockets of her black jeans. She took a calming breath, filling her lungs with the cedar-scented air. "Let's get something straight, Zeke. *You* are the one who needs protection. *I* am your bodyguard. I'm more than qualified for the role. I was on the force for six years. I've broken up riots, disarmed attackers, arrested murderers. I've proven I'm capable of taking care of myself and others. If you're not prepared to let me do my job, then what am I here for, Zeke? Your entertainment?"

She held his eyes as he absorbed her words. She sensed the turmoil in him as he considered her challenge. He'd been raised to protect those who couldn't protect themselves. Celeste admired that. But he needed to remember she wasn't in that category. Like Zeke—and like Zeke's mother—Celeste had been trained to protect herself and others. She was *not* going to let him get away with treating her like she needed saving.

Finally, he nodded his acquiescence. The motion was jerky with reluctance. "You're right. This will be your room. I'll take the one down the hall."

Celeste relaxed and followed him to the room in question. It was almost identical to hers. The patterned coverlet on the queen-size bed and the area rugs that surrounded it were warm tan and moss green. The intricate cedar carving above the headboard depicted maple leaves that seemed to be floating on an autumn breeze.

Zeke turned, nudging his chin toward the door behind them. "There's only one bathroom."

Celeste flashed a grin. "You must be thrilled to have your own room again. And to be sleeping in a bed. You get your privacy back."

Zeke grinned. "You weren't such a bad roommate. You were

neat and quiet. I'd still like to know how you were able to leave every morning without waking me."

"I'm sure you would." Celeste arched an eyebrow and moved toward the stairs. "I'm hungry."

That was one way to change the subject. The sound of Zeke's footsteps behind her reassured Celeste that he was willing to follow her lead—at least for now.

"How did you know TSG would need a safe house? Do you have a crystal ball?" Celeste posed the question after dinner Monday night.

Zeke stood in front of the sink, scrubbing a skillet. Memories of their meal were kept alive by the aroma of the blackened chicken and garden salad that lingered in the air and danced on his taste buds.

A few chuckles rolled past his lips in self-deprecating humor. "I wish we did have a crystal ball. I could use one right now. I certainly could've used it a year ago." He pitched his voice above the sound of the running water. "As I mentioned, we'd originally planned to offer it to high-profile clients and their families who needed to disappear from the media for a while. We have a couple of guards on retainer who maintain the cabin and its grounds at a moment's notice, including stocking groceries. They're discreet. My brothers and I regularly come out to check on it."

"Does it get a lot of use?" Celeste added the final dishes and silverware to the dishwasher.

"Not as much as we'd hoped." Zeke winced as he dried one of the pans. His stomach muscles clenched as he thought of how much money they'd sunk into this unicorn—and how little return they'd had on their investment. An example of his mismanagement of their company's money. "On the one hand, you want high-profile clients to know the space is available. On the other hand, publicity would compromise its security."

"I see your point." Celeste took the dishcloth from him to continue drying the pans and trays as he returned the items to their cabinets. "But it's been a good investment. Twice now, you've been fortunate enough to have it to keep someone safe, this time yourself."

"I guess." Talking about the safe house always made him tense. Zeke wouldn't add using the cabin for his own protection to their company's profit column.

"Don't sound so gloomy." Celeste turned to lead them into the great room. "It's not as though people can walk onto the resort from the street. There's security, including your own guards. If you promote it only to your exclusive clients, this safe house will pay for itself in time."

"Why hadn't I thought of that?" She'd given him hope.

"Sometimes you have to let go of control and ask for input." Celeste threw up her hands. "You should get a hobby."

Zeke gaped at her back as he followed her into the great room. "Have you been speaking with my brothers? They've started nagging me about my lack of social life."

Celeste snorted as she curled into the far end of the overstuffed brown sofa. "I wouldn't do that to you. I don't like it when Nanette meddles in my personal life."

Zeke settled onto the other end of the sofa. "Nanette's taken it to another level. Did you know she was going to ask me to be your date for her wedding?" Although it wouldn't take any persuasion.

"No, I did not." Celeste briefly covered her face with her hands. "How embarrassing was that? You'd think after all these years, I'd be used to her doing that, but I'm not."

"Does she try to fix you up a lot?" Zeke didn't like the sound of that.

"Yes." Celeste sighed. "I've told her a million times I don't need a date for her wedding. I can make my way to the church and reception with GPS."

Zeke was uncomfortable with the sense of relief he felt that she wasn't bringing a date. He covered it with a smile. "At least Mal and Jerry aren't trying to set me up."

"Yet." Celeste lifted her right index finger. "Trust me. That'll be their next step." She let her hand fall back onto the sofa.

He hoped she was mistaken. "So you declined to be in the wedding party because of the dress?" Zeke tried to imagine her in the fussy lavender gown. He couldn't. "I've never seen you in anything other than black pants or jeans."

Celeste didn't move, but Zeke sensed her stiffen. The warmth in her eyes cooled just a bit. "Wearing black clothing usually allows me to blend into the environment. People tend to overlook me."

That would be impossible. No one could overlook Celeste Jarrett. She was a presence that was hard to miss. He didn't correct her, though. Zeke was too surprised by the personal information she'd shared with him. That was the second time she'd shared something so intimate about herself. It gave him hope that maybe she would let him past the walls she hid behind and allow him to get close to her.

Zeke set those hopes aside for now. "Will you take on a new partner when Nanette moves to San Diego?"

"I don't know yet." Celeste stood and wandered across the room to the cold fireplace. "I think I'd like to run the agency by myself for a while." She turned back to him. A wisp of a smile curved her full heart-shaped lips. "Taking on a partner is a big decision, and I don't make big decisions lightly."

Zeke nodded his understanding. She'd already made the big decision of remaining in Columbus. He'd take that win and the opportunity to build on it.

Chapter 12

Jogging indoors had felt weird. Celeste preferred to run outside, rain or shine, hot or cold. But Zeke was right. Even on the relative safety of the wooded resort grounds, they should remain indoors as much as possible. They couldn't risk bumping into someone they might know. A couple of innocent, casual conversations later, their cover could be blown.

Their luggage had arrived last night. Celeste had insisted on going with Zeke to get their bags from the resort's management office. Even though they were staying in the Touré Security Group safe house, she was still his bodyguard. The thought may not sit well with him, but facts were facts.

Judging by Zeke's reaction, Mal had packed well. He'd seemed pleased with the clothing, shoes and toiletries his brother had loaned him.

The jury was still out on Nanette. Her business partner had been very generous in providing her with outfits and other items to get through the next few days. Celeste really appreciated her generosity. But after she'd pulled out the bright business casual clothing and bold exercise wear, she'd found sheer baby doll nightgowns, barely there lingerie and booty shorts. In September. Nanette's message was loud and clear. Her friend might as well have labeled the bags *Attire to Help You Get Your Groove Back*. The last thing Celeste remembered was a cherry red thong.

She'd decided it would be best to keep washing her sensible undergarments.

This morning, moving around undetected in a strange environment had been a challenge. But Celeste had had eighteen years of growing up with her paternal grandmother, Dionne, to develop her technique and another thirteen years to perfect it. Zeke hadn't found her in the exercise room—otherwise known as the basement—until after she'd run a mile on the treadmill, proving she still had mad ninja skills. She'd completed her five-mile run while he'd worked the strength-training machines. Then they'd switched places. The camaraderie had been nice, with easy conversation and laughter. It had continued as they shared breakfast, adding a few accidental—maybe on purpose—touches. Very nice. But for the past hour plus, she and Zeke had been closeted in their separate bedrooms, working.

A chord sounded from the clean laptop Mal had provided to her, indicating a new email had entered her Jarrett & Nichols Investigations account. The notification jarred her out of those enjoyable morning memories. Seated at the little pinewood desk centered between the two windows on her bedroom's far wall, Celeste checked her messages. Her eyebrows stretched upward in surprise. The sender was someone she hadn't seen or thought of in years, Sterling Jarrett. Her biological father.

The only thing Sterling had given her was life. After her mother had died in childbirth, he'd dumped the day-old Celeste with his mother and walked away. Correction: he'd also given her the obligatory annual visits on her birthday and Christmas, taking time away from his new family. What a guy. Celeste wondered again what kind of person had her mother been to have wanted anything to do with someone like Sterling?

His email's subject heading read, "Important Message about Your Grandmother." Celeste narrowed her eyes. Why was Sterling contacting her about Dionne? Her muscles were weighted with reluctance as she pressed the keys to open the email. His salutation caused a wave of nausea to wash over her.

My dearest daughter, It's been a long time. Please call me. I need to discuss your grandmother. With affection, Dad.

Affection? What was he up to?

Despite her aversion to any contact with him, she felt a fission of concern. What was wrong with Dionne?

Celeste grabbed her clean burner phone from the desk and tapped in the number he'd provided in his email. Her call connected on the second ring.

"Hello?" The sound of Sterling's voice triggered a flood of negative emotions from her childhood and youth.

Celeste braced herself, schooling her voice to be cool and in control. "Hello, Sterling. I got your email."

"Good morning, Celeste. I wish you'd call me 'Dad.'"

Celeste's eyes stretched wide. *Seriously?* She remained silent through the awkward pause.

Sterling continued. His voice was warm and caring. "How are you?"

Celeste went on immediate alert. She lurched out of her chair and paced the room. Her muscles were stiff with tension. She already felt out of sorts. She'd chalked it up to wearing someone else's clothes. Nanette's royal blue knee-length skirt and deep gold blouse were giving her an out-of-body experience.

This rare call from Sterling was making it worse. Celeste hadn't heard from him either by phone, mail or email in almost five years, since he'd sent her an email congratulating her on becoming a homicide detective. The message had read like a form letter. She suspected he'd been directed to send it.

Celeste drew a breath and kept her voice steady. "What can I do for you?"

Sterling cleared his throat. The sound seemed awkward, as though he wasn't comfortable with the distance between them. That was almost laughable since he'd created it. Celeste pressed the phone more tightly against her ear as she turned away from the pinewood dressing table and paced toward her queen-size bed. Through the phone, she heard a male news anchor announcing stock price gains and losses for Tuesday morning.

"Celeste, I'm sorry to tell you this." His voice was muted with grief. "Your grandmother has died."

Dionne was dead?

Celeste dropped onto her bed. She stared blindly across

the room through the windows. She'd spoken with the elderly woman less than two weeks ago. Celeste had gotten into the routine of calling Dionne on the first and third Saturday of each month, outside of obligatory calendar dates like the older woman's birthday and holidays. Dionne had sounded tired, but otherwise she was her usual grumpy, negative self. After every call, Celeste wondered why she bothered keeping in touch with the bitter woman. But she knew the reason. She may not have liked Dionne, but she'd been grateful that the elderly woman had taken her in rather than packing her off to a foster home. Other than surprise, Celeste didn't feel anything at the news. Shouldn't she have a sense of loss and grief? Shouldn't she have the same reactions that Meryl Bailey and Jayne Archer were experiencing?

"What happened?" Celeste filled her left fist with the soft cotton green-and-brown coverlet that lay beneath her.

"She had a heart attack." A thin thread of grief made Sterling's words seem heavier.

Celeste had been aware of Dionne's hypertension. The older woman had been managing it all Celeste's life. During each call, Celeste would ask about her health. She'd scheduled semiannual visits so she could take Dionne to her doctors' appointments. Had something unusual happened to trigger the attack?

Or was this investigation getting to her?

"That doesn't sound right." Leaning forward, Celeste rubbed the spot on her forehead between her eyebrows. "She'd been taking her medication and getting regular checkups. When did this happen?"

Sterling paused. "Wednesday."

Celeste jerked upright. It was like she'd been slapped. "Wednesday? As in, almost a week ago?" And Sterling was only telling her now? She tightened her hand on the fistful of the coverlet as though it were someone's throat.

"We've..." Sterling cleared his throat. "There was a lot to take care of."

With an effort, Celeste purged the emotion from her voice. "I'm sorry for your loss. Is there anything else I can do for you?"

A muted knock sounded on his end of the call. Was he at

work? "Hold on, Celeste. Come in." His voice became muffled. He must have put his hand over the receiver. A minute or two later, he returned to their call. "It's your loss, too, Celeste."

"Is it?" A trace of bitterness escaped into her tone. She couldn't blame herself too much. She was almost choking on the emotion. "Then why am I the last to find out?"

It hurt to always be the afterthought. Or not to be considered at all. After thirty-one years, you'd think she'd be used to it. But she wasn't. That was one of the reasons Celeste hadn't known how to respond to Zeke's accusation that she'd closed herself off. She hadn't known she was doing that. She wished he'd told her sooner.

Sterling's words broke into her self-reflection. "Mother told me you often called and visited with her. She said you'd sent her birthday and holiday cards." His smile came through the phone. "That's more than my children ever did."

His children. Did he realize *she* was one of his children? Probably not. He'd treated her as an obligation. A charity case. Her stomach muscles clenched at the painful memories. She forced herself to block out the past and focus on this call.

Sterling wasn't telling her anything new. Dionne had complained constantly that Sterling and his children had never called, emailed, or sent her letters or holiday greetings. They didn't seem aware that she had a birth date. The only time they visited was when they wanted something from her. Her tirades weren't meant to praise Celeste for spending time with the older woman. Celeste had the sense Dionne wanted Celeste to commiserate with her. The old woman seemed to forget she'd never given Celeste a greeting card.

She flexed the muscles in her neck and shoulders, hoping to ease her tension. "Is there anything else?"

Sterling's sharp breath echoed in Celeste's ear. "You don't sound upset at the news of your grandmother's passing. You should be grateful to her for raising you."

Wow. How dare he?

Celeste stood from her bed. She strained to keep her voice low. Zeke was working in his room, which was on the other side of the wall from hers. Or was he? Awareness swept down her spine like a warm evening breeze. Without turning toward the door, Celeste knew Zeke stood there, watching her.

She forced the image of him from her mind and struggled to stay focused. "*You* should be grateful as well. If your mother hadn't taken me in, you would've had to raise me yourself." Or perhaps he would've stuck her in foster care. "Her taking me in allowed you to pretend I didn't exist outside of holidays and birthdays." She regretted allowing her father to trigger her temper. She wanted more than anything to end this call. Right. Now.

He drew another audible breath, this time exhaling noisily. His displeasure didn't impress her much. "Your grandmother's funeral will be here in Chicago this weekend."

"Is there anything else?" Celeste's voice cooled.

Sterling's voice heated. "Are you going to attend?"

Celeste had no desire to see Sterling with the family he'd abandoned her for, the family he'd never let her be part of. She'd stopped yearning for relationships with them years ago.

Celeste straightened her spine. "I'm on a case. In fact, I have to get back to work now."

"Are you still a homicide detective, or are you running the place now?" His attempt to sound like a proud father missed the mark by a lot.

Celeste rubbed her eyes with the thumb and two fingers of her left hand. "You never cared about my career before. Why are you asking about it now?" She sensed tension in the silence on the other side of the call.

When Sterling finally spoke, his words were clipped. "Mother's death has reminded me how little time we have. I wasn't there for you as I should have been when you were growing up, but I want to be there for you now. And I want you to meet your siblings."

Was he kidding? She was a successful entrepreneur with a home and good credit. "I don't need you now."

Sterling's sigh was the sound of defeat. "Celeste, you're named in Mother's will."

All the pieces of the puzzle dropped into place: his call, the kind words, his interest in a better relationship with her. Celeste pictured her grandmother's modest home and her few belongings. She didn't think the elderly woman's estate would inspire this newfound paternal interest. Still, she was calling BS.

"Thank you for letting me know." Celeste ended the call. She was more drained now than after her hour-plus workout earlier in the morning. But she couldn't give in to the temptation to rest. There was still one matter to deal with.

She spoke without looking around. "Do you need something?"

How does she do that? How did she know I was here without looking around? And how does she walk around the cabin without my hearing her?

Zeke crossed the threshold into Celeste's bedroom. His steps were hesitant. "I'm sorry, Celeste. I didn't mean to pry. I wanted to ask when you might have time to discuss the case."

"We can talk now." She turned to him.

Celeste stepped forward, swaying a bit as though her legs were trembling. She came to an abrupt stop. Her features were pale and stiff. Zeke sensed her struggle to mask her emotions. His arms ached to wrap around her and offer comfort. She seemed uncertain and vulnerable.

"Are you sure?" He gestured toward the cell phone still in her grip. Her knuckles were white with tension. "Your call sounded upsetting."

Celeste looked at her phone as though she didn't remember she held it. She tossed it onto the bed beside her. "How much of that did you hear?"

Zeke's face warmed with embarrassment. "Most of it. I'm sorry, Celeste. I don't know why I didn't walk away."

That wasn't true. He'd stayed because he'd wanted to learn more about her. And he'd stayed because he'd wanted to comfort her, if he could.

Celeste nodded. Was that a gesture of acceptance? Forgiveness? Or a reflexive response?

"That was Sterling Jarrett. My father." Her eyes drifted to her cell phone. "His mother died. Six days ago."

"I'm very sorry for your loss, Celeste." Why had her father waited so long to tell her of her grandmother's passing? You know what? Forget it. He couldn't imagine a reason that would justify such a delay. Zeke would've been furious if someone had waited that long to let him know a relative had died.

"Thank you." She wandered the room. Her movements seemed restless and random.

Zeke tracked her steps. "How do you feel?"

"I feel fine. As I've told you, Dionne raised me, but we weren't close." Celeste was breathless, as though she'd been running. "So I don't know why she named me in her will."

"She cared about you." Zeke crossed his arms over his chest and braced his legs. Should he be worried that she was aimlessly wandering her bedroom?

"No, she didn't." Celeste paced in silence for several seconds. "I called her twice a month and visited a couple of times a year." She paused as though trying to catch her breath. "Why did I call her? Why did I keep in touch with her?"

She wasn't asking him, but Zeke answered anyway. "She was your grandmother. You cared about her."

"No, I didn't." Celeste shook her head, emphasizing her point. "I kept in touch with her because she lived alone, and I felt obligated to check on her. The last time we spoke, she accused me of calling to see if she was dead. I told her she was too evil to die. And I meant it. Apparently, I was wrong." She gasped, covering her mouth as if trying to take the words back.

"You were angry and hurt, Celeste." Zeke lowered his arms and stepped to the center of the room. He felt the emotions battering her: shock, anger. Sorrow. "You didn't mean it."

"Yes, I did." Celeste turned her back to him. She brushed a hand across her cheeks, then folded her arms beneath her chest. Her words were tight. "Dionne Jarrett had been hateful to me my whole life. She made me feel like I had to apologize for my existence every day. There were days she made me wish I'd never been born."

Her words were knives impaling his chest. "Celeste—"

"So why does her death make me feel so bad?"

Zeke caught her before she crumbled to the floor. He lowered them both to a seated position on the patterned rug. His back pressed against the foot of the bed. Wrapping her in his arms, he searched for words to comfort her.

"I'm so sorry, Celeste." He whispered the words against her hair. "I'm so sorry she hurt you."

"She made me feel like trash." Her voice was muffled against his chest. "So why do I care that she's dead?"

Her pain was his pain. Zeke swallowed the lump in his throat so he could speak. "Because you care about people, Celeste. That's who you are. It's the reason you went into law enforcement. It's the reason you rushed to the hospital when you heard Jerry had been hurt. It's the reason you volunteered to put your life in danger to protect me."

Celeste tightened her arms around him. She spoke into his chest. "I don't want anything to happen to you."

The intensity in her voice shook him. Zeke stopped breathing. Was she speaking strictly professionally—or did she feel something more? "I don't want anything to happen to you, either." His voice was so rough he didn't recognize it. "You have a big heart, Celeste." Why hadn't he realized that before?

She leaned away from him. Her hazel eyes were wet with tears. With jerky motions, Celeste drew her sterling silver ring from her right thumb and raised it so he could see the infinity circles on the band.

"My mother gave Sterling this ring before I was born." Her voice was a whisper he could barely hear. "It's the only thing I have of hers. Well, I guess it's not hers." She put the ring back on her thumb. "It belongs to him, but my mother bought it for him."

Zeke swallowed the lump in his throat and held her closer. "I'm so sorry." He wished he could think of something more meaningful to say but he felt overwhelmed. She'd already had so much pain in her life. Was this the reason she had trouble letting people get close to her?

Celeste pulled away and pushed herself to her unsteady feet. She resumed her pacing with tentative steps. "Sterling left me with his mother to raise me. Dionne was an angry person. She yelled all the time. All the time. She claimed my mother deliberately got pregnant to force her son to marry her. She'd hated my mother and transferred that hate to me. She hated everything about me, especially how much I reminded her of my mother."

Outrage propelled Zeke to his feet. He was shaking with it. "That was a cruel thing for your grandmother to do. Your parents' relationship had nothing to do with you. You were a child. She should *not* have taken her anger and resentment out on you."

Celeste's eyes were wide with surprise. "I—I appreciate your saying that." She turned away from him and scrubbed her face with her hands. "You've asked me how I was able to get out of my house without your hearing me and about my being able to sense when someone's near me." She faced him again. A faint smile touched her lips, but it didn't reach her eyes. "Those are some of the survival skills I learned growing up with Dionne. If she didn't know I was in her house or if I could tell where she was, then I could avoid her." Her smile spread. "Sometimes, I could go for days without seeing or hearing her. Those were wonderful days."

"I hate that your childhood was so miserable." Zeke clenched his fists at his side. "I wish I could go back in time to do something—anything—to bring you some joy."

Celeste shrugged. "You're bringing me joy now. I know we're on a life-and-death case, but honestly, you've made me laugh and smile more these past three days than I have in years."

Zeke closed the distance between them and drew her into his arms. "Then let me bring you more."

Chapter 13

Zeke lowered his head and pressed his lips to hers. Celeste shook in his arms as though she'd touched an electrical current. He groaned low in his throat and held her more closely. He loved the feel of her body in his arms, the touch of her lips against his. The scent of her. She raised up on her toes. Her body was warm and firm as she pressed herself against him. Zeke's heart began a slow, steady pounding against his chest. He opened his mouth just enough to sweep his tongue across the seam of her lips. Celeste parted for him with a sigh. His heart beat faster.

He swept inside, caressing her tongue with his own. Her arms slid up his torso and over his chest. Her small, soft palms cupped his face as she deepened their kiss. He burned from the inside out. Using his body, Zeke guided Celeste back toward her bed. His fingers fumbled as he tugged his wallet from his front pocket and tossed it onto the mattress. His hands shook as he worked to remove her clothing and coaxed her to take off his. When they were naked, standing in pools of their discarded garments, he stepped back. She was beautiful. Long, toned limbs; full breasts; tight waist and rounded hips. Her skin glowed in the late-morning sunlight leaking through the window blinds.

Celeste raised her right arm and drew her fingertips down his chest to his abdomen. "You're incredible."

Zeke shook his head. He could barely breathe, much less form words. "You're amazing."

Her smile seduced him as she pushed him onto the mattress behind them. She crawled onto the bed, balancing herself on her arms and legs over him. She closed her eyes and parted her lips as she lowered her head to kiss him again. Zeke held her waist, drawing her down to him as he deepened their kiss. Her skin was soft and warm against his palms. She tasted like peppermint and smelled like vanilla and citrus.

Zeke smoothed his hands down her sides and cupped her hips, pressing her against him. Celeste gasped at his touch. He drank in the sound, enjoying the feel of her against him. Her full breasts pressed to his chest. Her long legs tangled with his. He sent his tongue deeper into her mouth, mimicking the way he wanted to bury himself inside her. Celeste drew him even deeper. She rocked her hips against his. Zeke heard his blood rushing in his head. He felt his heart thundering against his chest. Or was it hers?

Celeste freed her mouth from his. She whispered against his neck. "You're making my head spin."

"You're making me burn." Zeke rolled them onto their sides. Drawing her back against his torso, he spooned behind her. He pressed his right knee between her thighs. "Part your legs for me, sweetheart."

Zeke paused, sensing her desire—and confusion.

Celeste's skin was warm. Fires burned across her breasts, within her belly and between her legs. Zeke trailed kisses down the side of her neck.

His voice, deep and seductive, whispered in her ear. "Part your legs for me, sweetheart." His right knee pressed against her legs, parting her thighs.

This was unexpected. "Zeke, I—"

He lowered his knee and wrapped his arms around her. He drew her closer to him. He nibbled, licked and kissed the curve of her neck. His hand caressed her thigh, her torso, her breasts. Long, slow strokes that fueled the fire inside her until Celeste thought she'd explode. Her hips rocked back against his, her body pleading for him.

Zeke whispered against the shell of her ear. "Do you want me, Celeste?"

"Yes. Oh yes." She gasped for air.

"Do you trust me?"

"Yes," she sighed.

"Part your legs for me, sweetheart."

Celeste raised her right leg. He pressed his knees between hers. Zeke slid his right hand across her hips and between her thighs to touch her there.

"Zeke." She moaned low and long. His fingers moved over her. Sweat broke out on her skin.

"I'm here." His voice was husky. "Let me hold you, sweetheart." His left hand caressed her breast as his right hand cast a spell.

His moved against her, matching her rhythm as her body took control. He trailed kisses down the back of her neck and across her shoulder. She shivered against him, and he held her tighter.

"Zeke." Celeste's movements became more desperate. She strained against him. "I can't."

"Yes, sweetheart, you can." He breathed the words against her ear. Her nipples pebbled against his palm. Zeke squeezed her breast gently. "I'm right here."

Celeste felt her tension building, tightening her muscles to a breaking point. The pressure was centered between her legs. She writhed and strained against Zeke's magic fingers as he coaxed awake a desire she thought was in a permanent coma. His other hand was molding her right breast, stroking and teasing her. Strange sounds came from her: raw groans, deep moans, thin whimpers. Her body burned and melted under his touch. Her thighs quivered. Her muscles trembled. Her pressure built and drew tighter, and tighter, and tighter. And then she erupted. Zeke held her. He kissed her shoulder and neck as wave after wave of pleasure crashed over her.

Celeste lay back with her eyes closed. She drew a deep breath and collected her scattered thoughts. Opening her eyes, she took

Zeke's wallet. She turned her head and caught his eyes. They were dark and heavy with desire.

She gave him his wallet and a smile. "Want to join me this time?"

He pulled a condom from his wallet. "Very much so."

Celeste took the packet before he could open it. "Let me."

She straddled his thighs. Her body still hummed with arousal. She held his erection and stroked her tongue over its length. His deep, broken groan stoked her desire further. Celeste fitted the condom onto him, then took him into her. With one strong move, he slid into her moisture. Zeke lifted his hips, driving himself even deeper inside her. Celeste gasped, rocking her hips forward. She arched her back as she moved with him. His thrusts filled her, stroking the embers of her passion into another inferno of need. He lowered his hands and grasped her hips, moving her on him as he pressed against her. Celeste could feel the perspiration covering her body.

"Roll with me, sweetheart." Zeke wrapped one arm around her. He rose up, then tucked her under him.

His body was a delicious weight on her. Celeste wrapped her legs around his hips and pressed herself harder against him. Zeke kissed her shoulders, nibbled her neck, teased her nipples. He covered her mouth with his. He rocked with her, kissing her deeply, endlessly. Celeste floated weightless on a wave of desire. Her legs strained as he pressed against her. Her back arched as he cupped her hips. Her blood rushed in her head. Her heart thundered in her chest. Her breath came in short, sharp gasps. Her muscles drew tighter and tighter. Then he touched her. Her body snapped. Celeste tightened her arms and legs around Zeke as he stiffened above her. Their bodies shook against each other as together, they soared over the edge.

Celeste drifted up to consciousness. She was so relaxed. More relaxed than she could remember ever feeling. A steady beat like a heavy tapping echoed in her head. What was that? What time was it? What day was it?

Where was she?

Stretching her arms and legs, she drew a deep breath, filling her head with the clean scent of soap and sandalwood. The tapping sped up, sounding more like a locomotive. The warmth seeping into her bones came from the warm, muscled, naked body beneath her. She opened her eyes and found herself staring across the broad expanse of Zeke's chest. She was snuggled against his left side. His arm was wrapped around her with his hand cupping her hip. Her left thigh lay across his narrow hips. Her palm rested over his heart close to her cheek.

Her body vibrated. Her skin burned. It all came back to her. It was Tuesday afternoon. She was in bed with Zeke in his cabin safe house. And they'd just made love. Her fingertips combed through the short hairs sprinkled across his chest.

Zeke's low, sleepy voice echoed in her ear. "Am I forgiven?"

"For what?" Celeste was aware they were lying above the sheets of his bed, naked. There was nowhere to hide. She gingerly removed her thigh from his hips.

Celeste had never felt this way before. Her heart ballooned in her chest. It struggled to contain its flood of emotions: joy, hope, excitement and something more that she didn't have the courage to identify. Yet. Were these feelings a result of the powerful physical connection they'd just shared? Or were they real? Did Zeke feel them, too?

Please let him feel them, too.

"For eavesdropping on your conversation with your father." Zeke opened his eyes. His voice sped up as though he wanted to share everything on his mind before she interrupted him. "It was inexcusable. I know I shouldn't have done it, and I'm very sorry for invading your privacy. But I heard the pain in your voice and couldn't walk away from you."

He'd stolen her breath. He'd stayed because he couldn't walk away from her while she'd been in pain. With those words, Zeke Touré continued to tear down the walls she'd built around her. He was making it harder for her to hide. Part of her didn't want to crouch behind those barriers anymore. He was dispelling the darkness and tempting her into the light. She felt seen. She felt valued. For the first time in her life, she felt neither the compulsion to apologize for being nor the instinct to battle for the right to exist.

It was a miraculous realization.

Celeste swallowed the lump of emotion threatening to choke her. Her voice was husky. "I think I can be persuaded to give you another chance."

"I appreciate that." Zeke sounded relieved. "And I want to say again how very sorry—and outraged—I am over the way your family has treated you."

"Thank you." Celeste took a moment to savor the feeling of having someone on her side. "That first night you were in my home, you said you wanted me to talk more about myself. I didn't want to."

"I could tell." Zeke rolled onto his side to face her. His voice was soft.

Celeste's hand drifted from his chest. "I'd never done that before. I didn't even know if I could." She gave him a weak smile. The words weren't easy for her to say. "But I've never walked away from a challenge."

He smiled into her eyes. "I didn't mean it as a challenge."

"I know. But I'm glad I took it that way, otherwise I would never have opened up to you. And I'm glad I did." Celeste took a breath, briefly lowering her eyes. "Having someone I feel safe confiding in, someone I can trust and who listens without judgment, makes a difference. Thank you."

"You're welcome. And I feel the same about you. Beneath your gruff exterior, you have a big heart, and you're easy to talk with." He flashed the grin that made her toes curl. "We make a good team."

A good team. As they lay in bed, naked, facing each other. A teammate wasn't the first comparison she would hope he'd think of. What had she wanted him to say? That she was the love of his—

"Yes, we do make a good team." Celeste found a smile.

Zeke rolled off his side of the bed, then turned to offer her his hand. "Let's hit the showers." He gave her a sexy wink.

Celeste smiled, letting him help her to her feet. The teammate analogy had great perks.

Chapter 14

"If revenge is the motive for Dean's and Art's murders, Damien Rockwell and May Ramirez don't fit." Zeke sat next to Celeste at the cabin's dining room table Tuesday afternoon. His palms itched with the urge to hold her hand. "They both have new jobs. They're doing well and have moved on. Damien's doing better now than when he worked for Art."

After getting dressed, he and Celeste had put together a quick lunch of salad and grilled-cheese sandwiches before joining Mal and Jerry for their case-status meeting. He hoped his inability to look away from Celeste wasn't too obvious to his highly observant younger brothers.

It wasn't only his strong feelings that drew his eyes back to her again and again. It was also the very un-Celeste outfit she was wearing. Celeste's and Nanette's fashion preferences couldn't be more different. All the times their paths had crossed, Zeke had never seen her in anything other than black. But today, Celeste was wearing Nanette's lime green capris and pink-white-and-gold blouse. She looked confident, vibrant, amazing. The blouse's square low-cut neckline framed her collarbone. Zeke could still feel her skin against his lips. His eyes strayed toward her again.

"Zeke's right." Celeste met his eyes, then looked to the laptop. The screen showed Mal and Jerry seated together in the Touré

Security Group conference room. "Damien accepted responsibility for sleeping on the job. May still seems irritated that Art apparently held her responsible for her coworkers' bad behaviors. But I don't think she would've killed him or Dean for that."

"Which leaves us with Chad and Agnes." Zeke stared hard at Jerry, looking for signs of pain or fatigue. He seemed better today. "We have to speak with them. They're part of this. Even if it turns out that they aren't viable suspects, they might have helpful insights."

"I agree." Celeste rotated the sterling silver ring on her right thumb. "I was going to arrange an interview with Chad, but that tail from our meeting with May distracted me."

"One or both of them could be working with Monica Ward," Mal added.

Jerry held up his right hand, palm out. "Slow your roll, cybersleuth."

Mal shrugged. "It's too early to rule out anything."

"Agnes is doing well also." Jerry wore another loose-fitting short-sleeved dark pullover. This one was copper. He must have bought several of them to accommodate the white plaster cast, which extended from his palm to halfway up his bicep. "She got married and retired to North Carolina with her very wealthy husband. Chad's the only one who isn't doing well."

Mal made a note in his smart tablet. "I'll look for any connections Chad may have to Monica Ward."

"That will be helpful. Thank you." Zeke was still restless. There was something they were missing. What was it?

Mal's words interrupted Zeke's stressing. "One of our personal security consultants is helping with surveillance."

"Good thinking." But they were still missing something.

Celeste sprang from her chair and paced past Zeke. "Agnes and Chad don't fit the revenge motive, either. We're missing something."

Jerry raised his voice. "You know we can't see you, right?"

"We're talking to an empty chair." Mal sounded almost amused.

Zeke shifted in his seat to track her movements as she paced from the dining room to the kitchen and back. Her strides were long and stiff with temper. Tension and impatience shot from her and battered against him. He felt her presence in the room with him, but her thoughts seemed miles away. It was as though she was running various scenarios in her mind.

Celeste ignored his brothers' comments as she marched back and forth beside him. "Where's the harm? As a result of their losing their job, what harm did any of the former guards experience? The loss of a house or medical insurance or the end of a marriage? It's not enough that Agnes, May, Damien and Chad lost their jobs. What harm did their job loss cause to trigger their killing spree?"

"The Invisible Woman makes a good point." Jerry referenced one of the characters from the Fantastic Four superhero comics, Dr. Susan Storm, a.k.a. the Invisible Woman.

Zeke and Mal exchanged smiles.

Celeste continued as though she hadn't heard the youngest Touré. "May and Damien got better-paying jobs with better benefits. Agnes remarried."

Jerry was right. Celeste was making very good points.

Zeke picked up her train of thought. "And Chad has been in prison for months. If he'd planned this elaborate revenge, would he have committed a crime that would have landed him in prison?"

Jerry shrugged his healthy right shoulder. "Prison would give him an airtight alibi—except for Monica Ward's connection to the case."

Celeste stilled. "This is about something more than someone's job. We probably have the right motive—revenge. But we have the wrong reason."

Zeke felt a chill blow through him. "You think the killer wants revenge for something else? Like what?" He searched his mind for the answer.

"I don't know. Yet." Celeste reclaimed her seat. She seemed to have worked off most of her tension. "We need to find other links between TSG, Buckeye Bailey and Archer that could be a motive for murder: professional or social connections, organizations, cases. Something."

"I'm on it." Mal tapped the keys on his smart tablet.

"I can do it." Jerry tossed his right arm. "Zeke and Susan Storm are questioning suspects. You're already looking deeper into Chad's background. I'll search for other connections between our three companies."

Mal glanced at Jerry's cast. "We'll discuss that later." He turned back to the computer. "You should know someone may be following me."

Zeke straightened in his chair. "Excuse me?"

Celeste leaned into the table. "Wait. What?"

"Why didn't you lead with that?" Jerry shifted to face Mal.

"Because of your reactions." Mal gestured toward the monitor. "We needed to review the case—"

Zeke interrupted him. "Have you received a threat?"

"No." Mal turned to Jerry. "Have you?"

"No, I haven't." There was an edge to the youngest brother's voice. "And we're not done talking about this."

"Why do you think you're being followed?" Zeke balled his hands into fists, straining to keep his voice even and fear from clouding his judgment.

Mal switched his attention from Jerry back to Zeke. "I've sensed someone watching me. And the same car keeps driving past my house."

"Is Grace all right?" Celeste asked.

"Yes." Mal ran his hand over his clean-shaven head. "It took some persuading, but I've convinced her to keep her distance from us until this case is over."

Zeke briefly closed his eyes. How many people had he endangered with his actions? He wasn't even certain what he'd done wrong. He'd responded to a request for a bid for a corporate-security account, and his bid had been accepted. Was that the transgression that had led to two murders and endangered his friends and family?

He opened his eyes and saw Celeste. He wouldn't let anything happen to any of them. "Have you assigned a consultant to yourself?"

Mal's eyes flared briefly in surprise. "No."

"I'll keep an eye on him." Jerry's words were grim.

Zeke's eyes dropped to Jerry's cast. "All right."

He recognized the uncertainty in his voice, but he needed to let go of some control. He trusted his youngest brother knew what he was getting into and what he was doing. Besides, Jerry was starting to moderate his impulses and taking more time to think things through. Symone was a good influence on his brother.

"We'll see." Mal's skepticism was a little louder.

Zeke shook his head. They needed to solve this case yesterday. He scowled. "Both of you be careful out there."

Jerry gestured toward the screen. "That's good advice for all of us, Number One."

Mal looked from Zeke to Celeste and back. "Watch each other's back."

After ending the videoconference, Zeke sat staring at the keyboard. What was he missing? What more could he do to keep his brothers safe?

A soft, warm weight settled on his right shoulder. Zeke looked up into Celeste's troubled hazel eyes.

"They're not helpless." Her voice was soft. "And neither are you."

"Thank you." Zeke covered her hand with his own. "Please keep reminding me of that."

Celeste felt the tension in the hard muscles of Zeke's broad shoulder course through her palm, up her arm and lodge in her chest. He was a man tormented, and her heart hurt for him. What could she do to help him carry this burden? What could she say to reassure him that, just as they had with The Bishop Foundation hostile takeover attempt, they'd bring the murderer to justice and his brothers would be safe. His brothers. The inseparable Touré trio.

She squeezed his shoulder, then let her arm drop to her side. "One thing the killer didn't take into account is how close you and your brothers are and how well you work together. In less than a week, they've moved you to safety, identified the top suspects and revealed the stalker."

"We couldn't have done any of that without you." Admiration

shone in his eyes. It made Celeste uncomfortable. Or maybe it was Nanette's clothes.

She stood and wandered the dining area, forcing herself not to fidget. "I'm happy to help. Problems are usually easier when you can share them." Zeke's silence was deafening. Celeste struggled against nervous chatter. It was a losing battle. "Besides, we're helping each other. The sooner we solve this case, the sooner we can tell my client who killed her husband and why."

"Who do you share your problems with?" Zeke's curiosity carried from the dining table behind her. "Is it Nanette?"

Celeste turned to him. She could feel that her smile was crooked. "I thought you didn't like it when people changed the subject from themselves."

"You didn't ask a question." Zeke's grin chased the tension from his chiseled features and revealed perfect white teeth. His voice was warm with humor. Had she helped to ease his burden?

Celeste shook her head, expelling an exasperated breath. "I'm never going to get the hang of this emotional sharing stuff."

"You're doing fine." He closed the laptop and rested his forearms on the table in front of him. "Is Nanette the one you confide in when you're troubled?"

Why was he asking? She'd like to know the reason for his curiosity, but she'd follow up about that later. For now, she wanted to keep the shadows from returning to his eyes.

Celeste wandered from the dining area into the great room. She admired the room's gleaming pinewood floor with its warm soft-brown-and-moss-green area rug. Her eyes lingered on the fluffy brown sofa and matching chairs with ottomans. The cabin was beautiful, but she preferred her bright, whimsical little home in Worthington.

"Nanette is a good friend, but she's not much of a problem solver. I can't strategize with her the way you can with your brothers." Celeste walked past the cedar-wood coffee table and paused in front of the stone fireplace.

"Why did you go into business with her?" Zeke's chair squeaked against the flooring, as though he was leaving the table.

"She asked me to." Celeste drew a breath, filling her senses with the fragrance of cedar pines. And with Zeke's soap-and-sandalwood scent. He was so close. "When I told her I was opening my own agency, she asked to join me. She was a good detective, and we could split the start-up costs. So I figured why not? Honestly, during these past almost-three years, she's been great at promoting the agency and bringing in clients."

"Celeste, why didn't you return to the department? Your lieutenant wanted you and Nanette back. Why did you turn him down?"

She faced him. This was the second time he'd asked that. His tone was more caring than curious. That was a point in his favor. If he was just being nosy, she wouldn't tell him the time of day. But there was something in his voice, his eyes, that made her want to tell him things she'd never told another soul.

Her smile was unsteady. "It's a long story."

His eyes smiled back. "Start at the beginning."

Celeste paced past him, gathering her thoughts. "Nanette was promoted to detective a couple of years before me. She was dating a detective in the robbery division. She and Roger kept saying his partner, Lee, and I should go out. Lee was handsome, intelligent and charismatic. So when he finally asked me out, I said sure."

Big mistake.

"Lee Martin." Zeke didn't ask.

Celeste frowned over her shoulder. "You knew him?"

Zeke shoved his hands into the front pockets of his gray pants. "I know he and Roger Strand were convicted and sentenced for the crime you and Nanette were charged with."

Celeste searched Zeke's features. His face was unreadable, but his tension reached her across the room. He was angry. With whom—and why? Was he angry with her? She had flashbacks of the reactions from some of the officers and detectives with whom she'd served. They seemed to think she and Nanette should've taken the fall for their "brave brothers in blue." They'd acted as though she and Nanette had done something wrong in defending themselves. Their betrayal had felt like a physical attack.

She turned to face the fluffy brown sofa again. It was easier than looking at Zeke and wondering what was going on in his very agile mind. "I thought I was in love. And Nanette, she was over the moon. She'd been practicing her authentic reaction to Roger's anticipated proposal. She was convinced he was going to ask her to marry him. And then Internal Affairs called. Nanette and I were accused of stealing property from the evidence room—money, drugs, jewelry. They had log sheets with our signatures and footage of us handling the evidence boxes. Even our union lawyers urged us to take a deal."

Zeke prompted her when she stopped. "How long had you and Lee been dating by this time?"

"Six months." Celeste marched to the bay window. "He was my first call after Internal Affairs, but he said he didn't want anything to do with me. He said associating with a dirty cop would be bad for his career. That's when I realized he'd set me up."

Shame enveloped her. Six months. She'd given him her heart, her mind and her body. If they'd been together much longer, she was sure she would've given him even more. She'd wanted forever with him. But their relationship had been a lie from the start. Anger, pain and humiliation were ripping her apart from the inside just as they had back then. Her muscles trembled from the effort to keep herself together. Willpower alone kept her on her feet. Celeste took deep breaths to combat the nausea.

"I'm so sorry, Celeste." Beneath Zeke's gentle words, she heard an edge of anger. "With all the evidence against you, how did you find the courage to fight them?"

"I owe everything to Eriq." Thinking of Eriq's steadfast belief in her helped Celeste breathe. Her relationship with the veteran detective was the best thing to come out of her time with the Columbus Division of Police. "Everyone in the department thought we were guilty—except him. He's been my mentor since the day I walked into the department. He's what I imagine a real father would be."

"He's very proud of you."

"That's nice to hear." Relief and gratitude washed away the residual feelings of anguish and shame. Celeste turned away from the window. "He'd warned me to be careful. He said Lee was too slick. But again, I thought I was in love. So when I was charged, I was ashamed to ask him for help. Before I could get my courage up, he was knocking on my door, helping me figure out what I needed to do to clear my name. Nanette and I fired the union lawyers and hired a defense attorney to represent both of us. Then we started our investigation. It wasn't easy."

Zeke took his hands out of his pockets and stepped away from the fireplace. "What did you do?"

Celeste allowed her mind to travel back to those planning sessions with Eriq and Nanette. Being proactive and involved in her defense had protected her sanity. "Lee and Roger must have been selling the stolen items. We found their fences. The ones who were willing to talk met with our attorney and linked Lee and Roger to the thefts. A forensic technician proved the footage was fake, and a handwriting expert testified that our signatures had been forged."

A glint of satisfaction lit Zeke's eyes. "And now Lee and Roger are in prison where they belong. I'm so proud of you for having the courage and strength to defend yourself. You constantly impress me."

The look in his eyes made Celeste believe she could do anything. "You're pretty impressive yourself, which is how I know we're going to keep your family safe and take down Dean's and Art's killer. We make a good team."

Zeke grinned as though she'd given him a gift. "Yes, we do."

After Lee, Celeste didn't think she'd trust anyone ever again. She'd envied Nanette for being able to find real love with Warren. Maybe like Nanette, she could trust again. Zeke wasn't Lee. He wasn't a slick, showy charmer. He was a sincere, caring, albeit controlling, protector. She trusted Zeke with her life, just as Zeke was trusting her with his.

Then why was she so afraid to trust him with her heart?

Celeste's eyes were crossing after her third review of Jerry's report on Chad Cooper. Her frustration rose as she sat at the desk in her bedroom in the safe house late Tuesday afternoon. Her attention drifted away from the laptop Mal had sent her toward the shared wall between her room and Zeke's. Had he found anything they may have missed the first two times they'd read Chad's file? Perhaps she should ask him. She closed the computer as she rose from her chair.

Her cell phone rang, stopping her in her tracks. Celeste checked the caller ID. Nanette. She'd never before noticed how very bad her partner's timing was. "Hi, Nanette."

"Hey, is everything okay?" Nanette sounded suspiciously concerned.

"As well as can be expected, considering an unidentified serial killer who's already killed two people is after my protectee." Celeste strained to catch background sounds. She wanted to know from where her partner was calling.

Nanette sighed. "Do you have any new leads?" Was she settling back onto her office chair or her living room sofa?

"Not yet." Celeste wandered her room. "We're going a little deeper into our known suspects' backgrounds. But that's not why you're calling." *Please don't let her try to convince me to move to San Diego again.*

"You've got mail." Papers rustled under Nanette's announcement. "I stopped by the office since you're, shall we say, on location, to check on the mail and messages."

"I appreciate that." So the other woman was probably calling from their office. One of the many benefits of having a partner: they could check the mail when you couldn't.

"Sure," Nanette continued. "You have a letter from a law firm. I don't recognize the firm's name but it's in Chicago. I thought it might be important. Don't you go to Chicago a couple of times a year?"

"Yes, I do." Celeste searched her mind for clues as to why a Chicago law firm was sending her a letter. "It's probably the firm handling Dionne's estate."

"Dionne who?" Nanette sounded confused.

"She's—she *was*—my paternal grandmother."

"Your *grandmother*?" Surprise boosted the volume of Nanette's voice.

Celeste winced as her eardrum took the punishment. "Sterling, my father, called this morning to tell me his mother had died." It still rankled her that he'd waited almost a week to tell her. Although why should she be surprised? She'd bet the only reason he'd called was that he'd known the law firm was going to contact her. He'd wanted to run interference.

"Your *father*?" Once again, Nanette's surprise was like a cymbal ringing in her ears. "Mind. Blown. Why haven't you ever told me your grandmother and your father were still alive?"

Celeste shrugged although Nanette couldn't see it. "You never asked, and I don't have a relationship with either of them."

Their exchange reminded her of the discussion she'd had with Zeke. He hadn't wanted to make assumptions about her life. Instead, he'd cared enough to ask her about her family. A warm feeling enveloped her.

Nanette's impatient breath brought Celeste back to their phone call. "It's obvious you're not close since you refer to them by their Christian names. I talk about my family all the time. And I call them 'Mommy,' 'Daddy' and 'Nana.' I figured all your family must be dead. I thought those Chicago trips were mental health vacays. You're pretty intense."

Memories of those biannual trips to check on Dionne played across her mind. "No, those weren't vacations."

Those four-day stays were the exact opposite. They were packed with doctors' checkups, dental exams and pharmacy trips for her grandmother. Celeste also checked the condition of her grandmother's house to make sure it was safe and in good repair. And the whole time, she endured her grandmother's familiar suspicious stares and hostile silences. What had compelled her to make those visits? She would rather have spent that time in her own lovely little home. In fact, from the minute she packed up her car for the six-hour drive, she was looking forward to the day she returned.

HBO's *The Wire* said it best. Every situation had two days: the day you get in and the day you get out. The stuff in between didn't matter.

"Anyway, Celeste, I'm sorry for your loss." Nanette's words were awkward and muted. "I remember when my maternal grandmother died. We'd been close. Her death was hard on me."

"Thank you." Celeste left it at that. She didn't want to explain that Dionne had been a virtual stranger to her.

"Of course." Nanette sighed. "Now, what should I do with the lawyer's letter? You're probably right about it being about your grandmother. I could scan it and email it to you. You know you can trust me not to read it. Unless you want me to?"

Nanette's insatiable curiosity was her superpower. It made her a great investigator.

Celeste shook her head in amusement. "I don't care if you read the letter."

"In that case, I'll read it to you now." Nanette's voice bounced with excitement. "But I'll still email a scan of it to you before I leave."

"Thanks, but I don't know why you're so excited. It's probably just an official announcement about Dionne's death." Celeste imagined Nanette reaching for her letter opener during their brief silence. In the other woman's opinion, there were few things worse than a papercut.

"Oh, girl, this is more than an announcement." Nanette inserted a dramatic pause. "According to this letter, you're your grandmother's sole beneficiary, and she's left you her, quote, 'sizable assets,' end quote. The lawyer asks that you contact them, quote, 'at your earliest opportunity,' end quote."

"*Sole* beneficiary?" Celeste massaged her brow. "Well, that solves the mystery of Sterling's phone call."

What were these assets, and how much were they worth?

Chapter 15

"Are you police officers?" Agnes Letby's image was projected onto Zeke's clean laptop early Wednesday morning. She removed her overly large red-rimmed sunglasses and squinted at the monitor.

The retired Buckeye Bailey Security guard and serial killer suspect looked like she'd joined the videoconference straight from the salon. Her hair was skillfully dyed a rich honey blond and swept high onto her round head, giving her a regal appearance. Her makeup was perfect. It took at least ten years from the sixty-two recorded on her employment files.

Agnes craned her neck as though trying to identify where she and Zeke were. This made Celeste doubly grateful to Eriq for securing permission for her and Zeke to use the same small meeting room at the police substation where they'd spoken with the detectives before taking refuge at the cabin safe house.

Mal and Jerry had vetoed Zeke and Celeste interviewing Agnes via videoconference. They'd raised the possibility of Agnes circumventing Mal's cybersecurity systems and tracking them to the safe house. This would be especially bad if Agnes was working with the serial killer.

Celeste accepted they had a point. But Zeke had a good argument as well. She and Zeke had conducted every other interview. They'd questioned Damien and May. They'd spoken with Dean's and Art's families. The information they'd personally collected could prove useful when meeting with Agnes. With their personal experience, Celeste and Zeke might think of follow-up questions or notice inconsistencies in Agnes's responses that Mal and Jerry wouldn't catch. The two overprotective younger brothers weren't completely sold on Zeke and Celeste's plan to interview Agnes from the substation, but they conceded it was better than sending Agnes a virtual invitation to the safe house.

"We aren't officers, but we're working with the police." Celeste sat beside Zeke, sharing the laptop screen with him.

Although she was wearing the most subdued items her partner had packed, she was still uncomfortable in Nanette's clothes. Judging by Zeke's reaction to her appearance, she'd chosen well. The emerald scoop-necked blouse had long flowing sleeves. The pencil-slim cream skirt was a little loose in the hips and a little short in the knee-length hem. Her black loafers didn't enhance the outfit, but wobbling around in Nanette's four-inch stilettos would've made her motion sick.

"Why did you decide to retire after you left Buckeye Bailey Security?" Zeke looked very handsome in his smoke gray suit, navy shirt and tie.

Agnes's chuckle was raspy, as though she was battling a cold. "I don't know who your sources are, but I didn't leave Buckeye Bailey. I was fired." She spread her arms, balancing her sunglasses in her right hand. "And at my age, I didn't think any decent security company would hire me. So when my lover suggested I retire and that we get married and move to North Carolina, I thought, 'Why the heck not?'"

Celeste didn't want to like Agnes, but there was something about the older woman that was drawing her in. "Congratulations."

"Best decision he's ever made." Agnes's big blue eyes twinkled. "How long have you two been together?"

Celeste blinked. She decided to let Zeke handle that question.

He responded with confidence. "This is our second case together."

Ah. Good one. "Yes, we're colleagues." *With benefits. Very nice benefits.*

"Really?" Agnes arched a thin brown eyebrow. "Did you forget I was a security guard? We're very observant." She winked. "Don't worry. Your secret's safe with me. You make a good-looking couple."

Celeste's eyes widened. It was time to regain control of the interview. "Ms. Letby—"

"Call me Agnes, hon." Agnes put her sunglasses back on. The large black lenses covered two-thirds of her face.

"Agnes." Celeste inclined her head. "How was your relationship with Arthur Bailey?"

"I wouldn't call what we had a *relationship*." Agnes's words held a thin layer of dislike. "I only saw Art when I collected my paycheck twice a month. We barely spoke. If he'd moved the agency into the twenty-first century and implemented direct deposit like we'd all asked him to I can't even count the number of times, I wouldn't have had to see him at all."

"How did you feel when he fired you?" Zeke asked.

Agnes removed her sunglasses again. She cocked her head as though in confusion. "Mr. Touré—"

Zeke interrupted. "Call me Zeke."

Agnes glowed. She glanced at Celeste, wiggling her eyebrows in approval. "Zeke, how would you have felt if someone had fired you unjustly?" She held up her hands. "I know Art lost the Archer account and couldn't afford to keep all of us, but May and I had been complaining about Damien and Chad for *months*—"

Zeke stopped her again. "You and May complained about Damien's and Chad's unprofessional behavior?"

Celeste was surprised as well. May hadn't mentioned that.

"You bet we did." For the first time, anger surfaced in Agnes's voice. "May's shift was between Sleeping Beauty—that's Damien—and Mr. No-Show, Chad. She told me she'd start her shift and find Damien sleeping, sometimes at the front desk. And Art had called me more than once to relieve May when Chad was late. He called it 'bonus shifts.'" She made air quotes with both of her hands. "I called it 'not hiring qualified people.' I'm sixty-two years old. Do you think I want to spend every day of my life at work?"

Celeste crossed her right leg over her left. Startled by how high the skirt rode up her thigh, she immediately put both legs flat on the ground. "Did you notice any tension between Art and either Damien, May or Chad?"

"May?" Agnes laughed. After her outburst, her temper seemed to dissipate. She put her glasses back on. "She was too busy looking for another job to waste energy on Art. So was I." She sobered. "But something was going on with Chad. More than once, when I went in to get my check, I heard them arguing."

Beside Celeste, Zeke tensed. "Did you ask him what it was about?"

Agnes was shaking her head before Zeke finished speaking. "I never asked. I didn't want to get involved. But Chad saw me outside of Art's office once as he was storming out. He claimed he and Art were arguing because Art didn't have his paycheck *again*."

Celeste caught the suspicion in Agnes's tone. "You don't sound like you believed him."

"That's because I didn't." Agnes crossed her arms over her ample chest. "Chad had worked for Art for what? A couple of months? I'd worked for him for years. In all that time, I'd never had any trouble with my pay. Not once. But he'd missed Chad's paycheck multiple times? And only Chad's? No one else ever complained about not getting paid. I know that for the last couple of years, Buckeye Bailey had been leaking money like a sieve. But I still didn't buy it."

Celeste held Zeke's eyes. If Agnes didn't buy Chad's story about missing paychecks, why should they? They couldn't put it off any longer. They had to speak with Chad. He may be the key to the motive behind the murders.

"Why hadn't May told us she and Agnes had been complaining to Art about Damien and Chad for months?" Zeke directed the question to the image of his brothers projected onto his computer monitor.

Mal and Jerry were in the Touré Security Group conference room. Even to his concerned eyes, they looked fine. Jerry didn't seem to be in as much pain over his broken arm. And they both appeared to have made it into the office without running into the stalker. He breathed a sigh of relief.

Seated beside him in the police substation's meeting room, Celeste seemed unusually quiet, as though more than this case was on her mind. Did it have anything to do with Agnes's comments about their body language?

Zeke hadn't been aware that he'd been telegraphing anything, although he wouldn't mind if people knew they were together. Now that she trusted him enough to open up to him, he wanted another chance with her. He'd thought he'd made that clear. Was she uncomfortable with the idea of their relationship becoming public knowledge?

Jerry shrugged his uninjured right shoulder. "The only way to know why is to ask her."

Mal rubbed the back of his neck. "Neither Damien nor Agnes had problems with their paychecks. May didn't mention any issues with her pay, right?"

"She didn't mention that she and Agnes had complained about Damien and Chad, either," Jerry muttered.

Zeke considered Celeste. She was so still. Almost preoccupied. Should he be concerned? "What do you think, Celeste?"

She was rotating the ring on her right thumb. Her mother's ring. "I think Chad was blackmailing Art. I think his missing 'paycheck' wasn't for his work. It was for his silence."

"What now?" Jerry frowned. "Where are you getting that from?"

"Of course." A light bulb went off in Zeke's mind. He addressed Jerry. "Agnes claimed Buckeye Bailey Security had been leaking money like a sieve. Is there a connection between Art's financial problems and his arguments with Chad?"

Mal ran a hand over his head. "Chad was showing up late to the point that Agnes and May complained about him, but Art wouldn't fire him. Maybe that's because of the blackmail material Chad was holding over Art."

Jerry spread his arms, looking from Celeste to Zeke and Mal. "But in the end, Art did fire him. And what does Chad's blackmail scheme have to do with us or Dean?"

"That's what we have to find out." Zeke was grim.

"I'll follow up with Meryl this afternoon." Celeste sounded terse. "I have a feeling she's still holding out on us."

"I'm afraid you're right." Zeke held her eyes. "We have to meet with Chad as soon as possible."

"Hold on, Number One." Jerry held his right hand up, palm out. "Mal and I have been talking. We think you going to the prison is a bad idea."

Zeke frowned at the monitor. "Why?"

"What?" Celeste spoke at the same time.

Mal gave Jerry the side-eye. "You can't go without security."

Celeste burst out laughing. "There are literally security guards in prison."

Jerry's scowl was stubborn. "If Chad's working with Monica Ward, they could set a trap for you if they know when and where you'll be. That could've been what happened the last time you were followed."

"What do you mean *the last time*?" Celeste lifted her right index finger. "We've only been followed *once*. *One* time."

She was right, but Zeke opted to stay out of it. He kind of enjoyed having someone defend him. Having Celeste defend him.

Mal broke the impasse. "Eriq got permission for the two of you to videoconference with Chad tomorrow afternoon. You can use that same room."

Celeste chuckled again. "You Tourés, you really look out for each other. It's nice."

"We're brothers." Zeke turned to Mal. "That reminds me. Are you still being followed?"

Mal looked thoughtful. "I don't think so, but I'm being vigilant."

Zeke was reassured. Mal's idea of vigilance was everyone else's definition of extreme paranoia. He had the best home-security system of anyone he'd ever known. Mal should be safe. He hoped.

Zeke checked his watch. "We might as well head back." He saved the notes they'd made on his computer. "We'll call you after our interview with Chad tomorrow."

Jerry inclined his head. "All right. Be careful getting back."

"Stay alert." Mal split a look between Zeke and Celeste before leaving the meeting.

"You and your brothers make a great team." Celeste's tone was thoughtful.

"I agree." Zeke studied the faraway look in her eyes. "And you were right. I need to get their input on TSG's business plan earlier. I'll talk with them about it." Although, like his brothers, Zeke didn't like admitting to failures.

He stood, extending his right hand to Celeste. She took it, sending heat up his arm. He didn't want to let go. One of the officers escorted them to Zeke's rental car. Eriq's orders.

Zeke navigated the car out of the parking lot and braked at a red light. "Is everything okay? You seemed quiet during our meetings."

Seconds that felt like minutes ticked by in silence. Zeke thought she was going to ignore his question or change the subject. The impression that, even after what they'd shared that morning, she was still putting up walls between them hurt. Then she spoke, and he breathed again.

Celeste's voice was low. "The attorney for Dionne's estate sent a letter to my office. I asked Nanette to read it to me. I'm not just named in her will, as Sterling had told me. I'm her sole beneficiary. That's why he called me. He's panicking."

Zeke's temper spiked on Celeste's behalf. "He pretended he wanted a better relationship with you, but you believe he's panicking because he was left out of his mother's will."

"I do." Celeste's voice carried to him in the cozy confines of the rented sedan. "Dionne constantly complained Sterling and his children were always asking her for money."

"Was your grandmother wealthy?" The traffic light turned green, and Zeke moved the car forward.

Celeste shrugged. "She didn't talk about her finances, and I didn't ask. I haven't asked her for money since I was sixteen. I left her house when I was eighteen, and I've been taking care of myself ever since."

That wasn't pride he heard. It was determination and resolve. Celeste Jarrett was her own person. She could take care of herself and wasn't willing to count on anyone else. Zeke was impressed. He was also concerned. Had she convinced herself that she didn't need anyone? Not even him?

She continued. "I'm not surprised he had an ulterior motive for calling me. But I am upset he thought I'd fall for it. He must think I'm a fool."

"Then he doesn't know you at all." Zeke regretted his sharp tone. He softened it. "What do you want to do?"

Celeste rotated the ring on her thumb. "I'll email the lawyer tonight. Let her know I'm in the middle of a case and ask what she needs from me."

Zeke took the Route 315 North on-ramp. "I'm here for you if there's anything I can do to help. You shouldn't have to go through something like this on your own."

"Thank you. I may take you up on that." Celeste's voice held a weak smile.

Zeke turned his attention back to the road. "Of course. I want to help you."

As much as you'll let me.

"Agnes Letby's words keep echoing in my mind." Zeke finished packing their bowls, plates, glasses and silverware into the dishwasher and straightened away from the machine Wednesday afternoon.

"Which ones? She used a lot of them." Celeste dried the large saucepan they'd used to make the lentil soup they'd had for lunch. She returned it to the dark wood cupboard beside the oven.

The kitchen was redolent with the scent of lentil and onions, as well as the vinaigrette and olive oil from their salads. As they'd prepared lunch, they'd moved together as though they'd shared scores of meals before. It was funny the way little things like that could ease a loneliness Zeke hadn't even known he'd felt.

"The ones about Buckeye Bailey Security's financial challenges." He rested his hips against the white-and-silver-marble counter and crossed his arms over his chest. "Agnes's specific words were 'For the last couple of years, Buckeye Bailey had been leaking money like a sieve.'"

Celeste's cell phone rang. She checked the ID screen before sending the caller to her voicemail. "Why can't you get that out of your head?" She strode past him on her way to the great room.

Had she brushed against him deliberately? He hoped so.

Zeke followed her. "I've told you before the similarities between Buckeye Bailey and TSG make me nervous. It's like watching my family's company in the future, if we aren't able to turn things around."

Celeste folded herself onto the far end of the sofa. "But TSG isn't leaking money like a sieve."

Wincing on the inside, Zeke paced the great room. Should he remind Celeste of the business mistakes he'd made? She must think he's a loser to have so badly steered his family's company. He felt sick, thinking of the decades of hard work his parents had put into their legacy, only to have him, in a handful of years, bring their investment to the edge of collapse.

"No, but as I've said, we haven't paid ourselves in months." He paused in front of the bay window. Instead of the rolling lawn and magnificent trees, he pictured his parents and his brothers. "We're working to pay our bills. That's not what my parents had planned for us."

"That's not the *aspiration* your parents had for you. But running a business is hard. Some days, you think you'll never see another client. Never get another paid invoice. I get it. And I'm sure your parents had those same feelings as they built their company."

His parents had mentioned more than once there were months when the company had struggled. Zeke had thought they'd hoped he'd learn from their experiences. Instead, he'd recreated those experiences, putting his own spin on them.

Zeke pinched the bridge of his nose as frustration swamped him. "Adding Archer Family Realty has helped, but we've got to do more to rebuild. And to protect ourselves in the future. If we were to lose even one client, it could destroy us like it destroyed Art."

"What are Mal's and Jerry's ideas?" There was a soft rustling from the sofa, as though Celeste had shifted to keep him in sight as he resumed his pacing.

Zeke paused again. "I haven't discussed it with them yet." He sensed the shock in Celeste's silence.

"Why not?"

Zeke expelled a heavy breath. "This isn't exactly an easy conversation to have."

"Yet you're having it with me." She broke off. Her voice stiffened. "Is that because my opinion doesn't matter?"

Shocked, Zeke spun to face her. Her eyes held his with an intensity that mesmerized him. "That's not true. In fact, it's the opposite. I want your opinion. You're a small-business owner, too. You know how challenging it is trying to forecast how the markets are going to affect our incomes. But I don't want you to think less of me because of bad decisions I've made."

Celeste's eyebrows leaped toward her hairline. "Now, that's just ridiculous, almost as ridiculous as you not having this conversation with your brothers."

Zeke paced toward the fireplace. "This was on me. And I've learned from my mistakes, but I don't want to let my brothers down again."

"I thought the three of you were equal partners?"

"We are."

"Then this was actually on *all* of you." She stood from the sofa and crossed to him. "Listen, I know you love being in control, but I'm sure you didn't implement your expansion plans without input from Mal and Jerry."

Zeke frowned. "Of course not. We discussed those business decisions."

Celeste braced her hands on his biceps. "You need to have this conversation with them, too. *Now.* Give Mal and Jerry bigger roles in developing your company's business plan. I'm sure they want to help. And you shouldn't take this on by yourself."

Zeke shook his head. "They haven't said anything to me about wanting to help develop the plan."

Celeste's eyes twinkled with amusement. "That's because you're a control freak and they probably didn't want to argue with you. They love you. You're very lucky."

"I know." Zeke's sigh was less burdened this time. "And

you're right. They were probably picking their battles. We tend to do that."

"You guys are phenomenal when it comes to brainstorming. You build off each other's ideas. I'm sure you can come up with some great strategies for keeping TSG thriving."

"Thank you." Zeke gave her a considering look. "Do you really think I'm controlling?"

Celeste's hazel eyes darkened. "Yes, but I love a challenge."

"And I love...challenging you." He pressed his lips to hers to keep from confessing what was in his heart—he was falling in love with the prickly private investigator. In fact, he may have already fallen.

Chapter 16

"You've been waiting for the business plan." Zeke was videoconferencing with his brothers in his cabin bedroom early Wednesday evening. "It's taken longer than expected. I've come up against a wall and don't have a clear idea of where to go from here."

His brothers, who were seated in the Touré Security Group conference room, watched him in silent anticipation. It was as though they expected him to say something more.

Jerry glanced at Mal before returning his attention to Zeke. "Is this where you finally ask for our input *before* you finalize the plan?"

Zeke rubbed his right hand across his eyes. "I deserved that."

Jerry expelled a breath on a broken laugh. "Yeah, you did, control freak."

Mal smiled. Zeke recognized the expression. His middle brother agreed with Jerry but didn't want to hurt Zeke's feelings. Celeste was right. He was a control freak—and it was past time he shared the responsibility of developing their business plan with his brothers.

Mal gestured toward Zeke. "I know you think you've made some bad decisions. Your previous ideas were ambitious, but we've benefitted from them, including recruiting contractors in other states—"

"Mal's right." Jerry interrupted. "Those contractors came in handy when we had to go to Florida to protect Grace's grandmother."

Mal inclined his head. "That's right. And we've hired a couple to keep tabs on Agnes. They haven't turned up anything suspicious on her. The safe house was a good investment, too."

"Yeah, it was a good idea to use it now and when we were protecting Symone." Jerry nodded again. "Mal's making a lot of good points. And using words instead of grunts to make them. So you need to stop kicking yourself over those decisions. They may not have turned out the way you intended, but they were good investments."

Zeke pinched the bridge of his nose. "I just wish we were making a return on these investments." He dropped his hand. "However, our priority—I think—should be finding a way to protect the agency from future market shifts. I need your help with that."

Mal and Jerry exchanged another look before Mal responded. "We've had a 57.7 percent increase in cybersecurity requests, and we've increased our client retainers almost a third over last year by 31.4 percent."

Jerry gave them a sheepish grin. "I can't rattle off numbers like the human spreadsheet, but personal security requests are up at least thirty percent. As you know, we've had to increase the number of training classes to keep up with demand without sacrificing quality—or our reputation."

Although encouraging, the news didn't ease Zeke's concerns. Those numbers reflected their current business. How sustainable was that income? It was impossible to tell.

Zeke straightened in his seat. "Those numbers are great. Corporate-security requests have increased a bit, too. But what about the future? What if corporate, cyber and personal security requests all drop? We need a feature of our agency that will help shield us from that type of market turn."

Mal's thick black eyebrows knitted in an expression similar to Jerry's. "We can monitor trends, but we can't forecast the future."

"Yeah, we'd need a crystal ball for that." Jerry shook his

head. "Things are going well now. We're paying down our debts. We'll be able to pay ourselves again soon and, hopefully, put away extra savings in case cash flow gets a little tight again."

Why couldn't his brothers understand his concerns for the agency's future? "What if we aren't able to set aside extra savings before the market shifts? What if AI replaces our corporate security or cybersecurity or personal security services? Or all three?"

Artificial intelligence was one of the market trends Zeke considered a very real threat to Touré Security Group's business. Not everyone would choose the personal touch over automated systems, especially if the price tag was lower. Zeke didn't want to cut costs to bring in more customers. He didn't think his brothers would be interested in that strategy, either. It hadn't worked for Arthur Bailey.

Mal pinned Zeke with an intense stare. "Art's financial challenges are a cautionary tale." It was as though his middle brother had read his mind. "He tried to build his business by underbidding projects to bring in clients. Mom and Dad didn't do that. Neither do we."

Zeke ran a hand over his clean-shaven head. "I know that—"

"Do you?" Jerry interrupted. "Then why are you panicking? We're doing well. That doesn't mean we can sit back on our laurels, but we don't need to run around like the sky is falling, either."

It was a struggle to remain seated when his body was vibrating with impatience. "I'm not panicking. I want to explore options that could help stabilize the company if technologies or market trends make things more challenging for our industry."

Mal spread his hands. "We can't add a division every time we need to supplement our business income. At some point, we'll become a jack of all trades, master of none."

Jerry raised a hand. "Wait a minute, Mal. Number One may be onto something." He lowered it again. "I've been giving this some thought. This is our third case involving an investigation. We were successful with our first two cases. I'm praying we're successful with this one, too. What do you think about adding investigative services to our agency?"

Mal lowered his head as though considering the idea. "We would be competing against Celeste's agency. She's more established and has better credentials. It also feels disloyal."

Jerry shifted toward Mal. "We wouldn't have to move into investigations. What if we asked her to collaborate with us? She could refer us to her clients who need services like personal, cyber or corporate security. We could refer her to our clients who need investigations like fraud, lawsuits, corporate espionage."

"That's a good idea." Mal nodded his agreement. "We could still collaborate on some cases. Investigations is a natural offshoot of security. And partnering with another company would help expand our client base."

Zeke sat perfectly still as his thoughts raced. "What if we asked her to join us?"

Jerry frowned. "You mean, like merging our two agencies?"

Zeke leaned forward, lowering his voice. "Her partner's getting married and moving to San Diego. Celeste doesn't want to relocate, but she doesn't want to run the agency by herself, either. What if we ask her to join TSG?"

Jerry's expression brightened. "Why not? The four of us make a good team. It could be the Touré Security and Investigations Group—TSIG."

Mal looked dubious. "Do you think that would interest her?"

Zeke spread his arms. "What wouldn't she like about the plan? She enjoys working with us. We enjoy working with her. She'd be the head of her division. She wouldn't be giving up anything."

"Except her independence." Mal arched an eyebrow. "Right now she's working for herself, making her own decisions. Collaborating on a case is one thing. Would she be interested in collaborating on her livelihood?"

Jerry shrugged. "You have a point, but we should at least ask her."

Zeke gestured toward Jerry. "I'll ask her. The worst that could happen is that she says no."

The idea of partnering with Celeste to take TSG to the next level the way his parents had worked together made him more excited about the future than he'd felt in years. He hoped this was a vision she could share with him.

"Meryl, tell me about Art's financial problems." Celeste had called her client on the burner phone Mal had prepared for her. She sat cross-legged on her bed in the safe house early Wednesday evening.

"What do you mean?" the widow asked. But Celeste heard something in the other woman's voice that told her Meryl knew what she was talking about. From the beginning, Celeste had the feeling her client was keeping secrets. Now she was certain of it.

Celeste called her bluff. "Buckeye Bailey Security was operating in the red. Art had had to cut guards even before he fired the four who were assigned to Archer Family Realty. What was behind Art's financial trouble?" She sensed Meryl debating whether to tell her the truth or continue to feign ignorance. "Meryl, this might have something to do with Art's murder."

"Art was sued." The words rushed out of Meryl. "Two years ago."

Celeste's hand tightened around the cell phone. "By whom?"

Meryl hesitated. The pain of this topic transmitted over the satellite connection. Celeste empathized with her client, but she had to keep pushing. Art and Dean had already been killed. Now Zeke's life was on the line.

Celeste held the phone even tighter. "Meryl, who sued him?"

Meryl sighed. "The children of the guard who was killed on duty."

Oh no. "What happened?"

The sound of running water in the background gave the impression of Meryl pouring herself a cool drink. The faucet shut off, and Meryl spoke. "It was the middle of March two years ago. I'll never forget it. It was a beautiful day. Or at least, it had started that way. Then Art called me late that morning. He'd gotten a call from a police officer. One of his guards had been shot multiple times while on duty. Art had gone to the hospital immediately, but he was too late. The guard, Sally Jaxx, had died."

Celeste briefly closed her eyes. Grief tried to drain her energy. She took a breath and kept going. "I'm so sorry. Did they catch the killer?"

Meryl's sigh shook. "It was domestic violence. The husband of one of the employees killed Sally and his wife before shooting himself. Sally had two children. Art met them at the hospital. They were devastated."

"Of course." Celeste's heart broke, imagining Sally's children's distress. "How old were they?"

Meryl hesitated as though trying to remember. "I think they were in their late teens or early twenties."

Celeste had seen enough tragedies as a police officer and a homicide detective to understand that saying that final goodbye to a parent was hard at any age, whether you were a tween, teen, young adult or middle aged. She'd never known her mother, but she still felt her loss. "Do you remember their names?"

"No, I'm sorry. I could look through Art's files to see if there are any papers with their names on it."

Celeste nodded. "Thanks, Meryl. That would be helpful. What about their father? Was he there?"

Another call was trying to come through Celeste's cell phone. She checked the screen. It was Sterling again. She'd sent his call to voicemail earlier. This time, she rejected it, then returned to her conversation with her client.

Meryl hummed. "I think Art had said their father had died. I'd asked because Sally had a different name from her children. She'd remarried, but I don't think their stepfather was in the picture, either. I don't remember what happened to him. But her children sued Art for negligence."

Celeste stood from the bed and started pacing the room. "On what grounds?"

"Art used to assign two guards to every shift. But he'd reduced those staffing levels to stay competitive. Sally's children claimed his lack of appropriate training to the contractors and inadequate staffing contributed to Sally's death. The court agreed with them and awarded them damages. They also wanted Art to go back to assigning two guards per shift. The cost of the additional staffing, plus his attorney's fees, were a big hit to the company's finances."

Celeste turned to walk back to her bed. Through the wall behind the headboard, she heard the periodic murmur of Zeke's voice. She knew he was having a videoconference with his brothers to discuss their business plan. She couldn't make out their words, but the lack of tension in their exchange indicated the meeting was going well.

She turned to pace away from the wall. "Is that the reason Art eventually went back to only one guard per shift?"

"That's right. Art didn't actually tell me much about the lawsuit. He said he didn't want to *burden* me with the company's problems." For the first time, anger entered Meryl's voice.

In Meryl's position, Celeste would've been irritated by Art's attitude, too. She was sure Art's business's assets affected their personal finances. Because of that, Meryl had a right to know and understand the things that impacted Buckeye Bailey Security.

"But you think the lawsuit was the reason Art's business suffered financially?" Celeste asked.

"I know it was." Meryl's tone was firm. "He had a hard time making payments to Sally's children. Operating expenses had increased, and a couple of his clients went out of business."

"Wow. That's a lot." As a small-business owner herself, Celeste could imagine the stress Art was under.

"Yes, it was. He was having trouble sleeping and eating. He'd lost a lot of weight. But he *didn't* commit suicide." Meryl was adamant.

Celeste believed her. Meryl said Art would have reorganized under bankruptcy protection before he ended his life. Based on their decades of marriage, Celeste was certain Meryl was right. She knew her husband. And there had been that threatening letter.

Celeste stopped pacing and stared blindly through the window. Beyond the maple trees and evergreens, past the rolling grass, she could see the river and the late-evening sunlight dancing on its surface. "Meryl, why didn't you tell me about this lawsuit when I first took your case?"

Meryl gave a tired sigh. "As I explained, Art didn't tell me much about the lawsuit. And if I'd brought it up, you might have considered it more evidence that Art had killed himself."

"I still would've investigated your case."

"I know that about you now." There was a smile in the older woman's voice. "You're not the kind to be dismissive like some people. You check the facts yourself."

Celeste was proud and a little embarrassed by the compliment. "I do my best."

Meryl hesitated. "And to be honest, Sally Jaxx's death was a dark time in the company's history. It wasn't just the lawsuit. Sally had been with the company for years. She was a really good person. Art was devastated. I just didn't want to relive that. I wanted to protect Art's legacy."

Was protecting her husband's legacy more important than finding his killer? Celeste didn't bother to ask Meryl that question. In the end, she'd been forthcoming about the lawsuit, and that was all that mattered.

Celeste turned from the window and paced back toward the wall behind her bed. "You said Sally had been shot on assignment. Where was she assigned to work that day?"

Meryl gasped, a short, sharp explosion that echoed in Celeste's ear. "She was working at Archer Family Realty."

Celeste stilled on her way to the dressing table. What were the odds? Sally had been murdered while working for Buckeye Bailey Security, which had assigned her to Archer Family Realty. Two years later, someone kills Art and Dean. "Sally's children sued Art for negligence. Do you know whether they also sued Archer Family Realty?"

Meryl spoke after a beat of silence. "No, I don't. Celeste, do you think... Could this be a coincidence?"

Celeste dragged a hand over her hair. "I don't believe in coincidences. I think we may have identified the real trigger that links Art's and Dean's murders." She turned toward her bed and the wall she shared with Zeke.

How does he fit into this?

"You want to know about Arty's death?" Chad Cooper fixed his eyes on Zeke. His image appeared through the lens of a computer in the prison's library Thursday afternoon. "Suicide, right? Was sorry to hear about it." He didn't sound sorry.

Zeke returned the other man's flat stare. "It wasn't suicide. Someone killed him."

He was seated beside Celeste. Her outfit today was a bright red miniskirt and a silk pearl white long-sleeved blouse that flowed over her curves like water. Zeke had enjoyed one long look at her before leaving the cabin, then consigned himself to keeping his attention on her beautiful hazel eyes.

They were using the same police substation meeting room in which they'd videoconferenced with Agnes the previous morning. They'd chosen to set up their laptop facing a wall without windows or framed photos, making their location more difficult to pinpoint.

The former Buckeye Bailey Security guard's appearance had changed a lot since he'd entered the prison system. He'd shaved his head, getting rid of the dirty-blond tresses that had rolled past his shoulders. He'd also added a couple of tattoos and a thick mustache with a three-quarter beard. If Zeke were estimating correctly, he'd also added about ten pounds of pure muscle.

"Someone killed Arty? Really?" Chad's eyes lingered briefly on Celeste before moving back to Zeke. "Are you sure? What's the motive?"

Celeste crossed her arms. "Why don't you tell us?"

"What?" Chad let out a surprised laugh. His brown eyes sparkled with it. "You think *I* killed Arty? How? If you haven't noticed, I'm already in prison."

Zeke narrowed his eyes as he tried to read the other man's body language, which was difficult on a videoconference. The camera framed Chad from the top of his tattooed head to the middle of his chest covered by the orange-twill prison uniform. He sat straight in his chair, with his hands apparently folded on his lap. His posture indicated openness. Still, Zeke believed Chad was lying.

Part of his skepticism was based on the revelations Celeste had shared with him and his brothers after her conversation with Meryl yesterday evening. The four of them—Celeste, Mal,

Jerry and he—suspected Chad was Sally Jaxx's son. They were waiting for Mal to confirm it.

"How would you describe your relationship with Art?" Zeke wondered if he'd seen a spark of anger in Chad's eyes. It had disappeared too quickly to be certain.

The fired guard shrugged. "He was my boss. I mean, we were friendly, but we weren't friends."

"How friendly were you after he tried to stiff you twice on your pay?" Celeste lobbed the question at their interview subject with taunting aggression.

"He didn't stiff me." Chad leaned toward his computer monitor. "The checks were late, but he paid me what I was owed."

Celeste shrugged. "They were still late. And then he fired you."

"He didn't fire me." Chad's features tightened as his temper built. He switched his attention back to Zeke. "Arty laid off a bunch of guards because TSG took the Archer Family Realty contract from him."

Zeke shook his head. "We spoke with the guards who'd been fired along with you. They confirmed that Dean Archer had complained about your unprofessional behavior. *You're* the reason Art lost the Archer contract."

Chad's nostrils flared with anger. "That's bull—"

This time Celeste laughed. "Are we supposed to believe everyone's lying *but* you? Just admit Dean Archer accepted TSG's contract *after* leaving Buckeye Bailey Security because of *your* sloppy behavior."

A muscle flexed in Chad's jaw. "You're pretty bold talking to me from behind a computer screen. Would your tongue be as sharp if we were face-to-face?"

Celeste leaned closer to the monitor. "You're pretty bold having other people do your dirty work for you. People like you don't intimidate me."

"Is that right? Then why aren't you here?" Chad spread his arms, indicating the prison. "When I heard you wanted to talk to me, I thought they meant in person. I don't get that many visitors."

"You're right. You don't." Zeke drew a printout of the prison's visitors log for the past three months. "In fact, you've only had one person visit you in the past three months. She's visited every week, though, at least once a week. Monica Ward."

Blood drained from Chad's face. Zeke felt a rush of satisfaction. *We've got you.*

He spoke when Chad remained silent. "Is she your sister?" It was a wild guess. After all, they had different surnames. But it was a gamble worth his life—or death.

Chad narrowed his eyes. "I don't know who you're talking about."

"I'll take that as a yes." Zeke held up the sheet of paper, angling it so Chad could read it through the camera. "Her signature's on this form. She's written your name and identification number on the visitor log. Does that help your memory?"

"I'm not denying that she's been here." Chad's voice cooled. He gestured toward his computer monitor. "You have the log. But what's that matter? You seem to think that's evidence. Evidence of what?"

"Conspiracy to commit murder." Celeste's voice was expressionless, but Zeke sensed her anger and impatience. "We can connect Monica to you, Arthur Bailey, Dean Archer and Zeke Touré."

No, they couldn't. At least not yet. Connecting Monica to the three of them would be a challenge, considering she wore disguises when she met with Dean, with Art's daughter and with Kevin. But Zeke remained silent because Celeste's bluff was a good one and could come in handy.

Chad sneered. "You're lying."

Zeke shrugged. "How else do you think we were able to identify her? Your sister was dating one of TSG's employees."

Chad swallowed before trying his own brand of bravado. "I still don't know what you're talking about."

"We're talking about murder and attempted murder." Celeste leaned back against her chair. She was generating enough frost to freeze every pipe in the substation. "You must really like it in prison, Chad. Your stay is going to be extended for a very, very, very long time."

Chad looked away, then back. "Obviously, I won't be able to

change your mind. You're not listening to me. You're only willing to believe what suits your vision of your case. Well, good luck with that." His eyes held Zeke's. "You'll need it." He ended the meeting, turning the screen to black.

Celeste sighed. "We've got them, both of them. And he knows it."

Zeke shifted in his seat to face her. "You were brilliant to follow your instincts with Meryl. The information she gave you about the lawsuit connected all the dots: Chad and Monica as the killers, and revenge against Art and Dean for their mother's murder as their motivation."

Celeste frowned at him. "But how do *you* fit into that?"

Zeke rubbed his eyes with his left hand. "That's the missing piece. Hopefully, Mal will find something."

Celeste looked at the black screen. "How much do you want to bet Chad's warning Monica right now?"

Zeke's muscles tightened with tension. "If he is, how will she react?"

Zeke's cell phone rang as he stepped out of the shower early Friday morning. He and Celeste had just finished their workouts. It wasn't yet 7:00 a.m. The call could only be from his brothers. Hopefully, they'd discovered more information about Monica Ward or Chad Cooper.

He dried his hands and grabbed the phone on its third ring. "Hey, wh—"

Jerry's voice was sharp with panic. "Mal's been shot."

Chapter 17

"Lean on me!" Celeste hissed as she tugged him closer to her, further impeding his movements as they crossed the hospital parking lot early Friday morning.

"Hurry up. I've got to get to my brother." Zeke struggled to keep from shouting his panic and frustration. He was sweating. It was from a combination of anxiety and the ridiculous costume Celeste had forced him into.

"That's exactly what Monica's looking for." Celeste had altered her gait, taking longer—albeit slower—strides. "Someone running across the lot toward the emergency room entrance. Perhaps to check on someone with a gunshot wound?"

After receiving the bare minimum details from Jerry about the shooting, Zeke had flown out of the cabin's bathroom. He'd found Celeste and explained why they needed to get to the Riverside Hospital Emergency Room. Right. Now.

Celeste had slowed things down. She suspected Monica had shot Mal at least in part to flush Zeke out of hiding. In case she was right, she'd insisted they wear disguises to the hospital. She'd been firm that Zeke wear her overweight old man's costume. She'd dressed as a gangly young man, stuffing her hair into a natural wig and attaching an adhesive and makeup that gave her chin and upper lip stubble.

Zeke gritted his teeth. "Have you considered your obsession with disguises is your subconscious need to hide from the world?" He felt her stiffen and regretted his comment.

"Listen, Gramps, that kind of talk is going to get you dropped in this parking lot." The spunk in her response reassured him that Celeste wouldn't hold his amateur psychology against him.

"This is killing me." Zeke was forced to waddle due to the extra padding he was carrying around his stomach, waist and hips, and Celeste's pressing down on his arm.

"I know, and I'm truly sorry. But this is for everyone's well-being, not just yours." Celeste was tapping the keys on her cell phone with her thumbs.

Was she staying in character as a gangly youth, or was she communicating with someone? "Who are you texting?"

"Jerry." Celeste dropped her cell phone into the front pocket of her baggy, faded blue jeans and used both hands to pretend to help him walk. "He and Mal are waiting for us in one of the examining rooms. Eriq and Taylor are with them. We're supposed to ask for Nurse Becky Hardy at the desk."

"Great," Zeke said on a grateful sigh. He tried to speed up, but Celeste held him back. It made for a long journey to the emergency room entrance.

The waiting area was packed. Zeke didn't sense any hesitation in Celeste's movements as he leaned on her. She set a course for the registration desk. Her gait remained steady and deliberate, much to Zeke's impatience.

She stopped in front of one of the nurses seated behind the desk. Her name tag read *Becky Hardy*. Becky had a warm, welcoming expression. Her brown eyes sparkled when she smiled. A wealth of thick red curls framed her peaches-and-cream face but clashed with her hot pink short-sleeved top. Zeke instantly felt that he could trust her.

Celeste lowered her voice. "We're here to see Detectives Duster and Stenhardt, please."

Becky's expression became more serious. Her big brown eyes considered Zeke before returning to Celeste. She stood and circled the desk. "Please come with me."

To Zeke's relief, the young nurse set a brisk pace to the examination room. Her curls swung around her head as though in a panic. Arriving at one of the closed doors, she knocked twice before pushing it open and stepping back.

Celeste inclined her head. "Thank you."

"Thank you, Nurse Hardy." Zeke tried to smile past the fake gray beard and mustache Celeste had affixed to his face, before following her across the threshold into the room.

Jerry sat in a chair beside the examining table. Mal was seated in the chair facing the table. Eriq and Taylor stood on either side of him. The middle Touré wore a sweat-stained slate gray wicking jersey and black running shorts. A white bandage was wrapped around his right upper arm. His face was stiff with anger, some of which eased when he saw Zeke.

"What are you both wearing?" Jerry split a look of humor and bemusement between Zeke and Celeste.

"They're disguises," Celeste responded before Zeke could. "Don't tease. It was hard enough convincing your brother to wear one."

Zeke gave Jerry a quick visual scan. He looked worried, but physically he was fine, except for the cast that was still on his left arm. He said he'd been walking laps around Antrim Lake in northwest Columbus while Mal was jogging. Zeke was grateful the two had been together and that Mal had only sustained a flesh wound.

Mal looked to Celeste. "You think Monica Ward shot me to get to Zeke. I agree. Thank you for taking care of our brother."

Jerry cleared his throat. "Yes. Thanks, Cece."

"Celeste is fine." She stepped aside, giving Zeke a clearer path to Mal.

Zeke heard the fear in Mal's voice. His brothers' care and sincerity humbled him. Zeke crossed to him, clenching his fist to keep from grabbing Mal in relief.

"How are you feeling?" He heard the scratchy tone of his voice.

"Angry." Mal looked up at him. "But I'll be fine. You should've stayed in the safe house. That's what it's for."

Zeke's eyebrows—the real ones—flew up his forehead. "Would *you* have stayed at the safe house?"

Mal's eyes never wavered. "No."

Zeke looked at Eriq and Taylor. "I'm surprised to see you two here so early, but I'm grateful."

In his dark gray suit, Eriq looked like he'd been up for hours. Today's bolo clip was silver and shaped like a white bass. "A friend was shot. Where else would we be?"

Taylor looked around the room. She appeared fresh and wide awake, in a trim black pantsuit. Her honey-blond hair was balanced on the crown of her head. "Are we sure Monica Ward didn't just mistake Mal for Zeke? Your family resemblance is pretty darn strong."

"I'm positive." Celeste's response was firm.

"How?" Taylor asked.

Celeste pointed to Mal. "Because Mal's still alive. If Monica mistook him for Zeke, the outcome would've been very different."

Eriq crossed his arms over his broad chest. "I agree with CJ." His tone was somber, bordering on funereal. "This means you three have been under surveillance for some time. Probably months."

Taylor crossed her arms. "The killer knew about your regular runs at Antrim, and when and how often you jog there. You may want to stay away from the lake and otherwise alter your schedules for a while."

"You're right." Mal looked disappointed.

Jerry groaned. "We've got to close this case. It's bad enough that I can't jog for the next six weeks because of this cast, but walking indoors on a treadmill is not my idea of a good time."

Mal looked around the room. "Based on the information Celeste got from Meryl on the lawsuit against Art, I was able to dig deeper into Monica Ward. Zeke and Celeste were right. She's Chad Cooper's sister and Sally Jaxx was their mother."

Celeste took a few minutes to fill Eriq and Taylor in on Monica and Chad's lawsuit against Art's company.

Mal continued. "Sally Jaxx was murdered two years ago on March 15."

Jerry interrupted. "So that's two and a half years ago."

"Correct." Mal nodded. "Which was three months after her application for employment with TSG was denied because she failed the physical fitness test." His eyes met Zeke's. "Your name and signature were on that declination letter."

Celeste blinked. "That's the missing piece that connects the revenge motive to Art, Dean and Zeke. Monica and Chad blame Art for not providing backup for their mother. They blame Dean because their mother was killed at his company. And Zeke because they believe that, if you'd hired their mother, she'd still be alive today."

"She very well might have been." Zeke scrubbed his hands over his face, surprised when he felt the fake beard against his palms.

"Don't blame yourself." Taylor was adamant. "She didn't pass the fitness test."

"You *can't* blame yourself." Celeste's eyes were wide with concern for him. "There are too many variables in life. Let's stay focused on the case." She turned to Mal. "Do you have an address for Monica?"

Mal rubbed the back of his neck. "I'm working on it."

Eriq rested his hand on Mal's left shoulder. "We'll give you a hand with that." He scanned the room. "With your help, we're closing in on the person who killed my friend. Thank you."

"No thanks necessary." Zeke dropped his eyes to the white bandage on Mal's sienna bicep.

For his part, Zeke didn't think he'd be able to sleep again until the serial killer was finally caught.

"I have a proposal for you." Zeke's words broke their companionable silence late Friday afternoon. He took a breath, stretching his emerald pullover across his chest. "My brothers and I want you to partner with us. We want to offer our clients your investigative services. In exchange, we'd ask that you refer our security services to your clients."

Celeste's skin warmed as her temper ignited. They'd finished lunch hours ago. She'd been thinking about the apples and grapes in the fridge. Snacks she could eat with one hand—or pitch at Zeke's handsome head.

With an effort, she kept her voice flat, without inflection. "You want me to bail you out."

"What?" Zeke's eyes widened. "No, it would be a collaboration. We'd refer each other to our prospective clients."

Celeste could barely hear his words above the buzzing in her ears. She knew he'd said something. Whatever it was, it wouldn't have made a difference. "Your company's finances are unstable. Your words. You said TSG's finances were on shaky ground. You need a source to protect your agency in case of a market shift. You see *me* as that source."

He was using her. Like others before him. Sterling. Dionne. Lee. Nanette. To name a few. Now, with a broken heart, she could add Zeke to the list. She'd thought what they had was real. He wasn't with her because he *needed* her. He was with her because he *wanted* her. At least, that's what she'd thought.

Zeke stood from the dining table to pace. "You're misunderstanding our intent. This would be a mutually beneficial partnership. The referrals would help each of us to grow our client base."

Celeste wanted to stand as well, but she was afraid she'd pummel him. He'd hurt her. She wanted to release at least a little of that pain. "And if your client used me, you'd take a percentage of the case."

Zeke stopped to frown at her. "That's right. Just as you'd get a percentage of any case we got from your referrals."

She still couldn't stand. Her knees were trembling. From nerves or temper? *When he looks at me, does he see his future—or his finances? And how pathetic was she? What made her think someone as intelligent, successful, kind and caring as Hezekiah Touré would have any interest in her?*

Fool! Fool! Fool!

"I appreciate the offer." That was a lie. She winced as she swallowed the bile in her throat. "But I don't need more referrals. I have as much work as I can handle from client referrals and law enforcement contacts. Besides, Nanette's leaving, remember? I'm taking on her clients. All of them."

Zeke dragged his hand over his head. He expelled a breath. "I hadn't thought of that."

He hadn't thought of her at all. He'd thought only of himself. And maybe his brothers. What he wanted. What he needed.

She'd thought he'd cared about her. He'd said he'd wanted to get to know her. He'd wanted more than a physical relationship. Had anything he'd said been sincere? Or had it all been part of his plan to get close to her so he could use her? Like Lee had. And Nanette. And like Sterling was trying to do.

"No. You hadn't thought of that." She was growing numb. Good. She pushed herself off her chair and locked her knees. "Is that what this seduction was about?"

Zeke's dark eyes flared with anger. His body stilled. "What?"

"Were you trying to make me more amenable to your persuasion to stay and help put your family's company back on solid ground?"

"Never." His voice was gruff. Tight. "How could you think that?"

She arched an eyebrow. "You wouldn't be the first."

His sharp cheekbones flushed. "Don't compare me to Lee Martin."

"Don't make it so easy." She collected her case files from the table, then stormed past him toward the stairs. "My whole life, people have been getting close to me just to use me." She spun back to face him, anger strengthening her limbs. "And you've been the worst of them."

"Celeste, that's not—" He tried to interrupt, but she wouldn't let him.

Celeste verbally bulldozed past him the same way he'd trampled all over her heart and soul. "All that crap about wanting to get to know me. Wanting me to share my thoughts, my feelings, my past with you." She stalked toward him, jabbing her finger into his chest. "Those were all lies! But I have to hand it to you. You put more effort into your act than the others did. Bravo."

Zeke took hold of her wrist to stop her attack. "It wasn't an act."

"Save it!" She jerked her hand free. Spinning on her heels, she headed back to the stairs, clutching her files to her chest.

"My feelings for you are real, Celeste." He aimed the words at her back.

It was like someone slid a blade between her shoulders. Was she bleeding? Celeste breathed through the pain.

Grabbing the banister, she pulled herself onto the first step. "Ah, so that's the reason you're asking me for referrals. Your *feelings*."

"Celeste, one has nothing to do with the other."

She looked at him over her shoulder. "Doesn't it? I'm done with being used." She marched up the steps on stiff legs, without another word.

Zeke's eyes drilled into her back. Let him look. She'd learned her lesson. This time was much more painful than all the others combined and multiplied by infinity. This time, she'd fallen in love. Zeke had broken through all her barriers. She'd never wanted to share her thoughts, her fears, her past with anyone before. But she'd allowed Zeke to get close to her. She'd thought he was opening himself to her in return. Instead, he was lulling her into a false sense of security. And she'd let him.

Fool! Fool! Fool!

At the top of the stairs, Celeste paused to let the pain pass through her. She crossed into her room, and with all her willpower, refrained from slamming her door shut. Instead, she closed it quietly behind her.

Celeste pressed her forehead against its cool surface, inhaling its cedar scent. She'd given Zeke her heart. He'd asked for her business contacts. She'd never make the mistake of letting anyone close to her ever again.

Chapter 18

"How did you mess this up so *badly?"* Jerry asked the question Zeke's mind had been shouting since Celeste had walked out of the great room minutes before.

They'd each retreated to their rooms, separated by a shared wall. Through that barrier, Zeke could hear her, speaking softly to someone. He couldn't decipher her words. With whom was she speaking? Were they discussing his colossal error in judgment? Did he have any hope of fixing his mistake? That's what he hoped his brothers could help him figure out.

"You or *we?"* Mal broke his silence. He was almost eerily still, seated beside Jerry at the Touré Security Group conference table. He'd loosened the black tie he wore with the pale gold long-sleeved dress shirt.

Since Zeke had texted asking them to join this videoconference call, his middle brother had been silent. Mal's dark eyes had seemed to assess Zeke's every movement and expression as he'd recounted his disastrous exchange with Celeste. Jerry had been the one to interrupt with commentaries and verbal nudges, prompting his narration. Anyone who didn't know the brothers would think Mal was silently gloating that he'd warned Zeke and Jerry that their offer wouldn't be as well received as they'd hoped. But unlike Jerry, Mal wasn't prone to gloating. He wouldn't take pleasure in I-Told-You-Sos. At least, not in the moment. That boast might come later. But right now, Zeke could sense Mal was trying to figure out what could have gone wrong and what Zeke wasn't telling them. Zeke could attest that there was a lot he was holding back.

"What does that mean, 'you or we'?" Jerry interrupted. The white cast on his left arm seemed to glow against his dark bronze short-sleeved shirt. Both brothers must have left their jackets in their respective offices.

Zeke kept his voice low. "Mal's asking whether she thinks all three of us are taking advantage of her or just me." He stood to pace. "She only accused me."

"Why are you walking away from the camera? You know we can't see you, right?" Jerry continued after Zeke ignored his exasperated question. "Why would Celeste think you were using her?"

"Because she has feelings for him." Mal's response exposed what Zeke should have realized himself. What he should have considered before he blundered in with his grand offer of working together.

"Oh." The light bulb came on for Jerry. "Do *you* have feelings for *her*?"

Zeke spoke with his back to the monitor. "I'm in love with her."

"So that's a yes." Jerry broke the brief silence. "Which means you've really screwed this up."

Zeke returned to the small wooden desk. His movements were stiff and jerky as he claimed his seat in front of the clean laptop. "That's right, Jer. I have. So how do I fix it?" His words dripped with sarcasm and impatience.

Jerry shrugged his right shoulder, glancing at Mal, then back to Zeke. "Just tell her how you feel. That worked for me and Mal."

Mal hadn't moved during their videoconference. "If he does that now, Celeste will think he's trying a new strategy to get her help with our company. She won't believe he's being sincere."

"Exactly." Zeke sank back against his chair. "I told her my personal feelings for her don't have anything to do with our professional lives, but she didn't believe me. She basically told me to take a flying leap into a shallow pond."

"Harsh." Jerry winced. "Look, we should scrap the referral plan. Celeste doesn't need our help. Once Nanette leaves, she'll be drowning in clients. She's probably going to have to contract with other detectives to help her."

"Jerry's right," Mal said.

Jerry frowned. "Why are you surprised?"

Mal ignored him. "Zeke, what's more important to you—building the company or building a life with Celeste?"

"Celeste." He felt guilty, but he owed his brothers the truth.

He wanted Touré Security Group to succeed. He owed it to his parents for the legacy they'd built for him and his brothers. He owed it to his brothers because it was their inheritance, too. And he owed it to himself. His parents had taught him to always give his best effort to every endeavor. But seeing his brothers' happiness after falling in love with exceptional women had made him realize their company's success alone could never fulfill him. He needed a partner. Someone who could help him see through the dark times. And someone with whom he could share the brighter days. His brothers had that. He wanted it, too.

"Good answer, Number One." Jerry's dark eyes twinkled with the mockery only younger siblings seemed able to manifest.

"Agreed." Mal nodded. "When Celeste's ready to listen, lead with that."

"Cyborg's right." Jerry inclined his head toward Mal on his right. Mal's shoulders rose and fell in a silent sigh. "Celeste needs to know that you meant it when you said your personal relationship with her doesn't have anything to do with our two companies. The best way to prove that to her is to take our companies out of the equation."

Zeke closed his eyes briefly in gratitude. "Thank you. Both of you. That's good advice."

"Good luck." Mal held his eyes through the computer's camera.

Zeke could tell he was remembering when he'd faced a similar turning point in his relationship with Grace. Zeke was heartened by the fact that things had worked out for the medical researcher and his brother. Hopefully, he'd also be able to fix things between himself and Celeste.

"We'll send you our bill and encourage you to let your friends know about our services, if they need similar help." Jerry gave him a cocky grin.

Zeke echoed Mal's anguished groan.

Jerry split a look between Zeke and Mal. "Too soon for the referral joke?"

Zeke leaned toward the laptop's keypad. "I'll catch up with you later." He ended the meeting then stood to wander the room.

When Celeste's ready to listen, lead with that.

He glanced toward their shared wall.

When would she be ready to listen to anything he had to say outside of the case? Would *she ever be ready?*

Celeste's cell phone rang minutes after she'd secluded herself in her bedroom. She pulled it from the front-right pocket of Nanette's scarlet linen pants. Maybe it would be a welcome distraction. She checked the screen. It wasn't. It was Sterling. Again. He'd already left several voicemail messages for her, all of which she'd ignored. She was tempted to ignore this one as well. But she was in a bad mood anyway. Perhaps she should just get this conversation over with.

She rotated her neck to ease the tension there and filled her lungs before exhaling. "Hello."

"Celeste. I'm glad I finally caught you." The irritation was evident beneath his words.

She didn't owe him any explanations. She didn't owe him anything. Let's just get to the point and get this over with. "Why are you calling?"

"As I've explained on the numerous voicemail messages I've left for you, we need to discuss your grandmother's estate." Sterling's patience seemed on the verge of unraveling.

Welcome to the club.

"I've already heard from your mother's lawyer." Celeste kept her voice down.

She was aware Zeke had entered his room shortly after she'd come upstairs. She could barely hear his voice through their shared wall behind her headboard. Was he speaking with his brothers? Were they discussing their failed plan to use her to help increase Touré Security Group's revenue base? What were they planning now?

Sterling's voice was loud in her left ear. It shattered her concentration. "What did she say?"

Startled, Celeste jumped. "Who?"

Sterling's sigh was short and sharp. "The lawyer. What did she say about Mother's estate?"

She hadn't said anything. Instead, Celeste had emailed the lawyer to explain she'd received her letter, but since she was working a case, Celeste wouldn't be able to meet with the lawyer right away. In the interim, they'd have to do as much as they could via emails and, when possible, phone calls until Celeste closed the case. But that wasn't the information Sterling was after. Even if it was, Celeste wasn't inclined to share those details with him.

She roamed the spacious bedroom. Her steps took her past her dressing table to the window in the front half of the room. The view overlooked the main entrance to the cabin. "What do you want to know about the estate?"

Sterling hesitated, as though her question had confused him. "Well, we should know what kind of condition she left her estate in. Is it carrying any debt? Is she up to date with her payments like her taxes, insurance and utilities? Does she have any liens against her home?"

Celeste mentally filed everything Sterling said to reference later. Experience had taught her that people hid their goals and motivations within their words.

"I'll be sure to ask the lawyer." Celeste moved on to the window on the left near the back of the room. "Anything else?"

She wanted to linger near the shared wall to catch any stray words that penetrated it. But it was a two-way street. If she drifted too close to the wall, Zeke would be able to hear her as well.

Sterling sighed again. He did that a lot. He'd recorded several sighs on his voicemail messages. "Celeste, surely you realize this isn't right."

She froze. She'd known those words were coming. And still they hurt—almost as badly as Zeke had hurt her. But not quite.

Her mother had been Sterling's first wife. Allegedly, he'd married her for love, and Celeste had been his first child. Despite that, Celeste wasn't a real member of his family. She was an outsider. Dionne had never accepted Celeste's mother so Sterling wouldn't accept Celeste.

Yet in the end, Dionne had left her...everything. "Why do you think your mother made me the sole beneficiary of her estate?"

"Who knows why my mother did anything?" Sterling's words had a bite to them.

"You do." Celeste resumed her walk about her room. She turned away from the windows and wandered toward the closet. She considered the colorful and admittedly pretty outfits Nanette had loaned her. Maybe it was time to rethink her all-black wardrobe. Hiding from people hadn't shielded her from harm. "If you had to guess, why do you think she left everything to me?"

"I don't know." Now Sterling was just being stubborn.

"Then let me try to guess." She let the sleeve of the soft pink silk blouse slip through her fingers. She propped her right shoulder against the wall beside the closet and stared blindly at the dressing table. "You and your children live near your mother in Chicago. Despite that, you rarely visited, and the only time you called was when you needed something. You didn't spend much, if any, time with her during the holidays, and you never helped her celebrate her birthday."

The silence was deep and tense.

"What gives you that idea?" Sterling sounded as though he was chewing glass.

"Your mother gave me that idea. In fact, I'm practically quoting what she'd tell me every time I called and visited." Celeste's gut burned with satisfaction.

"You only have her side of the story."

"It's her estate. Her side of the story is all that matters."

Sterling blew an irritated breath. His silence was longer this time as he apparently tried to work out his next steps. Celeste used the quiet time to try to make out what Zeke was saying, but his voice was too low and too deep. She knew he was speaking with his brothers and suspected she was the topic of their conversation. Since they were working this investigation together, if they were discussing the case, they would have asked her to join them.

The next time she saw Zeke, she'd have to play it cool. And she'd have to keep her guard up.

"We just want our fair share, Celeste." Sterling brought her focus back to their conversation.

"And that's what your mother believed she left you—your fair share."

"She left us nothing," Sterling snapped.

"Exactly." Celeste straightened from the wall. "I have to get back to work, Sterling."

"I don't even know where you live." Sterling's remark surprised her.

Celeste frowned. "Are you planning a visit?"

She'd been eighteen years old the last time they'd spoken in person. It was the morning she'd moved out of his mother's house, in a car she'd bought herself. She'd been on her way to Ohio to attend Franklin University. She'd wanted to go to college but had known she couldn't count on financial assistance from the adults in her life. Instead, she'd gotten a job, earned scholarships and applied for grants. But Sterling had still shown up minutes before she'd left. He'd tried to give her a paternal speech and take credit for the success she'd worked for. She'd driven off before he'd finished and had never looked back.

"I have your phone number, but I don't have your address." He was breathless. Was he climbing stairs? What was he doing? "Do you have my address?"

Time to cut this conversation short. "If I need to get in touch with you, I'll call."

"What are you going to do, Celeste?" Sterling caught his breath.

"I'm going to settle your mother's estate. After that, I don't know." She disconnected the call. With any luck, Sterling would wait to hear from her and stop leaving messages every other day.

Celeste's eyes strayed toward the far wall. Lately, it didn't seem as though luck was on her side.

Zeke's knock on her door made her jump. Slipping her cell phone into the front pocket of her borrowed slacks, Celeste crossed to the door and yanked it open. She took mean-spirited satisfaction in Zeke's surprised expression.

"I'm sorry to interrupt." His words were low. His eyes were wary. "Eriq and Taylor want to meet."

"She'd listed this address on her rental-car application." Taylor led Celeste and Zeke down a narrow hallway on the third floor of a three-story redbrick apartment building early Friday evening. She wore pale gray slacks and a boxy-cut navy blue jacket.

The building was in northwest Columbus, not far from Zeke's neighborhood. That was unsettling. He'd noticed the two police cruisers parked across the street. Were they waiting for Monica Ward's return?

Music, television programs and conversations carried into the hallway from the apartments they passed. If he spread his arms, Zeke suspected he could touch the walls on either side of the hall. The building must have been built in the early twentieth century. It smelled of mold and dust. Eriq's, Taylor's, Celeste's and his footsteps were silent on the thin moss green carpet. At the end of the hall, narrow French doors opened onto what appeared to be a stacked black-framed balcony. Natural light streamed through the glass doors, supplementing the hallway's fluorescent lighting.

Faux-maple-wood doors alternated along the paper-white walls. Taylor led them across the threshold of the door third from the end of the hallway. "We came to bring Monica in for questioning, but she was already gone. She must have realized we were getting close to her."

Zeke stepped aside for Celeste to enter. "Chad may have tipped her off after our videoconference with him yesterday."

"The apartment manager let us in." Eriq's voice carried from behind them. Zeke glanced back at the older detective. Eriq wore a dark brown suit. A copper clip in the shape of a walleye held his bolo tie in place. "It looks like Monica packed in a hurry. She's either moved to another location or she's left the city. We've put out a BOLO for her."

There was no way to predict how long it would take to get results.

Celeste stood a little more than an arm's distance from him. Zeke ignored the deep freeze wafting from her despite her warm blue blouse and red slacks. He turned his attention to the worn and faded efficiency unit Monica seemed to be using as her base of operations. He listened to Eriq's and Taylor's recount as he surveyed his surroundings. A shabby navy blue-cloth sofa bed dominated the space. It was open and unmade. Monica looked like a restless sleeper. Her plain white sheets lay tangled in the middle of the thin mattress beneath the single pillow. A chipped and scarred dark wood nightstand was positioned beside the bed.

Zeke started to cross toward it. Celeste grabbed his arm, stopping him. She released her hold just as abruptly and pressed disposable gloves into his chest.

He took them from her. "Thank you."

She turned away without a word. She still wasn't ready to listen. That was okay. He could be patient. She was worth the effort.

Zeke pulled on the thin, blue latex gloves as he approached the nightstand. His eyes moved over the moss green porcelain lamp. It was missing a shade. There were three quarters, two nickels, a dime and three pennies beside it. A five-by-seven-inch color photo was balanced against it. The image was of Chad Cooper and Monica Ward hugging a middle-aged woman who stood between them.

Off on their own were two contact lens cases. On a hunch, Zeke opened them. Each had a different tinted pair of lenses. In one case, the lenses were blue. In the second, they were green. He turned to find Celeste searching the closet. Two mannequin heads—one wearing a red wig, the other an ebony one—waited on a shelf.

"It looks like we've found Monica's disguises." Anger rolled over him. Zeke tightened his hands into fists to control it.

He met Celeste's eyes before she turned away to unload the

model heads. Taylor and Eriq helped her bag them. Zeke moved on to the kitchen.

That's when the stench hit him. The unmistakable, nauseating stink of dishes left too long in the sink. His eyes stung as he surveyed the cramped space. Coffee-cup stains dotted the off-white linoleum counter. Cupboard drawers and doors were left partially open. Dirt tracked the off-white flooring.

Zeke turned and hurried out of the kitchen so he could breathe again. "She hasn't left."

"Sure she has." Eriq swept his arm around the room, bringing Zeke's attention to the clothes strewn across the thin carpet. "She must have been in a panic when she packed up and raced out of here."

Zeke tracked Eriq's gestures. "I don't think that's what we're looking at. Monica's apartment isn't a mess because she packed in a rush. It's a mess because she's a slob."

Taylor's thin blond eyebrows knitted. "What?"

"Monica's not missing. She's just not home." Zeke pictured Jerry's room when they were growing up and his home before he started dating Symone. Yes, there were definite similarities between what he was looking at now and the nightmarish memories of his childhood. This was the room of a slob. "Her clothes aren't flung across the room. They're pooled on the floor."

Zeke thought of the police officers parked out front. They were an extra layer of protection. They could also be a deterrent. Monica would be spooked if she noticed them before they saw her. Then what would she do? Where would she go? Zeke briefly closed his eyes. He needed to close this case. As long as Monica was who-knew-where, his brothers and Celeste were in danger.

"I agree that Monica hasn't left." Celeste closed the closet doors. "She could be out looking for us. She could be anywhere. But she's coming back."

"What makes you so sure?" Taylor wore a plain white blouse under her navy jacket.

Zeke pointed toward the picture of Monica with her mother and brother. "Because she left that photo behind."

"And Zeke's still alive." Celeste appeared beside him. Frost still rolled off her. "She's not going to leave until she's accomplished what she's here for, regardless of what happens to her."

Zeke shrugged his eyebrows. "And there's that, too."

"You've convinced me." Eriq checked his watch. "In which case, we should get you back. We don't want you here when she returns." He stepped back and gestured for Celeste and Zeke to proceed him.

"All right," Celeste said over her shoulder. "We'll wait for your update."

Zeke followed her from the apartment. "Hopefully, we'll hear something soon."

They were steps away from the exit beside the French doors, which led to the stairwell, when something—or someone—snatched Celeste and dragged her out of sight around a corner.

Zeke's heart was in his throat as he rushed after her. The scene that greeted him almost caused his heart to stop. Monica Ward had found them. One of her arms was wrapped around Celeste's neck. Her other hand held a gun to Celeste's throat.

She caught Zeke's eyes and gave him an evil grin. "I knew if I waited, *you'd* find *me*."

Zeke didn't think he'd ever take another breath.

Chapter 19

"**W**ait!" Zeke's heart galloped like horses through a storm. "I'm the one you want. Let her go, and I'll come with you."

"You'll come with me anyway." Monica's brown eyes gleamed with malice. "I'm taking her for insurance." Her smile blinked away. Her pink lips thinned. Her voice snapped. "Go on. All of you. Lead the way."

Zeke hesitated. He didn't want to turn his back on Celeste. He knew Monica was capable of hurting him by hurting the people he loved. What could he say to make her let Celeste go?

Eriq's voice moved past him like a frigid wind. "We're not letting you take anyone."

Monica shielded herself behind Celeste's body. "Take your best shot." She arched a thin brown eyebrow. "I didn't think so. Now, *move!*"

He looked back at Eriq and Taylor. They both had their guns drawn, but everyone knew they wouldn't use them. They were in the narrow hallway of an occupied residential building. They couldn't risk a stray bullet penetrating one of the units and hurting—perhaps killing—someone. This wasn't a safe space to stage a shoot-out.

Zeke's heart slammed against his chest. He was sure they could all see his shirt waving against it. He glanced at Celeste again. She returned his gaze and rolled her eyes. Slowly. Deliberately. Twice. He could hear her in his mind: "I'm more than just a sparkling personality."

Did she have a plan? A better question: Would it work? There was so much at risk. Too much. Her life. Zeke took a steadying breath. She was a trained professional. And they were out of options. This was a situation that was out of his control. He had to step back and give her a chance.

Zeke turned and led the other four into the stairwell that exited into the rear parking lot. Like the hallway, the stairwell was narrow. And it smelled old. The walls and stairs were made of concrete and had been painted a utilitarian gray. There was a window at each landing that allowed in a meager amount of sunlight to supplement the fluorescent bulbs affixed to the walls and ceiling.

Zeke descended the first set of stairs. He was alternately cold with fear and hot with anger. He held fast to the gray metal railing to support his unsteady knees. Beneath the muted sounds of their footfalls, the silence was oppressive. Zeke stopped beside the fire engine–red door that opened onto the second floor and glanced over his shoulder. Taylor was a step behind him. Eriq followed her. Monica and Celeste were at least an arm's distance behind Eriq.

Monica held a fistful of Celeste's blouse to anchor them together. She seemed tense, as though she anticipated some eventual resistance. Celeste's features were expressionless. He couldn't tell what she was thinking. Was she nervous? Did she have any doubts about what she was planning to do?

What was she planning to do, and how could he help her?

"Don't even think about walking through that door." Monica pressed her gun into the back of Celeste's head.

Zeke's heart took a painful pause before trying to bulldoze its way out of his chest. He clenched his hands and continued down the stairs.

Another small window and another red door marked the first-floor landing. Zeke didn't have any illusions that the officers stationed on the street to keep watch for Monica would happen to glance toward that window and see them in the stairwell with their target. They were on their own. That's what they had to plan for.

Zeke had reached the ground level. The exit was perhaps three paces ahead of him. They'd run out of time. His mind raced through possible scenarios to get them out of this situation. Could he signal the officers? Eriq and Taylor both had guns. Could they shoot out the tires of whatever vehicle Monica used for her getaway? In doing so, would any harm come to Celeste?

He pushed through the exit and stepped out into the parking lot. It was empty except for the dozen or so cars standing in what appeared to be assigned spaces. He'd left their rented smoke gray sedan in a visitor's spot. Zeke tightened his fists as he walked into the lot. If Monica hurt Celeste in any way, he'd dedicate the rest of his life to making her life a living—

Behind him, he heard a muffled, "Oomp" and then a thud. Zeke spun toward the noise. Celeste stood above a prone Monica, with the killer's gun in her hands.

Her legs were braced apart on the asphalt. She pointed the weapon at the other woman. "Eriq, could you cuff her, please?"

Eriq grunted. "It took you long enough."

Zeke watched the other man wipe his upper lip with the back of his wrist. His hand shook slightly as he holstered his weapon before pulling out the handcuffs.

Celeste engaged the gun's safety before turning it over to Taylor. The detective secured the weapon in an evidence bag as Eriq read Monica her Miranda rights.

With two strides, Zeke crossed to Celeste. He locked his hands around her upper arms and searched her face. "Are you all right?"

Her crooked smile melted his heart. She rolled her eyes. "How many times have I told you, I'm more than just a sparkling personality?"

Zeke wrapped his arms around her and held her tight. "Thank God you're safe."

He could have lost her today. If that had happened, he would have lost himself. It was going to take him weeks to banish from his mind the image of her with a gun to her head. He held her even closer to him and breathed in her scent.

As ugly as this day had been, it had taught him one very valuable lesson: he needed Celeste Jarrett in his life. He had to find a way to make that happen.

"You didn't have to come into the agency." Celeste led Nanette into her office to retrieve her partner's suitcase and colorful wardrobe Saturday afternoon. "I told you I'd bring it by. It's the least I could do after you loaned me your clothes for a week."

Minutes before, Celeste had been at the Bailey residence, debriefing Meryl and her children on the investigation and capture of the person responsible for killing Arthur Bailey and the charges that were, at that moment, being brought against her co-conspirator. The meeting had been painful. Many more tears had been shed, but at least the family had closure and had received some peace in knowing their husband and father had not committed suicide.

Celeste wheeled the pastel purple suitcase out from beside her modular faux-maple-wood desk and turned it over to Nanette.

Nanette waved a dismissive hand. "I was out doing bridal stuff anyway. Besides, I wanted to know if the clothes worked."

Celeste frowned, tilting her head to the side in confusion. "Worked?"

"To turn up the heat with the sexy security consultant." Nanette grinned as she made herself comfortable on one of the sterling-silver-and-black-vinyl chairs at Celeste's small glass conversation table. "Tell me *everything*."

Celeste shook her head as she rounded her desk and took the black-cloth executive chair. "You do, of course, remember this was a homicide investigation and not some sort of reality-TV love connection? Someone was trying to kill my protectee." Even though they'd solved the case and the killer was in custody, that phrase still made Celeste's blood run cold.

"I know, I know." Nanette crossed her right leg over her left. She smoothed the material of her grape knee-length skirt over her right thigh. She swung her deep purple wedge-heel shoe above the thin gunmetal-gray carpet. "But you solved the case, and he's safe now. How did you solve the case?"

Celeste gave Nanette a summary of the past week, hitting

only those points that were relevant to the investigation. She watched her friend's eyes grow wider as she described the events of the last twenty minutes of the case.

Nanette interrupted as Celeste got to the part when Monica had grabbed her in the hallway. Her words were partially muffled behind her right palm. "Have mercy, Celeste! She held a gun to your neck?"

Celeste was glad she was seated as she remembered that moment. She didn't think she'd ever been that scared. "Yes. She'd seen the officers in their patrol cars and known they were looking for her. She avoided their notice by climbing the fire escape to the roof of the building and entering the third-floor hallway through the French doors."

Nanette shook her head. "That's crazy. What did Eriq and Taylor do?"

Celeste spread her arms. "They drew their guns. What else could they do? Monica was using me as a human shield. And we knew that many, if not all, the apartments were occupied at the time. We didn't know if other people were on their way up the stairs. We had to get out of the building before we tried anything."

"That's terrifying," Nanette said on a breath.

"Yes, it was." Celeste shivered as her mind played flashbacks of what seemed like the never-ending descent into the parking lot yesterday evening.

Monica had gripped the pearl white blouse so tightly against her that Celeste thought the buttons would pop. The cool metal of the gun's barrel had bitten into the skin between her shoulder blades.

She'd kept a steady pace as they'd walked the three stories to the building's ground floor. All the while, she'd held two thoughts in her mind. The first was that she'd only have one chance at getting the gun away from Monica and that would be when they stepped out of the stairwell into the parking lot. She'd remembered stepping up to the threshold sill when she and Zeke had entered through the rear door. She'd hoped that step would force at least some distance between her and Monica's gun. It had.

Celeste had taken a large step across the threshold and down into the parking lot. Moving as quickly as she could, she'd grabbed Monica's gun hand, twisting the wrist to make her drop the weapon, then continued twisting her arm to flip her onto the asphalt.

"What did Zeke do?" Nanette's question blessedly drew Celeste from the memory of that confrontation.

"He'd offered to take my place." That was the second thought she'd held in her mind.

Zeke hadn't hesitated. His first thought had been ensuring her safety, apparently at any cost. The fear and anguish in his eyes couldn't be mistaken. Celeste doubted he had a plan when he'd told Monica to release Celeste and take him instead. He couldn't have put something together that quickly. Still, he was prepared to turn himself over to someone determined to kill him in order to keep her safe.

"What?" Nanette pressed a hand to her heart. "Celeste, that man *loves* you."

Hope stole her breath. "Do you really think so?"

"Of course he does!" Nanette gaped at her. "The whole reason the two of you went underground in the first place was to keep him safe from that homicidal maniac. But as soon as she got her hands on *you*, he volunteered to give up his life for yours. *That* is love."

Celeste rose to pace her cramped office. "But that's the kind of man Zeke Touré is. He and his brothers. They're protectors. It's not just their business. It's in their blood."

Nanette huffed. "Girl, if all he was interested in was 'protecting' you—" she put the word in air quotes "—he could've said, 'Wait, let's talk about this.' Or, 'There's no way you're getting out of this.' But you said he offered to take your place. That's love."

Celeste leaned back against her desk. Her knees were shaking with nerves, hope and excitement. "I hope you're right. Because I'm in love with him."

Nanette screamed her joy. "I knew it! I knew it! I've never seen you as mopey as you were when you and Zeke stopped going out. So when are you going to tell him how you feel?"

Celeste tightened her grip on her desk behind her to keep from dropping to the floor at the idea of telling Zeke she loved him. "I don't know. I haven't thought about that. I mean, suppose you're wrong and I'm right, and he was just being chivalrous or something?"

Could someone as decent and kind as Hezekiah Touré fall in love with a misfit like her?

Nanette rose and crossed to her. She took her hands and held her eyes. "Celeste, I know you have trust issues. I have no idea what happened between you and the family you never talk about. But I realize what Lee and Roger did to us did a job on you. It did a job on me, too. If it weren't for you, I would be in prison."

Celeste shook her head. "We solved that crime together."

Nanette squeezed her hands. "No, girl, that was all you. And I know I've been leaning on you ever since. You carried the lion's share of opening this agency. You even helped me close the majority of my cases and never once asked for a share of my profits."

Celeste shifted with discomfort. "Where are you going with this?"

"You're worthy of being loved, Celeste." Nanette tightened her grip on Celeste's hands when she tried to pull free. "No, listen to me. Zeke is the first person you've shown any interest in since that punk Lee five years ago. I've lost count of the number of times I've tried to fix you up over the years, and you wouldn't give any of those prospects a chance. And they were good ones. Zeke is a good man. Eriq likes him, and he has a good reputation in the community. If there's any chance of having a relationship with him, take it. You deserve it."

Celeste tossed her a grin. "That's good advice. This bridal thing is giving you second sight."

Nanette gave her a shaming look. "It's more like you're finally listening to my excellent advice."

Celeste straightened from her desk. "Before I talk with Zeke, I think I'd like to add some color to my wardrobe. I enjoyed the way I felt wearing your clothes. The brighter colors made me feel seen. I liked that."

Nanette raised her fists in the air and screamed. "This is fantastic!" She spun toward the table to grab her handbag. "Quick, before you change your mind." She laughed. "Goodbye, Johnny Cash. Hello, Rihanna."

Celeste stopped mid-stride. "Wait. What?"

"Don't know how you did it, bro." Jerry lowered himself beside Mal on Zeke's steel gray leather sofa Saturday afternoon. Like his brothers, he wore dark knee-length shorts. His bronze short-sleeved cotton accommodated his cast. "I would've passed out if I had to lead someone down three flights of stairs while they held a gun on Symone."

Zeke sank into his matching armchair to the right of the sofa before his knees gave out. He wore rust-colored shorts with a black jersey. "I've already had one nightmare about it. I suspect there will be a lot more."

The brothers had just finished a celebratory lunch. Since Zeke's kitchen was out of commission because of the fire, Jerry and Mal had brought over sodas, salad and an extra-large, extra-cheese-and-pepperoni pizza. They'd claimed it was to celebrate successfully closing the case yesterday. That was probably partly true. But he believed it was mostly to do a reconnaissance of the area to make sure there weren't still threats lurking around him. That was fine. He'd done a similar surveillance of both of their neighborhoods as well as Celeste's yesterday and planned to do one again today.

"You didn't see what she did to disarm Monica?" Mal sat on the corner of the sofa closest to Zeke's armchair. He had on coffee-colored shorts with a cobalt shirt.

"No, but whatever she did, she moved quickly." Zeke gripped the chair's padded arms to keep at bay the fear and anger he'd felt yesterday afternoon. "I heard Monica cry out, but by the time I turned around, she was already on the ground and Celeste had her gun."

Jerry shook his head. His eyes were wide with amazement. "Celeste has some scary skills."

"When are you going to see her again?" Mal asked.

Good question. Zeke swallowed a sigh. "I don't know. I'm

trying to work up my courage. She was furious with me after I asked her to partner with us."

Jerry spread his arms. "But she stuck to your side like a shadow the whole time we were at the precinct."

"It was the other way around." Zeke tightened his grip on the chair's arms. "*I* was sticking to *her* side."

Celeste had been physically unharmed after the ordeal. She hadn't sustained a bump, bruise or scratch from the encounter with Monica. But it had taken hours to convince him she was okay. He couldn't stop touching her—her arms, shoulders, back and neck. He'd even checked the back of her head where for one horrible moment Monica had held her gun.

"I saw the way she was looking at you, Zeke." Mal looked from Jerry, who nodded his agreement, back to Zeke. "I think she's ready to talk with you again."

Jerry leaned forward, balancing his elbows on his lap. "Zeke, I know how scary it is to tell someone how you feel."

Mal interrupted. "So do I."

Jerry glanced at Mal before continuing. "But Celeste is worth the risk. She's good for you."

Mal nodded. "She makes you laugh. You're happier—and less controlling."

"She's a miracle worker." Jerry's voice was dust dry. "And she's a bad—"

The doorbell interrupted Jerry's praise. Zeke unfolded himself from the armchair and strode toward the front door. He sensed his brothers trailing him, as though they wanted to make sure danger wasn't on the other side. He checked the peephole. His heart stopped. His breath caught in his throat. It took him a moment to remember to open the door.

"Celeste." Was he dreaming?

She stood on his porch wearing an apricot pencil-slim, knee-length dress with cap sleeves and soft cream ankle boots with one-inch heels.

Celeste looked over Zeke's shoulders. She must have noticed Mal and Jerry behind him. "Is this a bad time?" She took a step back when he didn't respond. "I could come back later."

Jerry walked forward and offered her his hand. "Celeste,

hello. It's good to see you. Ignore my brother." He drew her past Zeke and into the house. He moved back to stand between Mal and Zeke. "Sometimes I think he was switched at birth. This is a good time. Mal and I were leaving."

Zeke's brain started working again. "Yes, they were just leaving."

Mal gave Celeste a big hug. "Thank you for protecting our brother."

Celeste's eyes stretched wide with surprise. She patted Mal's shoulders. "You're welcome."

Jerry gave her a one-armed embrace. "Yes, thank you so much for taking care of Zeke. You're amazing."

"I couldn't have done it without you guys. We make a good team." Celeste patted Jerry's right shoulder, then stepped back. She looked from Jerry to Mal. "Please tell Grace and Symone I said hello."

"We will." Mal gave her a smile before he and Jerry disappeared through Zeke's front door.

Zeke locked the door behind them, then faced Celeste. His heart was running seventy miles an hour. "You look beautiful."

"Thank you." A blush filled her cheeks. She smiled at him and his heart beat even faster.

"Please come in." He gestured with his right arm that she should proceed him. "Can I offer you something to drink?"

"No, thank you." She lowered herself to the right corner of the sofa. "I had lunch with Nanette."

Zeke was relieved. He'd forgotten that all he had was water and milk. He reclaimed his armchair. "How are you?"

"I'm better." Celeste rotated the ring on her thumb. "I met with Meryl and her children. They're very grateful to you and your brothers for helping to find Art's killers."

Zeke nodded. "Jayne sends her thanks as well."

"That's nice." Celeste looked around his living room. Zeke wondered what she thought of his decorating skills. She returned her attention to him. "Now that the case is over, I had a chance to speak with Dionne's lawyer. She's going to settle the estate, including the sale of Dionne's home. Her estate's worth a little more than a million dollars. Imagine my surprise."

Zeke's eyes widened. His eyebrows rose up his forehead. "Wow. Are you going to share it with your father?"

"No, that's not what Dionne would have wanted. If she had, she would have named him in her will."

"That's true. Are you going to keep the money?" A million dollars was tempting, but Zeke couldn't imagine Celeste having anything to do with her grandmother, including inheriting her estate.

"No." Celeste shook her head decisively. "I haven't taken money from Dionne since I was sixteen." A slow smile curved her lips and brightened her eyes. "I've decided to donate all her money, including the proceeds from selling her house, to The Bishop Foundation."

"What?" Zeke's jaw dropped. "That's wonderful, Celeste. Symone's going to be thrilled."

"The foundation does important work, supporting medical research." Her smile grew into a grin. "I'm excited about the donation."

"So am I." Zeke smiled. "I'm glad you told me. Thank you."

Her grin faded and her uncertainty returned. She straightened her shoulders and drew a deep breath. "Zeke, I owe you an apology."

"For what?" He frowned his surprise.

"I misjudged you. I jumped to conclusions when I should have trusted you." Celeste started to stand, then sat back down, as though her legs were unsteady. "It wasn't until Monica grabbed me and you offered to take my place that I realized you really do have feelings for me."

Zeke held Celeste's eyes. She was at least as nervous as he was. Knowing that gave him courage to bare his heart. "Celeste, I'm in love with you."

Celeste's eyes widened. The blood drained from her face. Her shoulders slumped. She buried her face in hands and sobbed.

Zeke leaped from his chair. He sat beside Celeste and took her into his arms. "Celeste, sweetheart, what did I say?"

Celeste slumped against him and continued sobbing into her palms.

Zeke was near panic. "Sweetheart, what's wrong? Please tell me."

Her voice was muffled behind her hands. Her words came in short bursts. "My whole life, no one has ever said those words to me. My whole life. Until you just did, I didn't realize how much I needed to hear them."

She was breaking his heart. His arms tightened around her. He wished he could go back in time and take all her pain away. He couldn't. There was nothing he could do about her past, but he could do his best to make sure her future was full of joy and love.

Zeke kissed her temple. "If you let me, I'll tell you I love you so often you'll get tired of hearing it."

Celeste chuckled. "Impossible." She drew back from him and looked up into his eyes. "I'm in love with you, too, Zeke. I'm sorry it took a near-death experience for me to realize it."

He smiled. "Let's not think about that now. I've never been so afraid in my life." He wiped the tears from her cheeks. "I understand you've had experiences that have made you reluctant to trust people, but I promise I will never do anything to betray you."

Celeste nodded. "I believe you. And I would never, ever do anything to betray or hurt you, either."

"I know." Zeke's eyes drank in her delicate features. Her beautiful wide hazel eyes, heart-shaped lips and high cheekbones. "I love you, Celeste, and I'm going to spend the rest of my life making sure you know that."

He kissed her, catching his breath when she parted her lips for him. He swept his tongue inside her, tasting her sweetness. He raised his head to take a breath.

Celeste whispered against his ear. "Say it again, please?"

He smiled. "I love you, Celeste."

"That will never get old," she said on a sigh, and kissed him again.

* * * * *

Romantic Suspense

Danger. Passion. Drama.

Available Next Month

Colton's K-9 Rescue Colleen Thompson
Alaskan Disappearance Karen Whiddon

....

Stranded Jennifer D. Bokal
Bodyguard Rancher Kacy Cross

....

 LOVE INSPIRED

Christmas K-9 Guardians Lenora Worth & Katy Lee
Deadly Christmas Inheritance Jessica R. Patch

....

LOVE INSPIRED

Christmas Cold Case Maggie K. Black
Taken At Christmas Jodie Bailey

....

LOVE INSPIRED

Dangerous Christmas Investigation Virginia Vaughan
Colorado Christmas Survival Cate Nolan

Keep reading for an excerpt of a new title
from the Romantic Suspense series,
ESCAPE TO THE BAYOU by Amber Leigh Williams

Prologue

Sneaking away to Mexico before the first week of college had been Sloane's idea. It was a bad one. But as with most bad ideas born out of teenage desperation, this one was especially enticing.

One last "free girls" weekend, Sloane had beckoned.

Grace offered a fast yes. Pia, hesitant, echoed it.

Free girls, Grace thought three long weeks later, dejected.

She hadn't seen Sloane or Pia in seventeen days. Where had they been taken? They had been abducted from the same house—the little waterfront villa Sloane had rented on the sly. Her well-to-do parents would have flipped if they had known what she was up to. The senator and his wife would never have allowed it. So Sloane had paid for everything on the spot in cash.

Cash had been the problem. Throwing cash around had been their undoing.

If they had been more discreet, would they have been taken? Would the men have even known they were there?

And Alejandro. If Grace hadn't met Alejandro, would she, Pia and Sloane still be free girls? Had she doomed them all?

"I want to see my friends," she told him.

Alejandro didn't look up from the television. Fútbol was on. He leaned forward on the couch, inches away from the screen, his dark eyes magnetized to the ball. "Bad girls don't get visits," he said in a flat voice accented heavily in Spanish.

She'd tried escaping again. Could he blame her? She only left the house he and the other men had dropped her off at two weeks before to "work," as they called it.

Work. She was from the hard streets of New Orleans. She knew what it was to work. This? What he made her do—it wasn't work.

It was criminal, exploitation... It would take her soul if she let it continue.

She'd made it farther this time. Through the little window of the bathroom into the alley. He'd caught her before she could hit the street.

He'd beaten her. She'd thought someone...*anyone*...would hear her screams.

No one came. No one stopped Alejandro from locking her back inside the house. This time he had tied her up.

The rope around her wrists burned. She'd stopped tugging at the bind. Her face hurt. There was something wrong with her right arm, her ribs. Every inhale was agony.

At least he'd been generous enough not to traffic her in this condition. He hadn't driven her to some strange man's apartment in the city and thrown her at his mercy.

She lay awake at night worrying about disease—about pregnancy. About her friends. Where were they? What were the men doing to Sloane and Pia? Were they even alive at this point?

"Please," she said through lips that had long gone dry. She felt the bite of tears, but she had none. He hadn't given her anything to drink in the last twenty-four hours. Her one meal a day was down to rations of aging bread and cheese. "Just tell me if they're alive. That's all I need to know."

At long last, Alejandro turned his face away from the television. The box's light flickered across one half of his profile. It shrouded the other in darkness. He was a handsome man. It was how he'd drawn her in. Handsome and charming with a smile quick as lightning and just as white.

Was his name even Alejandro? Or was that part of his scheme? How many other women had he drawn into his web—into this life that wasn't a life—simply by smiling?

Now his smile came slowly. Her heart galloped in fear. She

knew him well enough to know what that smile meant for her… for Sloane and Pia.

"Your friends have gone to a better place, carne fresca," he informed her. Then he turned back to the television, leaning back into the cushions of the couch as he scooped his beer off the side table and drank, satisfied.

He wasn't looking, but she turned to face the wall. Her lip split as she grimaced, her shame and grief big enough to bite. She was afraid it would eat her up.

There'd be nothing left for him then. Nothing left for him or the rest of them to take.

The sound of glass shattering made Grace instinctively duck—her nerves were on a hair trigger. She'd gotten quick under his "care."

She peered over the edge of the table. Alejandro slumped forward. He moved gradually, limply, to the floor.

Her lips trembled as his arm flopped toward her, the beer bottle rolling across the bare planks. His sleeve crept up his biceps, revealing the brand—the burned, black Aztec skull she'd noticed he and his men all wore like harbingers of death.

The door burst open, kicked off its hinges.

She ducked farther under the table. The rope cinched tight against her raw wrists.

A pair of boots crept across the threshold. She watched them cross the floor to Alejandro's prone form. They looked like cowboy boots—snakeskin. She didn't dare breathe or think or move as she watched a large hand remove the pistol from the small of Alejandro's back where it was wedged between his beltline and his skin.

"Grace?"

It had been so long since anyone had called her anything but carne fresca, "fresh meat." She blinked, coming awake on a startled inhale. Still, she didn't raise her head above the table-top. Instead, she peered at the boots.

She watched the jean-clad legs bend. Knees appeared. Then thighs. A leather belt, silver buckle, plaid shirt…

A bronze face. Long, dark hair fell from hairline to jaw. Eyes glittered at her, black as night.

"You," she said, recognizing him at once. She backed away.

He held up his hands. One held a pistol. He tipped it to the floor. "No, no. I'm not here to hurt you," he blurted.

His English was better than Alejandro's. And his eyes were kind. But he'd been at the house the night of the abduction. She'd seen him...with the men who'd taken Pia. "Where is she?" she hissed. Emboldened, she tried to grab him...his gun... The rope held her back. "Where's Pia?" she demanded.

He put his finger to his lips. "You mustn't yell. I'm here to get you out."

"Where is she?" she shouted.

His hand fit tightly over her mouth. His face was close to hers under the table, nose to nose.

"Listen," he told her. "I don't want to leave that rope around your wrists. But if you fight me, I won't have a choice. Do you understand, bonita?"

His hand was warm and dry. He'd just shot a man. Shouldn't it be cold or wet with sweat? She could feel the rough texture, calluses. There was strength there, and she trembled despite the endearment—despite the fact that his grip didn't hurt. Over the last few weeks, they had conditioned her for pain. She waited for it.

He reached for his belt. She heard the slide of steel. Her eyes widened when he raised the knife.

"I'm going to cut your binds," he said, his gaze holding fast to hers. "You must be very still."

She closed her eyes and breathed hard through her nose as the knife lowered to her wrists. She felt the cool steel against the sore skin of her wrists and whimpered.

One pull and her hands fell away from each other. Something in both of her shoulders ached with gratitude. "Ah..."

His hand loosened from her mouth. She gaped at him as he tossed the rope aside. "We must go now," he explained. "They'll be coming. Tell me you understand."

She nodded faintly. He retreated, motioning her to do the same. After a moment's hesitation, she crawled out from under the table.

"Back door," he said when she veered for the open one splintered around the locking mechanisms Alejandro had kept firmly in place when she was inside.

She turned to follow him through the house and nearly tripped over Alejandro's form. Covering her own mouth, she stared at the blood pooling on the floor. "You... You just killed him."

"What would you have me do instead?" He didn't raise his voice. He kept it even-tempered as he walked around the body. "Knock on the door and let him use you as a hostage?"

They made it halfway down the hall before she stopped. "Tell me about Pia. What happened to her and Sloane?"

"I'll tell you everything. But first we—"

"I'm not going anywhere with you," she said stubbornly. "Not until I know they're okay."

Frustration ticked across his face. "They're alive. And they know we're coming back for them."

"Alive?" She could hardly grasp the possibility. Hadn't Alejandro just told her the opposite? "Sloane and Pia are...alive?"

"Si. They're alive."

It seemed too good to be true. She resisted when he tried to move her toward the back door again. "I don't believe you."

He made a noise in his throat. The trembling strengthened. His eyes reminded her vividly of Alejandro's—dark, practically liquid.

Where Alejandro's had been hard and cold, like smooth volcanic rock, this man's sparked with heat. They contained firestorms. She didn't know what to make of that.

Stepping closer, he lowered his face toward hers. "'Free girls code.' Does that mean anything to you?"

Free girls. Her heart leaped. "Oh...oh my God." The bite of tears was back. A sob worked at her throat, and she gasped.

"Now you believe me?"

"Take me to them. Please."

He took her hand. "This way."

"I need your name," she insisted as she followed.

"Javier," he whispered before sticking his head out into the alley behind the house. It bisected others surrounding the tight-knit neighborhood where there were no yards, no gardens, no trees...just stone and walls and pavement. "Javier Rivera."

She dropped her voice to a whisper. "Why are you doing this, Javier?" she asked as she trailed him into the alley. "Why are you helping us?"

He stopped long enough to check around the corner. "Because it's the right thing to do, Grace. Stay close. Entiende?"

She nodded fervently. "Si."

Pressing his finger to his lips for quiet, he lifted his gun hand before coaxing her around the first in a series of blind corners.

Subscribe and fall in love with a Mills & Boon series today!

You'll be among the first to read stories delivered to your door monthly and enjoy great savings.

WE SIMPLY LOVE ROMANCE

MILLS & BOON

JOIN US

Sign up to our newsletter to stay up to date with...

- Exclusive member discount codes
- Competitions
- New release book information
- All the latest news on your favourite authors

Plus...
get $10 off your first order.
What's not to love?

Sign up at **millsandboon.com.au/newsletter**